Faith-Filled Fiction™
www.faith-filledfiction.com | www.vikkikestell.com

LAYNIE PORTLAND, SPY RESURRECTED

Laynie Portland | Book 4
Vikki Kestell
Also Available in eBook Format

BOOKS BY VIKKI KESTELL

LAYNIE PORTLAND

Book 1: *Laynie Portland, Spy Rising—The Prequel*
Book 2: *Laynie Portland, Retired Spy*
Book 3: *Laynie Portland, Renegade Spy*
Book 4: *Laynie Portland, Spy Resurrected*

NANOSTEALTH

Book 1: *Stealthy Steps*
Book 2: *Stealth Power*
Book 3: *Stealth Retribution*
Book 4: *Deep State Stealth*, 2019 Selah Award Winner

A PRAIRIE HERITAGE

Book 1: *A Rose Blooms Twice*
Book 2: *Wild Heart on the Prairie*
Book 3: *Joy on This Mountain*
Book 4: *The Captive Within*
Book 5: *Stolen*
Book 6: *Lost Are Found*
Book 7: *All God's Promises*
Book 8: *The Heart of Joy—A Short Story*, eBook only

GIRLS FROM THE MOUNTAIN

Book 1: *Tabitha*
Book 2: *Tory*
Book 3: *Sarah Redeemed*

LAYNIE PORTLAND, SPY RESURRECTED

ISBN-13: 978-1-970120-02-8
ISBN-10: 1-970120-02-9

LAYNIE PORTLAND, SPY RESURRECTED

Laynie Portland | Book 4
Vikki Kestell
Also Available in eBook Format

LP

How strong are the cords of love?
Can they reach into hell and back?

LAYNIE, TOBIN, AND JAZ narrowly escape the hit squad sent by the Ukrainian mob—the third attempt to kill members of Director Wolfe's staff. Whatever the task force does and wherever its people go, the enemy is right there, always one step ahead.

Wolfe admits that his organization has been compromised—that a mole within his staff is feeding information to the Chechen separatist group All Glorious for Allah. Before their enemy can strike again, Wolfe orders the task force members to immediately abandon their homes and the team's headquarters for safer grounds.

The task force, with Laynie leading it, has just reestablished itself within the protective walls of Broadsword when Wolfe receives a coded letter from Cossack, his deep-cover asset in Chechnya. In the letter, Cossack reveals that he has knowledge of a large and significant terror attack scheduled for New Year's Eve. He also alludes to the leak in Wolfe's organization and his fear that passing details of the attack through normal channels will blow his precarious cover.

Cossack insists on passing intel on the impending attack to the one person he feels he can trust, the operative who foiled the assassination attempt on Vassili Aleksandrovich Petroff, Russian envoy to the UN.

Cossack's demand sends Laynie halfway around the world to a covert meeting in the city of Tbilisi, Georgia. *It sends her to her death.*

ACKNOWLEDGEMENTS

Jesus, Jesus, how I trust Him!
How I've proved Him o'er and o'er;
Jesus, Jesus, precious Jesus!
Oh, for grace to trust Him more!

Thank you as always
to my wonderful team,
Cheryl Adkins and **Greg McCann**,
for their loving hearts and
unfailing dedication to this work.

Thanks also to **Lora Doncea**
for coaching my writing style into
this century's fiction standards!

Dedicated To

TobyMac and all his family.
Thank you for your commitment
to proclaim the gospel of Jesus Christ
year after year and season after season
and for your steadfast testimony
as you walk through the agony
of losing your son, Truett.

Truett died by accidental overdose
after taking amphetamines
cut with fentanyl.
The danger is real.

Scripture Quotations

Cover Design

Vikki Kestell

HYMNS

Amazing Grace
Lyrics, John Newton, 1772
Public Domain

Away in a Manger
Attribution Unknown
Public Domain

Blessed Assurance
Lyrics, Frances J. Crosby, 1873
Public Domain

Jesus Paid It All
Lyrics, Elvina M. Hall, 1865
Public Domain

'Tis So Sweet to Trust in Jesus
Lyrics, Louisa M. R. Stead, 1885
Public Domain

What Child Is This
Lyrics, William Chatterton Dix, 1865
Public Domain

Laynie Portland
SPY RESURRECTED

PART 1:
THE GRAVE

LP

AUTHOR'S NOTE

Some of you, my dear readers, expressed disappointment when *Renegade Spy* ended on a "cliff-hanger." If this was you, I offer a small consolation: I had originally thought to end *Renegade Spy* with what is now Chapter 1 of *Spy Resurrected.*

When you've finished Chapter 1, I think it very possible that you will thank me for *not* leaving it as the conclusion of *Renegade Spy*.

Big hugs,

—Vikki

Chapter 1

November 29, 2001
Tbilisi, Republic of Georgia

LAYNIE FOLLOWED THE RIVER north from Holy Trinity Cathedral, walking steadily toward Tbilisi's Dezerter Bazaar. She was in no hurry and paused several times, staring into shop windows at colorful wares, using the windows' reflections to surveil her surroundings.

To check for a tail.

Seraphim had said she and Wolfe would arrange for a man from the US embassy to observe her during her stay. She'd spotted him when she landed at the airport. She'd even caught a glimpse of him on her way to the cathedral.

But not afterward.

I lost him when I left the cathedral. If I was able to "make" him, surely any too-interested party would have, too.

She pursed her lips. *Can't have someone tagging along when I meet up with Cossack.*

A gust of wind buffeted her. Glancing at her own image in the window, she was grateful for the faded caftan and headscarf of a Muslim woman with contact-lens-brown eyes staring back at her. Her clothing's thick fabric was a welcome barrier between her and the icy breeze.

Still, she shivered. From the cold? Or from some sixth sense, a premonition warning her of danger? Carefully scanning her surroundings again, she spotted nothing of concern, no one who triggered an alarm.

Dressed as I am, I'm as nameless and unknown as anyone can hope to be in this city.

Laynie's fingers strayed toward the hard outline of the mobile phone tucked into her bra. The phone rested in the hollow below her breastbone.

Jaz will be monitoring my phone's signal in real time. So long as my phone has a cellular connection, she will be tracing my progress.

Laynie visualized Tobin's worried eyes peering over Jaz's shoulder and drew comfort from the image. *I'll be back soon, Quincy. We'll have plenty of time to "figure things out."*

At Queen Tamar Avenue, she turned right. If the glut of pedestrian traffic converging at that intersection and moving in a common direction was any indication, the bazaar was not far ahead.

She rehearsed her instructions. *I am to find the fish market on the edge of the bazaar and look for a sign indicating fresh-caught Black Sea and Caspian seafood. At noon, I am to ask for beluga caviar.*

It would be up to Cossack to initiate contact with her after that.

THE MAN CODE-NAMED COSSACK ran his gaze around the stuffy tea room. Cossack occupied a table just inside the tea shop's entrance. The shabby, hole-in-the-wall shop was situated diagonally across the road from the city's famed Dezerter Bazaar. His table afforded him a clear line of sight to the fish market on the corner. Cossack kept his back against a plastered pillar and his chair angled so he could monitor the tea room's occupants while he kept watch on the seafood stalls without appearing to do so.

The angle of his chair would also allow him to spring to his feet and flee through the rear of the tea room should circumstances warrant a hasty escape. A reliable motorbike waited for him out back, ensuring his quick departure.

Cossack's clothing—the apparel of a man from the steppes of eastern Ukraine or perhaps the Caucasus Mountains to the north—were not in keeping with the dress of westernized Georgians, but they were not all that uncommon a sight in the city either. He wore a turban, tunic, and vest over loose-fitting pants stuffed into stout boots. A thick wool cloak over his shoulder prepared him for the impending winter nights.

The tail of his turban hung down the right side of his face and looped about his neck. The skin around his gleaming amber eyes was creased and burned to bronze from a lifetime in the sun. His thick brows and beard, once glossy black, were shot with silver, but his beard had more to say about the man. While it sprung thick and wiry along his left jaw, little facial hair sprouted on the opposite side where, years before, the fiery shards of an exploding mortar round had struck him. Seared him. Instead of bushy whiskers, yellowed scar tissue mottled his cheek and jawline.

The innocuous scarf trailing from his turban did its job veiling the scars. Cossack fingered the scarf out of habit. It would not do for the fabric to shift—for it disguised a man whose features were too remarkable to go unnoticed. A man upon whose head the Russian Federation had placed a sizable reward.

The Russian "wanted" posters referred to him as Arzu Labazanov, the name he had taken years ago. However, from Ukraine across southern Russia to the Caspian Sea, Cossack's exploits as a smart, ruthless fighter and strategist, a general in the cause of Chechen independence, had earned him the designation "Dark Destroyer"—*Temnyy Razrushitel* in Russian.

He and his militia had been a bloody thorn in the side of the Russian Federation for more than two decades. And those who hunted him for his role in the ongoing war against Russian domination? They knew him by his scars as well as his reputation.

Cossack was a man, too, whose alliance with the Chechen-Islamist militia All Glorious for Allah must never be questioned by its leaders—and yet the tea house in which Cossack waited this day was nearly three hundred miles from his militia's stronghold in the Caucasus Mountains. His presence in Tbilisi, should he be seen and recognized, would raise questions and unwanted scrutiny.

Because his face could so easily betray him, Cossack rarely left his stronghold in the Caucasus Mountains. On the odd occasion that he did so, he hid his scars and arrayed loyal followers around him. While he observed from the shadows, his proxies did his bidding.

As they would today.

However, the men he depended on today were not drawn from the ranks of his Chechen militia. Over the past six years, Cossack had recruited a number of Chechen refugees, those who had fled their war-torn country to live in Tbilisi. Cossack had chosen only men who were Christian by heritage. Cossack knew that Christian refugees were unlikely to be known by the Islamist radicals of his own militia or AGFA.

When the tea room's owner set a fresh glass of steaming tea before him, Cossack placed a sugar cube between his front teeth, lifted the glass of hot tea to his lips, and sucked the fragrant brew into his mouth. Closing his eyes momentarily, he savored the sweetness that joined the tea as the sugar melted.

Cossack raised the steaming glass of tea to his lips again, employing the motion to casually sweep his eyes across the fish market. Deshi and Chovka, two of his men, loitered out of sight in the nearby bazaar. Bulat, another man loyal to Cossack, worked with his father and brothers behind the counters of the Dezerter fish market. Cossack's gaze noted but did not linger on the bright blue shirt Bulat wore or the counters where Bulat oversaw his family's selection of seafood.

Cossack set the glass of tea on the table, dropping his eyes at the same time. It was nearly noon. Midday. He and his people were ready, waiting for Director Wolfe's operative to appear. He would surely show himself. Soon.

In the coded message he had sent to the director, Cossack had instructed the director's operative to peruse the stalls of the fish market. He was to look for a sign advertising "fresh-caught Black Sea and Caspian seafood" and ask for beluga caviar. When the director's operative did so, Bulat would signal Cossack's men loitering in the bazaar. As the director's operative moved back into the flow of the pedestrians, Cossack's men would flank him, identify themselves, and escort him to a vehicle waiting in sight of the tea room.

Cossack would pay for his tea, mount his motorbike, and rendezvous with them at a predetermined meeting place.

These carefully scripted moves were necessary to protect Cossack's deep cover within his Chechen militia. The men of his Chechen militia were faithful, both to him and to the cause of Islam, the holy struggle. They would die as willingly for him as they would for Allah—but they only *thought* they knew their leader. Cossack had been embedded in Chechnya for so many years, had lived as one of them for so long, that his identity and his allegiance to the twin causes of Chechen separatism and the ascension of Islam were indisputable—so much so, that Cossack himself sometimes forgot that his role was an alias, a means of gathering and conveying intelligence to his western handlers.

Unfortunately, his own agency had been infiltrated by those who hated America and sought her downfall. For months now, Cossack had maintained operational silence, afraid to pass intel up the chain of command, worried that the moles within the agency would intercept the intel and trace it back to him. When the intelligence he had painstakingly gathered reached a point worth the risk, Cossack had been forced to employ unorthodox and unapproved means of communication to bypass the moles and reach the director.

Now, with vital details in his hands but uncertain of whom he could trust, Cossack had requested a face-to-face meeting with the agency operative who had stymied AGFA's plot to assassinate a highly placed Russian dignitary. Why? Because no agent loyal to AGFA would have saved the Russian. Cossack felt certain the operative could be trusted.

Soon, with the help of his secret Tbilisi cell, Cossack would meet the director's operative and hand off the intelligence he had collected. He would, at the same time, institute new communication protocols with this man, again ensuring the smooth flow of intelligence from Cossack to the director.

Cossack set his tea down and picked up his newspaper with both hands. He used its open pages like a shield while he kept one eye on the fish market. Cossack tracked Bulat's bright blue shirt as he haggled with customers over the price of the day's catch. So far, the director's operative had not shown himself.

A Muslim woman approached the stalls and began to peruse the selection of fish. Cossack's gaze passed over her. Stopped. Returned to her. The woman sauntered along the fish market stalls as though looking for a particular item.

Cossack's eyes narrowed. *What is it? What did I see?*

Muslims bought their meat only from halal butchers who would slaughter the animals as dictated by the Quran. Although the Quran did not require a halal butcher for *fish*, Muslims still tended to buy all their foods from fellow Muslims. Yes, it might be unusual for a Muslim woman to shop the public fish market . . . but it was not completely out of the question.

That's not it. Something else.

He picked up his tea, brought it to his mouth, and skimmed his eyes over the woman, taking inventory. He used the edge of his scarf to dab at his mouth and assure himself that it covered his scars. Just then, two women and a man shouldered their way past the Muslim woman.

What is it?

Ah. All three were shorter than the Muslim woman.

Is that it?

Yes. The Muslim woman was tall, taller than most Georgian women, Muslim or not. She retraced her steps, paused, leaned across the stall toward Bulat's blue shirt. She must have spoken, because Cossack saw Bulat's head jerk incrementally.

Why?

Cossack thought the woman spoke again, perhaps repeated herself. After a moment's hesitation, Bulat nodded. He reached behind him and retrieved something that he handed to the woman. A small red bag. The woman slung the bag over her forearm and moved away.

Bulat had marked the Muslim woman as the director's operative.

Cossack sat back and exhaled. The director's agent, the one who had saved Vassili Aleksandrovich Petroff from a terrorist chemical attack not many weeks back? That operative was a woman?

I have been too long in this part of the world. I presumed the director would send a man.

He frowned and considered the unanticipated twist.

Does this affect the plan?

No. As long as the woman is not part of the corruption within the agency—as long as she conveys my intelligence to the director without being intercepted, I need not change the plan.

The intelligence must reach him. Nothing else matters.

And it mattered a great deal.

Less than three months after the attacks of 9/11, new assaults against the US were in the making. In fact, the next terrorist action was mere weeks away, a series of coordinated New Year's Eve attacks across the US eastern states to further demoralize America—to soften her up for the *coup d'état*, a stroke so brazen and devastating that it would drop America to her knees, shake her economy, and trigger her fury. The attack would pit America against the Russian Federation—which was the objective.

All of the attacks are engineered to point back to Russia.

And when tensions between America and Russia escalated to all-out war? Russia's attention would swing away from Chechnya and her former Soviet Bloc states, providing the opening for every separatist militia to strike in concert under the direction of AGFA and its ruthless, single-minded leader, Mohammed Eldar Sayed.

Sayed.

Should the moles within the director's organization intercept this woman? And should she be found to be carrying the specifics of the next plot? Then AGFA would know that *they* had a leak. Sayed would know he had been betrayed from within.

Two things would happen. First, Sayed would goad AGFA into a more tightly controlled structure and move to purge anyone he deemed a possible leak. Proof of guilt would not be required—Sayed was merciless. He would cut off every possible avenue of treason no matter how loyal or close to him.

Second, Sayed would order his generals to alter the plans.

Cossack thought on the tenuous alliance between his militia and AGFA, the fragile trust Sayed had bestowed on him and his people.

For more than twenty years, Cossack had fought for Chechen independence. He had cut off every tie from his past, had given himself fully to the Chechen cause, had espoused Islam, and had been more than "careful." He told those who asked that he had been born in eastern Ukraine to a Chechen man and a Ukrainian woman, that his father had filled his childhood with tales of Chechen glory and independence. He spoke *Laamaroy muott* Chechen, the dialect of the southern mountain tribes as the native he pretended to be. He spoke fluent Russian with a Chechen accent, and he spoke passable Arabic.

He had taken particular pains to ensure that no one knew he spoke English.

More than once, other militia leaders had spoken English in his presence—much of it broken, all of it heavily accented—thinking their conversation was private. Cossack had come away with important facts and a sense of how they viewed him.

He had lived this hard and lonely life to infiltrate the radical Islamists, to keep his fingers on the pulse of the Chechen wars with Russia, and to pass on to his handlers at home any immediate and long-term intelligence he could gather. He was the eyes and ears of the US as closely embedded with the radicals as he could get.

Would it all be in vain?

I and my militia would certainly fall under Sayed's suspicion. At the very least, he would box us out while they changed their plans. At worst, he would move to purge us. Either way, the attacks would go forward—and I would not be privy to the altered plans. The US would have no warning.

The possibility of exposure caused Cossack's gorge to rise. He ground his teeth. *That cannot happen.*

Cossack watched as his men, Deshi and Chovka, stepped from the shadows and drew alongside the woman. It was time.

Throwing some coins on the table, Cossack rose and threaded his way toward the tea room's back exit to retrieve his motorbike.

LAYNIE UNDERSTOOD THAT THE innocuous red bag dangling from her arm marked her as the director's operative. She had not taken ten steps before two men converged on her, one on either side. They kept their faces and eyes forward as did Laynie. Outwardly, the men appeared to be ordinary shoppers in the bazaar, unknown and unrelated to her—until the man on her right nudged her elbow.

"Follow," he whispered in heavily accented English, never turning his face or eyes in her direction. "We have car."

He walked on, and Laynie fell in a little behind him while the second man dropped behind her. As they reached the street at the edge of the market, a black late-model Russian-manufactured Lada Riva sedan pulled to the curb. The man ahead of her threw open the rear door. Laynie did not hesitate. She climbed in and scooted toward the opposite door. The man got in after her.

The second man took the front passenger seat. As he closed the car door, he hissed to the driver, "Go!"

The driver edged away from the curb and expertly maneuvered the Riva through the congested foot traffic. A block later, the pedestrians thinned. He sped up and turned onto a wider road where traffic flowed in both directions—cars, vans, trucks, and motorcycles moving as fast as their drivers chose. The driver of the Riva was obviously accustomed to navigating through the chaotic melee, and they sped onward, dodging other vehicles, changing lanes without notice.

No one spoke.

Several blocks later, the driver slowed as the car approached a busy intersection. One vehicle ahead, a woman had left the curb on their right, dragging a small cart filled with produce directly into the path of ongoing traffic. In response to the slowdown, horns blared, drivers cursed in frustration, and tires squealed as they sought purchase on the asphalt.

With her head bent toward the pavement, the woman in the intersection seemed either heedless of the danger or oblivious to it.

Laynie's driver stomped his brakes to avoid rear-ending the car in front of them. About then, the woman lifted her head and raised a shaking fist. She rained down curses on the cars and their drivers before continuing her slow progress across the intersection.

As traffic began to move, Laynie's driver looked to the right and let up on the brakes. Laynie glanced right, too, just as the driver turned his head to the left. Suddenly the driver shouted. Laynie's head snapped left in time to only glimpse what was bearing down on them from that direction.

She cried out as the heavy truck plowed into them, striking the front side of the Riva including the driver's door at around forty miles an hour.

Metal shrieked and crumpled. The truck's forward motion carried the sedan across the sidewalk and slammed it into a high retaining wall. Moments later, the truck reversed, leaving its bumper embedded in the Riva's frame.

THE TRUCK BACKED, TURNED in the direction from which the Riva had come, and idled in the intersection. The driver swore as he fought the gearshift, trying to force it to move. The truck's transmission protested then acquiesced as the driver, sweating and laboring with furious intent, at last jammed it into gear and stomped on the accelerator, lumbering away from the accident, slowly picking up speed.

The Riva, its right side mashed against the retaining wall, blocked the sidewalk. Concerned pedestrians drew near to render aid. Other vehicles stopped and disgorged their drivers and passengers. Many hands worked to wrench open the driver's door and the passenger door behind him. The driver's door, however, was completely caved in. The steering column had crushed the driver's chest and his head lolled unnaturally. The would-be rescuers muttered to each other that it was too late for him and set to work prying the rear door open.

Uniformed Tbilisi police rolled up in two unmarked cars followed by an ambulance. Brandishing batons, two policemen drove the civilians away from the wreck and demanded that they move their vehicles out of the intersection. The remaining officers took over the work on the rear door behind the driver's seat. The paramedics wheeled a lumpy gurney to the Riva, ready to transport accident victims as they were extricated. The officers labored feverishly, shouting at each other to hurry, because the car sizzled and steamed. Thick black smoke roiled from under the car, and the smell of gasoline was everywhere.

With a tortured screech of metal, the door behind the driver's seat gave way, and the paramedics pushed the gurney closer. Only one of the car's occupants, the man in the far rear seat, stirred. He tried to move, but the mechanism that adjusted the seat ahead of him forward or back had given way. The passenger seat, along with the weight of the passenger's dead body, sat on his right foot, crushing it. A woman sat beside him, behind the driver. Hands reached for her unconscious figure first, but the driver's seat, pushed backward, wedged her in place.

The smell of gasoline . . . and the odor of something on the edge of burning filled the air with choking fumes. The conscious passenger struggled urgently to free himself and screamed for the officers and paramedics to help him.

"Hurry! Hurry! Please! My foot is stuck!"

The smoke thickened. Flames shot out from under the car's crumpled hood, and onlookers shouted warnings. The police and paramedics backed away, their frustration apparent to the crowd as the heat began to scorch them.

It was too late to save the passengers.

The man in the rear seat shrieked with fear until—with a gasping *whoooomp*—the gas tank ignited and the back end of the car lifted six feet off the ground. When it crashed back down onto the street, fire and flaming debris rained down thirty feet in all directions.

Not all the onlookers had heeded the police's commands to move back nor did they escape injury from the falling debris. Even the police and paramedics retreating from the burning vehicle suffered minor cuts and burns. A fire truck arrived to put out the inferno. The paramedics shook their heads, loaded their gurney into the ambulance, and drove away. Soon after, the police, too, left the scene.

TEN MINUTES AFTER DRIVING away from the tea room, Cossack arrived at the prearranged meeting place, an abandoned house with a partially caved-in roof. All seemed as it should be when he climbed from his motorbike and walked it up the drive to the house and its dilapidated garage. His men would have arrived before him and parked inside the garage. Their orders were to maintain the illusion of the abandoned house. No lights. No opened curtains.

No signs of activity.

But something felt "off" to Cossack. He scanned the muddy drive, looking for tire tracks in the damp earth. He saw none. He pried open the side door to the garage and peered inside.

It was empty.

His stomach churned with sudden anxiety. *Do not panic. They will be along shortly. Perhaps an accident stalled traffic on their route.*

He stowed his motorbike inside the garage out of sight and waited. When they still did not arrive, he began to truly worry.

Where are they? How could they not be here by now?

He retrieved his motorbike, straddled it, and coasted down the drive to the road. He then started the engine and drove off, planning to backtrack along his men's most likely route.

As he drove, he questioned himself and his planning. *Could Sayed know that I came to Tbilisi? Could my plans have been found out? Is my cover blown?*

He shook his head. *I think not. I've been too careful. No one from Chechnya knows I am here, not even the most trusted captains in my militia who think me in Turkey buying arms. And for this meeting, I have used only men carefully recruited over the years, Chechen Christians whose families fled to Georgia because of the war, men who would be utterly unknown to my militia.*

His analytical mind spoke back to him. *You are thinking of your end of this operation. If there are leaks, they must be on the director's end.*

Cossack turned onto one of the busier streets his men might have taken. Traffic coming at him was not as dense as the traffic going the opposite direction.

Odd . . .

Lifting his eyes and searching far down the road, he spotted a smudge of black smoke. The discomfort in his gut intensified, and he tasted bile in his throat. He hawked, spat it out, and drove toward the source of the smoke.

That logical part of his mind spoke again. *Could the operation at the director's end have been compromised?*

Yes, he admitted.

Could the moles in the director's organization have had the director's agent followed to Tbilisi?

Quite possibly.

He relaxed a little. *If so, my end of the operation should be secure, my cover still safe.*

Less than two minutes later he came upon the smoldering ruin of a car and the remnant of the crowd that had watched it burn. Cossack's heart thudded as he recognized the Riva's remains. The sedan had been pushed into a high stone wall. Whatever had hit the unfortunate vehicle had been big enough to pancake its front end against the wall and crush the driver's seat.

Although the firemen had doused the vehicle, the car's burned framework continued to smolder and radiate heat. The door behind the driver hung ajar on blackened, warped hinges.

What happened? Did anyone get out and escape the flames?

He dismounted and walked his motorbike past the wreck, staring into the rear seat, forcing his disbelieving mind to acknowledge what he saw. He slowed, stopped, put down the bike's kickstand, and drew nearer to the charred wreckage.

He squatted a few feet from the open rear seat. Heat and residual smoke from the fire wafted around him as he took stock of what he saw.

The human remains within the wreckage were misshapen—spines twisted grotesquely, arms contorted by superheated flames, the jaws of the skulls frozen in agonized gapes or grimaces.

He swallowed and forced himself to count. Then recount. No, there was no mistaking the charred outlines of the corpses.

Four of them.

CHAPTER 2

LP

AN INCESSANT CHIRPING ROUSED Jaz. She rolled from her cot and remembered too late that she wasn't in a real bed—or how near to the floor her cot was. She landed on the cold gym floor with a bone-jarring thud.

"Ow."

Dragging herself onto her knees, she found her chair and climbed into it. The screen before her was a blur until she'd wiped her eyes several times.

What time is it? Right. Oh-dead-thirty.

She wiped her eyes again. The clock on her computer read 3:17 a.m. Blur or not, she already knew what the chirping meant—she'd lost the signal from Bella's phone.

She checked the carrier Bella's phone was on. No problems. No outages.

Tobin appeared beside her, his hair tousled, his face bleary. They had both set up camp in the gym.

"What's up?"

"Lost the signal to Bella's phone."

"Where was she when—"

"Yah, yah. Hold your horses. I'm getting to it, Yank."

Jaz retraced the last cell towers the phone had pinged off of, then zoomed in on an online map of Tbilisi.

"Huh."

"What? What does 'huh' mean?"

"Dunno for sure. Her rendezvous with you-know-who was set for noon. That's just seventeen minutes ago, Tbilisi time. Her phone pinged continuously from . . . around here," Jaz jabbed the map, "that's near her hotel, before it moved up this river about two miles, then over to here."

She poked the map again. "That's the bazaar."

"So, she made her rendezvous."

"Yah. I'd say so, but . . ."

"Where is she now?"

"Dunno. Her phone dropped off the carrier's network three minutes ago."

Tobin chewed his lower lip. "Think you-know-who took her phone and pulled the battery from it?"

"Good OPSEC if he did."

"Then we should expect her phone to reconnect when they're done meeting."

"Sounds right." She fiddled with a new stick of Black Jack gum but didn't unwrap it.

"What?"

"Nothing. Just . . . gonna wait up for a while."

"Tea?" Tobin suggested.

"Better make it coffee."

"Really?"

"You overcaffeinated Americans have ruined my love for tea. 'Sides, I don't want to sleep again until I've reacquired her signal."

"Me, neither. Coffee it is."

Tobin wandered off to fire up the task force's coffee maker.

COSSACK LEFT THE SCENE with the horrific images burning behind his eyes. As bad as they were, he'd seen too many brutal deaths in the last twenty years for the images to throw off his thinking.

The director's operative is dead. Men from my Tbilisi cell are dead.

A number of important questions nagged at him. *Was the car crash a fluke, an accident? How likely was that?* He shook his head. *Worst case, it was intentional. If intentional, then the operation had been compromised—from Wolfe's end.*

Cossack sighed within himself. If the mole inside the director's organization had given Sayed the identity of the director's operative, that meant that Sayed's people had followed the woman from the US to Tbilisi. And from her hotel to the market.

Sayed.

Cossack shuddered. *It is, perhaps, a mercy that my men died with the woman. If they had been taken alive? Sayed's people would have interrogated them. As loyal as they were to me, under torture they would have eventually given my description to Sayed. Yes, it was a mercy for them to have died quickly. And a relief for me.*

He checked himself into a cheap Muslim boarding house where his tribal dress drew no comment, paid cash for the room, and wheeled his motorbike inside. He locked the door behind him and gave himself over to analysis of the situation.

*My cover should be intact, but the New Year's attacks are still in motion. Even if I don't possess every nuance, I can give the director sufficient details for his people to unravel the rest, if—*if*—I can convey what I know without the intel being intercepted.*

He thought of the dead woman in the car's charred remains. *At the very least, the director needs to be told his operative is dead.*

He preferred breaking the bad news directly to Wolfe—something of a trick since the director's calls could very well be monitored and even recorded by the moles in his organization.

His next steps would require forethought and planning.

TOBIN STALKED OUT OF the bullpen and began to jog the perimeter of the gym, trying to calm his mounting anxiety. It was after seven in the morning now, and Jaz had not reacquired Bella's cell signal.

Settle down, Quincy, before you blow a gasket.

Jaz was beginning to really worry, too—as evidenced by the number of Black Jack gum wrappers scattered on the floor around her workstation. She hadn't even tried to toss them in the trash can.

Tobin broke from a jog to a trot. *How long should her meeting with Cossack have taken? An hour? Two hours? Surely not four hours!*

After forty minutes of running, he moved to the free weights, making himself count off reps aloud in an attempt to distract his thoughts.

BO OPENED THE GYM door. He noted Tobin's punishing workout and Jaz's slumped shoulders. He took one look at Jaz's stormy countenance and backed out of the doorway. He went looking for Richard and found him in the kitchen drinking his own morning coffee before starting breakfast.

"Something amiss, Bo?"

"If I had to guess from Jaz and Tobin's behaviors, I'd say something's up."

Richard picked up a phone and called the landline on Jaz's desk in the gym.

Her answer was more of a snarl than a greeting. "*What?*"

"Sitrep, please, Miss Jessup."

Jaz was slow to answer. "We . . . we lost Bella's cell signal around three this morning."

"And haven't reacquired it?"

Jaz kinda liked the old man and really didn't want to curse at him. She sighed and curbed her acid tongue. "If I had reacquired her signal, I would have said so."

"Noted. I'll apprise Seraphim of the situation."

COSSACK WAS READY. He waited until an hour after midnight before mounting his motorbike and riding off in the direction of the US embassy.

The embassy was located north of the city, off Georgian-American Friendship Ave. Many of the embassy employees lived in this upscale area of the city, including a certain cultural attaché.

NATHAN COLLIER WOKE FROM sleep and was immediately alert. What had awakened him? He reached for the Ruger semiauto he kept in the bedside table's drawer. Slithered from his mattress to the carpet. Froze in place, his senses alert.

There. That's what had awakened him. The soft strains of music rising from somewhere in his house. The attaché—known to the ambassador and a select few of the embassy staff to be the resident CIA station chief—should have been alone in his home. He had secured the doors and windows himself before he retired for the evening—and he had very good locks.

The music was coming from downstairs . . . from his study?

What? That's one of my CDs, Schubert's "Serenade."

The haunting violin solo and piano accompaniment were unmistakable.

With the Ruger held out in front of him, Collier crept down the stairs. He took his time, and reached the bottom floor after three minutes of careful stop-and-go movement.

The house's first floor was dark except for the pale splash of light coming from the open doorway to his study. Collier crossed the entryway then crept along the wall until he reached his study's door. The open doorway offered him an angled view inside. The lamp sitting on his desk was on, its dimmer switch dialed low, the articulating lampshade canted toward the door, leaving the remainder of the room in the dark.

Collier glimpsed a figure standing in the shadows beyond his desk. The window next to him was open. A cool breeze rustled the curtains.

"Please come in, Mr. Collier," his visitor invited quietly. "I mean you no harm."

The man's English held the edge of a slight accent.

"Who are you?"

"Not an enemy, I assure you. Quite the opposite. Please—time is of the essence, as they say. I have urgent business to attend to and require your assistance."

Against his better judgment, Collier felt drawn to trust the intruder's invitation. To a degree. With the Ruger half-raised and ready, he walked into the study. His right hand reached for the light switch on the wall.

"Please don't. I need to preserve my cover, and we already have sufficient light to conduct our business."

"Which is what, exactly?"

"I left a piece of paper next to the phone. I would ask you to dial the number written on the paper—and, oh—feel free to lower your weapon. I'm unarmed."

Collier lowered the Ruger a few inches. "The number. Whose is it?"

The man in the shadows chuckled. "It's an unlisted number possessed by very few people, but you'll recognize the man when he answers."

"You could have made the call yourself. Cut out the middleman. And all this drama."

"Ah, but I'm not altogether convinced that the call will be unmonitored and unrecorded. I'd rather not have my voice on tape, you see. The consequences of blowing my cover could be unpleasant. And permanent."

"You're not CIA. I'd know you if you were operating in Georgia."

"Consider me a cousin of the kissing variety."

"That's not enough to convince me to help you."

A pause. Then, "Did you, by chance, assist an American woman into the city quite recently? In the past day or two?"

Collier had received orders to put a man on the woman, a passive observer. The man he'd assigned had followed her from the airport to her hotel when she arrived and, the following morning, from her hotel to the unfinished Holy Trinity Cathedral.

Not many hours later, he'd called Collier. "Sir, after walking the cathedral grounds, she went into a restroom outside the cathedral."

"And?"

"And she never came out, sir."

"You *lost* her?"

"Yes, sir."

Collier had cursed the man up one side and down the other, but he said nothing of it to his visitor.

"I assist many US citizens when they visit this country. It's my job."

"Well, this citizen is dead, and you need to tell her handler what happened."

Collier's head snapped up. He broke into a cold sweat.

"Explain, please."

"She kept an appointment at noon. I suppose that's noon yesterday, since it's now past midnight. Shortly after the rendezvous, the car she was riding in was hit by a large vehicle. I estimate it was a commercial truck, although the driver didn't stick around. It was . . . a terrible accident. The front of the car was badly crushed. Then the vehicle burned.

"I watched her keep the appointment, you see. Four individuals left the bazaar in that car including the woman of whom I speak. I personally witnessed four burned corpses in the vehicle after the fire was put out. No one escaped."

"You're sure it was an accident?"

"I didn't see it happen, so I cannot say one way or another. I came upon the scene perhaps twenty minutes after."

Collier moved toward the desk and picked up the piece of paper with the number on it. The country code was US. The area code, 202.

Washington, DC.

"Stay on that side of the desk, in the light, if you please."

Collier reached across his desk for the phone and dialed the number. The call on the other end rang six times. "No one's picking up."

"Be patient. The call is being forwarded. It's just past four in the afternoon there. He'll answer."

Collier listened to the phone ring another six times. He was getting ready to hang up when the call connected.

"Wolfe here."

Collier's mouth fell open. "*Director* Wolfe?" Collier certainly knew who Jack Wolfe was, even if Wolfe had never heard of him.

"Who's this?"

"Nathan Collier, sir. Tbilisi embassy."

Wolfe did not reply, and Collier heard the faint sounds of traffic on Wolfe's end of the call. When Wolfe remained unresponsive, Collier sensed the man was steeling himself to receive the grave news Collier was to deliver.

"Sir?"

"Yes. I'm . . . here."

Collier made himself continue. "Sir, it is half past one in the morning in the Republic of Georgia. I was asleep in my house until I heard music coming from downstairs. When I investigated, I found a man standing in my study. In the dark. He has asked me to convey to you that . . . a woman of your acquaintance was involved in a fatal car crash yesterday—that is, about twelve hours ago."

The silence deepened. Then, "Can you put your visitor on the line?"

"Sir, he's concerned that this call may be monitored. His voice recognized."

"Yes, I see."

Collier waited several seconds. "Sir?"

"Give me as much detail as you are able to, please."

Collier repeated the few details his "guest" had given him. "He is certain the burned car had four bodies in it."

"Accident or intentional?"

"My visitor did not witness the actual crash, sir."

"I understand." He paused a moment, then said, "Listen up, Collier. I need you to do several things for me. First, locate the body. Find out where it was taken and claim it. Arrange for it to be shipped to the States ASAP. Do whatever is necessary to expedite the process. Then I need you to interview the police and fire department personnel who were on scene and as many witnesses as you can locate. I want firsthand interviews. I want you to determine who caused the crash."

"Begging your pardon, sir, but my chain of command will expect—"

"Leave your superiors to me. Just do as I've asked of you. It's important."

"Yes, sir."

Collier's visitor stirred from his place in the shadows and spoke softly. "Turn your back to me, please, Mr. Collier."

"What?"

"Turn around. I'm going to place a small package on your desk. Count to five very slowly then retrieve it. I've written instructions on its back. Follow them to the letter."

Reluctantly, Collier turned away from his desk. He heard the whisper of the manila envelope as it landed on his blotter. He counted to five before facing his desk.

In his ear he heard, "Collier? What's going on?"

"Sir, my 'guest' has just . . ."

Collier peered into the shadows. He could no longer make out the dark profile of his visitor.

"Hey, you. Are you still here?"

When his visitor did not answer, he twisted the lampshade toward the shadow. No one there. He pointed the lamp at the open window. The end of the curtain now hung outside the window casing.

"One moment, sir." Collier picked up the package and scanned the instructions on it.

"Sir, my guest has departed. Out the window. I will collect the body as you've requested and . . . and make all the appropriate arrangements and investigations. I'll require shipping instructions for the body. Should I look for an encrypted email?"

"No. I can't trust that it won't be intercepted . . . even before it leaves my end."

Collier was taken aback. "Your end?"

Wolfe ignored Collier's comment. "I'll send sealed instructions via diplomatic courier." He emphasized his next words. "I want you to examine the seal on my instructions carefully when you receive them."

"I will, sir. Ah, Director Wolfe?"

"What is it, Collier?"

"I won't presume to ask your business, sir. However, I am wondering, why me? You don't really know me, but you are placing . . . a great deal of trust in me. I am wondering why, sir."

"You're right. I don't know if I can trust you. But your visitor picked you, Collier, and I trust him. Whatever he's asked of you? Do it."

"I understand. Thank you, Director."

"Goodbye, Collier."

"Goodbye, sir."

Collier hung up slowly.

He dropped the Ruger on his desk and stepped to his bar. He poured himself two fingers of bourbon and drank it down, neat. After closing and relocking his study window, he sat down at his desk to consider one of the strangest encounters of his intelligence career. He read the instructions on the sealed package a second time.

Collier,

Once you retrieve the woman's remains, have them placed in a metal casket then have the casket sealed and prepared for shipping. You are to assign a two-person unit to guard her body, 24/7, from the moment you retrieve the body until it is delivered. Mind my words—the remains are not to be left unattended, not even for a moment. Ship them to Wolfe personally *with unalterable instructions that the casket is not to be released to anyone but* him. *The assigned guards are to stay with the body until Wolfe dismisses them.*

The envelope had one last line of instruction. Collier reread the concluding line, stared at the package, and shook his head.

Whatever vital information was enclosed in the package he held? The Director would not receive it until he, personally, opened the casket.

CHAPTER 3

LP

DIRECTOR WOLFE SHUT HIS mobile phone and stared at it in his hands for a long moment. Then he looked out his car's window and fixed his eyes on the scenery flashing by.

He perceived none of it. Instead, he saw only the appalling image Collier's description had painted in his imagination. The tall, blond form of the fearless woman he admired and respected . . . charred and twisted beyond all recognition.

Accident or intentional? The crushing weight inside Wolfe's chest insisted it was no accident.

I failed you, Bella. No, I failed you, Laynie! *I sent you into danger, and my efforts to protect you were woefully inadequate. Somehow, despite our precautions, the enemy knew you were coming . . . and was waiting for you.*

It occurred to him that the fake email he'd sent to smoke out the mole in his upper organization had yielded nothing. The "canary trap," as it was called, had been ignored. Why?

He could think of only one answer—because the mole had already obtained the details of the actual op. Despite the silo he'd built around Bella's mission, the mole within the task force had obtained and communicated the operational particulars to his or her superiors—and had done so right under their noses.

But who? Who could it be? Was it Seraphim? Richard? Tobin? Jaz? Wolfe shook his head. They were Bella's closest friends! But they were also the only people within Broadsword's perimeter who were privy to the operation's particulars.

I don't believe it. I know these people—and I didn't rise to this position by not being able to spot a liar when I hear one. There has to be another answer, another explanation.

He pushed the distressing thoughts of Bella's last moments aside and focused on the conundrum he faced.

The mole can't be one of Richard's people either. It became obvious to us that the team harbored a second mole before *I relocated the task force to*

Broadsword. So, if it isn't Seraphim, Tobin, or Jaz, that leaves just the remaining six members of the task force.

Wolfe ground his teeth together. *This leak is like a cancerous arm. The only certain means of excising the cancer is to cut it off—amputate the whole limb.*

Disband the task force.

He shook his head. *But I can't do that. Not with the certainty of a New Year's attack only weeks away and the progress we have made toward figuring it out. No, we have to flush out the mole—and soon—so we can stop the attacks.*

Wolfe focused on his short conversation with Collier. He made himself slow down and run through it multiple times. *Collier's visitor could have been no one but Cossack. At least he believes himself still safe—and I trust the man. I know he will find a way to convey the details of the upcoming attacks to us.*

Sighing, Wolfe turned his attention back to the matter at hand. Bella's death. He had to break the news to the team. Her team. He had to rehearse the awful details while the traitor within its ranks gloated behind a façade of grief.

I will be watching their reactions. I will personally interview every member of the task force. We cannot let up until we have uncovered the leak.

Wolfe felt suddenly sick inside—he would have to notify Bella's family. No, not Bella's family. Laynie's family.

I'm sorry, Laynie. You deserved better from me.

I pray that the God you so recently found has received your soul and granted you peace. I pray, too, that he will forgive me for vowing that I will never rest until every snake hiding in my organization is hunted down and destroyed.

He cleared the lump from his throat. Still, his voice rasped when he spoke to his driver. "Parker?"

"Sir?"

"You have a go bag with you?"

"Always, sir. In the trunk."

"Good. Back to my condo, pronto. I need to grab mine. We'll be gone overnight."

"Yes, sir. Where are we headed, sir?"

"Broadsword."

IT WAS DARK WHEN Wolfe's car arrived at the Broadsword checkpoint and the guards waved it through. Richard was waiting on the front porch when Wolfe's driver pulled up to the cabin.

Wolfe clenched his jaws and climbed from the back seat.

"Good evening, Director."

Wolfe shook his head. There was nothing good about this evening. "Would you please ask Seraphim to join me in the conference room? And I would like you to join us."

"Is it bad news, then? About Miss Bella?"

"Yes, I'm sorry to say it is."

Richard had difficulty speaking. He finally managed, "I'll find Seraphim, sir." He would have stumbled had Wolfe not caught his elbow and steadied him.

Pulling himself upright, Richard lifted his chin. "Thank you, Director. I can manage now."

Minutes later, Seraphim and Richard entered the conference room. Richard closed the door behind them. Perhaps sensing the purpose for Wolfe's unannounced visit, Seraphim had set her face in stone. While Wolfe spoke, neither she nor Richard said anything other than to ask a few clarifying questions.

"I'd like you to assemble the task force, Patrice," Wolfe said, "so I can break the news to them."

"I should do it," she answered. Then her chin wobbled, and her face contorted. "But . . . I don't think . . . I don't think I can."

Wolfe's hand covered hers. "It is my responsibility, not yours. I was the one who sent her."

"Pardon me, Director," Richard whispered. "I would appreciate if you would allow me to bring Bo and Harris into this meeting. I wouldn't want them to hear it afterward."

"Yes, of course . . . only, I want to do it soon. As soon as we can assemble everyone."

SERAPHIM SENT OUT A group text message, summoning the team to the gym. They arrived by ones and twos looking around at each other, some wondering aloud at the late-evening meeting.

Tobin walked to his desk and sat down. He glanced at Jaz when she took her seat and noted Lance and Sherman standing against a wall. Richard, Bo, and Harris were also present, Richard's expression carefully blank.

It wasn't until Wolfe walked in that the gravity of the summons began to dawn on Tobin. His eyes jinked from Wolfe to Seraphim and back. When he was unable to make eye contact with either of them, his shoulders tightened.

Then Wolfe began to speak.

"Ladies and gentlemen, I have called you together to convey sad news."

A low murmur ran through the gym. Tobin's heart stuttered. He choked on his own breath.

Wolfe said, "I received word a few hours ago that yesterday noon, local time, our friend and coworker Bella was involved in a serious car accident."

He paused. "A fatal accident. Bella and the other passengers in the car perished at the scene."

All around them, Wolfe's news was met with denials followed by sobs and curses.

Tobin gasped. He muttered, "Marta? Lord Jesus . . . no! Please, no!"

Rusty, weeping unashamedly, jumped to his feet and shouted what others were thinking.

"No, that's not right! She can't . . . Are you sure? Are you *sure?*"

Wolfe nodded, slowly. "I received my information, through channels, from a firsthand witness."

He waited a moment, allowing the team to process what they had heard before adding, "I understand your pain. I feel it just as deeply. Bella was . . . extraordinary. She was the heart and soul of this task force. I don't know how she managed it, but she pulled all of you together—complete strangers—and, within days, showed you how to work together. She fashioned you into a powerful, cohesive team. She exacted your best efforts, insisted on everyone's full participation, and demanded that you respect each other. She made you . . . more than a team. She made you a family, and we will mourn her as a family."

Of those gathered in the gym, a few attempted to stifle their shock and grief until they could get away and find some privacy, but many were shaken, openly weeping.

Jubaila stood. "Director Wolfe? Please. Can't you tell us anything more? Where is Bella? I mean where is her . . ." She didn't finish.

Wolfe nodded. "I understand your need for information, to try to make sense of her demise. I can add only a few details to what I have already told you. Bella was out of the country when this happened, and we are working to bring her home. However . . ."

Wolfe's voice failed him momentarily. He swallowed, cleared his throat, and tried again. "What I can tell you is that the car she was in . . . caught fire after the accident."

Tobin shuddered. *O God, my God! Please, no! I cannot bear this. Oh, Marta!*

Wolfe said softly, "The car burned. None of the passengers escaped the fire. Bella—"

Seraphim, seeing Wolfe struggling, came and stood next to him. "The Director will arrange for Bella's remains to be shipped back to the States . . . not to us, but to her family."

She looked around, making eye contact with the task force members. "Because of Bella's injuries, there will be no viewing. In fact, out of respect for her family's privacy . . . and to safeguard this task force and its ongoing work, none of us will attend Bella's burial."

Into the stunned silence, Wolfe cleared his throat and nodded. "Thank you, Patrice." He added, "Seraphim is correct. We cannot attend Bella's burial. But that does not mean we won't pay our respects to her. We will hold a memorial service here. At that time, we will properly honor her—as she deserves."

Within Tobin's heart, every hope and dream he'd nurtured fractured and crumbled. He pulled in on himself and wept like a child.

Within his agony, he kept remembering their last words. "*I couldn't let you leave, Marta, not without telling you how I feel. I love you. Come back to me—in one piece, hear? We need more time, you and I, to figure things out.*"

"*Quincy Tobin, I can't promise you anything except, God willing, I will come back. And if it is his will? We'll have plenty of time to, you know. Figure things out.*"

"No more time," he babbled softly. "No more time for us! Oh, Lord! Why? Why wasn't it your will for us?"

Tobin sat up and scrubbed his face with his shirtsleeves. He saw Jaz prostrate on her keyboard, her whole body shaking and quivering.

He stood and rolled his chair over to hers, sat, and placed one hand on Jaz's shoulder. He was crying again, heedless of his own weeping—only that his tears, as they tumbled down, felt like the shards and slivers of his broken heart.

Jaz shuddered under Tobin's hand.

"No," she keened softly. "I can't believe it! I *don't* believe it!"

Tobin couldn't answer her, but inside he was screaming, *I don't believe it, either.*

The meeting began to break up. Some team members stood in small knots, hugging and comforting one another. Others fled the gym, seeking the privacy they needed to mourn.

Tobin remained with Jaz.

Eventually, she lifted her head a few inches off her keyboard. The black eyeliner and mascara that were such a part of her "trademark" look now streaked her cheeks and chin.

"Tobin."

"Yeah, Jaz?"

"I can't stay here. I . . . I can't. I can't bear it."

"Can't stay here? Do you mean here, in the bullpen? Or . . . here, with the task force?"

"There is no task force without Bella."

You're not wrong there, Jaz, Tobin thought.

"But where would you go? The Ukrainian mob. You know they are looking for you."

"I don't need Wolfe's protection from them. I never did. I have the means to disappear and never be found. I just kind of got roped into this and thought it might be fun for a while, but now . . ."

"You can't go yet, Jaz. Not until we've honored Bella like the director said. It wouldn't be right for you to leave before then."

She sniffed and scrubbed a hand across her face. "Yah. I suppose you're right."

"MARSHAL TOBIN."

Tobin raised his chin. Wolfe stood over him.

"Sir?"

"I need to notify Bella's family. In person. I would like you to come with me."

Marta, Tobin screamed within himself. *Not Bella, but Marta.* My Marta!

"*What are you grinning at?*"

"*Grinning at the best news I've heard in days, sweet Marta.*"

"*Dork. You know that's not my name, right?*"

"*You may have mentioned it once or twice.*"

No, her name wasn't Marta. Nor was it Bella. It was *Laynie*—and now he was supposed to tell Kari that her only sister was dead?

Memories of the night Wolfe and his team had intercepted Laynie and reunited the two sisters rushed into Tobin's mind. He had seen them running to each other. Embracing. Sobbing with love and wonder.

It had been one of the most profoundly joyous scenes he had ever witnessed. The two sisters had talked from Lincoln all the way to Kari and Søren's home in RiverBend, often touching hands during the drive. Tobin had thought their love a holy thing. An unbreakable bond forged in and through fire.

He flinched as he reminded himself that, in a few hours, he and Wolfe would dispense grief and loss to Laynie's sister. They would become the instruments to destroy that joy.

Tears stung his eyes. *You'll always be Marta to me. My Marta.*

Tobin had done death notices before. He knew how to compartmentalize so he could perform this sacred duty with honor and dignity. He choked down the tears. Forced the pain to the back of his mind and locked it there.

I will grieve later, he told himself.

His heart added, *You will grieve forever.*

"Yes, sir. I'll go."

"I'm having my plane prepped and fueled. We'll leave here in thirty minutes, spend the night at a hotel near LaGuardia, and fly out early tomorrow morning."

CHAPTER 4

THEY LANDED IN LINCOLN, Nebraska, around ten in the morning. Two agents, a man and woman, met them. The woman handled the introductions.

"Agent Julie Knox, sir. This is agent Joel Brooks."

Wolfe and Tobin shook their hands. Wolfe asked, "Do you have Max Thoresen's current location?"

"Yes, sir," Knox replied. "I have a man keeping tabs on him. He was last reported to be in class, but that class just ended. We expect him to return to his dorm shortly." She gestured toward a Suburban. "My agent has spoken to Max's resident assistant and has secured the dorm's library as a private space for the notification. The RA will bring the young man to you there."

"Very good."

They parked near Burr Hall. Tobin and Wolfe followed Knox into the dorm and down a hall to the library. Max arrived moments later.

Wolfe spoke. "Hello, Max."

The tousled-haired young man recognized Wolfe and Tobin and grinned. "Hey! What are you guys . . ."

Wolfe and Tobin's stoic, unchanging expressions halted Max's greeting.

He glanced from Tobin to Wolfe and back to Tobin. "What's going on?"

"I'm afraid we have bad news, Max. It concerns your aunt."

HALF AN HOUR LATER, Tobin explained to Max that they needed to leave for his parents' farm to break the news to them.

"We can take you along with us, Max. We have a car and a driver waiting for us."

"Yeah. I should be there for them."

He climbed into the seat behind Wolfe and Tobin and kept to his own thoughts during the drive.

It was early afternoon when they exited the freeway near RiverBend and began the last leg of their journey toward the Thoresen's farm. Tobin twisted in his seat to look behind him.

"How are you doing, Max?"

"Okay, I guess. I'm just . . . worried about Mom and Shannon. And Grandma Polly and Granddad Gene. This is gonna hurt them something awful."

Tobin nodded. "Your mom and your aunt had a special bond."

"So did Shannon and she's . . . she's sensitive, y'know?"

"Yes. Your aunt told me." He thought a moment. "When do your brother and sister get out of school each day?"

"Usually three, I think. The bus drops them at the bridge around three thirty."

"So, they won't be at home when we arrive?"

Max shook his head. "No. Maybe that's a good thing."

Tobin silently agreed. When he turned forward, he saw that they were riding the bluff near the Thoresen farm. The road descended toward a creek. Before they reached the creek and its bridge, they turned off the road and followed the gravel drive to Kari and Søren's house.

Tobin saw the curtains move when they pulled up at the front of the house. Max jumped out as soon as the driver put the Suburban into park. At the same time, Kari Thoresen opened the front door. Max ran to her.

"Max? What is it?"

She seemed surprised when Tobin and Wolfe exited the vehicle. When she saw their grave expressions, she crumpled in Max's arms. "No! No, no, no!"

Wolfe and Tobin quickened their steps and helped Max guide Kari into the house. They sat her down on the sofa in the room that doubled as Kari's office and the living room. Wolfe pulled the chair from her desk to the sofa, sat in it, and leaned forward, eye-level with Kari.

"Ms. Thoresen? I'm sorry to be the bearer of bad news."

"No! I don't want to hear it!"

"I'm sorry, but your sister, Laynie, was in a vehicle accident two days ago. She did not survive."

"No. That's not true. You . . . you're lying." Kari dared Wolfe to contradict her. "Please. Tell me it's not true!"

"Ms. Thoresen . . . Kari, I'm sorry, but Laynie is gone. She died in the accident."

Kari whimpered and covered her face. "Oh, Lord Jesus! Lord Jesus! Please help me!" She sobbed into her hands and rocked back and forth.

Tobin looked to Max. "Where's your father, Max? Your mom needs him."

"He's probably across the creek. I'll . . . I'll go find him."

Max grabbed a set of keys from a hook near the door to the garage. Moments later, they heard the sound of a car backing away from the house, leaving Wolfe and Tobin alone with Kari.

Kari twisted her fingers together and stared at her hands. "Tell me what happened."

Tobin looked to Wolfe, who nodded. They had already discussed what details they would release to Laynie's family and who would relate them.

Tobin reached out and took one of Kari's hands. "Your sister was out of the country on assignment."

"What country? What was she doing there?"

"I'm sorry. I'm not at liberty to discuss the details of her assignment, including where she was."

As Kari set her jaw and gathered herself to argue with him, Tobin couldn't help but observe how much she resembled Laynie doing precisely the same thing. His forehead puckered, and tears sprang to his eyes.

Kari noticed. "You . . . you were the sky marshal on that other plane the hijackers tried to take down on 9/11, right?"

Tobin brushed his fingers across his face. "Yes. That was where I met . . . Laynie."

"Was there . . . was there something between you and her?"

Tobin tried to smile. "It was early days for us, but yes. We had hoped for more time to . . . wait on the Lord. To explore the possibilities."

It was Kari's turn to offer comfort. "I'm sorry, Marshal Tobin. I didn't realize."

He nodded. "Like I said, our relationship was young. When she . . . when she gave her life to Jesus, I think she began to hope for a different future than the one she'd been . . . locked into for so long."

"Laynie's salvation was the answer to prayer. Generations of prayer."

"Generations?"

"Yes. Generations of our family and their friends. From April 1911 forward."

"She never said."

"She hardly understood it herself. It's the proverbial 'long story.'"

"I'd like to hear about it, if you're willing to tell me. Sometime . . . later."

His words brought them back to the present and their shared grief. "You asked what happened, Ms. Thoresen?"

"Yes. And would you please call me Kari?"

"I would be honored to do so, ma'am. What . . . what we know so far is that a truck or a large vehicle hit the car she was riding in. She was with three other individuals." He paused a beat. "The car was damaged significantly. Everyone in the car, including Laynie, perished."

Kari's lips trembled. "Where is she? I want to see her."

This was the hardest part for Tobin, hardest because the thought of Laynie dying in such horrifying fashion wrung his own heart. "No, ma'am. You don't want to see her. The accident must have damaged the fuel tank because the car . . . the car burned."

"Laynie? She was in the car when it . . . burned?"

"Yes, ma'am. She and her fellow passengers."

Wolfe stepped in. "We are bringing Laynie home, Ms. Thoresen. However, because of her . . . injuries, the casket will be sealed . . . and should remain sealed."

Kari stared straight ahead as she struggled to process the news and sank into a deep trough of silence that neither Tobin nor Wolfe ventured to disturb. Several minutes later, they heard vehicles in the driveway and the slam of car doors. Søren burst through the front door, Max behind him.

Tobin and Wolfe drew back from the sofa to give them space, grateful that Kari's husband was there to comfort her.

Søren dropped to his knees in front of his wife. "Kari? Max told me. Are you all right?"

"No. My heart is broken, Søren. Shattered. They keep saying Laynie is dead, a car crash, but it can't be true! Oh, what am I going to tell Shannon and Robbie? How will we ever tell Polly and Gene?"

Søren pulled Kari into his arms. "We will tell them together, my love. The Lord will help us. He will help us all." He looked to Wolfe and Tobin. "Thank you for coming to tell us in person."

"You . . . and Laynie deserve our best," Wolfe said gently. He cleared his throat. "When you're ready, we'd like to discuss the arrangements."

"Isn't it too soon?" Søren asked. "We haven't even told our other children or Laynie's parents."

"We understand. However, it's important that we remain here until we've had some conversation around the arrangements."

Tobin watched Søren's eyes flick from Wolfe to himself. Tobin moved his head incrementally up and down, answering Søren's unspoken question.

Yes. We have more to say.

Søren's impatience grew. "Can you at least give us a little space and time? We will want to talk about the arrangements privately. As a family."

"Of course. We'll step outside. Call us when you are ready."

Wolfe jerked his chin and headed for the door. Tobin fell in behind him.

Tobin blew out a long breath and stretched his neck and tight shoulders. Then he inhaled, filling his lungs with fresh, bracing air. "I'm going to take a walk, Director. Clear my head."

He didn't wait for Wolfe to answer. Tobin set his feet moving away from the house and found himself wandering down the slope toward the creek that ran along the property line. When he reached the creek's bank, he fixed his gaze on the deep green waters and watched them flow by, dancing over the rocks in the creek bed on their way to the river some distance away.

He looked downstream to his right and noted the bridge that spanned the creek and the unpaved road that wound away from the creek to eventually turn into the farm on the other side of the creek. His eyes took in the well-tended fields opposite him and, at the far reaches of the fields, studied the rustic barn and the equally antiquated house just beyond it.

What sights have these old buildings witnessed over the many decades they have stood there? Tobin wondered. *What tales could they tell of the heroic men and women who poured their lives into this land?*

KARI WENT TO HER DESK and stared out the window. She watched Tobin trudge down to the creek, place his hands on his hips, and gaze out at Søren's family homestead and beyond. Dejection slumped his broad shoulders.

"Marshal Tobin is hurting as much as we are."

Søren stood behind her and wrapped her in his arms. "As always, you are more insightful than I am," he murmured. "You picked up on his loss. I was too engrossed in my own sorrow to see his."

Kari sighed. "Did I pick up on something else? That this Director Wolfe hasn't told us everything?"

"You didn't get that wrong. There's something about the 'arrangements.'"

Kari looked down at the clock on her desk. "Shannon and Robbie won't be home from school for another hour and a half. And we don't expect Gene and Polly until dinner time."

Gene and Polly Portland lived in the little casita behind Kari and Søren's house.

"I think I'd like to hear whatever else these two men have to say. Get it over with so we can be alone with our children and their grandparents . . . to grieve." Her voice caught on the last of her words.

Swallowing down her pain, she pointed to the tangled branches of an old apple orchard far back on Søren's land. "Many of our family members are buried on that knoll over there."

"Is that where you're thinking you'd like Laynie laid to rest?"

Kari nodded. "Yes. She should be near us, near her mama and dad. Home. At long last."

"Would you like me to ask them inside again?"

"Give me a few minutes. I think I'll make some coffee and sandwiches for them. I need to use my hands and mind on an ordinary task. Something to ward off this terrible sense of disbelief."

Søren placed a kiss on the tender skin of her neck. "I married a kind woman."

Kari shuddered and sniffed. "What would I do without you, Søren Thoresen?"

TOBIN WALKED UPSTREAM along the creek bank, then looked back, surveying the road they'd driven in on. It topped a bluff, then dropped away toward the creek, revealing a broad hollow on this side of the water. Although winter was already making its entrance and the land was stark and bare, he liked what he saw—the Thoresen's house, nestled in the hollow between the creek and the bluff behind it, set apart and sheltered from the wild prairie's expanse.

A small structure farther up the hollow caught his eye, and he left the creek to examine it more closely.

Why, it's a house. A really old house, he realized. He could hardly believe that people had actually lived in such a tiny structure. Someone had added a porch to the front of the house—a porch with at least half the area as the house itself. More recently, someone had fenced in the house, not to hide it, but to set it apart.

To cherish it, perhaps? Mark its significance?

Tobin unlatched the gate and walked around the house. At most, it had two tiny bedrooms, tacked on as an afterthought, and he estimated the structure's total area at less than four hundred square feet.

My apartment in Germantown is bigger than this—and yet whole families spent their lives here. Was this part of the "generations" Kari mentioned?

He marveled that the house was still standing until, looking closer, he saw that the foundation had been shored up, rotted posts replaced, and new shingles added to keep out the rain.

A whistle caught his attention. Wolfe, signaling him. Tobin latched the gate behind himself, respectful of the family treasure within the fence.

"They've asked us back inside," Wolfe told him.

KARI INVITED THEM TO sit at the family table just off the kitchen. "It's past lunchtime, and I figured we could all do with some sustenance. We can . . . discuss the arrangements after we've eaten."

Tobin realized he was starving when his stomach knotted at the sight of hot soup, a mountain of sandwiches, and a plate of home-baked cookies. "This looks great. Thank you."

Wolfe agreed. "Yes, thank you. You're very kind."

The men, including Max, dug in, devouring soup, sandwiches, and cookies. Conversation among the five of them was stilted until Tobin, looking for something to cut the silence, mentioned the old house.

"You've done a great job preserving that old place," he said. "It's just hard for me to imagine anyone actually living in it."

Kari smiled. "My great-grandmother, Rose, came west on the train in 1881. She had recently lost her husband and her three young children. She was thirty-three and utterly alone when she got off the train in RiverBend."

"Why? Why did she do that?"

Shrugging, Kari said, "I believe she came looking for consolation, for a purpose to her broken life. What she found was Jesus."

Tobin's chewing jaws slowed. "You're saying she lived in that house?"

Søren answered. "According to my grandfather, when she saw the creek, this hollow and the house sheltered in it, she fell in love with them. 'Course, it was springtime. The prairie really is beautiful in the spring. Not like now when everything is dead and dry.

"Anyway, it was a vacant homestead, up for sale by its owners through the local bank. The house wasn't in much better shape at that time than it is now, but Rose's husband had left her some money. In fact, she was quite well-to-do. She shocked the entire community when she up and bought the homestead, the very land where we sit right now."

"Wait. Your grandfather told you this?"

Søren and Kari exchanged amused looks. Søren said, "Yes, my grandfather, also Søren Thoresen. I'm his namesake. Grandpa lived into his nineties and spent many hours recounting our family's history to me."

Wolfe looked from Søren to Kari. "Your families share history, then?"

"More than that—our families are intertwined," Kari answered. "Søren's great-grandfather, Jan Thoresen, owned the homestead opposite us, across the creek. He was a widower, and my great-grandmother, Rose, eventually married him." She tilted her head toward her husband. "That made Søren's grandfather—"

"Grandpa Søren," Søren interjected.

"Yes. When Rose married Jan, Jan's son, Søren, became Rose's stepson. Then Jan and Rose had a daughter, Joy. My grandmother."

"So, you two are . . ." Wolfe, confused, left the statement hanging.

"We're related, but distantly. We share the same great-grandfather, Jan, but different great-grandmothers. That makes us half-cousins two or three times removed—or some such thing."

Tobin glanced at his empty plate, then at the table. The food was gone, the remainders vacuumed up during the short conversation.

Kari addressed Max. "Max, would you mind going to your room for a bit? Your dad and I need some time alone with these gentlemen."

"Sure, Mom." He leaned over and kissed her on the cheek. "I'm awful sorry about Aunt Laynie. 'Specially since we just found her again. I . . . I'm glad I got to meet her. She was pretty amazing."

"She was, wasn't she?" Kari sniffed and wiped her eyes. "Thank you, Max."

After Max excused himself, they adjourned to the living room.

Kari looked from Wolfe to Tobin. "You wanted to discuss the funeral arrangements. What about them?"

Wolfe nodded. "I've given orders for Laynie's remains to be brought back to the US. I don't have an arrival date yet, but I've asked the embassy to expedite the process. Inside of a week, I should think."

"Send us the arrival information. We can take it from there. We're going to bury her here, in the family cemetery."

When Wolfe did not agree immediately, Kari's eyes narrowed. "What? Do you have an objection?"

Wolfe and Tobin didn't want to make things harder for this family, but they needed to speak the truth about the possible dangers still at play.

Wolfe cleared his throat. "Not an objection. More of a concern."

"What concern?"

"We think it would be very unfortunate if certain parties should connect your sister, via her death, to Elaine Granger, the woman against whom these, er, parties hold something of a vendetta."

Kari's response was harsh. "You sound like a bad lawyer dancing around an insupportable argument without ever making his point, Mr. Wolfe. If my sister is *dead*, what does it matter?"

Wolfe leaned closer and spoke softly. "Then let me be plain. While fleeing through Canada after 9/11, Laynie—as Elaine Granger—earned, inadvertently, the ire of a certain crime syndicate when their electronic financial records were swept up in an FBI raid. We're convinced that the syndicate has copies of the records, but that's not the point. The point is that the FBI also has them.

"These records are encrypted, and the FBI hasn't cracked the encryption yet, but it's only a matter of time until they do, which is causing the syndicate a great deal of heartburn. The syndicate would like nothing better than to get their hands on the individual who arranged the FBI's raid on their facility . . . and on anyone associated with the event. Even remotely associated."

"Remotely associated? What does that mean?"

"I'm saying that this syndicate, based out of New York, is still actively hunting the individual who gave the FBI probable cause for a raid, and Elaine Granger was the reason the syndicate got involved with this individual, this hacker, in the first place. We are, of course, keeping this person, who later became Laynie's friend, safe."

"Safe? The way you kept Laynie safe? I feel for this unnamed person you say was Laynie's friend." Anger dripped from Kari's mouth.

Søren squeezed Kari's hand. "Sweetheart, let the man talk, please." He looked at Wolfe. "Go on."

It was time for Wolfe to be blunt. "I'm sorry, but the Ukrainian mob won't care that Laynie is dead. They have a reputation for visiting the sins of the fathers upon their children, and if they were to discover that Laynie had a family? They would come for you and your children."

Kari went deathly pale. She opened her mouth. Nothing came out.

"You need to understand that the mob wants the person who stole their records, and they want her in the worst way. If they came here to RiverBend, to your home, you could tell them you know nothing, that you've never met this person. You could swear on the Bible that you don't even know her name, *and it would not matter*. The mob's thugs would feel it necessary to satisfy themselves and their bosses that *none* of you are holding out on them. They would show no mercy."

Kari began to shake in Søren's arms. She couldn't stop. The horrific news Wolfe had brought them was bad enough. The picture he painted of danger to her family—her children—was too much. She leaned her face into Søren's chest and sobbed.

Søren said through gritted teeth, "You obviously have a plan. Tell us what we should do."

Wolfe nodded. "I understand your family spends Christmas in New Orleans each year?"

"Yeah. What of it?"

"Take the family to New Orleans a couple weeks early this year. Bury Laynie in New Orleans before Christmas. Quietly. Just the immediate family. No publicity. My people will handle all the arrangements, thus keeping her name and yours apart. You'll return to RiverBend after Christmas, and the Ukrainians will never connect Laynie to you. Your family . . . *your children* will be safe. I swear it."

When neither Kari nor Søren spoke, Tobin added, softly, "It's what she would want you to do. She loved all of you deeply. Nothing mattered more to her than keeping her family safe."

Kari, her face mottled and wet with tears, acquiesced. "All right. We'll do it your way."

Wolfe released his breath. "Thank you." He withdrew a business card from his pocket. "We'll have Laynie's remains delivered directly to New Orleans, and we'll be in touch as soon as we know when they will arrive. If you have any questions, call me at this number—any time, day or night."

Signaling Tobin to follow, Wolfe showed himself out.

CHAPTER 5

SERAPHIM, TOBIN, AND JAZ huddled around the conference room table. It was early morning, still dark outside. Wolfe had returned Tobin to Broadsword the night before. Even though the room was soundproof and Harris was posted in the living room to watch the door, the three of them kept their voices low.

"I spoke to Director Wolfe last night after he dropped you off here, Tobin. He wants the three of us to follow up on his 'canary trap.'"

"What's a canary trap?" Jaz demanded.

"It's a form of disinformation. In order to keep her real mission a secret from the mole high up in his organization, Director Wolfe manufactured a fake, disingenuous mission package for Anabelle."

"Bella," Tobin and Jaz said in unison. They glanced at each other and shrugged.

"She didn't like being called Anabelle, Seraphim," Tobin said softly. "She preferred Bella and asked that we call her that."

Seraphim nodded. "I'll try to remember, but our priority is uncovering the mole in the director's organization and plugging the leak right here on our team."

"Understood," Tobin replied.

Jaz said nothing. Her grief had progressed to the anger stage, and that anger smoldered not far under the surface.

Seraphim, one cautious eye on Jaz, said, "About the trap. The director sent an email to five high-level deputies in his organization outlining Ana—I mean *Bella's*—mission parameters."

"I don't understand," Jaz said. "Why would he give away operational details?"

"He wouldn't, of course. Like I said, it was a ruse to keep their attention off her actual operation, but it was also a means of smoking out the mole. Bella had garnered something of a reputation as a renegade, someone who would bend the rules, even defy orders and work outside her mission parameters. The email stated that Bella had again disobeyed orders.

"In the email, the Director gave instructions that any agent in the field who spotted her was not to intercept her, but was only to surveil and report her actions. He varied the faux mission details slightly in each of the five emails, added that his instructions were need-to-know only, and sent the emails out."

"Varied the details how?" Jaz asked.

"Different destination cities and arrival times. Varied descriptions of Bella. We put five female agents on the ground, one in each city at these arrival times, all of them tall and slender. In each email, we varied Bella's hair color and style to match the female operative's color and style and described the clothing she would be wearing. Then we put eyes on the agents and waited."

"Waited for what?"

"For someone to disregard the email's instructions and, instead of reporting Bella's movements, try to capture or take her out. We had the agents covered, of course, and would have taken whoever was sent to capture or kill her. The point was, if one of the agents were to be attacked, we'd have narrowed down the pool of suspected moles."

"And?"

"And nothing. That's the problem. Our people were in place to follow the five fake Bellas at all five destinations, but no one made a move on her. Wolfe wants to know where we messed up."

"That's easy enough," Jaz snarled. "Our own precious mole right here managed to obtain the real scoop on Bella's destination and mission. Whoever it is? He or she fed it to their superiors, which warned them off the trap. *It also painted a bullseye right on her!*"

"Mind your temper, Jaz. I can't have you going all shirty on us."

"What the **blank** does that mean?"

Tobin gently lowered his palm to Jaz's arm. "Jaz, 'shirty' is Brit talk for *keep your shirt on* or calm down."

"How I act doesn't change the facts one iota. Someone here is responsible for Bella's . . ." Jaz couldn't finish.

Seraphim leaned her forehead on clenched fists. "You aren't wrong, Jaz. The task force has six other members. One of them leaked Bella's mission and as good as killed her."

"Eight," Jaz ground out. "You're leaving off Bella's protective detail. Lance and Sherman."

"Okay. You're right. Eight possible moles."

Tobin's brow furrowed in concentration. "How. How did they pass the info? If we knew that, we'd have the mole."

Jaz's rage bubbled closer to the surface, reddening her complexion. "Well, I can't exactly go back in time and figure that out now, can I?"

Seraphim asked, "No, but . . . what if we gave the mole something new to report? Could you be ready then?"

Jaz considered the questions, a little of the heat leaving her face. "Maybe."

"We need better than 'maybe,' Jaz, if we're going to set another trap."

"No restrictions?"

"No. None."

"Yah, okay. I can do it. Give me . . . give me a couple hours."

FOR A SECOND TIME, Collier dialed the number his "guest in the shadows" had given him. The call rang eight times before it was picked up.

"Wolfe here."

"It's Collier, Director."

"Report, please."

"Sir, it took a couple days to cut through the red tape—I had to obtain the local health officer's release form—but I claimed your friend's remains. I personally oversaw them being placed in the burial casket and sealed and the casket placed in a shipping container. I accompanied the remains to the airport and booked them through to their destination—exactly per your orders."

Meaning I did not leave them alone in the airline's care. They have been under continuous two-man guard since I claimed them and they will remain under guard until they are delivered. To you.

"You're certain they are my agent's remains?"

"Yes, sir. The coroner identified the four bodies to me—three male, one female. He attested to the female remains when I claimed them."

Collier broke into a sweat just thinking about the scene in the morgue. Four covered stainless steel autopsy tables in a row and the four charred corpses the coroner insisted on unveiling to him.

"You received my shipping instructions?"

"Yes, sir. I have arranged shipment to the location you specified and to *you*, personally. As I was instructed."

Wolfe hadn't directed Collier to ship the remains to him. His instructions were to send the remains to one Charles-Pierre Lavalle, owner of the New Orleans funeral home with whom he'd contracted Laynie's memorial service and internment. Collier was acting on someone else's orders.

Cossack.

Wolfe's hesitation was almost imperceptible. "Thank you, Mr. Collier. I appreciate your attention to detail."

COSSACK HAD LEFT TBILISI soon after speaking to Collier. He rode north on his motorbike until daybreak before he pulled off the road into a grove of trees where he hid himself and his machine. Exhausted physically and mentally, he wrapped himself in his cloak, lay down in a thicket, and slept.

When he woke, he judged the time to be past noon. He'd slept six hours without disturbance, long enough to fortify himself for the grueling journey ahead. He had hours ahead of him before he reached his militia's stronghold in the mountains. His route, so far, had been easy. Cossack's destination would take him in the direction of the Georgia-Chechen border, but he would leave the road before he reached it and then the way would become difficult, his progress slow and arduous.

The most direct crossing from Georgia into Chechnya wound through the eight-mile-long Pankisi Gorge, also known as the Gate of Wolves. The gorge's only road followed the Argun River and was cut into steep canyon walls that plunged down into the river.

The gorge eventually opened to a valley on the Chechen side of the border. The valley had been occupied by Chechen Muslims for as long as anyone could remember, and the gorge had been used for generations to smuggle arms and radical jihadis into Chechnya. It was also infamous for skirmishes and all-out battles between Chechen-Islamic separatists and Russian forces.

Last year, when the Russian military defeated Chechen forces, the Russians had instituted direct rule over Chechnya, including taking control of the border between Georgia and Chechnya along the Pankisi Gorge. The route through the mountains was now dotted with checkpoints, the road tightly controlled by Russian military. The Russian stranglehold over the gorge had made using the direct route to cross into Chechnya impossible for insurgents such as himself.

Cossack and his militia, hunted by Russian troops, had been forced into the wilds of the mountains where they were determined to forge another route from Georgia into Chechnya. They had also resolved to establish a winter stronghold for their ranks deep within the forbidding mountain terrain, but this goal was not without its challenges.

The Lesser Caucasus Mountains, running northwest to southeast across Georgia and Armenia, boasted many notable caves and cave dwellings because of their soft, easy-to-carve sedimentary rock. Those caves and cave systems included the monastery complex built into the sides of Mt. Gareja in the Kakheti region bordering Azerbaijan, and Vardzia, another cave monastery etched into the slopes of the Erusheti Mountains. These cave systems were well known and frequented by tourists. They were also far south of the area where Cossack needed to hide his men.

The *Greater* Caucasus Mountains that stretched northeast and southwest between Georgia and Chechnya were roughly the length of California. These wild, primitive mountains, in contrast to the Lesser Caucasus range, consisted of harder, less malleable rock. Nevertheless, Cossack knew that Sayed's All Glorious for Allah operated out of a mountain stronghold in eastern Chechnya.

Sayed had not yet trusted Cossack with the exact location of his stronghold, but Cossack knew that Sayed's militia used their cave system to stockpile the arms and supplies that enabled them to winter in the mountains.

Weary of the continual danger of moving his men from place to place, Cossack and his lieutenants determined to search out their own mountain stronghold. He and his second-in-command, Rasul, sent several two-man parties into the rugged mountains to hunt for defensible locations. Cossack wished their sanctuary to reside south of Chechnya, just within the boundaries of the Republic of Georgia—thus providing them with a measure of safety from Russian troops—but not too far from the Chechen border. They wanted a home base from which they might mount sorties into Chechnya and return across the border to relative security.

One of their search parties reported finding a few small, unconnected caves in a densely treed ravine several miles east of Pankisi Gorge. They enthused over the ravine, telling Cossack and Rasul, "The terrain is so rugged that we can hold both ends of the ravine with only a few men. One end of the ravine can be reached from the road leading to Pankisi Gorge—and we have found a foot route from the caves through a narrow pass that crosses the border farther east into Chechnya."

When Cossack had initially viewed their find, he rejected it. "The caves are too shallow to winter in. It would take tremendous effort and not an insignificant amount of time and money to deepen them," he told Rasul. "We should focus our energies on consolidating our control over Chechnya."

They made that decision in the spring of 1999.

A few months later, Sayed and other Islamist leaders proposed invading Dagestan, the Russian province east of Chechnya, bordering the Caspian Sea. Cossack had advised against the move and had warned of Russia's likely retaliation. "If we rouse the Russians' anger with a new offensive, we risk losing the Chechen territory we now hold—the ground our people have bled and died to gain." He had not objected too forcefully, sensing that the leaders of the other insurgent militias might question his loyalty to the dream of a new Islamic caliphate.

In August, ignoring Cossack's counsel, Chechen and Dagestani Islamist militants took the provincial government and declared Dagestan to be an independent Islamic state—the Islamic Republic of Dagestan. With their own people in control of the government, they soon began the work of giving unbelievers a choice—convert, leave, or die.

Two months later, the army of the Russian Federation responded. The army rolled into Chechnya in force, intent upon recapturing Chechnya's capital, Grozny. A long, costly winter battle ensued, a bloodbath that would become known as the Second Chechen War. The campaign ended in May 2000 when the Russian military defeated the Islamist militias in open battle and reestablished direct Russian rule over Chechnya.

Cossack lost many of his men to the Russian military, as did Sayed and the other Islamist militias. But while Sayed had a mountain sanctuary to flee to, a secure stronghold in which to lick his wounds and regroup, Cossack did not. It was then that Cossack changed his mind about the hidden ravine high in the Georgian mountains east of Pankisi Gorge.

Gathering his decimated troops, he spoon-fed them the dream of a safe harbor. "We will build a home in the mountains—a sanctuary hidden from Russian gunships, a stronghold inaccessible to Russian troops. We will descend from our mountain aerie into Chechnya, terrorize the Russians and inflict damages on them, then return to our stronghold. They may try to follow us—but we will ensure that they never find us."

He formed foraging parties and sent them to "liberate" what they needed from the Russian invaders. An element of a foraging party would harass the Russian troops, drawing them out, striking when feasible, distracting them, then withdrawing without taking casualties. While the Russians were busy defending themselves, the other part of the raiding party would attack Russian supply depots and steal all they could carry.

Each raid was planned to worry the Russians like a dog worries a bone—all while robbing them blind. Cossack's men lost their discouragement and entered into this form of guerrilla warfare with renewed zeal. They spent weeks stockpiling stolen materials and supplies in the foothills before porting them to the ravine by way of a treacherous route known only to them. With hope revived, they labored without complaint.

Over the late spring and summer, Cossack's militia chiseled and blasted their way into the mountain, enlarging and connecting the caves, slowly carving out a deep and complex cave system with spring-fed water and multiple points of egress should they be attacked.

The road Cossack traveled this day by motorbike took him into the foothills of the Caucasus Mountains north of Tbilisi. Here he observed snow along the roadside, snow that covered the mountainous terrain through which the road wound. Had he continued up the winding road, he would have encountered Russian checkpoints guarding the Pankisi Gorge. The gorge, however, was not Cossack's route.

Less than a half mile farther up the road, he spied a marker only he and his people would recognize and turned off the road. He hauled his motorbike over the trunk of a fallen tree and wheeled it through the dense woods until he reached an unmarked and rock-strewn path leading away from the main road. Before he continued on, he returned to the fallen tree near the road and brushed away the signs of human disturbance in the snowy drifts and muddy ground.

Cossack pressed on. He knew the way to his militia's sanctuary. It was strewn with rocks, patches of snow, and debris washed downhill. The "path" was often far too treacherous and too damaging to his tires to ride on, but he knew from experience when to dismount and walk.

Soldiers of his militia were posted at critical junctures along the route. Their job, should they detect an intrusion, was to give early warning to other soldiers up the path.

A Russian patrol that stumbled upon the "path" might deem it unusable and ignore it. A patrol bent on following the path would, after half a mile, find their progress blocked by a rockslide of obvious age based on the lichen growing on the fallen rocks.

Cossack's soldiers had constructed a bypass above the landslide and had cleverly hidden its starting point yards before the rockslide. The bypass wound up a steep, nearly vertical slope and across a portion of the rockslide they had stabilized with rock, timber, and mortar.

The soldier that met Cossack at the bypass's starting point attached a short rope to the motorbike's steering column. Together, the soldier and Cossack pulled and pushed the machine up the slope. They carried it across the rockslide and down the other side where, several hundred yards farther, Cossack could remount his machine and ride a much-improved path the remainder of the way to his militia's hideout.

He was worn through when he arrived at his militia's stronghold near midnight. The advance guards, recognizing him, allowed him to pass and radioed ahead to announce their leader's return.

As he dragged his weary body from the motorbike, Rasul's familiar voice greeted him.

"Welcome home, Arzu. Did you meet with success?"

"Mostly—praise be to Allah. Hassan agreed to our terms. However, he cannot fill our order for another six weeks."

"We must be patient, then." He slapped an arm around Cossack's shoulder. "Come. You must be tired and hungry. I will have my woman fix you something to eat."

"Thank you, but I would rather sleep, my friend. I can eat tomorrow."

"As you wish, my general."

They walked in companionable silence to the entrance of the militia's cave system. The entrance was so close to a precipice that they could proceed only single file until they stooped to enter the cave. They took a narrow tunnel to the right and parted at Cossack's spartan living quarters. It was not more than a shallow niche that branched off from the tunnel. It contained a cot, a short stack of boxes that served as a desk, and a trunk containing his clothes. A blanket hanging in the doorway was the extent of his privacy. He left it pulled aside except when he lay down to sleep.

He'd no sooner sat on his cot to tug off his boots than a gangly young insurgent appeared at the entrance to his room. The youthful recruit had little to offer in the way of fighting skills, but he was adept in the use and maintenance of long-range radios.

"*As-Salamu Alaykum*, little brother," Cossack said.

"*Wa alaykumu s-salam*, General! Sir, I wished to give you a message that came while you were gone."

"From whom?" Cossack asked. "I am very weary at the moment. Perhaps it could wait?"

"From Hassan, sir. Yes, of course. I will give it to you in the morning."

Cossack cursed silently. Supposedly, he had just spent three days with the Turkish arms dealer!

"Wait," Cossack said. "It could be important. Did you write it down?"

"Yes, sir. Always. I . . . it was short, so I memorized it and left the paper by the radio."

Cossack was already putting his boots back on. "Never deliver a message without bringing the written version—for the receiver's sake, eh? Not everyone can recall details the way a young mind can. We will go, and I will read it myself."

"Certainly, sir. I apologize."

"Did you report the radio call to your supervisor?"

"No, sir. I was told it was for your ears only."

"Very good. Very good." Cossack patted a pocket with feigned absent-mindedness. "You return to your post. I will be along shortly."

As soon as the boy left, Cossack pulled out a cloak he hadn't worn for some time. He donned the cloak, drew a scarf over his head to hide his turban, and removed a compact Russian Karatel from his clothing trunk. He had taken the combat knife from the body of a Russian Spetsnaz he had killed in battle. He slid the knife into his waistband.

Just in case.

Stepping from his room, he checked the tunnel in both directions. Being the middle of the night, few of his soldiers were up and about other than the guards stationed far enough from the cave entrances to provide early warning should an attack be imminent. As Cossack moved stealthily toward the mouth of the caves, he thought it fortuitous that the radio was located at the very entrance of their cave system.

Their best climber had carried the radio's antenna on his back and climbed as high up the ravine's face above them as he could. Once he had secured himself to a narrow ledge, he bolted the antenna to solid rock. When he climbed down, he fastened one end of a one-hundred-and-fifty-foot coil of wire to his belt and climbed back up to the antenna and connected the wire. The remaining wire on the ground had reached inside the cave—but only just. Out of necessity, they had named the closest niche to the entrance the radio room.

Cossack also thought it fortuitous that the radioman had not shared the message with anyone else—anyone such as Rasul.

When he arrived at the radio room, the young soldier was its only occupant. The boy jumped to his feet and offered Cossack the slip of paper. "The message, sir."

"Yes, yes, but now I need to relieve myself. Follow me outside and read it to me."

"Sir, the light . . ."

"Bring a flashlight."

Cossack set a brisk pace to the edge of the ravine close the cave entrance. His men had built a short wall of rocks as a safety precaution after one of the soldiers had stumbled in the dark. The man had fallen from the precipice and been dashed to death on the rocks below. After the rock wall was built, his soldiers—as young men would—had subsequently made a sport of relieving themselves into the void.

While Cossack did his business, the boy read the message to him, "I have received your order and can fill it by mid-January. When will you come for a visit? I enjoy our long conversations and wish to see you again. Hassan."

When will you come for a visit? Cossack repeated to himself. *How unfortunate.*

When he finished his business, he reached out his hand. "The message, please."

As Cossack reached for the paper, he looked into the boy's face. The young man hadn't yet lived long enough to learn artifice, how to hide his thoughts and feelings—the skills one needed to survive in such a cruel world. Doubt was written in the radio operator's slack mouth, growing distrust and fear in his wide eyes—and the prescient sense of danger.

Instead of taking the message, Cossack grabbed the boy's wrist.

"I am sorry," he whispered.

It was over quickly. Cossack jerked the boy toward him, twisted around so the boy's back was to the precipice, and used both hands and his considerable strength to shove him. The boy's legs hit the low rock wall. Off-balance, he started to fall backward. His hands groped the air even as he tumbled over the edge and pinwheeled into the darkness.

The boy screamed as he fell the first fifty feet. Cossack heard his body thump on the rocks and continue tumbling down into the ravine.

"What was that?" a voice called out.

Cossack hurried into the cave before the guards arrived to investigate. The boy had dropped the flashlight. It lay on ground close to the stone wall, still burning where it would tell the tale Cossack needed it to tell.

SERAPHIM, TOBIN, AND JAZ met again the following day. Jaz's anger hadn't abated. She reported her progress in short, terse statements.

"I've tapped every form of communication in and out of this place—email, landline, mobile phone. If anyone so much as breathes into their phone, I'll know it. So far, nothing."

Tobin muttered the obvious. "They know to keep their head down. We won't catch them until we've given them something to report."

Tobin and Jaz looked to Seraphim. She shook her head. "I'm working on it. I can't just throw information out there. Has to be both critical and believable."

She asked Jaz, "How do you monitor communications when you're away from your laptop?"

"I've written code so that my laptop alerts my mobile phone when new communications arrive or leave." She thought for a moment. "Everything is pretty much dependent upon the broadband service coming into Broadsword. If that cuts out, my surveillance goes kaput."

Seraphim rubbed her eyes. "Understood."

COSSACK AROSE IN THE morning and made his way through the tunnels to the militia's largest room. It was used as a common area for passing the time and for strategy meetings prior to a sortie. Here, three women prepared meals and the men gathered in squads to eat.

As Cossack strode into view, his men stood and greeted him.

Several of them murmured, "Welcome back, General."

He nodded to them. One of the women brought him tea. He'd taken two sips when Rasul joined him.

"We lost a man last night, Arzu."

Cossack's head came up. "Who? What happened?"

"One of our radio operators fell into the ravine. He must have tripped in the dark and gone over the wall."

Cossack cursed. "Stupid fool. We cannot afford such losses! Good men do not grow on trees."

Rasul pulled at his beard. "I found it odd that the man had a flashlight with him and still tripped in the dark. It was lying by the wall, still on."

"Then he was careless!"

"I shall scold the men and reprimand the radioman's supervisor."

Cossack drained his tea. "Yes. And afterward? I want that wall built higher. The radioman's supervisor is to oversee it. Personally."

"Yes, General."

The boy's death and the public chastisement would both serve as potent reminders to the men not to take the nearby precipice lightly.

CHAPTER 6

TOBIN HUFFED A LISTLESS sigh. It was midmorning, exactly a week since Wolfe had delivered the devastating news of Laynie's death. He sat at his workstation in the bullpen and, around him, the task force labored, tasked by Seraphim but driven by their own dogged, hardened determination.

They had by this time compiled a list of seventeen bulletin boards hosted by Kazakhstani ISPs and frequented by individuals with jihadi ties. With Jaz instructing them, the team learned new tricks, and they actively monitored the seventeen sites and their multiple public and private chat rooms, hacking the private chat rooms and their now not-so-private conversations.

Jubaila and Soraya were on the hunt. They drilled down into Muslim chat rooms in southern Russia and its neighboring countries, identifying radical chats. The two women spoke the languages used in the messages. They employed keyword searches to set up alarms and logged possibly relevant conversation s. They identified individuals with ties to radical Islamist groups and passed them on to Rusty and Brian.

Rusty and Brian followed the threads, tracing the radicals to their hiding places. Jaz taught them to hack the communications of a suspect and his associates—anyone from whom they caught even the faintest suggestion of suspicion. Rusty and Brian kept drilling down, widening the net, snagging jihadis associated with their Chechen suspects, some of them leading back to the US.

Jaz showed Gwyneth how to follow the money, how to burrow into electronic funds transfers and track the funds from bank to bank and country to country. Gwyneth took to her new role with a speed and passion that did not bode well for those she pursued.

Vincent, for his part, kept a running account of their progress, collating data. He also created a database of individual profiles, making it simple for the team to cross-reference their finds with that of their teammates, adding their data to already established profiles, creating relationship graphs between and among the profiles.

And while Gwyneth traced money and suspicious actors, Jaz monitored communications inside Broadsword. *All communications.* She hacked cell phone providers and dug into text histories. She read every email in and out of every account at Broadsword and investigated the senders or recipients of every email she found. She learned facts about her coworkers she wished she hadn't—things such as bad breakups, weird habits, and comments about herself before the team had coalesced. All these she set aside to focus solely on hunting down their mole.

"Poor little mole," Tobin overheard her whisper, "You have no idea that Vyper is lurking outside your little hidey hole. You are unaware of my presence as I slither through the tall grass, silent and sure as death, but I am here—oh, yes—waiting patiently for you to give yourself away. And when you do? Your little lizard brain might sense danger, and you might duck back into your hole, but I will slither in after you, hapless little mole. Your last sight on this earth will be my fangs . . ."

No one on the task force—including Tobin—believed everything the task force was doing at this point was completely legal. With tacit, unspoken agreement, they had crossed that bridge and burned it behind them the evening Wolfe had announced Bella's death. Warrants required applications, and warrant applications were reviewed. Until the spy high up in Wolfe's organization was identified and excised, no task force warrants would be placed where the spy might see them.

Seraphim had picked up the reins of task force leadership and spurred the team on, but she carefully refrained from micromanaging them. Or asking about methods.

As for Tobin? He took his turn daily on perimeter guard duty, but compared to the other task force members, he had little to do . . . except to think on all he'd lost.

Lord, what am I still doing here? I have no necessary role with the task force any longer. Why hasn't Wolfe released me to go back to the Marshals Service? At least there I could bury myself in my work.

He thought about demanding that Wolfe send him home, but he couldn't bring himself to pull the trigger. He didn't know which was worse—the torture of remaining with the team when he knew *she* was never coming back, or the finality of leaving Broadsword and the task force to return to his real life.

His old and empty life.

Oh God. How I need your comfort and your guidance right now! In the name of Jesus, I am asking that you help me. Please show me what—

Tobin's phone vibrated. Jarred out of his sorrow and morbid reflections, he flipped the phone open. Found a text message. A text without a sender's name or number.

He eased back in his chair, yawned and stretched. Used the maneuver to nonchalantly scan for inquiring eyes. He dropped his attention back onto his phone and clicked open the message.

Stables. Five minutes.

Tobin closed his phone and stared up into the gym's rafters, arguing with himself.

I don't have the energy or the emotional reserves to deal with another crisis.

Yeah, but maybe we have a line on the mole.

Huh. About time. We're past due.

He grabbed his mug. Sauntered to the coffee maker and filled it. As he gulped a swig of the strong brew, he scanned the bullpen.

Yup. One team member missing, and he hadn't noticed the departure.

He took another gander around the room. No one else seemed to have noticed the departure, either. Nodding to himself, he returned to his desk. He started to lift the mug to his mouth again when his stomach cramped and acid rose in his throat. He'd been drinking far too much coffee lately, using it as one of the few comforts he allowed himself. Even that was failing him.

He had found no relief from the unrelenting desolation in his heart except when he closed himself in with the Lord and searched his Bible. The occasional "word in due season" granted him a small measure of solace, transitory though it was.

He set his mug down and pulled on his jacket. "Back in a few," he said to no one in particular.

The weather this morning was gusty and downright cold, so he headed directly for the stables. Blustery winds had scoured a recent snowfall and beat it into brittle bits of ice—bits that stung like shards of glass hitting his face. He was glad to reach the warmth of the stable.

He shut the door behind him and found Jaz waiting for him in the tack room.

Tobin shoved his hands in his pockets to warm them. "What's up? Why the secrecy?"

She stuck out her chin. "I didn't want to advertise that I'm busting outta here today . . . and that you're going to help me."

"Whoa. Hold on there, missy. I'm not doing that."

"Yes, you are. I've tapped the landlines and hacked every mobile phone and email account in this place—and I mean *all of them*, including Seraphim's. For an entire week, our precious mole hasn't squeaked, burped, or farted. Nothing. Nada."

She growled an afterthought. "Whoever the mole is, they have to know that I'm just waiting for them to stick their traitorous little head out of their hole."

"Waiting to pounce," Tobin supplied. "I get it."

"Exactly. Well, even though the mole is playing it safe, I just read an email from Wolfe to Seraphim giving her the details of Bella's funeral—day, place, and time. It's *the day after tomorrow,* Tobin! Bella's family is going to bury her in less than forty-eight hours. In New Orleans of all places." Jaz's expression, the corners of her eyes lined with new creases, was a shifting mosaic of pain, sorrow, frustration, and anger.

"You want to go—and I understand why you do, Jaz—but Wolfe has already decreed that he won't allow it. Is that what's got you riled up?"

"Me at a funeral? Not on your life. Nasty, loathsome things, funerals. I don't do funerals."

"Good, because Wolfe has put a great deal of care and effort into orchestrating Bella's funeral so that the Ukrainian mob doesn't ever connect her and her family to *you*, little missy—the not-so-brilliant hacker who thought handing the mob's financial records to the FBI was a good idea!"

Jaz lifted her upper lip and growled through her teeth at Tobin.

"Not an attractive look, *Vyper*. But back to my point, you go down to NOLA, start messing around, and the mob somehow sniffs you out? Sure, you might give them the slip, but how long before they wonder *why* you were in NOLA? Before they figure it out, make the leap from you to Bella, then Bella to her family? The mob will hunt down Bella's sister and her sister's children and torture them—all on the *off chance* they might know where *you* live."

Tobin leaned into Jaz's face. "Is that what you want? Is it?"

"No! I mean, why would you think I'd want that—of course I don't! But . . ."

"But what? Your job right now is to find our mole while the task force finds AGFA's fentanyl lab and figures out how they plan to use fentanyl to attack our nation's New Year's celebrations. Besides, if you don't want to attend Bella's funeral, why do you need to leave Broadsword?"

Jaz practically spit at him. "Because I'm not convinced that the remains they're getting ready to stick in the ground belong to Bella—and this is the last chance we'll ever have to prove whether they are or aren't."

Tobin's temper heated. "Now that's just crazy! Wolfe already told us they were. He said Cossack was on scene right after the firefighters put out the fire."

Every word Tobin uttered about the death of the woman he loved was another blade, slicing him to the core. He said them anyway. "*Cossack saw the bodies in the car.* Are you saying he lied to us?"

"No, but Cossack went by what the coroner told him, and all the coroner said was that he received four sets of remains—three male and one *female*. Well, that's not enough for me."

Tobin flushed with indignation. "Stop it. Just stop it, Jaz. Bella is *dead.* You have to accept it. You need to . . . let go of the fantasies. She's not . . . she isn't coming back. Ever."

Jaz folded her arms and stepped back. "You. You of all people . . . I expected more from you, Tobin. I really did."

She wasn't prepared for what happened next, how Tobin exploded and lunged for her. He grasped both her upper arms in iron vises, shoved her against the rough boards of the tack room, and roared into her face, "Me, of all people? Me? I loved her, Jaz! I *still* love her, and I always will! But because I loved her, you think I should latch on to some unlikely, improbable, and utterly *stupid* scenario where Marta *wasn't* in that car?"

For a long, charged moment, they stared each other down, venting rage and sorrow in equal parts. Then Tobin watched Jaz's face fall in on itself and fracture . . . into tiny, aching pieces. When she collapsed, sobbing, he caught her and folded her to his chest. He rocked back and forth and wept with her. In that moment, they were two frail, damaged people grappling with and mourning a shared loss.

"Sh-she . . . she . . . she was the-the only f-f-friend I-I . . . ever . . ."

"I know, I know."

"I-I-I—" Jaz couldn't catch her breath.

"Careful now. Hey, Jaz. C'mon. Breathe. C'mon, now."

But she'd opened the door, and now she couldn't subdue the anguish or push it back into the box where she'd stuffed it. Her wails intensified. They stripped away the façade she hid behind—the bold purple-tipped hair, the tats and piercings, the "cool" and unflappable Goth exterior. She was just a hopeless, brokenhearted woman, keening for her friend. Tobin held her, shed his own tears, and waited for her long-repressed suffering to run its course.

"I can't . . . I can't bear it!" she wailed. "It hurts so bad. I should never have . . . let her get inside. I-It hurts too much."

"I know," Tobin soothed. "I feel you, I truly do."

He patted Jaz's back awkwardly, mulling over what she'd said earlier, rejecting it . . . but coming back around to it. He pulled back so he could see her. "Jaz, help me understand what you're saying, okay? You want to go down to NOLA and prove that it's not Bella in the coffin?"

He pulled out a handkerchief—one he'd used to wipe his own eyes—and offered it to Jaz.

She sniffled and blew snot into Tobin's handkerchief.

Note to self. Toss handkerchief. Get a clean one. "I mean how . . . how would you even go about proving it's Bella—or not Bella? Did you hack her dental records or something?"

"No, don't be ridiculous—well, I did poke around a bit, of course, but she lived in Europe and Russia for a long time, and I couldn't even find any dentists where she'd been a patient, let alone any records. Besides, dental x-rays aren't digital. Yet."

"Then what would you expect to find if—hypothetically—you could reach NOLA before the funeral?"

"I-I . . . it's just that I-I did some research on how human bodies burn."

Tobin cringed and shuddered.

"Sorry. I'm sorry. I know how morbid I sound, but I found out that it's not that easy to burn a body . . . completely. And, well, if Bella was in the car, her back against the seat, that part of her, against the seat . . . might not have sustained as much damage as the front of her."

Tobin wanted to throw up. Instead, he shook his head and gaped at Jaz like she was crazy. "And?"

"And I . . . I bandaged Bella's back after the car bomb, remember? The one where you nearly died?"

"Oh, *that* car bomb. And here I thought you meant a different one," Tobin sneered. "Get to your point, *Vyper*."

Jaz sneered back. "My point is, Bella had cuts on her back—remember that? Cuts that the hospital stitched up, Tobin—*remember?* When she'd mostly healed, you took the stitches out of them—all except that one really deep cut under her left shoulder blade. I pulled those stitches a few days later. Myself."

Something clicked inside Tobin. "You're saying even if she's burned, we'd be able to find—or not find—those cuts?"

"Not us. We'd need a doctor, a specialist. A pathologist who knows how to look for them. Who could tell us . . . if he finds them. Or not."

Tobin's expression softened and fresh tears appeared in his eyes. "Dunno, Jaz. I don't think I can make a place in my heart for false hope. If I were to start to hope and things didn't pan out, I . . . I don't know if I would survive it."

Jaz touched his cheek—the only time Tobin had seen Jaz exhibit anything even approaching an intimate gesture. "Quincy, Wolfe's people haven't been able to find the truck that hit Bella's car. It was a *hit-and-run*. And of all the cars in Tbilisi, it was *her* car that got hit? Do you think for a minute it wasn't intentional? A setup? That our mole—right here at Broadsword—didn't burn Bella? Figuratively *and* literally?"

She dropped her hand, but not her argument. "Please. Stop thinking about false hope and feeling sorry for yourself. Look at this rationally, and ask yourself this question: Do you want to live the rest of your life not knowing—*for certain*—that it was her they put in the ground? Do you?"

When Tobin didn't answer, Jaz whispered, "*I* need to know, definitively, one way or the other. I can't . . . I can't stay here, stay on the task force, not knowing the truth. Can you?"

When Tobin still didn't respond, Jaz added, "Plus, I can't fall asleep because I keep thinking . . . that if Bella isn't dead, then she's *somewhere*. Because, if that's not her body down there in NOLA, then that not only means she's still alive—it also means AGFA took her."

Jaz shivered. "And if they have her? Then they've had her for a week already. And what do you think they are doing to her? No! I can't! I can't live with the possibility—as unlikely, improbable, and utterly *stupid* as you say it is—running around in my head like a never-ending, never-stopping hamster on a wheel, never leaving me alone, never letting me sleep."

Tobin stirred and looked at Jaz, saw the hollows hanging under her black eyeliner and the sharp, jutting points of her cheekbones. They spoke of pain and many wakeful nights.

She whispered, "I can't live like this, Tobin, not knowing. I'd rather die. Don't you understand?"

Tobin stepped back from her and studied his feet. Finally, he shook his head. "I get it. No, I can't live that way either. It *is* better to know for certain—one way or another."

"Well, good," a voice called from a nearby stall. "If I had to stand here much longer listening to you two cry, moan, and wring your hands without coming to a decision, I think I would have puked."

Bo stepped out of a stall and folded his arms.

"Why? You gonna help?" Jaz demanded.

"Heck, yeah. At the very least, I can smuggle you guys out of here."

Tobin drew himself up. "That right?"

"Yeah, that's right."

Tobin nodded. "Well, all right then. Let's figure this out. We're on a clock."

SHORTLY BEFORE NOON, Bo approached Richard. "Misty's got some swelling going on above her near fore fetlock, and I'd like the vet to take a look at it. Thinking I'd load her up and take her down the mountain after lunch. Get it checked out. You know Doc Riley won't come up here, the way the roads can change with the weather. Might visit the feed and supply while I'm down there, too."

Richard, preoccupied with the meal preparations, nodded. "I concur. Be back before dark, though. There's another front moving in, and we're expecting more snow."

"Roger that, sir."

After lunch, Bo hitched a Broadsword pickup truck to a horse trailer and backed the trailer up to the stables. He blanketed the mare, led her outside and up the ramp to the trailer, and fastened her halter to the trailer's bridle hook.

Five minutes later, he raised the ramp, locked it in place, and drove toward the perimeter gate's guard shack. Another ten minutes later, he passed the last of Broadsword's cameras. Shortly after, he reached the state road. He drove half a mile, pulled onto the shoulder, and let down the trailer's ramp.

Tobin and Jaz clambered out, carrying overnight bags. Both of them were shivering.

"Told you two to dress for the weather."

"We did," Tobin chattered. "Pretty cold back there."

"Well, get in the truck. It's warm enough."

When Bo pulled back onto the road, Jaz said, "We need to make a detour and stop at our old apartments."

"What—the apartments the Ukrainians hit? The site of Bella's infamous run-and-jump across the third-story balconies?"

"Yah, those," Jaz muttered.

"What do you need from there that's so all-fired important?" Tobin asked.

"Camouflage," Jaz answered.

BO RETURNED TO BROADSWORD as twilight was giving way to darkness. He unloaded Misty, no worse the wear for her ride down the mountain and back, rubbed her down, and fed and watered the horses under his care. After he'd parked the trailer and the truck, he went looking for Richard.

He probably needed to find Richard . . . before Seraphim found *him.*

Richard was where Bo knew he'd be—in the kitchen, overseeing today's kitchen assistants, Gwyneth and Brian, and their dinner preparations. When Bo came through the back door to the kitchen, Gwyn pursed her lips and looked at the floor. Brian side-eyed him.

Uh-oh. Guess the news is out.

"Richard, could you spare a minute for me?"

Richard turned to his assistants. "Any questions?"

"Lots," Brian muttered, "but not about dinner prep."

Bo followed Richard to the conference room and shut the door behind them. Richard didn't sit or speak. He simply folded his arms and waited.

"Sir, you know by now that I took Tobin and Jaz down the mountain."

"That's not the information I'm waiting to hear."

"You want to know why—and I hope, when I tell you, that I still have a job here."

"Unlikely. We'll see."

"Okay, so I was in the stables before lunch when Jaz and Tobin came in. They . . . they didn't know I was there. I overheard them talking—Jaz talking, mostly. She isn't convinced that Bella is dead."

Richard's brows lifted. "Indeed."

"Yes sir. She kept telling Tobin that she couldn't stand the thought of not knowing . . . knowing for sure that it was Bella's body—Oh. Forgot the part where Jaz told Tobin she'd read Wolfe's email to Seraphim about Bella's funeral. It's in New Orleans, day after tomorrow, sir."

Richard's brow switched direction and dove into a frown. "And what action did Miss Jessup propose that might alleviate her misgivings?"

"She and Tobin . . . hope to get a pathologist to look at the remains. Miss Jessup is convinced that a pathologist would be able to ascertain whether or not the body is Bella's."

"Director Wolfe's contact in the city where Bella died may not have known her personally, but he assured us that she got into the car and died only minutes later. Besides, how could a pathologist's simple physical examination prove otherwise . . . given the body's condition?"

"Begging your pardon, sir, but Jaz—Miss Jessup—said Bella had cuts on her back."

"Cuts?"

"From the car bomb Tobin told us about. Bella was hit with shrapnel when the bomb blew. I guess Jaz helped dress the cuts after Bella was released from the hospital. Some of the cuts required stitches, and Jaz mentioned a particularly deep gouge under Bella's shoulder blade."

Bo swallowed. "Jaz also said that the car crash was hit-and-run. I hadn't known that, sir. She said the accident had to have been intentional. If it was, that means it was coordinated by this Islamic terrorist group the task force is following."

Richard unfolded his arms and sat down. He didn't speak for a long moment.

"What was Marshal Tobin's response to Miss Jessup's idea?"

"He hated it—at first. Frankly, so did I, and I wasn't going to let them act on it. Until . . ."

"Until you lost your good judgment, Bo?"

"No, sir. Until she convinced me of something."

"Which was?"

"Which was . . . if we weren't certain that it was Bella's body her family was putting in the ground, we'd never be at peace about Bella's death. She also said if it *wasn't* Bella's body, then Bella was still alive, and if she *was* alive, then those terrorists had her."

"That was the part that convinced you to compromise the security of this place and the task force, was it?"

Bo pulled himself fully erect. "Sir, any whiff of our plan to leave would have been reported by the mole in our midst."

"Everyone here knew the three of you were gone within an hour of your departure."

"Yes, sir, but we got away clean."

"Be that as it may—"

"Sir. We don't leave our people behind—not ever. And until we prove that it is or isn't Bella's body, we'll never know with certainty that she's not in the enemy's hands."

Richard said nothing for several minutes. Then he stood. "Agreed."

Bo stammered. "W-what?"

"We'll deal with your lapse in discipline later. Right now, I need to speak to Ms. Seraphim." Richard reached for the door. "Oh. Word to the wise? I suggest you avoid her until tempers cool."

"Yes, sir. I will, sir. Thank you, sir."

CHAPTER 7

TOBIN AND JAZ RENTED a car in Germantown, and they drove through the night to reach their destination, stopping only to gas up, use the restrooms, switch drivers, and grab to-go food on the sixteen-hour trip. They used a credit card Jaz pulled from her pocket for all their expenses, a card under the name of Gretchen Sønntag.

"Who's Gretchen Sønntag?" Tobin demanded.

"Someone I invented. Not to worry—there's real money behind that card. More importantly, neither Wolfe nor the Ukrainian mob have ever heard of her."

"If you say so."

"I do say so."

Dawn was breaking over the water when they drove onto the causeway that spanned Lake Pontchartrain. Tobin yawned and nudged Jaz awake. "We're here, more or less. We should check into a hotel."

She sat up and looked around. "Agreed. I could use a hot shower."

They paid for two adjoining rooms, showered, and changed into fresh clothes. When Tobin knocked on Jaz's door, she was on her laptop, plugged into the hotel's broadband service.

"What are you doing?"

"Pinging someone's cell phone. We'll grab something to eat, then make a house call."

"Room service?"

"That would be best . . . in case Director Wolfe already has a team scouting the city."

"Speaking of Director Wolfe and a team looking for us . . . your appearance presents quite a memorable profile."

Jaz mumbled, "Don't fret. Got it covered."

Tobin ordered a pot of coffee and enough food for three people. While they ate, Jaz explained their next moves.

Tobin frowned. "But how did you know—"

"You think I've been sitting on my hands for a week? The phones and email accounts at Broadsword aren't the only ones I've tapped. I've been monitoring the communications of everyone connected to Bella."

Tobin didn't know whether to be appalled or impressed. He went with impressed. "I like the way you think, Jaz—although it fits a criminal's profile better than a legit government employee.

"I'm accustomed to coloring outside the lines." She swallowed the last of her coffee. "Gimme five minutes. Then let's roll."

Tobin wasn't surprised when a complete stranger emerged from the bathroom, covered from head to toe. He was stunned. "What in the bloody blue blazes . . ."

"Like you said, my normal appearance is memorable. In this, no one will see the real me. They'll be too busy ogling the hijab."

"But . . . where in the world did you find this getup?"

"I flew from Vancouver to DC under this cover. I've had the tunic and headscarf in my go bag since we moved into the apartments, and we all grabbed our bags the night the Ukrainians attacked us."

"Then why the stop at our old apartments? I thought Wolfe's cleaners had removed all our personal stuff."

"They didn't know to look under the carpet in the bedroom closet." She winked as she offered him a Canadian passport. "Meet Fawzia Niazi."

RUTH GRAFF STUDIED HER reflection in the mirror of her hotel bathroom. *You look tired, Ruth. Tired, old, and worn out.*

"Who are you kidding?" she told her image. "You *are* tired, old, and worn out. And hurting."

She'd wept when Kari phoned her with the news. She'd wept for everything Laynie had fought to overcome, for the hope of a future without guilt and shame. She'd wept for her dear friend Kari . . . and, having gotten to know Laynie, she wept for her own loss.

"You've seen and heard too much pain and sorrow in your line of work, Ruth, old girl. And the hits just never seem to stop coming."

Sighing, she left the bathroom, pulled on her coat, and picked up her handbag. "Lord, I just didn't expect Laynie's story to end this way, y'know? Yes, I'm so very glad that she gave her heart to you before . . . before she met you in person, but I had hopes she'd find some love and happiness in this life first."

She grabbed her room key and dropped it in her purse. "Who am I kidding? Like any of that matters to her now, right?"

Ruth smiled a little. "*No eye has seen, no ear has heard, and no mind has imagined what God has prepared for those who love him.* At this very moment? Laynie wouldn't trade a moment in the glory of your presence for this wretched place. We're the ones wishing for more time with her. Guess we'll have to be patient until it's our turn."

She closed her hotel door behind her and headed for the elevators, preoccupied with thoughts of the luncheon Kari was hosting at a local restaurant. Kari had reserved a small, private room for the lunch, leaving Shannon and Robbie at her New Orleans' home with her housekeeper, Azalea Bodeen. After lunch, the family plus Ruth would discuss and finalize the details of Laynie's memorial service.

"We consider you family, Ruth. You were Laynie's friend and confidant. She trusted you, and we want you with us," Kari had insisted.

The elevator doors slid open, and Ruth stepped into the car—but before she realized what was happening, an individual darted from the vending machine niche into the elevator with her. The woman dropped a bucket filled with ice cubes between the doors. The bucket kept the doors from closing.

Kept the elevator right where it was.

The Muslim woman rounded on her, and Ruth drew back. "What are you doing? What do you want?"

"It's okay, Ruth. You know me. When you went to DC to counsel Bella, I . . . I checked your hotel suite for bugs and found some—remember now?"

Ruth's eyes widened. "No!"

The woman loosened her scarf. She reached her hand in, close to her ear, and pulled out a strand of black hair. Black hair tipped in fluorescent purple.

And Ruth caught the faint but distinctive scent of licorice gum.

"You!"

"Shhh." Jaz tucked her hair in and tugged the scarf back into place.

"What are you doing here?"

"We need your help."

"You and who else?"

"Marshal Tobin and I."

Ruth's reaction swung from alarmed to confused. "Kari told me that I was the only non-family member allowed to attend the service. That Director Wolfe wouldn't let any of you come. Secret stuff about Laynie's enemies and danger."

"We're not here to attend Bella's funeral tomorrow, Ruth. The thing is? We're not convinced that the body they shipped back here is hers."

"*What?*"

"I need you to arrange for a meeting between us and Bella's sister. We'll explain then."

"I don't think so. Your interruption will only cause Kari more grief, Jaz."

"I'm asking you to set up this meeting with Kari. Please. If nothing else, let her decide for herself."

Something else occurred to Ruth. "Wait a minute. How did you know where to find me?"

"Duh. I'm a cyber spy, remember? I pinged your phone. Once I had triangulated your general location, I located the three hotels within range of the cell towers, hacked their reservation systems, and found you here."

Ruth muttered, "Why doesn't that make me feel better?"

"Please, Ruth. We need to speak to Kari, and it needs to be today."

"What—so you can tell her you're 'not convinced' Laynie is dead? Why would you announce a false hope to her family the day before they bury her?"

"Because if Bella isn't dead, she's in the hands of the enemy. And if the enemy has her? Then we're leaving her there, and there's no telling what classified information they are extracting from her—or what they are doing to her to extract it."

Ruth jerked back. Stunned. Aghast.

Jaz pressed her point. "We have come up with a relatively quick method of determining whether the body is Bella's or not. Kari has the authority and means to make it happen. Together, we can find the truth. And whichever way it turns out? We won't spend the rest of our lives wondering. That's the bottom line, Ruth. Tobin and I need to know, and Bella's sister deserves to know."

Ruth sighed and turned inward. *Lord? What would you have me do here? I don't want to be the cause of more pain . . .*

She imagined herself introducing Jaz and Tobin to Kari and Søren and the consternation that would follow. Then she heard Jaz's words in her head. "*Because if Bella isn't dead, then she's in the hands of the enemy. And if the enemy has her? Then we're leaving her there, and there's no telling what classified information they are extracting from her—or what they are doing to her to extract it.*"

Ruth studied Jaz before speaking again. "You said you had a method of determining whether the body was Bella's or not. Then you said Kari has the authority and means to make it happen. What 'means' are you referring to?"

"I heard that Kari is wealthy. We'll need an experienced pathologist with the right instruments to make the examination. It takes a hefty chunk of change to motivate someone to drop what they're doing and examine a body on our timetable."

Jaz wasn't accustomed to pleading, but she did now. "Please. Give us an opportunity to speak to Kari."

Ruth gave in. "All right. I'll provide the introduction. As upsetting as your visit will be, I know Kari. She's never been one to tolerate uncertainty. The moment you introduce doubt into the equation, she'll shift to your point of view."

She snorted a small laugh. "And as I'm on my way to her now, I suppose you two can tag along."

"Knew I could count on you, Ruth." Jaz nudged the bucket of ice out of the elevator doorway into the hall. "Let's go."

Ruth shook her head and muttered to herself, "Well, shoot. Not the first funeral in this family I've disrupted."

RUTH REHEARSED HER LINES as she drove toward the restaurant. A glance in the mirror told her Tobin and Jaz's rental was right behind her.

Lord, this is crazy, isn't it? So please. Please don't let me hurt Kari or her family any more than they are already hurting.

They arrived at the restaurant. Ruth inquired at the hostess station and was shown to the small private dining room where Kari, Søren, Max, and Laynie's parents, Gene and Polly, would be waiting.

Ruth halted a couple feet from the room. "Wait here," she told Jaz and Tobin.

She opened the door and went into the room. Søren, Kari, and Max stood and came forward to greet her.

Kari hugged Ruth. "It's so good to see you, Ruth. Thank you for coming."

Søren hugged her, too. Max—who'd met Ruth on only two occasions—offered his hand.

"Look how tall you've grown, Max!" Ruth marveled.

Kari took Ruth's arm. "Pretty much what everyone says to him these days. Come sit down, Ruth. Lunch will be served shortly."

But Ruth stopped. Besides herself, the only occupants of the room were Kari, Max, and Søren. "Where are Laynie's parents?"

Kari sighed. "All this has been so hard on Gene and Polly. They've lost their son and now their daughter. I hate seeing the pain they are in and what it is doing to them, particularly Polly. She's rejoicing that Laynie is in heaven, but . . . but her body is so tired and weak. At the last minute, Gene thought it better that they stay home with Shannon and Robbie."

"I'm sorry to hear that. However . . . their absence may be providential."

"What do you mean?"

Ruth took Kari's hand between both of hers. "Kari, you know I would never purposely hurt you, right? And Søren, you know I have only love and the best of intentions toward your family, yes?"

Søren looked from Ruth to Kari. "You're a great comfort to Kari and our family. We will always be grateful that you came to share this time with us, Ruth."

Ruth smiled. "You may not be thanking me for coming after you've seen who I've brought with me."

Kari cocked her head. "What's going on, Ruth?"

"A change in plans, I think." She released Kari's hand. "One moment, please."

Ruth opened the door and gestured into the hallway. A man and a woman appeared in the doorway. Søren immediately recognized the large—*very* large—man but not the hijab-wearing woman beside him.

"Marshal Tobin?"

"Yes, sir. Sorry to barge in on you like this."

"We . . . we were told you weren't allowed to come to the memorial service."

"Officially, we aren't even here, sir. Begging your pardon, may we intrude on your family gathering for a few minutes?"

Søren gestured them inside, and Tobin made introductions.

"This is one of my coworkers, Miss Jessup."

Jaz was untying her scarf and didn't acknowledge Søren or Kari until she'd removed it. "Whew. Stuffy." She nodded to them. "Jasmine Jessup. Please call me Jaz. Bella is a friend of mine."

Søren, trying hard to maintain a hospitable manner, said, "So, both of you have flown the coop to attend the funeral service?"

"Not exactly," Tobin supplied. "Uh, we realize you are sitting down to lunch shortly, but Jaz and I have come from the DC area to speak to you and your wife . . . on an urgent matter. May we have a few minutes of your time?"

Søren looked from Jaz to Tobin and back. "What you're wearing. It's a disguise?"

"Yes."

"Are you the hacker who stole the Ukrainian mob's financial records?"

Jaz nodded.

"But if they have followed you here . . ."

"They haven't. I promise."

Søren wasn't convinced, but he shrugged his acquiescence. "Kari, what do you think?"

Kari motioned Jaz and Tobin to the table. "Let's let them speak, whatever it is."

Jaz sat but didn't wait to get started nor did she mince words.

"Mr. and Mrs. Thoresen, the time to act is **bleeping** short, which is why Marshal Tobin and I are here. We're unconvinced that Bella died in that car accident or that the body shipped back to the States is hers. We aren't saying it isn't her, but we'd like the opportunity to prove, one way or the other, that it is or isn't. We need your permission to have a pathologist examine the body. Since you are burying her tomorrow, it must be today."

Thunderstruck, Kari stammered, "Y-you what?"

"We need your permission—"

"I heard you. I just can't believe what you said."

Tobin forestalled Jaz with a heavy hand on her arm. "Please forgive us for our rather blunt start. I'll back up a bit. Just yesterday, we came to the realization that we have no actual proof that the body recovered from the car accident is Bella's. Director Wolfe has only the word of an onlooker. And so, rather than suffer from uncertainty and regret the rest of our lives, we are here to suggest that perhaps you, too, would appreciate the certainty of knowing that it is your sister you are burying tomorrow."

"Her body was burned beyond recognition," Kari muttered.

"We believe we have a means of determining if it is her body or not."

"How? By what means?"

Tobin cleared his throat. "About six weeks ago, Bella and I were nearly killed by a car bomb."

Already hanging on every word, Max breathed, "*Holy cow.*"

"You know that you cannot repeat a word I say here, right, Max?" Tobin asked.

"Sure, sure. No problem."

"Thank you. To continue and make a long story short, Bella and I were far enough from the explosion that we only suffered minor injuries."

Jaz rolled her eyes. "About lost your kidney, Tobin."

"Not germane to the present situation, *Miss Jessup.*"

"Whatever."

Tobin pressed on. "All you need to know is that Bella, who was running away from the bomb when it exploded, received a number of shrapnel wounds to her back, some deep enough to require stitches. To sum up, any decent pathologist could examine the body, even though it is burned, and determine if it shows any recent cuts."

"Speaking of the body," Jaz interjected, "what arrangements have you made?"

"Director Wolfe made all the arrangements, even provided the cemetery plot so our names would never appear in any records," Kari said. "He chose and paid for the funeral home, too. He rented the facility for two full days for our exclusive use."

"And Bella's remains?" Jaz asked.

"I understand that they arrived by plane this morning and would be delivered to the funeral home." Kari glanced at her watch. "About now." She stared hard at Tobin and then Jaz. "Say, only for the sake of argument, that I was willing to go along with this 'suggestion' of yours. How in the world could I locate and hire a pathologist on such short notice?"

"I already took care of that," Jaz said. "Dr. Sydney Huber. Recently retired but highly reputable. I've booked him for the day. He's waiting for me to forward him directions to the funeral home."

"But how would you pay—"

"I posed as a partner in your lawyer's firm and promised him $25,000. Used your lawyer's firm to keep your name out of the transaction. You'll need to arrange payment of the actual fee, of course. I don't kite checks. Anymore."

Tobin stepped on Jaz's foot.

"Ow."

"Less is more, *Vyper*."

Kari waved her hand. "Stop it. What about—"

"I also emailed Dr. Huber an airtight nondisclosure agreement, the template of which I may or may not have pilfered from your law firm's network. Dr. Huber is to bring the signed and notarized NDA with him. The agreement states that he stands to lose his entire fee should he, in any manner, speak of or refer to today's, er, activities. Ever."

Kari, hands flat on the table and red in the face, spit back, "It appears my lawyer's firm needs to upgrade their security."

"Most definitely. And, as I may be freelancing soon, I could forward you a bid if you like."

Tobin interjected, "We don't have time for this. Like Jaz said, the time to act is, er, *short*."

Kari glanced at Søren. "What do you think?"

"Harebrained scheme from start to finish. Would never get off the ground in Nebraska."

"Agreed. And?"

"This isn't Nebraska. It's New Orleans. Anything goes here. I think you should do whatever will give you the most peace of mind, Kari. No regrets, right?"

"Right. No regrets." She looked to Max. "What do you think?"

"I'm with Dad on this, Mom. We should know for sure. *You* should know for sure."

Kari reached over and hugged Max tight. "I love you, Max."

Tears stood in his eyes. "Love you, too, Mom."

Kari lifted her chin to Tobin. "What are you waiting for, Marshal? Time is short."

CHAPTER 8

THEIR THREE-CAR CARAVAN arrived at Lavalle's Legacy Funeral Home. Kari led them inside where they were greeted by a pleasant but somber older gent.

"Good afternoon. I'm Charles-Pierre Lavalle, the owner of this establishment. I'm afraid we are closed today through the weekend, but perhaps I might be of assistance when we reopen on Monday?"

"Thank you, but we already have business with you. I believe my sister's remains should have arrived here today for her service tomorrow. We'd like to see them."

"*See them?* Oh, dear. I'm afraid, that is, I cannot—would not—recommend such a thing, and I, uh, that was not my understanding—"

Tobin shouldered his way past Søren and Max and pulled his badge from his pocket. "Pardon me. US Marshals Service. Which room, please?"

"I do apologize, but, well, you see, I cannot—"

Tobin was accustomed to reading people and their unconscious cues. As Mr. Lavalle delayed, he also flicked his eyes. Toward a hallway.

"Thank you," Tobin said. He gestured with a jerk of his head and marched in the direction Lavalle had unintentionally indicated. When Jaz ran to catch up with him, Kari, Søren, Max, and Ruth did, too, leaving Mr. Lavalle alone in the lobby.

"Wait! Please . . . oh, dear."

As Kari had mentioned, Lavalle's was a small establishment. The hallway led to only one door with a nameplate that read Embalming Room. Tobin threw open the door and charged in. He took in the room in a glance—sinks, cupboards, counters, stainless steel tables, equipment, and paraphernalia, a lone metal casket resting on a trestle—and three individuals, one standing behind the casket.

Tobin came to an abrupt stop.

Jaz ran into his back. "Tobin! What . . ."

Tobin spoke, but not to her. "Director Wolfe, sir?"

"Marshal Tobin. I wondered if I wouldn't see you here." He murmured to his companions, two armed behemoths in suits, "Wait in the lobby until I call you."

"Sir, our orders were to—"

"And you have delivered the remains to me as ordered. Well done. Now wait in the lobby, please."

"Yes, sir." The guards made their exit, side-eyeing Tobin as they left.

Tobin said, "I'm assuming Richard called you?"

"He certainly did." Wolfe glanced at Jaz. "Nice getup."

"It's effective," Jaz muttered.

Wolfe then addressed Kari and Søren. "Mr. and Mrs. Thoresen. A visitation today was not part of the agreed-upon arrangements."

Kari moved toward the casket. "Perhaps we wanted to acquaint ourselves with this place before the service tomorrow. Check on the arrangements. May I ask why *you* are here?"

"I was required to sign for the body at customs. Arrange for transport from the airport."

Kari placed a trembling hand on a corner of the casket. "I see that you've removed the shipping container."

"Entirely in keeping with tomorrow's service."

Kari stroked the soft metal patina under her hand. "We agreed that the casket should remain sealed, did we not?"

"Yes. Given the conditions, that was the wise decision."

Kari pointed to the end of the casket. "Then why this?" She pulled the crank handle from the casket's keyhole and held it up. "As you said, opening my sister's remains—given their condition—wouldn't be wise."

Wolfe pursed his lips. "Some aspects of the arrangements are classified, I'm afraid."

Kari shook her head. "That's not good enough. Why are you really here?"

"I'm not at liberty to answer your questions, Mrs. Thoresen. Why don't you tell me why *you* are here?"

"It seems that my law firm has hired a pathologist to examine the remains."

"Oh?" Wolfe seemed surprised.

"We need to know for certain that this is my sister's body, that she truly is . . . gone."

Wolfe looked to Tobin and Jaz. "Is that what this is all about? Why you two broke security, why you are here?"

Jaz nodded. Tobin answered, "Yes, sir. You see—"

Kari interrupted. "None of that matters at this point. The pathologist will be here shortly. Until then, I'll just keep this." She held up the crank handle.

"I see. However, I must insist—"

A tap sounded on the door. Søren opened it to the funeral director.

"Pardon me. There's a gentleman in the lobby. Says he is here to meet a Ms. Brunell?"

Jaz lifted her hand. "That would be me."

"You're making awfully free with my attorney's name," Kari grumbled.

"I'm surprised no one has hacked his offices before now and robbed him blind." Like an impressive card trick, a stick of gum appeared in Jaz's hand. She unwrapped it, folded it in fourths, and popped it into her mouth—all one-handed. She grinned around the gum. "Just imagine what I could do for your attorney's cybersecurity."

"Frankly, I'm terrified." Then Kari half-smiled. "Let's meet this pathologist, shall we? Since I seem to be on the hook for his fee?"

"Hold on there," Wolfe protested. "What is it you have planned?"

Jaz answered. "The pathologist is going to tell us if the body in that box is Bella's."

Wolfe opened his mouth to protest again, but Jaz forestalled him. "It will be a short exam. We believe we have a simple but definitive means of proving whether it is her or not."

Kari added, "And don't even consider calling your guards to remove us, Director Wolfe. I'm not leaving here until I'm satisfied this is or is not my sister."

Wolfe folded his arms. "Fine, but the point of my making the arrangements was to provide a buffer between Bella and her family—*your* family—for their safety. I require, therefore, that no one identify themselves to this pathologist except for—" He pointed at Jaz. "Ms. Brunell, did you say? Furthermore, I will remain in the room to observe the process."

Her hand again caressing the casket, Kari nodded. "All right."

"I need agreement from everyone, please."

Søren, Ruth, and Max nodded. Tobin and Jaz did the same.

Jaz addressed Mr. Lavalle. "Show the gentleman in, please—after which, you may excuse yourself."

Wolfe added, "Mr. Lavalle? Before you go, I want to remind you of our contract. Absolutely nothing that happens here today ever leaves this place—not without you and your business incurring serious repercussions."

"I know, I know," the frazzled man tossed over his shoulder.

Søren spoke up. "Uh, Kari? Why don't we let our friends handle this while you and I and Max wait . . . elsewhere?"

Kari swallowed, then nodded. She handed the crank to Tobin, then she, Max, Ruth, and Søren left the room just as Mr. Lavalle showed the pathologist in. He was short and chubby in a down-south, Boss Hogg sort of way, and he dragged behind him a sizeable stainless steel case on wheels. One of the case's wheels rolled with an annoying squeak.

"Dr. Huber?" Jaz asked.

"That's me." His eyes widened a little as he sized Jaz up. "Ms. Brunell?"

Jaz, in return, blew a bubble and popped it. "Yes, I'm Ms. Brunell. You have the signed NDA?"

"Uh, certainly." He produced it. Jaz examined it and handed it off to Tobin.

"This way, please." Jaz led him to the casket and waited until Lavalle left, closing the door behind himself, before addressing the doctor.

"As I said in our email communications, these human remains are said to belong to a friend of ours who perished in a traffic accident where the car caught on fire and burned."

"But you are unconvinced that they are your friend's remains?"

"Yes, that is the gist of our concern."

Huber removed a small notebook and a pen. "Gender, female. Race?"

"Caucasian."

"Age?"

"Forty-six."

"Height?"

Jaz sought Tobin's eyes. He answered, "Between five foot nine and five foot ten."

"Five foot ten," Wolfe said quietly. "One hundred thirty-six pounds at her last physical."

"Dental records?"

Jaz replied, "No. We have no means of positively identifying her remains other than one possibility. A little over a month ago, our friend sustained several cuts on her back. Cuts that required stitches. The deepest cut was under her left shoulder blade."

"Ah. Very good. That recent an injury—if the burns haven't penetrated too deeply into the derma, should be visible under magnification."

He looked around the room. "I require a table where I can unpack my case and remove a few instruments."

Tobin pointed to a wheeled cart against the wall. "Like this?"

"That will do. Also, if I could prevail upon one of you to roll that embalming table alongside the casket after I have opened it? Yes, that one. And I will require the assistance of one of you gentlemen to lift the body from the casket and place it on the table. I will do a complete examination of the body, both posterior and anterior, that is, front and back, and will need assistance to flip the body over when it is time."

"I—" Jaz, for all her bravado and steely demeanor, fled the room.

Tobin did not move, but the color drained from his face. "I don't think I can . . . see her like that, Director."

Wolfe placed a hand on Tobin's shoulder. "This is not the job for you. Go on, now. I'll do it." He removed the crank from Tobin's hand. "You have my word. I will take care of her."

Tobin, tears glistening in his eyes, followed Jaz from the room.

WHILE KARI WAS USING the restroom, she heard someone else come in. When she left the stall, she found Jaz leaned against a wall.

The woman had yanked the hijab from her head, revealing damp, purple-tipped hair. She had her face pressed to the cool wallpaper.

Kari washed up, but Jaz didn't move.

"Are you all right . . . *Ms. Brunell?*"

"Very funny."

Kari hesitated, then put her hand on Jaz' back and scribed gentle, soothing circles on it. "Would you like me to bring you some water?"

"I'll be okay in a minute. Just . . . couldn't stay . . . in there."

"Me, neither. Not for love nor money—and it's okay."

Jaz was quiet, and Kari continued to rub her back until Jaz whispered, "If . . . if it turns out that it is Bella . . . and she's really dead? I'm sorry for putting you through this."

"Thank you. But if it turns out that it isn't, er, Bella? I will be grateful to you forever."

Jaz lifted her face a little to study Kari. She quirked a wan smile. "You're a lot like her, y'know."

Kari smiled back. "That's a compliment in my book." She gave Jaz's back a final pat. "Come on now, Ms. Brunell. Mr. Lavalle made some coffee for us. I could do with a cup."

"I'll be right there. Need to ditch this sack I'm wearing."

"Why? Not your best look? I thought it rather suited you."

Jaz groaned. "Give me a break."

They found Tobin, Søren, Ruth, and Max in the reception hall. Tobin sat apart, staring at his coffee. Max sat before a plate of assorted pastries and was sampling them with the gleeful gusto only teenagers possess. Søren and Ruth were talking quietly with Mr. Lavalle.

"I hope we're not inconveniencing you," Kari apologized to Lavalle, "or eating someone else's. . . *wow*. That's quite a selection. Beignets, cannoli, Danish, cream puffs . . ."

"No inconvenience at all. These were brought in an hour ago for your sister's memorial service tomorrow." He gestured at the spread. "I was told to expect a dozen mourners, but Mr. Wolfe ordered enough for at least fifty."

"In that case . . ." Jaz dumped her wad of gum and made for the éclairs.

Kari took a deep breath and reached for a cannoli, steadfastly refusing to entertain thoughts about what was happening across the lobby and down the hall in that other room.

AN HOUR PASSED BEFORE they heard voices in the lobby and a case on wheels squeaking its way across the lobby carpet. Dr. Huber and Wolfe joined them. Wolfe's two guards followed him into the room. When Wolfe pointed out Mr. Lavalle, they escorted the man from the room and did not return.

Everyone but Dr. Huber looked to Wolfe for answers, but his hard, unyielding expression gave nothing away. And instead of joining the others who were waiting for Dr. Huber's report, Wolfe retreated to a far corner of the reception room, flipped open his mobile phone, and made a call. Occasionally, when he raised his voice, a phrase could be overheard.

"Then find her!" and "Yes, it's urgent."

While Wolfe withdrew to make his call, Dr. Huber spotted the pastries. "Ah! Delightful. May I?"

"Be my guest," Kari murmured.

Dr. Huber selected a raspberry tart. He bit into it and squeezed his eyelids shut. "Oh, bliss! Quite, *quite* wonderful."

He had dispatched the tart and was selecting a second one when he came to himself and realized that the room's temperature had dropped precipitously . . . and that he was the recipient of chilly and downright hostile stares. Ms. Brunell, the woman with black, purple-tipped hair, actually scowled at him.

He dropped the tart and wiped his fingers. "I beg your pardon. You are, of course, awaiting the results of my examination."

"It *is* why you're here," Ms. Brunell growled.

"Yes, yes. Of course." He glanced toward Wolfe, still on his phone in the corner.

"We're not waiting for him," Jaz decided. "Get to it."

"Certainly, certainly."

Søren gripped Kari's shoulders, and Max held her arm. Ruth, seated at the table, put her face in her hands. Tobin and Jaz stood side by side, their expressions impassive.

Huber found his notebook, stood, and began to read. "The subject of the examination was an adult Caucasian female between the ages of twenty-five and fifty."

He glanced up in apology. "I am unable to fix the age more accurately than that without a complete exam."

He continued. "Because of the constriction of the body as it burned, I was also unable to determine exact height or weight. My estimate, based on the length of femur and tibia, was consistent with a female of five foot nine or ten."

Kari's grip on Søren's hands tightened.

"I excised a layer of burned fabric from the subject's back, no doubt the subject's clothing. After applying a chemical to aid in debriding the burned epidermis on the subject's back, I used a high-magnification lens to study the underlying dermis—the connective tissue beneath the epidermis. I took tissue samples, cutting through the dermis layer down to the hypodermis or subcutis—the fatty tissue below the dermis."

He looked up. "I found no scars on the subject's back indicative of recent trauma, no evidence of cuts deep enough to have required stitches. In particular, based on the information you provided, I paid careful attention to the area surrounding the subject's left shoulder blade. I found no indication of trauma below or near the subject's left shoulder blade."

He was quick to add, "Of course, the absence of trauma is not as definitive as the presence of trauma."

"What does that mean?" Søren demanded.

Tobin seemed to deflate. "It means that *not* finding the cuts isn't necessarily the proof we're looking for."

Wolfe had finished his call and joined them. "Let the doctor finish."

Dr. Huber nodded. "Thank you. Let me see. Ah, yes, here we are. As I said I would, I performed a complete examination of the body, both posterior and anterior."

His brows twitched, signaling puzzlement. "I am a little hesitant to speak with confidence without laboratory confirmation, but . . . the type and severity of the burns on the anterior of the body suggest the direct application of an accelerant or ignitable liquid."

He looked up from his book. "Wasn't this assumed to be a fire resulting from an auto accident, the ignition of gasoline fumes?"

Jaz ignored his question. "Explain about the accelerant or ignitable liquid."

"Perhaps you do not know, but bodies, in and of themselves, are not that flammable. The addition of an accelerant, such as an ignitable liquid, will cause the body to burn hotter than it would without chemical assistance, but only where the IL was applied. Whatever material an IL is applied to will burn hot and leave nothing of said material behind."

"So?"

"Ah, that is the rub. I found very little of the subject's clothing on the body's anterior torso, even though I found significant fabric fiber residue from the knees down. The marked difference between the anterior torso and lower body suggests to me that the subject's torso may have been doused with an ignitable liquid."

Kari choked and gagged. Tobin clenched his fists until his finger joints cracked and popped.

Jaz moved the doctor along by saying, "Please include those findings in the written report. Have you anything else to add?"

"Yes, yes. My examination of the mouth suggests that the subject had less than optimal dental care in her lifetime. The typical adult has sixteen teeth on the top and sixteen on the bottom. This count does not include the so-called wisdom teeth. The subject in question had no crowns or fillings. The subject was, however, missing three adult molars, the lower right six-year and twelve-year molars—numbers 30 and 31 by the Universal Numbering System, and the lower left twelve-year molar, number 18."

Kari, Søren, Ruth, Tobin, and Jaz looked at each other, their questions unspoken. Tobin shrugged. None of them could say, with any confidence, whether or not Laynie had been missing molars—until Wolfe again demanded their attention.

"Listen up, people. Our friend underwent a full physical exam in October. The physical did not include a dental checkup. However, moments ago, I spoke with the physician who performed the exam. She attests to looking in our friend's mouth and throat during the course of her exam and . . ."

Wolfe stopped. Swallowed. Coughed once. He seemed to have something stuck in his throat.

"What?" Kari shouted.

Wolfe swallowed down the lump that had choked him. "She attests—and she noted this observation in her records at the time—that she saw evidence of good dental care and that her patient . . . her patient was *not* missing any teeth."

"It's not Bella," Jaz breathed. "It's not her!"

The room erupted in tears and rejoicing.

"Not her!" Kari sobbed. She and Søren embraced—Max and Ruth joined them.

Tobin grabbed Jaz, yanked her to her feet, and crushed her in a hug.

Before the babble of jubilation got out of control, Wolfe squashed it. "Quiet! I want silence—not a word more, if you please." He gestured to the pathologist. "Dr. Huber, we thank you for your time and expertise. You may go now."

Dr. Huber withdrew an envelope. "The invoice for my services?"

Wolfe took it. "I'll handle it."

"And you are? I don't believe we were introduced."

"Here's my card."

"But there's no name on this card—only a phone number!"

"My direct line."

"Really? But this is not at all what I contracted with Ms. Brunell. I would feel more comfortable with payment from Brunell and Brunell—as agreed upon."

The cold stare Wolfe turned on the man would have frozen flowing lava. "I am making it my responsibility, my *honor*, to pay you, rather than this attorney. I personally guarantee you will receive full payment within two weeks. If you are not in receipt of your fee by then, feel free to call me."

Huber, less than convinced that he'd ever see his fee, grumbled to himself, pocketed Wolfe's card, and grabbed the handle of his wheeled case.

He glanced at the table, still grumbling, when the raspberry tarts caught his eye. "I believe I'll just have another of these." He grabbed a napkin, selected a tart, sniffed, then grabbed a second tart. With back stiff, tarts and napkin in hand, he left the room. The irritating squeak of his cart's wheel marked his movement through the lobby and out the funeral home's front entrance.

Silence reigned in the reception room as Wolfe locked the door behind Dr. Huber. Wolfe remained unmoving for several moments, his jaw clenching and unclenching.

Finally, he spoke. "Mrs. Thoresen."

"Director Wolfe?"

"I am so sorry."

Kari nodded. "At the moment, all I have room for is gratitude and great relief."

Wolfe sighed. "Yes. I have a heart full of that myself. Still, you must know how very sorry I am to have put you through this ordeal although . . . we're not out of the woods yet."

Kari's tone changed. Hardened. "Director Wolfe?"

"Yes, ma'am?"

"*Find my sister.*"

"Yes, ma'am. That we will. Tobin? Miss Jessup?"

"Sir?" Tobin answered.

Wolfe jerked his head. "You two. With me."

Tobin and Jaz followed him out of the building. They huddled near his car, waiting for him to speak. Neither of them had seen Wolfe as shaken as they saw him now.

"We've been well and truly had," Wolfe finally said.

"Well, no duh," Jaz muttered. "And we've lost an entire week. *An entire week . . .*"

Wolfe withdrew a packet from his suitcoat. "Yes, but we do have this."
Tobin asked, "What is that?"

If it's what I hope and pray it is, it's the intel Cossack intended to pass to Bella."

"But . . . how did you come by it?"

"Cossack had it placed in the casket, under the body. It must be why the casket was under 24/7 two-man guard during transit—and why the shipping instructions required that I, personally, sign for its delivery."

As Wolfe shook off his shock, he surged into action. To Jaz and Tobin, he snapped, "Grab your gear from your rental car. You're coming with me. We'll read the intel, patch in Seraphim and the task force, and work while we're on the road."

He called to the two guards who had accompanied the casket and pointed them to Tobin and Jaz's car. "You're dismissed with my thanks. Take their rental. Turn it in at the airport and return to base."

INSIDE THE RECEPTION HALL of Lavalle's Legacy Funeral Home, Kari was again sobbing in Søren's arms. Max tugged on her elbow. "Mom? Why are you crying? Doesn't what the doctor said mean that Aunt Laynie isn't dead?"

"Not precisely, son," Søren said softly. "Yes, we now know that the body we almost buried isn't Aunt Laynie's. What we don't know is where Aunt Laynie is . . . or if she is alive or dead."

Kari wiped her face. "She cannot be dead. I don't believe that the Lord would have stopped us from burying this body only to find that she is dead anyway."

"Then why are you so sad?"

Fresh tears sprang to Kari's eyes. "Because now we don't know where she is. No one does—not even her agency, despite Wolfe's promises."

Max shook his head. "Mom? That's not entirely true."

He leaned in close to Kari and whispered, "The Lord knows exactly where she is."

THE LORD IS MY STRENGTH and my defense . . . He is my God, and I will praise him . . . my father's God . . . I will exalt him. The Lord is a warrior; the Lord is his name.

Darkness.

Deep cold.

The Lord is my strength and my defense . . . He is my God . . . I will exalt him.

So cold!

May these words of my mouth and this meditation of my heart be pleasing in your sight, Lord, my Rock and my Redeemer. Keep me safe, my God, for in you I take refuge.

Cold. Dark. Empty.

Can't stop shivering.

Lord, where am I?

Laynie Portland
SPY RESURRECTED

PART 2:
SHEOL, THE REALM OF THE DEAD

LP

CHAPTER 9

THE SOUND OF MUFFLED, barely audible words drew her, bit by bit, out of her sleep. Slowly, slowly, the whispers brought her to awareness.

"Whaffever faffens . . . worffy of the gospel of Christ . . . whaffever faffens . . . worffy of the gospel of Christ . . . Whaffever faffens . . . worffy of the gospel of Christ . . ."

Whatever happens?

She'd awakened partially once before, only to plummet into senselessness again. She struggled to sort her thoughts, to put them in order and to make sense of . . .

Where am I?

The darkness surrounding her was a tangible thing, an impenetrable shroud. No matter how she widened her eyes, utter blackness engulfed and enveloped her.

Hands? Feet? No movement that she could tell.

She had opened her eyes, but no other part of her body responded to her command.

Wait. Did I actually open my eyes? Or did I only think I opened them?

Panic flexed its claws and tried to bury them in her skull. She opened and scrunched her eyes furiously, hoping to prove to herself that she was opening them. She came close to convincing herself that she could open them.

But only close.

She tried again to move—move anything. Move any part of herself. Almost immediately another muffled whisper floated around her.

"Buff whaffever were gains to me . . . consider loss for the sake of Christ . . ."

That's me. Me talking. Trying to. At least my mouth works, although I think there's some sort of tape over my mouth.

She wanted to push her tongue out and feel for the tape, but could not part her teeth. Tried to suck in a breath through her mouth. All she could manage was to lift her top lip a fraction and inhale through her teeth.

They must have poked holes in the tape in case my nose stuffed up and I couldn't breathe through it.

Those small efforts had exhausted her.

I'm so weak. So very weak. Is that it? Why I can't move . . . or feel?

She took inventory again. Less desperate. Calmer. More focused.

The physical weakness. And the cold. Both part of why I can't move much, but it can't be all, can it?

The answer slapped her in the face.

Drugged. I've been drugged. How long? When?

What happened?

There it was—she couldn't recall what had happened to her. Or where she was when it happened.

Oh, Laynie! Where are you? In a real mess—that's where you are.

She laughed softly—and heard herself laugh.

Okay, mouth and ears work. Not positive about the eyes just yet. Mouth? Oh, yeah. What was it I was saying that woke me up?

The rasping whisper flowed from her. "Whaffever faffens, conduct yourselves in a manner worffy of the gospel of Christ, Philiffians 1:27."

Oh, wow. How many times did I read Philippians? Enough times for the Holy Spirit to bring a portion of it up from my subconscious when I needed it.

"Fank you, Lord."

The fog over her thoughts receded a bit more. She blinked her eyes several times. *Yes, I can open them, but I think that wherever I am is enclosed. Confined.*

She sniffed. Heard herself sniff. And smelled something . . . something "off," something rank, but she was unable to put a name to it.

Focus on your feet, she told herself. *Concentrate.*

She couldn't move them. *Do my feet feel anything?*

Yes. Cold. Numbing cold.

I'm cold all over. So cold, that I've lost sensation?

That didn't make sense.

She struggled to lift her head. It was too much effort. However, she must have gotten it off whatever surface she was lying on, because when she stopped trying, her skull thumped back down.

Progress. I can move my head an inch or less. Try . . . try rubbing two fingers together.

She focused on the index and second finger of her right hand. Nothing. She tried curling her fingers—

What did I just feel?

Her index finger had touched something. *Oh. It's the tip of my thumb.*

She rubbed her thumb along her forefinger and tried to turn her wrist. Encountered resistance.

My wrists are tied. Or bound. Taped like my mouth, maybe.

And some other sensation, like the top of her hand ached a bit.

Guess that's progress.

She sniffed again, trying to recall, to identify the unpleasant odor. Then it hit her. Sweat. And urine.

I've been here long enough for my bladder to let go.

The sharp claws of panic sprang to life. *Have they left me here? To die?*

Her heart thudded in her chest, and she opened her mouth—rather, tried to. Another whisper floated out. "I consider everything . . . a loss because of the surpassing worth of knowing Christ Jesus my Lord . . . for whose sake I have lost all things."

Yes, Lord, she spoke within her heart. *Knowing you is the surpassing worth of my life—I see that now. I would willingly lose everything . . . as long as I never lose you.*

She began to drift again. *My system is still flooded with drugs.*

Before she sank under the weight of the drugs, she acknowledged that it would take her body hours to flush the narcotics, whatever they were, from her system. But without food and water when she next woke, would she have the strength to break free of whatever prison she found herself in?

Moreover, would she remember how she had gotten here?

Chapter 10

TOBIN RODE SHOTGUN IN the passenger seat beside Wolfe's driver.

"Quincy Tobin," he said to the driver.

"Tom Parker." He glanced behind him. "Don't mind me. I'm just the hired help."

"Hired help with a Top Secret security clearance," Wolfe deadpanned without looking up.

Tobin chuckled—amazed that the weight of grief he'd been carrying had lifted. "Nice to meet you, Parker. I'm sort of in the same boat as you. You know—don't mind me. I'm just the hired gun."

Parker laughed without making a sound. "Good to know," he said softly.

In the rear seat, Wolfe worked the seal on the package open, unwrapped layers of packaging, and began leafing through the several sheets that comprised the package's contents. Jaz slid close and attempted to read what he held.

"Miss Jessup?"

"Sir?"

"You're lurking. I'll be forced to file a harassment complaint with HR if you don't get off my shoulder."

"Well, I can't see what the **bleep** you've got there."

"If you'll allow me to scan through and get a sense of what it is, I can then offer you half of the intel while I read the rest."

In the front seat, Tobin and Parker slid glances at each other. Parker's eyes had gone wide at Jaz's less-than-deferential behavior.

Tobin was amused.

"She's an acquired taste," he said—loud enough for the backseat to hear.

Wolfe snort-laughed under his breath. Like Tobin, the relief coursing through his blood was better than knocking back a couple of stiff drinks. He was euphoric.

Jaz was not. "You think this is a joke, Tobin?"

She rounded on Wolfe. "And do you? You're all fired up just because the body they shipped to us isn't Bella's, so just like that, you've moved on to stopping a terror attack? Do you think an impending attack is why I want to see what's in the package? Do I have to remind you and Tobin that Bella's still missing? That burned body doesn't prove she isn't dead. It only proves that body isn't her. *So where is she?*"

When neither Wolfe nor Tobin responded, she sat back, folded her arms, and huffed.

Wolfe leaned toward her. "I'm sorry. Sorry that I can't do anything to find Bella while we're on the road. What I can do is analyze the intelligence Cossack risked his cover and life to pass to us. Sorry if that makes you think I don't care about finding her, because I surely do."

"Careful. I'll have to file a harassment complaint if you don't clear outta my **bleeping** personal space, *Director*."

Parker sort of choked.

Tobin whispered to Parker out of one side of his mouth, "Like I said. An acquired taste."

THEY HADN'T GONE FAR when Wolfe suggested they stop for lunch—not for fast food but for an actual sit-down meal. None of them had eaten since breakfast. When Tobin gave his hearty assent, Wolfe pointed Parker to an upcoming restaurant. Parker maneuvered into the right lane and turned into the parking lot.

"Nope. No, this won't work," Jaz objected. "Drive on, Parker."

"You don't pay my driver, Miss Jessup. Kindly refrain from giving him orders," Wolfe reminded her. "This restaurant is fine."

"Does it offer complementary broadband service?"

"I sincerely doubt it."

"Then it's a no-go. Also? It's too snooty for my needs."

"Your needs?"

"Yah. I require space to unpack my laptop and spread out. Means I won't be sharing a table with you three. Need my own workspace—and any 'lah-dee-dah' restaurant *you* choose will look down their noses at me. Draw unwanted attention."

Parker, who was driving aimlessly around the parking lot, glanced in the rearview mirror for Wolfe's instructions.

Wolfe heaved a sigh. "Drive on, Parker."

They exited to the main road, and within fifteen minutes, Jaz vetoed Wolfe's next choice for lunch. And the next. And the one after that.

"Director, if you'd let me pick, we could avoid this stalemate," Jaz told him.

Wolfe sought Tobin's attention. "Marshal?"

Tobin just lifted one shoulder.

"Fine," Wolfe ground out.

Five possible eateries later, a disgruntled Wolfe found himself sharing a corner booth with Parker and Tobin. Jaz, occupying her own table across the aisle, ignored them and set to work. Wolfe was not pleased with Jaz's choice. They were in a common, second-rate café attached to a third-rate hotel. All because said hotel's blinking sign boasted free broadband service in their rooms and café.

"I'm unaccustomed to dining where the tables are topped in cheap laminate and come standard with ketchup and mustard dispensers, Miss Jessup."

Jaz had plugged her laptop's cable into the café's service, and was watching the computer boot.

"Sorry, but I need to check the status of the 'traps' I've set to snare our mole. For that I need broadband service and space to work." She speared him with an arch look bordering on disdain. "You *do* want me to find the mole, right, Wolfey?"

Parker flinched, wagged his head slowly back and forth, and mouthed "Wolfey?"

Tobin, beginning to enjoy himself, just grinned.

Wolfe turned to Tobin. "I'm not paying you people enough to work with her, Marshal."

"She's usually not *quite* this bad, but I was going to ask about hazard pay. You know—what with the car bomb, almost losing a kidney, the Ukrainian mob assassination attempt, being forcibly uprooted from my home twice now, and so on."

"What?" Parker's level of "stunned" clicked up a notch.

"Parker's not 'read into' the task force's day-to-day activities, Marshal Tobin."

"All due respect, sir? Please don't change the subject. We were talking hazard pay."

"Noted." And ignored. Wolfe opened his menu and scanned through it. "Unbelievable. Eight kinds of greasy burgers, three versions of oily fries, and ten flavors of sugary soft drinks—and that's just lunch. Positively barbaric."

"Better than what Bella's been eating, I wager," Jaz growled across the aisle.

Wolfe reddened. "Point taken. And thank you for the reminder, Miss Jessup."

Jaz returned her eyes to her screen. "Order me a chef's salad, ranch on the side, and iced tea when the waitress comes," she said. "No telling what's in that mystery meat they serve as hamburger." She pecked furiously on the laptop's keyboard, oblivious to anything else, while the men ordered.

When the food came, Jaz picked up her fork and took a bite, her focus still on her screen. The men had taken six bites to her one when they heard her fork clatter on the floor. Her eyes were glued to the screen while she typed furiously.

When Jaz didn't seem to notice she'd dropped her fork, Tobin asked, "Jaz? Everything all—"

"Got you. *Got you*, you slimy, stinking *weasel!*"

Wolfe and Tobin slid from the booth. They pulled empty chairs to Jaz's table. Sat on either side of her.

"What do you have, Miss Jessup?" Wolfe asked, keeping his voice low.

"I have the task force's mole, sir."

"Who? Who is it?" Tobin demanded.

Wolfe pulled his flip phone, "I'll call Broadsword. Richard will have him or her in custody before we leave this sorry excuse of a restaurant."

Jaz was still reading when her face fell. "It . . . it's not going to be as simple as that, I'm afraid."

She opened a new file and began copying and pasting into it, toggling to another screen and back, faster than Tobin or Wolfe could follow, ignoring their whispered demands for more information. Then she yanked the power and broadband cables and grabbed her laptop and its case without shutting the laptop down. "I took screen grabs of what you need to read, and the battery will keep my laptop going for a couple of hours—but we need to go. Now."

Wolfe dropped a wad of cash on Jaz' table. They left their food and ran for the car.

"Parker," Wolfe ordered, "Push the speed limit."

"Yes, sir."

Tobin had crowded into the back seat, sandwiching Jaz between him and Wolfe. Jaz pushed her laptop away until it perched on her knees so that Tobin and Wolfe could view the screen while she explained what she'd uncovered.

"I've been monitoring every phone at Broadsword, hoping to catch the mole texting, calling out, or receiving a call, but it occurred to me that the mole would likely have a second phone, one I know nothing about."

"A burner," Tobin supplied.

"Yah." She unwrapped a stick of gum, folded it, and shoved it into her mouth. "But, the thing is, Broadsword is in range of only one cell tower. Just one tower provides cell service up that mountain, you know."

"I do know. You have no idea how much we paid to have the provider build that tower so far off the beaten path," Wolfe murmured.

"Figures. Cell service is as necessary as Internet is these days. Richard told me Broadsword had high-speed DSL. *That* had to have set you back ten, fifteen grand or more, so why not your own, private cell tower?"

"Get on with it, Miss Jessup."

She shrugged, twirling a half-empty pack of gum in her left hand while gesturing with her right. "I wrote a program to monitor any and all cell activity pinging off that tower. Once I ruled out the mobile phones at Broadsword—the ones I knew about—I customized the program's code to ignore them."

"Ignore them?"

"Just the pings to the tower. I track the communications of all our phones in another program."

She pointed to her screen. "Turns out Broadsword has a couple of distant 'neighbors'—houses not actually near Broadsword land, but close enough to the cell tower to piggyback their cell service off of it. Not entirely your own private cell tower after all, Director. Anyway, I had to identify and rule out the neighbors' phones, too."

Her jaws moved like pistons between sentences. "This morning a new phone pinged the tower. New to me, that is. That's what my program was checking for—previously unidentified pings. When we sat down in the restaurant, I saw the new phone. Then I hacked into its service provider and read the text message records."

She toggled to an open file. "I've pasted the screen caps of the most recent texts in chronological order, earliest to latest." She pointed. "Here. Read."

Tobin and Wolfe leaned closer. Noted the timestamp. Thursday, 2:16 p.m.

Unusual activity.
Two TF members
left grounds without
permission
Uproar over unauth
departure

"That was two days ago," Jaz reminded them.

"That's our task force mole?"

"Undoubtedly."

A reply text followed.

Who? Find out
where they have gone.

"Who's replying to our mole, Jaz?"

"Has to be your *other* mole, Director. The 'bigshot' mole in your staff."

"Can you trace the phone to my, er, bigshot mole? Identify him?"

"Not yet. His phone pinged off several cell towers in DC, which doesn't help us or tell us anything we hadn't presumed. When we're back to Broadsword, I'll build the code I need to 'snare' him."

Jaz sighed. "Getting back to the task force's mole? Continue reading. You need to see this."

The mole at Broadsword texted again.

Want proof of life

Tobin and Wolfe sucked in their breath at the same time.

"I told you it wasn't going to be simple," Jaz said softly.

Check email

"Email? You assured me you were monitoring everyone's email," Wolfe growled.

"Yah, well I'm not *omniscient*. Once I deduced who the mole was, I went hunting and uncovered a second email account. New and well hidden—just not well enough to keep me from finding it once I knew it was out there."

"But you deduced the mole's identity first?"

"By the demand for proof of life. Keep going."

A grainy photo appeared on the next page of her screen shots—a frightened woman embracing a young child. The photo had a date and time stamp. 12/06/2001 2:23 p.m.

"Our task force's mole is a man, and he has a family," Tobin muttered.

Wolfe sat back. "Explains why we couldn't understand how one of our own could be a traitor. He's being coerced. Who is he, Jaz?"

She slid a stick of gum from the pack one-handed, not even aware she was doing it, then flipped it end over end and slid it back into the pack.

"See, I have the personnel profiles of our task force members on my hard drive. None of us are married or have kids. That leaves exactly two possibilities."

Tobin wagged his head sadly. "Lance or Sherman."

Wolfe groaned. "I would trust either of those two men with my life . . . but Lance isn't married."

Jaz's sad eyes met Wolfe's. "Yah. Our mole is Sherman—and your other mole has his wife and kid."

They read the screen grabs of the next text message.

Tobin and Jessup
no word where

The reply followed.

You have until dark
or wife loses 2nd finger

Tobin shook with rage. "They cut off one of his wife's *fingers?*"

"Settle down, Marshal. It's the fastest way for a kidnapper to gain a mark's cooperation. You know how this works."

Tobin leaned his face against the window. "Bo helped us get off Broadsword's grounds undetected. He was the only person to know where we were going."

"Yah, true," Jaz said. "And Bo must have gotten back to Broadsword before dark. Look."

The mole they believed to be Sherman texted at 6:49.

New Orleans
Garineau funeral

"How could Sherman have found that out?" Tobin demanded. "Bo wouldn't have ratted us out to him or anyone else!"

Jaz answered. "Look, once the team noticed we were AWOL and that Bo's truck was the only vehicle to leave Broadsword after lunch, they'd put two and two together fast enough. Everyone including Seraphim would realize that Bo helped us 'escape.' I figure Bo knew he had to come clean to Richard when he got back, including why we were going to NOLA. However, knowing we had a mole, Bo wouldn't have said a word to Richard in the open. They would have used the conference room."

"That room is built like a SCIF. How could Sherman have listened in on their conversation?"

"It's true that the conference room is soundproof, but it's not bug-proof. I mean, yes, Richard's people do scan the room each morning, so that means Sherman would have bugged the conference room as soon as the other mole threatened to cut off his wife's finger. A one-off event. And he would have removed the bug as soon as he had the information he needed."

"Miss Jessup, if bugging the conference room was a 'one-off event,' how could Sherman have overheard the details of Bella's mission to Tbilisi?" Wolfe asked. "We discussed the operational details in the conference room and *only* in the conference room."

Jaz recalled her last conversation with Bella. The moment when Bella told her about the mission and asked Jaz to monitor her cell signal.

"*I'm flying to Tbilisi, Georgia, to meet Cossack. In person.*"

"*What the *blank*! Why would you do that?*"

"*Because the next attack is only weeks from now, Jaz, and Cossack says it will outstrip 9/11.*"

Jaz gulped over the remembered exchange. "Oh."

"Oh?"

"Um, Bella and I, we walked around the house just minutes before she left. We were too far away from anyone to be overheard . . . and yet, because all the other conversations about the mission were held in the conference room, somehow we *had* to have been overheard."

She pursed her lips. "If Sherman obtained the intel from our conversation while we were outside walking the perimeter, then he must have a parabolic listening device. No telling how many times he's used it."

"Well, he won't use it again or pass further intelligence to our enemies. Like I said earlier, I will have Richard's men take him down the moment we hit Broadsword."

Jaz looked up at Wolfe. "We can't take Sherman into custody, Director."

"I am aware of the jeopardy it puts his family in, and it distresses me. However, our first priority is cutting off the flow of information to Sherman's handler."

"That's not what I meant when I said we can't have Richard take Sherman into custody."

Tobin studied Jaz. "Selective disinformation?"

"Absolutely. Keep reading."

Notify when they return
Find out what they did

"They don't know what we've uncovered," Tobin said. "They don't know *we know* that the body we have isn't Bella's—or that we have uncovered the identity of the task force's mole."

"Which is why we can't tell anyone at Broadsword what we've figured out," Jaz said softly. "We have to leave the task force in the dark. For now."

Wolfe slowly nodded. "I concur." He thought for a long moment. "The way I see it, we have three intertwined problems. One, the impending New Year's Eve attacks—where, when, what, and how to stop them. Two, Bella's well-being—if she's alive and if she can be rescued. Three, how we handle Sherman—what disinformation to construct to our advantage and how to feed it to him."

He added, "What if we gather the task force members, including Lance and Sherman, and announce that the three of us attended Bella's memorial service. I can concoct the details—how touching it was, what we shared with her family, how appreciative they were that we came. We let Sherman report that info to his handler."

Tobin said, "I get you, and it's a good idea . . ."

"But you don't like it."

"No, sir, not a bit. That burned body isn't Bella, and I want to shout the truth of it to the heavens."

"The burned body isn't Bella. Hmm. You know . . ." Jaz drummed her fingers on the side of her laptop. "We've been so relieved that it's not her and distracted by the intel Cossack smuggled to us that we haven't dissected what 'it's not her body' means. I'm talking from AGFA's point of view."

Wolfe invited her to continue. "Do tell."

"Gotta ask ourselves, who *is* this woman whose body was supposed to be Bella's? And how did she end up in the car with Cossack's men?"

"Right—"

"I mean, did the terrorists abduct Bella before she met with Cossack's men and replace her with a living, breathing reasonable facsimile, a woman who could initially fool Cossack's men? Or, did the terrorists 'just happen' to have a dead body at the ready, a body the same height and weight as Bella?

"Either of those scenarios leads to the same two conclusions. Conclusion one, the car crash was no accident. It was intentional. AGFA knew Bella was coming to Tbilisi *and* they had worked out a plan to abduct her."

"So—"

"*Not finished.*" Jaz raised a finger. "Hence, we know Bella is still alive."

Tobin frowned. "How do you figure that?"

Jaz bent a look of disdain on him. "Because, Tobin, they wanted us to believe she was dead. If AGFA simply wanted to kill Bella, they would have done so. Instead, they went to a great deal of effort to abduct her and, while doing so, convince us that she was dead."

Tobin and Wolfe slowly nodded their agreement with Jaz's point-by-point lecture.

"What next, Director?" Tobin asked. "How do we find Bella?"

"Sir," Jaz said. "What if we . . . confront Sherman—just the three of us. Tell him we know he's being coerced. Ask him to help us expose the other mole . . . and save his family. I mean, what other hope does he have of saving them?"

Tobin looked at Wolfe. "You *are* the spy master, sir. You know how to do this."

Wolfe started to shake his head, then stopped and pulled in on himself.

"Let me think on it."

Chapter 11

TOBIN AND JAZ HAD DRIVEN straight through from Germantown to New Orleans. For the return trip, Wolfe insisted they do the same. Tobin and Parker switched off on the driving, catnapping when it was the other person's time to drive.

Wolfe and Jaz spent the remainder of daylight studying the documents Cossack had smuggled out in the unknown woman's casket. The intelligence he'd supplied was both important and helpful—but it didn't contain the key the task force needed to unlock the attack.

Jaz tipped her head back and rested it on the seat back. The muscles of her neck were stiff and sore from bending over the documents. Eyes closed, she silently reviewed the portions of the intel that validated the task force's working assumptions.

AGFA is providing fentanyl to the New York branch of the Ukrainian mob—check. *The New Year's Eve attacks will also utilize fentanyl*—check. *Unlikely that the mob knows about the impending attacks right in their backyard*—check. *In fact, everything in Cossack's intel confirms Rusty's fentanyl theory*—check.

Jaz snickered to herself. *Far you have come, my young padawan apprentice.*

She moved on to the new intelligence Cossack had given them. *The attacks will occur in ten cities in the same time zone.*

"No doubt timing the attacks to occur simultaneously. A blitzkrieg strategy—looking to maximize fear and chaos."

"What's that?" Wolfe asked.

"Sorry. Just going over Cossack's intel."

She returned to her thoughts, trying to tease out any new hints to the puzzle the team so desperately needed to assemble.

Ten cities, but not a clue as to which ones. Perhaps not, but couldn't we . . .

Jaz's forehead furrowed, and she cursed the fact that she couldn't plug into the Web while on the road. She started a mental list of tasks for when she was back at Broadsword and reconnected to the Internet.

Not to worry. By analysis and elimination, we will identify most of the targets. Rusty and I will make quick work of it.

She smiled when she pictured the eager young man with freckles and reddish-brown hair. He'd grown on her. They were partners and "buds," although she was the senior partner. She'd even developed real affection for him—as a friend.

Yes, they'd run up against the usual pitfalls of a partnership but had survived them. A couple weeks back, Rusty had gathered the courage to send out tentative feelers, signaling he'd like to be more than friends. Jaz had signaled back that she preferred things as they were.

In a complete reversal of her usual *modus operandi*, Jaz had let him down gently, and he'd taken it well enough. *Gently?* Not at all the way she usually handled unwanted male advances. Meaning she hadn't, with heartless intent, demolished Rusty's male ego in the process.

To think I didn't "do" friends before . . . before becoming part of this team. Okay, this amazing *team.*

From far out in left field, Harris' grinning face popped up, and Jaz shivered. How she detested that man and that presumptuous smirk. So completely self-satisfied. So opposite her, so full-on *macho* to boot. Harris. Huh! A complete and utter . . . dork.

Dork? What am I—in kindergarten?

But it was the only label that fit . . . or that she found herself willing to employ. Jaz waggled her head and felt her neck *pop*, sending relief down her entire spine.

Harris. Yah, a full-on, card-carrying dork. *Going on and on about the merits of this gun versus that gun and what ammo was better and why—while I stand there bored out of my brain not even pretending to be interested. Why, that man is the last male on earth I'd ever consider . . .*

Jaz shivered again. *Last man I'd ever consider? Consider for what? And what's with the shivering business?*

She snickered again with sly amusement. *Wait—I've got it. I* might *be induced to consider him for target practice. Yah. Heh-heh-heh. Target practice . . . with Harris as the target.*

She crammed Harris' face into a box at the back of her thoughts—stuffed him there *twice more* before he finally stayed put—and yanked herself back to the task at hand.

Select and list top twenty east-coast cities by population.

Research public New Year's Eve celebrations.

List venues by capacity and popularity.

Analyze event security measures—rank venue security by order of vulnerability.

Distill list to top twenty candidates for terror attack.
Best-guess AGFA's targets.

LATER—HOW MUCH LATER she couldn't tell—Laynie's aching body raised her to consciousness again. Her head throbbed and her throat felt like sandpaper. She was beyond thirsty. She was parched.

Then . . . she heard something. Words. In an unfamiliar tongue. They sounded distant, muffled but like her whispers had sounded.

The words were followed by scraping, clawing, and a *scree* so close to her head that she instinctively tried to shy from it.

Light struck her eyes, light so bright that she moaned.

The voices were atop her now, one ordering, another replying, but she did not speak their language. Hands touched her. She wanted to pull away from them—even fight them—but she had no strength except to moan.

She felt a slight tug at her arm. A moment later, a familiar warmth coursed through her. It overspread her body, and she sank, sank, sank . . . down, down, down.

She floated on a cozy, comforting wave that rocked her gently. *Nice.* No pain. No fear. She heard the words echoing inside her and nodded her agreement.

Whatever happens . . . conduct yourselves in a manner worthy of the gospel of Christ . . . For it has been granted to you on behalf of Christ not only to believe in him, but also to suffer for him . . .

Yes.

"*FAUGH!* HOW SHE REEKS, Kameta!" The young woman drew back and spit on the floor. She wiped her mouth and wrinkled her nose in distaste.

Her companion unhooked the empty saline bag from the inside of the crate's lid and hung a full one. "Is that not why you are here? To clean her? Get to it."

Kameta had been a nurse most of her life. She had worked in hospital wards for decades, but she had grown gaunt and gray from a lifetime of labor and the ruinous effects of a two-pack-a-day smoking habit. Unable to hold down a full-time job but still needing to support herself and her addiction in her old age, she took whatever work came her way.

As she adjusted the IV line's drip rate, she muttered, "Your stink is not much better than hers, Amina. You might want to shower more than once a month, eh?"

Amina sulked at Kameta's rebuke. Was it her fault her family rarely had hot water?

Kameta checked the thick tape binding the patient's hands together and examined the transparent film dressing over the catheter inserted into the back of the woman's hand. Other than a spot of bruising around the catheter, things looked fine.

Nodding to herself, she picked up the syringe she'd injected into the catheter's medication port, capped the needle, and placed it in a small sharps container.

"Let me know when you have finished cleaning her and changing her gown, Amina."

"Almost done."

"And change her blanket if it is soiled."

"Yes, yes. You don't need to tell me."

Kameta squinted at the girl. "I will check your work. She had better not stink when you say you are done or have any sores from ill-treatment. Tomorrow morning is the last time you and I will attend this woman, and I do not want any complaints about her care that might affect my fee."

"Yes, I know! I will be thorough."

While shrugging on her coat, the old nurse said, "After I've changed the dressing on her ankle, you will help me turn her on her side." Kameta pulled a pack of cigarettes from her coat's pocket and shuffled toward the other end of the disused factory where she usually smoked.

"Don't I always?" Amina grumbled as she started her distasteful chore. She had accompanied Kameta to this place for eight days, three times each day, to clean and change Kameta's patient. The hours they were ordered to tend the woman were not ideal—one o'clock in dead of night, nine in the morning, and five in the evening. The odd schedule made the notion of "each day" laughable since they attended to the woman every eight hours. Three times every twenty-four hours for eight days, Kameta picked Amina up in her rattling old car and brought her to the old factory. And at the end of each visit, they turned the unconscious woman from side to back or back to side to prevent bedsores.

Unlike Kameta, Amina had no formal nursing training. She merely followed Kameta's orders. The disquieting man who had hired Kameta seemed to trust the old woman. He trusted Amina only on Kameta's recommendation. He had inspected Amina in stolid silence before approving her, but he had also made Amina swear to say nothing to her family or friends about this job or about the patient who was, quite obviously, not a patient by choice.

Amina was glad she and Kameta would not see him again until he came to take the woman away.

Truth be told, Amina had set her heart to care little for the unconscious woman. She needed the money too desperately to worry about what she was paid to do. As long as she did as she was told and kept her mouth shut, she would soon receive enough money to buy her family a decent-sized load of coal. December was cold in Tbilisi, and Amina was happy at the prospect of a warm house for a change. Maybe even a hot bath.

And who knew? This job might lead to others. Perhaps then her father would look at his unmarried daughter with something other than sadness and disappointment.

As she finished her chore and tossed the soiled rags and gown into a plastic bag, she scrutinized the patient's long blond hair. Even unbrushed for days and dirty, it was hair to be envied. Amina's own hair was a muddy brown. Nondescript and stringy.

Amina looked down. A pair of the nurse's scissors had sprung into her hands. Before Kameta came back, before she gave it thought, Amina snipped a strand of the patient's hair and held it up, marveling at its color, the high- and low-lights in it.

Kameta's trudging footsteps announced her return from her cigarette break. In a panic, Amina threw down the scissors. They landed on the floor. She grabbed them up and laid them back on the dressing kit Kameta brought.

Amina glanced down, startled to see the thick strand of hair in her hand. The plodding steps were close now. Unable to think of a better hiding place, Amina twined the hair around her finger and tucked it into her bra.

"Are you done?"

"Yes. All done."

Amina sneered at Kameta behind her back. The cloying stink of cigarette smoke was every bit as disgusting as the body odor Kameta criticized her for.

Soon my mother will have a load of coal in the basement—not the pitiful scraps of wood and lumber she and Father must scrounge for just to light a fire in the fireplace. We will have coal in the furnace to heat the whole house—and to heat water. Perhaps as early as tomorrow night, I will draw a bath, a whole tub of steaming hot water!

With the money left over after paying for the coal, I will buy shampoo—pretty, nice-smelling shampoo—and I will wash myself all over with it. When I am done bathing, I will put on clean clothes. Then I will smell nice, too, and my hair will be clean and shiny.

Amina was smiling to herself when Kameta unwrapped the dressing kit, drew on a pair of sterile gloves, and cut the old dressing from the patient's foot. The patient had a deep laceration above her left ankle. "From a car crash," Kameta had told Amina.

Initially, the foot had been swollen and bruised, so swollen with pooled blood that Amina had wondered if bones were broken. But Kameta seemed only concerned with how the thirteen stitches she'd placed above the woman's ankle were healing.

For the first day or two, the laceration had been red, puffy, and hot to the touch. Kameta had fussed over the wound. The old nurse had cleaned it, daubed it with antiseptic cream, and watched it carefully.

She had no antibiotics to administer, and the man who hired her was not around to buy any. The only medication he had provided were the vials of liquid that Kameta injected into the patient's IV to keep her unconscious.

"I will remove the stitches today," Kameta announced. She snipped and tugged until the threads came free, washed the healing wound, applied more antiseptic cream, then lightly bandaged the wound so it could breathe.

"There. Done."

Together, the two women turned the patient onto her right side and covered her with a blanket. Checking a last time to assure herself that the patient was stable and unconscious, Kameta gestured to Amina. The two of them replaced the lid on the wooden crate and hammered it back in place.

When they left the rusting Tbilisi factory, the moon was high in the sky. For a change, they were in good spirits. They would return at nine in the morning to perform their final ministrations on the woman—and to receive their wages.

Chapter 12

LP

JAZ SAT UP, RUBBED HER eyes, opened them to daylight. "Must have fallen asleep."

"You and me both."

"What time is it? Where are we?"

"Half past seven in the morning. Less than thirty minutes from Broadsword."

She looked up front. Tobin was driving. Parker was dead to the world, his face plastered against the passenger-side window.

Wolfe said, "I want to go over our plan and priorities with you and Marshal Tobin before we roll into the compound."

"Yah. Okay."

Tobin nodded that he was listening.

"Breakfast should be over when we get there. Since Sherman notified his handler that you two went AWOL, stirring up his handler's concerns, our first task is to assure Sherman that everything is fine. We need him to text his assurances to his handler, so I'll call an immediate meeting of the full task force and include Lance and Sherman. What they'll hear is that the three of us attended Bella's memorial service. I've fabricated some notes on the service and will deliver them to the team.

"Marshal? When we've assembled for our meeting, position yourself where you will have eyes on Sherman at all times. Do *not* let him out of your sight."

"Yes, sir."

"When I dismiss the meeting, my hope is that Sherman will immediately text his handler. Miss Jessup? I want you monitoring Sherman's phone so that we know the moment Sherman communicates with his handler."

"Yes, sir. The minute I plug into Broadsword's DSL, I'll be able to tell you when Sherman's phone pings the cell tower."

"Good. As to your suggestion that we bring Sherman over to our side? I have decided to go with it—but only after Sherman relays the details of our trip to NOLA to his handler. We want Sherman to tell the mole we attended

Bella's memorial service. We don't want the mole to suspect that we're on to him—in particular that we know the burned body in the car wasn't Bella's.

"Once Sherman has reassured his handler, we'll take him, get him in a room, and crack him like an egg. He will be made to see that working with us is the only possible means of recovering his family alive. Hopefully, he will then spill the handler's ID. I'll be putting a strike team on alert as soon as we reach Broadsword."

Tobin asked, "What about the task force after you've taken Sherman? Our teammates shouldn't be kept in the dark about Bella any longer than necessary. They are gonna be mad enough as it is when they realize your rendition of Bella's memorial was pure baloney."

Wolfe chuckled softly. "No, you're right about that. Tell you what, the minute we have Sherman in custody and have plugged that leak, we'll tell the team the truth about Bella."

Jaz cut back to Wolfe's previous statements. "What if Sherman doesn't know who his handler is?"

"As crafty as this traitor has been, that's a distinct possibility. However, if we find that is the case, I believe I have another way to ID Sherman's handler."

He dropped his voice. "You said the only activity between the two burner phones has been texts, that they have never spoken. We need to change that. We'll need a legitimate and urgent reason for Sherman to call his handler and get him to pick up the call. That should do it."

Jaz frowned. "Do what? I don't follow."

Wolfe raised one brow. "You think I won't recognize the voice of a man or woman who reports directly to me? If we can get our traitorous mole on the line with Sherman, I should know who it is immediately."

Jaz smiled, not something she often did.

Wolfe smiled in return. "Feels good to think something might be going our way for a change, huh?"

TOBIN STOPPED THE CAR BRIEFLY at the guard shack, waking Parker with a start. When Tobin had cleared the security checkpoint, he drove into the compound and pulled the car alongside the cabin's porch. Broadsword had snow, and lots of it, but a path from the car up the cabin's steps had been cleared as had a path from the house to the gym and the track the guards patrolled inside the fence's perimeter.

Richard, impeccably dressed as always, stood waiting for them with Seraphim and Bo at his side. The three of them nodded a greeting, but waited without speaking as Wolfe walked up to meet them. They immediately went inside, leaving Parker, Tobin, and Jaz to deal with luggage.

That suited Jaz fine. She was itching to get to her desk in the bullpen so she could "plug in." She trotted upstairs, dropped her bag on her bed, grabbed her laptop, ran out the back door, and hotfooted it across a shoveled path to the gym. As soon as she pulled the door closed behind her, the task force's collective attention turned her way.

"Hey."

Not one voice responded, but six sets of eyes brimmed with resentment. More than a touch of accusation.

Maybe out-and-out anger?

"Tough room," Jaz mumbled to herself.

She slid into her chair, pulled out her laptop, plugged into power and DSL, then booted it up. She jerked upright in surprise when she realized that her teammates—to a person—had converged on her desk.

Vincent, Jubaila, and Soraya's expressions were foreboding. Brian and Rusty had their arms crossed. By the look on Gwyneth's face, she was in charge of this rabid mob of the Third Estate—along with Jaz's imminent introduction to Madame la Guillotine.

Gwyneth glared at Jaz. "*Really?* You and Tobin figured that we—the lowly peons you left behind—would be *just peachy* with you two sneaking off to Bella's funeral without us? Is that it?"

"I, uh—" Jaz's hand snaked out to snag the unopened pack of Black Jack on her desk.

Rusty beat her to it. He snatched up the pack. Held it over the trash. Slam dunked it for two points.

Jaz's lips parted and she stared with longing at the trash can. She looked up. Her gaze skipped from one teammate to another. The collective level of "disgruntled" she encountered could have powered Broadsword for a month. And they were *daring* her to dumpster dive.

"Um, well, you see . . ."

"Shut it, Jaz. You've got no excuse. I'm so mad I could spit."

"Mad? I'm furious," Jubaila sneered. "*You excluded us.*"

"And we *don't do that* on this team," Soraya reminded Jaz.

Brian chimed in, "Yeah. In the immortal words of Desi Arnaz, *Lucy, you got some 'splainin' to do*. Serious explaining."

Jaz's thwarted fingers twitched and spasmed. If a machete were to sever her digits, Jaz was convinced they would crawl across her desk toward the trash under their own steam. "Sorry. I, um, have something I need to do right now—for Director Wolfe."

"Oh! Oh, *my*. For the Director. For him *personally*, huh?" This was from Vincent, sarcasm frosting every word—a rarity.

Vinny, you need to limit your exposure to Brian, Jaz thought.

From the doorway Wolfe answered, "Yes. For him *personally*."

The torch-toting mob led by Madame DeFarge melted away. All except Rusty. He lifted two fingers, pointed them at his eyes, whipped them back at Jaz, and hissed, "I. Am. Watching. You."

"Sheesh." Jaz had never much cared what people thought about her . . . before. She was shocked at how much the team's unified censure stung.

She yanked the trash can toward her and dug for her gum.

Wolfe walked to the front of the bullpen. "Gather 'round, people. I have important things to share with you this morning." Seraphim was with him. So were Richard and Bo, their presence a departure from the norm. Tobin, Lance, and Sherman entered through a door at the rear of the gym so they wouldn't disrupt Wolfe's address.

While her fingers were busy tearing into the pack of Black Jack and stuffing two sticks of gum—make that three—into her mouth, Jaz casually slid her eyes around to Tobin. He was leaned against a wall a couple yards behind Sherman. He dipped his chin once without looking at her.

Jaz chomped the gum into a wad, tossed it around in her mouth, and calmed. As soon as Wolfe began to speak, she put her fingers to her keyboard and set to work.

"I understand that Seraphim explained to you where Marshal Tobin, Miss Jessup, and I have been the past three days. Yes, we attended Bella's graveside service. I'm certain you all have questions—the foremost one being, why were we allowed to go and you were not?

"Here are the facts. Bella's family asked us to attend her memorial service. To be clear, they asked for all members of Bella's team to attend. They expressly wanted *you* there, you who worked closely with her and grew to appreciate and even love her. I know you would have been honored to do so.

"However, the problems all clandestine agents must deal with during their active career—and often after it, I'm sorry to say—are the enmeshed matters of safety and security. Safety for the operative and security for the agency and its intelligence network. Anonymity is the only method that protects our intelligence network and ensures the safety of an operative, in the field and out.

"As you are already aware, the woman you knew as Bella did not exist. Anabelle Garineau was a cover identity—one of many legends given to her to keep her true identity hidden from those who would have sought to harm her or her family. Yes, harm her family. Even after her death, Bella's agency and I, as its director, are honor bound to guard her true identity lest we place in jeopardy those she loved."

Wolfe coughed to clear the thickness from his throat. "How and why would her family face possible harm after Bella's death? The answer is not a simple one, but I will try to explain. You see, this woman, one of the finest agents I have ever had the pleasure of knowing, lived twenty-some years in the field. She gave her entire life to this work, to providing us with the information we needed to stay ahead of our foes.

"To her credit, Bella infiltrated some of the highest levels of our adversaries and stole many valuable secrets. Put plainly, she made powerful enemies—enemies who have long, unforgiving memories.

"As director, I made the decision that the individuals on the team closest to her would be permitted to attend her memorial. They would represent this task force, the people she was so *very* proud of. Bella's family, deprived of her company for most of her adult life, was touched and grateful as we described the woman we knew and appreciated—their daughter, their sister, and their aunt."

Rusty startled Jaz when he rose from his seat. "Director Wolfe? May I speak?"

A flash of consternation crossed Wolfe's face. It was gone as quickly as it appeared, but Jaz was certain he was as uncomfortable in the moment as she was.

Sniffles and muffled sobs around the bullpen tore Jaz from her own reflections. It dawned on her how angry, how *hurt* she would have been to be left out of the scenario Wolfe described. Now she realized that the team—those who didn't know Bella could still be alive—needed to grieve. Needed to memorialize her.

"Er, of course, Rusty," Wolfe answered.

"Thank you. I just want to say how grateful I am to Bella. I was only a lowly IT help desk nerd, but when Bella made me a full member of the task force, she gave me a voice. She insisted that my ideas had value—that my contribution to our team was as good as anyone's was. I'll never forget her for that."

One by one, the members of the task force stood and said something about Bella. Most related touching moments with Bella and said something to honor her. Brian's tribute, of course, was edged with witty sarcasm, but it was still, unmistakably, heartfelt.

When he finished, the room went silent. Until, one by one, the team members looked at Jaz.

What? Oh, crap—they expect me to say something?

Unable to forget that the body shipped back to the States was *not* Bella and that the memorial her family had planned had actually *not* taken place, Jaz still found herself on her feet.

Utterly uncomfortable expressing sentiment or emotion, she mumbled, "I-I learned a lot from Bella . . . about tenacity. About courage. I personally witnessed her confront danger and possible death and do the fearless thing anyway. I also watched her take charge of this group—or, shall I say, 'this motley crew'?—and mold us into something far greater than anything I've ever been part of. She was—and always shall be—my friend."

Jaz sat down and buried her face in her hands. *Argh! Please tell me I didn't just adopt Spock's epic line from "The Wrath of Khan!"*

With the team's tributes over, Wolfe thanked them. Before he dismissed them, he encouraged them to press on in their hunt to uncover AGFA's attack plans.

No one appeared to realize that Tobin had said nothing.

While her teammates dried their eyes and consoled each other in their common grief, Jaz stared at her hands and the half-empty pack of gum she twirled from finger to finger, around and round.

Huh. I hadn't planned on getting all mushy. Guess I got caught up in the moment—which wasn't such a great idea, given what we now know. And I wonder what everyone's going to think when they find out Wolfe led them on. That Bella may still be alive.

They'll probably nominate me for an Oscar—right before they call for my head on a pike.

THE TEEMING CITY OF BAKU, Azerbaijan, woke early each morning. The city, built on the Absheron Peninsula, was the largest and busiest port on the Caspian Sea, receiving ships and their cargos from Russia, Kazakhstan, Turkmenistan, and Iran. Unlike the Black Sea, the Caspian had no outlet. Crane operators hovered over massive cargo ships and conveyed their sea cans directly onto railcars bound for ports on the Black Sea. At those ports, other ships would take delivery of the sea cans, exit the Black Sea through the Bosporus Strait, and continue on to their destinations.

Some sea cans arriving at the port were off-loaded to the dockyards. There, dock workers toiled endlessly to empty cargo containers filled with all manner of produce and other foods. The workers would load the contents of these containers onto commercial trucks that made their way to warehouses outside the city where the cargo would be inventoried and scheduled for delivery.

Baku had a population of two million mouths to feed. Hundreds of trucks left the warehouses each day and entered the city to deliver food to grocers and markets. Other delivery trucks traveled inland and supplied the stores that filled the pantries and cupboards of the peoples of Azerbaijan, Georgia, and Armenia.

With such bustling commerce, trucks entering and leaving Baku were an ordinary sight. So were trucks traveling the roads that connected the three southern Caucasus nations. In fact, Yaver, who owned a small refrigerated truck, made the 360-mile trip from Baku to Tbilisi three times a week.

Today, on his return trip to Baku, Yaver's truck would contain a shipment of wine from a reputable Georgian vineyard. The grapes had been specially grown and vinted for the patriarch of the Russian Orthodox Church in

Azerbaijan. The vintner and his helpers had bottled and crated the wine, twelve bottles to a crate, had carefully stacked the crates on pallets four crates high and four crates wide, and had lashed the crates together to stabilize the pallets and their loads.

When Yaver arrived at the vintner's warehouse near 7:30 a.m., he backed the truck to the loading dock and lowered the truck's ramp onto the dock. A forklift operator carrying two pallets, one stacked atop the other, drove across the ramp and into the truck, depositing the pallets in the front left corner of the truck. He deposited his second load of pallets to the right of the first pallets and backed out of the truck.

The vintner's men then entered the truck and strapped the pallets to the truck walls to prevent shifting. They repeated this careful dance until the vintner's shipment was loaded.

After Yaver and the vintner had signed the required paperwork, Yaver left the warehouse for Baku. Unbeknownst to the vintner, however, the truck made a second stop before leaving Tbilisi.

Yaver backed his truck through the high doorway of an old and rusting factory at a quarter to nine. He parked in the middle of what had been the loading area and sat in his cab, waiting and picking his teeth.

He did not wait long. Minutes before nine o'clock, he heard the approaching car. It rattled its way into the factory yard and died with a shudder when its driver turned it off. He climbed down to greet the two women.

"Any problems to report?" he asked.

"No, sir," the old crone replied.

"Good. Please tend to your duties one last time. Oh—and wrap her in all the blankets you may have. Then I will pay you."

He accompanied the two women to the corner of the factory where they lifted away a pile of old cardboard and uncovered the crate. He watched as they performed their tasks. When they had finished, they layered their charge with three blankets, tucking them under her.

When they had nailed the crate's lid back on, he spoke. "You guarantee she will sleep?"

"For eight hours or longer, sir," the gaunt old woman testified. "I packed another bag of saline inside and a prepared dose of the medication. One need only inject the medication into the port near the catheter eight hours from now."

"Very good," Yaver murmured. "You have done well, both of you, and have earned your pay." Their eager eyes followed his hand as it dipped into his pocket . . . and as he withdrew the snub-nosed revolver.

"Thank you for your service."

He shot the old woman first. The younger one, stupefied, then realizing what was coming, thought to run. He saw it on her face, in her wide, terrified eyes.

She died before her brain could convince her feet to move.

Yaver wiped down his gun, walked it back to the cab of his truck, and wedged it under his seat. He returned to the crate wearing heavy gloves. He grasped the thick rope handle protruding from one end of the crate and dragged the box out from the corner, pulling it toward his truck.

He fished the old woman's car keys from her coat pocket before he dragged the bodies into the corner and covered them with the same pile of cardboard that had covered the crate. Next he drove the old woman's car to the other side of the factory where, when the factory closed down, workers had filled the yard with the factory's machines. He drove the car behind some of the rusted equipment, turned the car off, and left the keys in the ignition.

As he walked back inside the factory, he checked his watch. Only 9:35. Time to spare.

Twenty-five minutes later, he greeted the three men he'd hired to reload this special shipment. After Yaver let down his truck's ramp, he pointed to the crate resting on the brick floor and explained what he wanted. The men unstrapped the two front pallets and cut the ties lashing the crates to their pallets. They carefully but quickly unstacked three layers of wine crates from the two pallets.

At Yaver's direction, they positioned the new crate to bridge the two pallets. It took the same space as four wine crates. The crates the men had removed—except those the new crate replaced—were then stacked in their original positions, surrounding and above the new crate, concealing it completely. The men lashed the two pallets together instead of separately and re-secured the pallets to the truck walls.

Yaver opened one of the removed wine crates and withdrew a single bottle. He placed the bottle on his truck's passenger seat and covered it with his coat. The three men who had helped him modify his shipment took possession of the remaining crates as their payment for less than an hour's work.

One of the men pointed his chin at Yaver and, with a good-natured laugh, said, "We shall toast you tonight, my friend."

"Many times," another man agreed with a chuckle.

Yaver grinned. "And I, you."

The men had no idea that, as a Muslim convert, Yaver no longer drank alcohol. In fact, the three men had no idea he was Muslim. As was the plan.

After his helpers drove away, Yaver climbed into his cab and continued on his way, his refrigerated truck maintaining the truck's cargo at a constant temperature of fifty-five degrees.

Hours later, he arrived at the border checkpoint between Georgia and Azerbaijan. Two Azerbaijani border officers waved him forward for inspection. Yaver, with his frequent crossings, was known to the two officials

They greeted him familiarly and asked the usual questions.

"What are you carrying this day, Yaver?"

"Today? A special cargo—a shipment of wine to His Holiness himself in Baku."

"No! Really?" the first guard exclaimed. "Very special, indeed."

Yaver rolled up the truck's freight door and waved his hand at the pallets and crates. The officer climbed up into the truck and peered into its depths. He saw only more pallets and crates, all the same.

The second officer, not as religious as his partner, stared at the wine and remarked, "Would that a bottle or two of His Holiness's wine were to go missing! With so many crates, I wonder if the absence would be noted."

It was not a subtle hint.

Yaver smiled and waggled his brows. "Maybe a bottle does go missing, eh?" He casually scanned to the left and right. "Would you be interested in finding it?"

"I would indeed."

At the officer's signal, Yaver pulled down the cargo door and locked it. Then he gestured to the officer to follow him back to the cab. Yaver climbed into his seat and shut the door. His hand closed around the bottle near his side and pulled it across his lap, keeping it below the window but in full sight of the man.

The officer glanced away, reached his hand through the window, and brought it out. He tucked the bottle into his coat and nodded to the driver.

"Another perfect inspection, Yaver. Have a good evening, and we will see you on your next run."

CHAPTER 13

JAZ BURROWED INTO THE cell tower's data. She waited and watched for Sherman's phone to ping off the tower. A copy of text messages between him and his handler wouldn't be available instantly, but her job at the moment was to let Wolfe know when the exchanges between Sherman and the mole began and when they ended.

The wait wasn't long. Not more than ten minutes after the meeting dismissed, his phone pinged on the cell tower.

Sherman has updated his handler—Wolfe's mole, the traitor responsible for Bella's abduction.

She waited fifteen minutes longer. When no other activity occurred, she sent her own message, a single word to Wolfe's mobile phone: *Done.*

WOLFE, SERAPHIM, RICHARD, BO, and Harris were waiting in the conference room for Jaz's signal. All of them knew their roles in the takedown. When Wolfe received Jaz's message, he texted Tobin, who was keeping an eye on Sherman.

Tobin's quick reply provided Wolfe with Sherman's location. Wolfe then passed that information to Richard. He, Bo, and Harris left the conference room to act out their predetermined parts. Bo and Harris were armed and prepped to take Sherman into custody, but the plan called for isolating Sherman and taking him by surprise—no one wanted any unnecessary violence.

To that end, Richard went in search of Sherman. He spotted him, as Tobin's message had said, walking the Broadsword perimeter with a regular guard and his dog. Richard waited until Sherman and the guard were opposite the back door leading outside from the kitchen.

Sherman and the guard both halted when Richard, the usual apron tied over his crisp shirt and tie, waved to them from the kitchen doorway.

"Sherman? Could you spare a moment? I require a pair of strong arms."

"Be right there."

Richard closed the door and withdrew to the dining room. Bo and Harris had already arranged themselves in the living room, out of sight.

Sherman left the guard and headed toward the kitchen door. As he opened it, Tobin left his observation point and quick-stepped to close the distance between himself and the back door.

Sherman shut the kitchen door behind him, and Richard waved him into the dining room. The large table, usually expanded by four leaves, was pulled apart.

"Over here. The table slides are stuck. I need another body on one end to help me push them together."

"Sure thing, Richard."

Sherman moved into the dining room. Bo and Harris, guns out, stepped into view. At the same time, Tobin came through the back door.

Stunned, Sherman looked from one face to another. Even Richard had his sidearm drawn. Before Sherman could react further, Wolfe appeared. His expression was pained, but obdurate.

"We know you're the mole within the task force, Sherman. No, don't make a move—that will not save your wife and son."

Tobin holstered his weapon. He reached around Sherman and removed the man's sidearm before it could tempt him further. Bo, without moving the muzzle of his gun off of Sherman, took the gun from Tobin's hand.

Sherman's face twisted in agony. "You don't understand! I didn't want to—I would never willingly betray my duty! But I had no choice—he . . . he said he would kill my family."

"We know, Sherman. That's why we're going to offer you an opportunity to save them." Wolfe ordered Tobin, "Cuff him and take him to the conference room."

WHILE BO AND HARRIS stood post outside the conference room and Tobin and Jaz looked on impassively, Wolfe and Seraphim took first crack at breaking the mole's hold on Sherman. It was obvious that the man was demoralized. Wolfe intended to give him hope—in exchange for his cooperation and everything he knew.

"We have read the texts between you and your handler, Sherman," Wolfe said gently. "We know this person has your family and has threatened to kill them. We even know he had one of your wife's fingers cut off to prove to you that he means business. And we know that whenever you balk at doing what he demands, he threatens to cut off another of her fingers."

"Sh-she plays piano. Now she'll never play again. And my son! The things he said he would do to my boy—" Sherman hung his head and wept.

Wolfe placed a hand on Sherman's shoulder and squeezed. "I am so very sorry."

Sherman tried to master his emotions. "Sir, you need to understand that, in spite of his threats against my family, I did not give him what he wants most."

Wolfe's lips compressed into a tight line. "What do you mean by 'what he wants most?' What is it he wants?"

"H-he desperately wants to know where we are, sir. But when you pulled us from Griffin Industries? I told him we'd been brought to our new location in windowless trucks, that none of us knew where we ended up—only that we were somewhere in the mountains, surrounded by armed guards."

"And he believed you?"

Sherman's tone was plaintive. "Yes, sir. He still regularly demands that I determine our location—he threatened to kill my son if I didn't find out! But I held on, kept playing dumb. I knew if I gave in that he'd call in another attack, like the one on Jaz, Bella, and Marshal Tobin's apartments. I-I did what I could, sir, to protect the task force. Please believe me!"

Tobin interrupted, his fury barely in check. "*You gave him Bella!*"

"I-I did. I'm sorry. I had to give him something—he was running out of patience! But Bella is so smart and savvy that I hoped . . . I hoped she would outwit them."

"That's supposed to excuse what you did?"

"No. I know it doesn't. But please believe me—I didn't want Bella to be hurt. I didn't want any of this to happen."

A long moment passed before Wolfe said, "I believe you, Sherman. I appreciate that you did what you could for us . . . under difficult circumstances."

"Thank you, sir. So, what about . . . what about my family?"

Wolfe exhaled before speaking again. "Listen carefully, Sherman. We have a plan. A plan to trick your handler into giving up your wife and son's location. Once we have their location, we'll send in the FBI's Hostage Rescue Team to free them. But we need your help."

"How can you expect me to take such a risk?" Sherman whimpered. "He said they would kill Carole and Teddy should anyone attempt to storm their location."

Wolfe looked at Seraphim. They hadn't foreseen Sherman's fear as an obstacle. Seraphim shook her head once. Wolfe knew what it meant. He'd drilled it into his people over and over.

The mission always took precedence—meaning the safety of the many outweighed the safety of the few.

Wolfe backed off and went at Sherman from another direction. "Do you know who your handler is, Sherman? Have you seen him? Do you recognize him?"

"No. I don't know who he is. I've never seen him, either. We've never spoken directly. Only through texts and photos . . . and the package. The package arrived first—a few days before we moved the task force to Broadsword."

"A package with your wife's finger inside?"

"Yes, and the burner phone. They came with a picture of Carole and Teddy . . . and instructions."

"We're going to get Carole and Teddy home safely," Wolfe assured him. "Here's our plan. We're going to prep you to tell your handler that you have some urgent information. You'll text that you have the info, then you're going to immediately use your phone to *call* your handler."

"He won't take a call. I-I tried once. I was told not to again."

"Right. Okay. In that case, we'll have you text him with part of the urgent info—minus a critical piece. The info will shake him up. He'll text you back, asking for the missing piece, but you won't reply. The urgency of the info will make your handler anxious. When you don't respond, he'll grow more concerned. After we've let him stew long enough, you'll text only the words, 'We need to talk.'"

"What info?"

"You know we're dealing with terrorists, cold-blooded murderers, don't you, Sherman?"

He hung his head again. "Yeah. I know."

"The events of 9/11 showed our enemies that it was possible to throw the US into chaos. All Glorious for Allah first tried to assassinate Petroff. Now we know that they are planning at least two more attacks. They intend to kill thousands of American citizens, hoping the FAA will halt air travel, banks and the stock market will tumble, and industry will grind to a standstill. More than that, the terrorists will attempt to frame Russia for the attacks. Why? Because they want to pit the two superpowers against each other. Is that what *you* want?"

"Of course not!"

"And do you really think these mass murderers will honor their 'promise' to spare your wife and son?"

Sherman couldn't answer. His shoulders heaved in despair.

"Listen to me, Sherman. You need to face the facts and take hold of our offer. It's the best and *only* shot you have at saving your family. But if you turn us down? You'll not only be partially responsible for the murder of thousands of Americans, you *will* lose your family in the bargain."

Sherman wept and moaned—and Wolfe let him. He knew the man and his character. He was confident that Sherman's sense of right, duty, and simple logic would prevail. Wolfe's offer was the only means of saving Sherman's family.

After grieving another five minutes, Sherman quieted.

"This is your last opportunity, Sherman," Wolfe whispered. "Will you help us?"

The man shook himself. Wiped his face on his sleeves.

"Yeah, I will."

WOLFE ORDERED BO AND HARRIS to take Sherman into the library and keep him secured and isolated. When they closed the door behind themselves, he expected to immediately set to work on their next moves, but Jaz held up her hand.

"This isn't grade school, Miss Jessup."

"I wasn't asking permission to speak, sir. I was calling a halt."

"And why is that?"

"You told us you'd come clean to the task force as soon as we had Sherman, sir. You should tell them now, before we move forward another inch."

"I agree," Tobin added.

"This isn't a democracy—"

"I also agree," Seraphim interrupted.

Wolfe harrumphed. "Now is *not* the time. It's more important that we identify the traitor and—"

"It is exactly the time," Jaz cut back in. "We kept the team in the dark for one reason—to convince Sherman and his handler that you, Tobin, and I had attended Bella's memorial service, that we hadn't figured out AGFA had faked Bella's death. Okay, we did that, and the team will see your reasoning. Then we needed to take Sherman down without him warning his handler. We did that, too, and the team may be able to swallow your logic.

"However, we're past those reasons. If you tell the task force the truth about Bella now, your credibility with them might be strained, but it won't be ruined. If you choose not to tell them now, then I will. And sir? In my humble opinion, if you don't do it yourself at this first reasonable opportunity, I sincerely doubt you'll be able to show your face to them again."

"Agreed," Seraphim added.

Tobin nodded firmly.

"I see."

Wolfe was a pragmatist. His people watched him calculate the time it would take to inform the task force. Weigh it against Seraphim, Tobin, and Jaz's objections and the resistance he would face if he refused their "request."

"All right. Let's go."

Five minutes later, Wolfe, with Seraphim nearby, again presented himself before the task force. Less than two hours had elapsed since he dismissed them from Bella's impromptu memorial.

"I have some announcements—all good news. However, I must warn you, the good news came at the cost of misleading this team, of taking advantage of your trust."

Jaz smirked behind her hands. Wolfe, the consummate spy-turned-bureaucrat, was spinning his bombshell revelations just right.

"I hope, when you've heard what I have to say *in its totality*, that you will forgive my lack of candor this morning."

Yup. Setting expectations. Softening them up. Jaz treated herself to a fresh stick of gum.

Brian, eyes narrowed, said, "You'll understand if we reserve our forgiveness until you explain?"

"Of course. I'll also add that both of my announcements, while having a significant upside, have a downside as well. Shall I begin?"

As the task force members nodded for Wolfe to continue, Jaz laughed up her sleeve.

Oh, Director Wolfe, you are truly priceless.

"My first announcement is that we've identified the mole here at Broadsword and have taken him into custody."

No one in the bullpen moved. Then they began to scan the gym, checking to see who was missing.

"Who? Who is it?" Brian demanded.

"The mole is Agent Sherman," Wolfe said softly.

The team was stunned. Rusty was the first to ask, "Sherman? Sherman gave away Tobin, Jaz, and Bella's apartment location? To the Ukrainians?"

"It's more likely that he gave that information to his handler, and his handler fed it to the Ukrainian mob."

"But . . ." Gwyneth spoke next. "You *are* saying Sherman passed the details of Bella's mission to Tbilisi to his handler? That it was *Sherman* who got Bella killed?"

Wolfe spoke slowly and distinctly. "Did Sherman get Bella killed? For two reasons, my answer is no."

Jaz sat back, further amazed at how Wolfe was able to craft the perfect response on the fly. She cut her eyes toward Tobin. He was slowly shaking his head, as astounded as she was.

Wolfe continued. "I'm certain you feel a great deal of animosity toward Sherman, and I share your rancor. However, you should know that Sherman's handler, the other mole, has Sherman's wife and young son."

He let that fact land and settle where it collided head-on with the team's outrage. The shock of Sherman's situation blunted the edge of their anger immediately.

Before the task force's anger could recover, Wolfe added, "The other mole—the real traitor—threatened to kill Sherman's family if he did not cooperate. He also promised to make them suffer. As proof of the seriousness of his threats, he cut off one of his wife's fingers and mailed it to Sherman—can you imagine the horror?"

Brian cussed aloud, careless of who heard him, but he wasn't the only one swearing a blue streak.

In the lull after Wolfe's announcements, Vincent said, "You said you had two reasons Sherman didn't get Bella killed. What's the other?"

Wolfe waited until he had everyone's attention. "Yes, while it's true Marshal Tobin, Miss Jessup, and I went to NOLA to meet with Bella's family, what isn't true is that we went to attend Bella's burial. You see, we brought in a pathologist to examine the remains shipped back from the Republic of Georgia."

He paused. "As it turned out, they weren't Bella's."

FORTY MINUTES LATER, Wolfe, Tobin, and Jaz were still answering questions and apologizing to the team for the morning's emotional ups and downs.

"You're saying you *think* Bella was abducted, but you aren't sure, is that it?" Rusty demanded for the third time. "You know the body in the car wasn't hers—but that doesn't prove she isn't dead?"

"That's it," Wolfe said. "Like I said earlier, there's a downside to the news."

"You're saying not knowing if Bella is alive or dead is *a downside?* That's putting it mildly," Brian grumbled. "What I want to know is what are we doing about it?"

Others were angry that they'd been duped into displaying their grief during a mock memorial.

"You tricked us into pouring out our hearts so you could trap Sherman. I get that. But you didn't have to play along, Jaz," Rusty half-shouted. "You stood there and made us all . . . you know—"

"Made you what? Say it—I made you *cry?* Well, you guys made me cry first. And when I didn't stand up and join in memorializing Bella, the bunch of you stared at me like I didn't care about her. What was I supposed to do? Sherman was right there, watching and listening. I had to play along. We had to make sure that what he reported to his handler wouldn't rouse the traitor's suspicions."

Grudging mumbles circled the bullpen.

"Besides," Jaz replied with a shrug, "nothing I said was untrue."

"Well, what's next?" Jubaila asked. "Now that you have Sherman?"

"Now," Wolfe said, "we use Sherman to reel in the traitor."

WOLFE, SERAPHIM, TOBIN, and Jaz returned to the conference room to brainstorm their strategy, beginning with the text message Sherman would send his handler. The message was to be intentionally vague, worrisome and subject to the mole's interpretation at the same time.

Wolfe said, "Our primary objective is to manipulate the mole into asking for a phone call with Sherman. We'll start by knocking the mole off-balance through a series of text messages. Then we'll agitate him, make him need more detail and force him to ask for a call."

Wolfe added, "At present, it's clear that Sherman is emotionally fragile. We'll need for him to pull himself together when his handler decides to speak to him directly. Until then, it is easier to have Jaz send the texts exactly as we craft them."

"And I will triangulate the mole's location by the cell towers his phone pings. If we're lucky, we'll catch him while he's on the move, and I will track his general direction," Jaz explained.

"Too bad we can't do better than that," Seraphim muttered.

"Technology will get us there someday. Just not today—but I will need your laptop to record the call."

"Sure. But how will you record the mole's side of the conversation?"

Jaz pursed her lips. "I happen to have a little piece of, um, electronic *tech* that I attached to the phone. It will pick up both voices and send it to the laptop."

"That wouldn't be considered an illegal wiretap, would it?"

"Not touching any wires, cross my heart. And this tech isn't illegal."

"Uh-huh. But perhaps the way you have previously used it *was?*"

Jaz sidestepped Seraphim's question with, "We're way past legal vs. illegal. Besides, we're not planning on using what we glean in a court of law, are we?"

Seraphim slowly shook her head.

"Okay, then I need your laptop. At the same time Sherman is on the call, I'll plug a headset into your laptop, enabling Director Wolfe to listen to the person on the other end of the call."

Jaz installed the software, set Seraphim's laptop to record the call, and plugged a splitter into the laptop's headphone jack, then added a second pair of headphones for herself.

"Are we ready?" Wolfe asked.

When Jaz, Seraphim, and Tobin nodded, Wolfe gave Jaz the go-ahead signal.

Jaz keyed in the text they'd agreed upon. At Wolfe's nod, she sent it.

Something going down
Don't know what
Lots of activity

Intentionally vague and concerning.

As soon as Jaz sent the text, she turned to her laptop to await the traitor's reply and mark the towers where the phone pinged. The response came immediately.

Need details

"No surprise there," Jaz told the others. She started inputting the next message. When Wolfe nodded, she sent it.

Not sure
Task force behind
closed doors
I've heard words
PREPPING
and OPERATION

They waited. Wolfe turned to Jaz. "Have you triangulated the mole's phone?"

"Yah. Nothing unexpected there—your office building in DC is smack in the center of the triangulation."

"The traitor's office, too," Seraphim said.

Jaz raised a jubilant whoop. "No! He's on the move."

Wolfe smiled. "We can expect him to ask for a call soon. Let's get Sherman ready."

He and Tobin left to fetch Sherman.

Tobin and Wolfe appeared with Sherman. Sherman appeared to have shrunk. Fallen in on himself.

"We need to know before you dial that number. Can you do what we've asked of you, Sherman?"

"Yes. I have to. My wife and my son are counting on me."

Wolfe donned the headphones that would allow him to listen in on the call. Jaz slipped on her headset and bent over her laptop.

Sherman pressed the buttons to call his handler's number. Jaz was already recording the call. She and Wolfe were ready to listen. On her own laptop, Jaz watched the traitor's movement.

A text arrived.

Call me immediately

"Finally," Jaz breathed.

"Wait," Wolfe ordered. "Let the traitor sweat. Give him enough time to show Jaz where he's headed."

They waited until Jaz whispered, “Based on the speed the handler’s phone is pinging from cell tower to tower, I’d place him on a highway, headed northeast. General direction of Baltimore.”

“All right. Sherman? Make the call.”

Sherman pressed the call button. They heard the call ring through.

Sherman’s handler picked up the call and without a preamble demanded, “I need to know everything you know about what’s going on, Mr. Stadler—and do I need to remind you? Your wife and your son’s lives depend upon your usefulness to me.”

Jaz realized she hadn’t even known Sherman’s last name, so she almost missed it—the wave of shock that rippled across Wolfe’s face. Just as quickly, a hard, stony ruthlessness replaced it.

Whoa. He knows who it is, all right.

Sherman had years of habit and discipline under his belt. He slid seamlessly into his professional demeanor. “I can report that they are gearing up for something big, but I don’t know what. We’re not allowed inside the gymnasium while the task force is working on anything classified—and whatever is going on must be classified as all get-out, because Lance and I and two other guards have been posted six feet from every entrance into the gym. No one in, no one out, and we can’t hear a thing.”

“But surely you’ve heard some rumor, some indication of what they are working on?”

Wolfe and Seraphim had haggled over the exact piece of bait to hang from the hook. Sherman’s response had to be entirely plausible and yet not over the top. They didn’t want to send the mole into a panic.

“I have heard something, twice now, but I’m not familiar with the term. Not sure I’m even saying it right.”

“What term?”

“Fenta-something. Like I said, not sure what it means.”

Stunned silence. Then, “Can you be more explicit?”

“Just fenta-something. Fentazole or fentanaide, close to that.”

“Was the term fentanyl?”

Sherman, as cool as an April morning, answered, “Maybe. Sounds about right.”

“And what, precisely, did you hear concerning fentanyl?”

“Well, that’s the thing. I didn’t hear anything else. For some reason, everyone keeps talking about New Year’s Eve. The task force must be planning a big party, I guess.”

Another long silence, then, “Yes, that must be it. Thank you, Mr. Stadler. Do not call me again unless I give you permission.”

“I understand—now what about my family?”

"They are in good health and will continue to be in good health . . . for the present."

The caller hung up. Sherman looked around. "Did I do all right?"

"You did fine, Sherman," Wolfe replied. He opened the door and called Harris. "Take him back to the library. Guard him well."

After Harris took Sherman from the room, Wolfe turned to Jaz. "Tracking?"

"I've just lost the signal, so I assume the mole powered down the phone as soon the call ended. However, the phone's movement had stopped about a minute before I lost the signal."

"Does that mean we might have the general area where Sherman's family is being held?"

"Very general. The phone was last pinging a mile the other side of the DC-Maryland border, just north of New Hampshire Avenue Northeast. Best I can do is place it inside a five-mile radius."

Jaz studied Wolfe. "You know who the mole is, the traitor, don't you, sir?"

"I do."

He lowered his voice and revealed the traitor's identity to Seraphim, Tobin, and Jaz. The three of them recoiled at the revelation.

In response to their incredulity and anger Wolfe added, "We now have the traitor's identity, but on the off chance we have yet another unidentified leak here at Broadsword, we'll tighten our OPSEC even further. We'll redouble our scans for listening devices to ensure that our classified work spaces remain secure, and we'll widen the distance between us and Broadsword staff.

"In fact, after you've informed the task force, I want *not a hint* of the traitor's name to touch our lips—not mine, not yours, nor any member of the task force, even in this room or the gym. In all conversations and communications we'll employ the code name 'Rosenberg' to refer to the traitor's identity—Rosenberg as in Julius Rosenberg and his equally guilty wife."

He stared at each of them. "Got it?"

Seraphim, Tobin, and Jaz answered together, "Yes, sir."

"Good. Meanwhile, I want you, Jaz, and the entire task force digging into every facet of Rosenberg's life—and I mean *everything*. Connections to AGFA and Ukrainian mob, clues that will lead us to Sherman's family, clues as to who abducted Bella and where they have her. Divide the tasks among the team. Spare no effort or expense and *leave no stone unturned*."

Jaz's green eyes held a glint of malevolent glee. "You needn't motivate us, sir. No, indeed. This will be our pleasure—and we'll work fast."

"Thank you. I'll remain here at Broadsword to coordinate with the strike team for Rosenberg's takedown and HRT's rescue of Sherman's wife and son."

YAVER AND HIS TRUCK reached Baku that evening. He drove to an empty warehouse on the outskirts of the city where he joined another driver named Emil. Yaver and Emil unloaded enough crates of wine from Yaver's truck to reach the longer crate and haul it out.

"It has been eight hours," Yaver told Emil. "We must hang a new bag of fluids and inject the drugs to keep this woman Sayed wants so badly unconscious. Allah willing, she will remain unconscious—and alive—until you reach your destination."

"*Ya Allah!* I would not wish to be the man who fails Sayed, would you?"

Yaver shook his head vehemently and they set to work without wasting more time. They pried open the crate, checked the woman's condition, changed out the saline bags, and injected the drugs. Then they turned their attention to the other man's produce truck. It was a small truck destined for the rural community of Botlikh in Dagestan, Russia. The driver had already unloaded a portion of the cargo, making a narrow hole for the crate. The men slid the long crate into the truck and finished surrounding it with boxes of cabbages, bags of potatoes, and fruit imported from Iran.

Their last task was to repack the crates of wine into Yaver's truck.

"What will you do about the missing crates?" Emil asked Yaver.

Yaver laughed. "The Patriarch's clerk is not as faithful as the Patriarch might wish. The man is not averse to a few crates 'falling off the back of the truck' if it fattens his wallet. He will attest to receiving the entire shipment and pocket what I pay him for the wine. Later on, records will show the rate of wine consumption quite inexplicably increasing—to account for the missing cases."

Emil slapped Yaver on the back. "A good arrangement, Yaver. Very good! Well, I must be off if I am to reach Botlikh and my rendezvous inside eight hours."

The men parted company. Yaver's truck would spend the night in the warehouse, and he would deliver the wine in the morning.

Emil, the produce driver, however, had a long night ahead of him. He headed northwest on Azerbaijan's M1, to the border crossing at Samur, Azerbaijan, on the Reka Samur River. There, he would cross over to the Russian checkpoint of Yarag-Kazmalyarskiy Tamozhennyy. Since he regularly delivered produce to the mountain villages of the Republic of Dagestan, and as the border guards were well compensated, the examination of his produce truck was cursory.

Once in Dagestan, he drove north, following the coastline until he reached Novyy Khushet. At the junction, he turned west. This was the harder portion of his route. The road twisted and turned, up and down, through the rugged foothills of the Greater Caucasus Mountains. Botlikh was at the far end of the tedious 100-mile drive, with his rendezvous point another ten miles beyond.

It was an hour past midnight when he passed Botlikh. The houses, many generations old, sprawled across the foothills, hanging to the rocks and hills by their fingernails. Like many mountain villages in Dagestan, Botlikh was a poor, obscure community that could boast a population of no more than 11,000. It was, however, not far from the border of its sister Russian republic, Chechnya.

He did not stop, but continued west, then north. Eventually, he took a right turn onto an unpaved road that led up a canyon. Far down the road, headlights winked on, then off.

His rendezvous.

He pulled over. Men surrounded his truck.

One of them yanked open his door. Another shined a light in his face, blinding him to what lay outside the circle of light. He raised his hands to show he was not armed.

"*As-Salamu Alaykum*," someone in darkness said.

"*Wa alaykumu s-salam*," Emil answered.

"Do you have General Sayed's package?"

"Yes. I would ask some help in digging it out."

The light clicked off, and Emil stepped down from the cab. As his eyes adjusted, he counted four men watching him and noted two pickup trucks parked behind them that had seen many years on mountain roads.

Emil jerked his head. "This way, please."

He unlocked and rolled up the rear door. Pointed. "Straight through here. If we unload the boxes of produce from here back, we will unearth the package."

He was careful to use a nonspecific term. From what he'd heard, Sayed was more suspicious than most men and did not like people—even his own—mouthing the details of his business, even when such knowledge was impossible to avoid.

The men worked with a will at the direction of their leader, a large and muscular man. At his command, they were mindful of Emil's true cargo, stacking it with care on the ground to get at the hidden crate, repacking the truck with the same care as when they'd dragged the crate out. Two men carried the crate toward one of their pickup trucks.

Emil touched the arm of their broad-shouldered leader. "It has now been eight hours since the *package* was last sedated. I wish to caution you that the drugs will be wearing off soon."

"We will shortly be where the drugs will not matter, but thank you for the notice."

Emil got in his truck and Sayed's men in theirs. The last Emil saw in his rearview mirror were the taillights of the trucks as they moved farther into the mountains.

IT WAS MONDAY, AND Collier was in his office at the US consulate in Tbilisi. He hung up with his caller, sat back, and considered his next move. A minute later, he left his office and entered the consulate's SCIF. Within the walls of the SCIF, with the door locked behind him, he was confident that the call he was about to place would not be intercepted or the number he dialed flagged and reported.

He had committed the number to memory ten days ago—following the visit of his uninvited, middle-of-the-night guest. The call rang and rang. He looked at a clock. Nine in the morning in the Republic of Georgia. Six in the evening in Washington, DC. He let the call ring.

After ten rings, someone picked up. "Wolfe here."

"Director Wolfe, Nathan Collier speaking."

"Mr. Collier. Do you have information for me?"

"Yes. I've compiled witness interviews and my conversations with the police. I will forward them to you by courier—although the upshot, in my opinion, is more than a little confusing."

"Tell me."

"I've distilled the following facts from my interviews. Several eyewitness accounts agree that, just prior to the accident, a female pedestrian stepped into the intersection. Traffic snarled and ground to a halt to avoid hitting her."

"The car my agent was in?"

"Second from the intersection when this occurred."

"Then?"

"The driver of the vehicle behind your agent told me that, as the line of cars pulled forward, a dump truck drove into the intersection from the left and hit your agent's sedan. The witness said, and I quote, 'The truck was lumbering along, quite fast for its size, and it looked to me that it swerved toward the car ahead of us. There was no reason for it to veer. Perhaps the driver was drunk and lost control. That's what it looked like.'"

"And perhaps it was intentional," Wolfe opined.

"Yes, it very well could have been, for the same witness and his wife both declared that immediately after crashing into the car, the truck driver backed up, turned, and drove away without a backward glance."

"What do the police say?"

"Ah, things get a bit more interesting—and confusing—at this juncture. Bystanders declare that the emergency response was quick. Two unmarked police cars and an ambulance. Near instantaneous, in fact, the witnesses say. A pair of police officers pushed back the growing crowd. Another pair worked to free the passengers in the seat behind the driver while the paramedics rolled a gurney to the car."

Collier hesitated, struggled to frame his next words. "I don't want to read my own conclusions into the witness accounts, sir, but what the closest witness said next seems . . . odd, perhaps astonishing."

"Push on, Collier. I'm fairly certain the 'astonishing' testimonies of your witness won't surprise me at all."

"Oh?"

When Wolfe didn't respond, Collier continued. "The driver of the car behind your agent described the paramedic's gurney as having 'lumpy blankets' piled on it rather than a flat, uncluttered surface. Later, just before the explosion, when the smoke obscured the wreckage and everyone, including the paramedics, pulled back, the witness caught a glimpse of the gurney. The astonishing part? He said, and I quote, 'Until I read in the papers that all the vehicle's passengers died at the scene, I was convinced the paramedics had pulled at least one victim from the car.'"

This time, Wolfe's reply was a soft and understanding, "Ah."

"Sir?"

"Finish, if you please, Mr. Collier."

"Yes, sir. I'll now condense my conversations with the police—as conflicting as they are."

"Conflicting how?"

"They dispute my eyewitness accounts. You see, the police insist that when their officers first arrived on scene, the fire truck was already putting out the blaze."

"I see." Wolfe seemed unsurprised.

Collier's patience snapped. "If you 'see,' sir, then either I'm blind or you're 'seeing' a lot more than I am."

"Only because I have more pieces of the puzzle than you have, Mr. Collier. Let me guess the rest of the police's testimony. The dump truck—it was stolen, yes?"

"The day before the accident. How did you know?"

Wolfe chose not to answer the question. "Do you have anything further to tell me?"

Collier huffed in frustration. "In point of fact, I do. I asked my contact on the police force to do me a personal favor—keep my investigation in mind should any strange, out-of-the-norm incidents crop up. My man on the force rang me this morning, right before I called you."

"Do tell."

"Yes, sir. Yesterday, four kids skipping school were exploring the old industrial area of Tbilisi. They wandered into an abandoned factory and were chasing each other around. You know, the usual games kids play. During their antics, a boy lifted a pile of cardboard, thinking to hide under it.

"Instead, he discovered the bodies of two women. They were both local, one elderly and one in her early twenties. They'd been shot. Close range, center mass."

"I'm interested in a local murder, *because?*" "I'm getting to it. In the corner with the bodies were two trash sacks. They were filled with empty and discarded bags of saline, soiled bandages, dirty washcloths, and hospital-type gowns. Nearby, the police found a hypodermic needle disposal container. The police say the drug residue in the sharps container appears to be a benzodiazepine—a particularly strong one with a long half-life."

Wolfe's skin began to itch. "Earlier, you said this information was confusing. Why?"

"Because, according to the police, the evidence suggests that someone was kept there. For days, possibly a week. Sedated."

"That's it, then," Wolfe said to himself.

Collier gave up trying to understand Wolfe's cryptic commentary. "One last thing, sir."

"Yes?"

"The younger victim? When the coroner undressed her for autopsy, he discovered something. A hank of hair. Not ripped from the scalp, but evenly cut, around twelve or fourteen inches long. Blond hair."

A shudder ran down Wolfe's back. "How long had the two women been dead?"

"No more than twenty-four hours, possibly less."

Collier heard Wolfe whisper to himself. "She's alive. As of yesterday, she was alive."

"Sir?"

"My agent, Mr. Collier. This entire debacle has been a charade, an elaborate piece of misdirection. Someone wanted my agent and wanted her *alive*. He also wanted us to think her dead."

"But the body I shipped to you . . ."

"Not her, Collier. *Definitively*. Not her."

Chapter 14

LP

LAYNIE WOKE TO THE GROWL of a truck laboring uphill. She was still in total darkness, the air stale and thick, but she could tell by the sway and jounce beneath her that she was on that truck.

I'm moving. Being taken somewhere. Not a commercial truck. More like a pickup. Rough, winding terrain, moving uphill, so not within the city of Tbilisi—or any city for that matter.

She wasn't cold any longer. In fact, she felt overly warm. Fabric scratched her neck. She rubbed her chin across it.

Wool. A blanket?

She was less fuzzy-headed than the last time she'd woken. This time, she tried to put together who had taken her. And why.

I'm weak, but maybe the drugs are wearing off.

How long? How long have they had me? Is it day or night? What kind of surface am I lying on? What is this "thing" I'm in?

The many questions crowding in only raised her anxiety, and her breath quickened.

Stop that. Not helpful. Stay calm.

Calling on the disciplines she'd learned in survival training, she attempted to calm herself. For a moment it worked—and then, it didn't. Adrenaline, already triggered, coursed through her veins and induced panic. The panic insisted that she move, run, flee, but her limbs only twitched in response. Without consciously planning to, she tried to sit up. Her forehead slammed against a surface six or eight inches above her. Something hard and rough scraped her forehead.

Wood. Unfinished wood.

I'm in a box. They've put me in a box, nailed the lid down—and I can't move, can't get out. Wait. A coffin?

Laynie felt the scream that boiled up in her chest. It scrabbled hard for her mouth but she was unable to open her jaws. The scream piled up in her throat instead, clogging, choking, and strangling her. She heard her muffled cries, but could not give voice to them. Could not part her teeth. She began to hyperventilate and gasped for air.

Laynie, my daughter.

She was trembling all over, choking and wheezing, when the calming words broke through her terror. She swallowed the fear stuck in her throat and whispered, "W-what?"

Laynie, my daughter. I am here.

Every muscle, bone, and tendon in her body melted. Liquefied. Her heart and lungs unclenched, and she could breathe again.

Laynie knew the source of her peace. "Thank you, my Jesus."

A while later, she felt her right index finger tingle and itch. Unconsciously, her thumb scratched it.

I can feel my fingers?

She arched her back and stretched a little.

Ohhh! So very stiff. Feels good to stretch—Wait. I arched my back? Maybe I can move other parts of my body.

Laynie concentrated. Her bound hands lifted a couple of inches. She rested, then tried again. She managed to raise her hands higher.

I want to feel that ceiling over me. I want to know if it is nailed down.

She kept at it, lifting her hands every few minutes, resting when she needed to. She was so thirsty that her mouth felt like it was filled with glue and sand, but she kept at it.

Then it happened. The back of her right hand encountered the boards above her. Straining, she twisted both hands and got her index finger on the rough surface. Yes, it was wood. An unfinished wooden lid. She used her shoulder muscles to shore up her weak arms and hands, to push on the lid. It creaked a little, one side looser than the other, but she couldn't sustain the effort for long. Trembling with exhaustion, she let her hands fall.

She didn't remember drifting off.

ARMED WITH THE IDENTITY of Wolfe's mole—a lead that might prove to be the "big break" they so desperately needed, a lead that would bust open every dead end including Bella's location—the team threw themselves into their work.

They ate at their workstations while delving into Rosenberg's life. Richard prepared hot meals for the team and conscripted two guards to lay them out in the bullpen. The team napped at their desks. Woke and kept working. They stopped only to stretch, use the restroom, or tank up on more coffee.

Wolfe and Seraphim walked over from the house to check on their progress.

Jaz, eyes on her monitor, and a great frown of concentration on her face, growled at them, "Go away. We'll let you know . . ." She didn't finish her sentence.

The task force had been at it for close to two days when Jaz called the house. "Director Wolfe? The task force requests the pleasure of your presence in the bullpen. Seraphim, too."

"You have something?"

Jaz laughed. "Some*thing*, sir? No. We have *lots*."

Vincent had logged their findings on the whiteboards. All Jaz and the team had to do was walk Wolfe and Seraphim through the bullet points.

Before Jaz began, she asked Rusty, "You have Rosenberg's present location?"

"According to the last badge swipe, still in the director's building. Last use of official email, fifteen minutes ago. Last use of office desk phone, three minutes ago."

"You hacked my building's badge access log?" Wolfe asked.

"And your department's phones and your employees' emails. You said spare no effort or expense. Leave no rock unturned."

Wolfe slowly nodded. "Well done."

"Thank you, sir. Brian? Please report to Seraphim and Director Wolfe what we've learned about Rosenberg's communications."

Brian leaped to his feet and pointed to the relevant bullet points on the board. "As you already know, when we acquired Sherman's burner, we hacked its call log and obtained the only number texted or called—Rosenberg's burner. When we hacked Rosenberg's call log, we found something interesting.

"Rosenberg's burner phone has been used to call Sherman and only Sherman—except in a single instance. Once and only once, it called *this* number." Brian indicated a number on the board and waggled his brows with conspiratorial fervor.

"We think that call was a mistake, *an accident,* but for us it was a happy accident. It gave us another number to excavate. Of course, we hacked the new number's call log and found that all of *its* calls or texts were between a *third* number."

Wolfe stopped him. "Wait. You're starting to lose me."

"Get in line," Seraphim snorted. "I'm already in a muddle."

"I'm sorry." He nodded respectfully. "We anticipated that explaining our progress might prove confusing, so we've labeled the phones and Vincent has created this flowchart as a visual. Let me step you through our logic."

He slowed and added, "Think of this process as a daisy chain. When we found a new phone number, we mined that phone's contacts—which has provided us with more numbers and more contacts. A chain."

Wolfe and Seraphim nodded.

"Go on," Wolfe said.

"In the same way patient zero is the starting point in an outbreak, we've designated Sherman's phone as Burner Zero—our starting point—and we'll call Rosenberg's phone Burner One. Understand that our traitor is careful. Never stores a number on the phone to be redialed. Always erases the call log. Used Burner One to communicate exclusively with one person, only Sherman—*until* two weeks ago."

"That's when Burner One accidentally called another number?"

"Exactly. How did that happen? Couldn't have been a 'pocket dial,' an accidental redial, because he erased his call logs after every call to Sherman."

"So . . ."

"So we believe that Rosenberg uses *two* separate burner phones, Burner One to communicate exclusively with Sherman, and Burner Two to communicate with the people holding Sherman's family—the kidnappers. Rosenberg must have mixed up the two phones, accidentally dialing the kidnappers from Burner One instead of from Burner Two."

Brian grinned at Wolfe and Seraphim. "This is where it gets fun. When Rosenberg accidentally called the kidnappers from Burner One instead of from Burner Two, it gave us the kidnappers' phone—we've labeled it Burner Three—and once we had Burner Three's number, we were able to hack its call records. The only phone Burner Three has ever called is Burner Two."

"I think I'm with you," Wolfe said, "but how did you know Burner Two belonged to Rosenberg?"

"Good question, sir, and the answer is deductive. With the exception of the unintentional call from Burner One, Burner Three has only ever called or been called *from* one number—the phone we've labeled Burner Two. Burner Two has to belong to Rosenberg because there's no other possibility."

"Then you hacked what you believe is Rosenberg's second phone, this Burner Two?"

Brian was positively vibrating. "You better believe it."

"And found?"

"The mother lode, sir."

Jaz interrupted. "Excuse me, Director and Seraphim. We've arrived at a junction. Before we go further, I'd like Gwyneth and Soraya to report."

"What? This is just getting good. I'd rather hear the rest of what Brian has to say."

"For the sake of continuity, please bear with us."

Wolfe's frown told the team he didn't like having "the mother lode" yanked out from under him. With a grudging shrug, he said, "It's your show."

"Thank you. Gwyneth?"

Gwyneth went to the board and gestured to a series of bullets. "Soraya and I were tasked with doing a deep dive on Rosenberg's financials. We looked for inconsistencies and deviations from the norm. To make a long story short, we found a second checking account.

"The account in itself was an oddity worth our scrutiny, but its activity was more so—an initial payment to an attorney of just less than five thousand dollars, then three payments over the following three months to the same attorney, each payment exactly three thousand dollars. Also, the attorney was the *only* payee from this account. This was exactly the kind of loose thread we were looking for.

"When we, er, browsed the attorney's bank records, we found payments of the same amounts, each minus five hundred dollars—the attorney's fees, we think—designated to a rental management firm. When we hacked the rental management firm, we found that the payment from the attorney had been applied to the lease on a house—a house whose address places it across the DC-Maryland border, north of New Hampshire Avenue Northeast."

"Where Jaz last triangulated Burner One," Wolfe finished for her.

Jaz replaced Gwyneth at the board. "That's right, sir."

"Are you saying we have the kidnappers' location?"

"That's what we're saying, sir."

"What? Why didn't you lead with that? We can have HRT rolling inside twenty minutes."

"We didn't lead with that information because we can also tell you that, unlike Burner One, Burner Two, Rosenberg's second phone, was not used exclusively to call the kidnappers. It has also been used to call or take calls from a satellite phone purchased in Azerbaijan—a phone used only in Chechnya and Dagestan, Russia."

"And you think the satphone belongs to AGFA?"

"Yes, we do, sir. It may belong to Rosenberg's contact within AGFA, possibly someone in AGFA's leadership. Either way, it's *the* most promising lead we've had in a long time—because, sir, a satphone can be tracked by its radio emissions. It takes the right equipment and a trained technician, but the results are accurate to within yards of the phone's transmission location."

Wolfe replied, "I can appropriate the equipment and technician from the FBI and put them on it."

Jaz followed up quickly. "Sir, a few minutes ago, I said we were at a junction, a crossroads, and we are. With the information we have, two distinct paths lie before us. On one path, we free Sherman's family and take down Rosenberg, not necessarily in that order. But if we arrest Rosenberg, we may lose all hope of stopping the attacks or finding Bella."

Wolfe lifted his chin. "You're suggesting that if we arrest Rosenberg, we might very well provoke AGFA, cause them to rethink or alter their plans—which would put us back to square one in our efforts to foil the attacks and find Bella."

He frowned and leaned back, thinking aloud. "Unfortunately, I see a more immediate problem. Sherman can't keep up his pretense with Rosenberg for long. What if he spooks Rosenberg, who then flees the country? One wrong inflection, and we lose everything."

"Actually, sir, I'm saying let Rosenberg escape and lead us to Bella."

Seraphim stared at Jaz. "You can't . . . You want us to risk Bella's life—"

Tobin, who had been a passive observer up to this point, interrupted. "Bella is already at risk—or she's dead and we just don't know it. The fact is, the longer victims of abduction are missing, the less likely it is they'll be found alive. We'd be taking more of a risk if we continued to sit on our hands."

"We are *not* sitting—"

"Sir," Jaz jumped back in. "Something else Gwyneth and Soraya turned up in Rosenberg's financials? A one-way open-ended ticket under an alias from DC to Toronto, Toronto to Moscow, Moscow to Grozny. This information lets us anticipate Rosenberg's next move, perhaps even provoke it. I'm suggesting that we provoke Rosenberg to bolt, flee the country, and lead us to AGFA's headquarters. Perhaps to AGFA's fentanyl lab. *Perhaps to Bella.*"

"We can't afford to lose Rosenberg—"

"We won't. Here's why. First, Rosenberg doesn't know that *we know* about Burner Two. Doesn't know that *we know* Burner Two is used to communicate with AGFA. And Rosenberg isn't likely to ditch the phone, but will continue to use it to reach out to AGFA, right? We need the FBI ready and waiting to track the satphone's radio emissions the next time Burner Two calls AGFA's satphone."

"I'll take care of that."

"Thank you, sir. Second, I suggest you position a team of your best operatives in Grozny to await the arrival of Rosenberg's flight. They then follow Rosenberg to AGFA's base of operations. To Bella. Yes?"

Wolfe studied his hands for a minute, looked to Seraphim. "What's your opinion?"

Seraphim thought for a moment. "They are right about several things—we're running out of time all the way around. To free Sherman's family. To stop the New Year's Eve attacks. To find and save Bella. This is the best play we've had in a while."

"Actually, it's the only play we've had since Bella left for Tbilisi," Tobin pointed out. "She's been missing eleven days now. Whatever we do, we need to do it now and do it smartly."

Seraphim asked Jaz, "Can you cut off the kidnappers' phone so that it can't receive calls?"

"Absolutely."

"Can you also send a text from the kidnappers' burner to Rosenberg's burner or make it look like the text came from the kidnappers' burner?"

"Spoof a call from Burner Three to Burner Two? Not a problem."

Seraphim turned back to Wolfe. "If we do this smartly, as Marshal Tobin suggested, if we send HRT to save Sherman's family and then send a text from the kidnappers to spook Rosenberg into fleeing the country, we will save Sherman's wife and son, and perhaps send Rosenberg running to AGFA.

"Either way, we can have eyes on Rosenberg and have our people prepped and in place, ready to follow."

Wolfe considered his options and reached a decision. "All right. I approve. Miss Jessup? Marshal Tobin? You're with us in the conference room to map out the operation."

LAYNIE'S EYE OPENED TO darkness yet again, but something had changed.

The truck has stopped.

She heard voices raised in greeting, in victory and celebration. Then grinding metal close to her—a tailgate being lowered. More voices and excitement.

Hands laid hold of the box and dragged it from the truck bed, carried it along with shouts and exclamations. Moments later, the box jarred to a stop. Laynie heard sounds she'd heard before—scraping, clawing, the wrench of wood and nails. Before the lid was lifted, Laynie closed her eyes, determined to pretend she was still unconscious.

Cool air wafted over her as the lid was lifted away, and a brilliant glare struck her face. After days of darkness, the light, focused directly on her face, was a violent shock. It burned her. Her eyelids scrunched, and her head twisted, trying to escape the pain.

"So. She is awake. Get her up," a man ordered in Russian.

The light moved and a pair of hands jerked her to her feet.

The earth whirled about her. She could not stand. Her head lolled, and she swayed, nearly toppled, but again a pair of hands held her up. Then someone behind her slipped a dark bag over her head. It stunk of mildew, but she didn't have the strength or will to protest. Even with nothing in her stomach, nausea overwhelmed her, and she gagged.

Another voice in accented Russian shouted, "Fools! She's not been upright in more than a week. Even without an injured foot, she would not have the strength to stand. Sit her here. I will remove the IV catheter from her hand."

She was dragged forward and pushed down to sit on a box. A glow of light, perhaps a flashlight, penetrated the fabric of the bag over her head.

She felt a few tugs followed by the cold sting of alcohol on her skin. The same voice that removed the catheter said, "I need to cut the dressing on her foot and examine the wound."

Wound? Laynie fell forward and gagged again.

"Pull that bag up a bit, off her nose and mouth, and bend her over—unless you wish her to vomit all over herself."

A disgusted voice answered, "She already stinks—she has fouled herself many times."

"As you would have, too, if you'd been nailed into a box for days."

Days? How many days?

The doctor—that was the label Laynie put on him—lifted her foot into his lap and snipped away. Laynie, shivering in the night air, now felt an icy breeze on her left foot.

I don't have any socks or shoes on. Whatever I'm wearing is flimsy, and it's cold here. Really cold. She shivered and grew colder by the moment.

"Ah. The stitches have already been removed. The wound is healing well. Good. No need to rebandage it."

"May we go now?"

"Yes—but don't expect her to stand or walk without support. It may take her days to recover her equilibrium and muscle tone. And get something warm to wrap about her. General Sayed will not be pleased if she comes to him ill."

The breeze reached out its icy fingers and stabbed her in the chest.

Sayed!

Someone pulled the bag down over Laynie's mouth and chin. A man dragged her to her feet and swept her up into his arms. He was large and solid. She was actually grateful for the warmth of his body against hers. He strode away with her, other men ahead of and behind them.

Suddenly, the wind died. The men's chatter and noise changed. All sound went hollow and echoed.

We're not in the open air any longer.

With no warning, Laynie's keeper dumped her onto a hard seat. She didn't know up from down. She tried to keep herself from falling sideways, but her hands were still bound. Her fingers scrabbled against cold metal before the man who had carried her climbed in beside her and shoved her upright.

The seat on which Laynie sat jerked and shuddered. Crawled slowly forward. Gained a little speed. Her "keeper," as she thought of him, spoke. In front and in back of her, she heard other men, three or four, answering. Talking to her keeper and to each other.

She labored hard to make sense of what her ears told her. Her mind sifted through past experiences, trying to tell her where she was.

An old train. Perhaps. A carnival ride? No. What, then?

It came to her in a rush. *Neither of those. A mining car. I'm in a mineshaft, in an old mining car. A string of three cars, by the sounds of them.*

They are taking me into a mountain—into Sayed's stronghold.

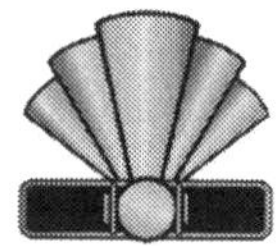

Chapter 15

WINTER HAD SET IN. Six inches of new snow lay on the ground outside the caves housing Cossack's militia. With the next good storm, they would see feet, not inches of snow. Then hiking in or out of the stronghold would be next to impossible.

Why is it that Sayed and his men have no difficulties leaving their stronghold? What do they have that we do not?

Cossack, his men, and the few wives Cossack had allowed his officers to bring with them would survive within the mountain, although the conditions were harsh and primitive. The caves generally maintained a steady temperature that, while less than comfortable, would never drop to freezing. His men had stockpiled supplies for the winter. They had gathered enough wood and painstakingly packed in a load of coal. A constant fire in an old stove warmed the largest cave, a sort of common area where his men both ate and slept.

The wives cooked and washed clothes for everyone, but Cossack had drawn the line at allowing children in the stronghold . . . or "loose" women to service his men. Some militia leaders viewed non-Muslim women as fair game, taking female prisoners for such purposes. Cossack was not one of those leaders. On the other hand, with several feet of snow confining the men to the tunnels except when on guard duty, long months of inactivity could negatively affect discipline and morale. Cossack had devised a strict schedule of work and training to offset boredom.

Routine and discipline will keep the men in shape and prevent restlessness. Perhaps a few harmless diversions such as games will also help to balance morale.

"General?"

"Yes?"

"General Sayed is on the radio, sir." This radio operator was a mature soldier, battle-tested and dressed for the cold.

"Tell him I will be there shortly."

Cossack strode toward the radio room, stopping at his niche to grab his cloak on the way. The common area, far back from the entrance, might be warm enough, but the radio room was never warm. Even though his men had built a wall and a door to screen out the wind, the temperatures at the mouth of the caves could be brutal. No wonder the radio operator was dressed for the outdoors.

Sayed's unscheduled radio call concerned him. After the pounding they had taken at the hands of the Russian military over the past spring and summer, the militias had agreed to hunker down and recover over the winter.

If Sayed wishes our assistance with some previously unannounced plan, it will take days for us to break trail to the Chechen border. My men would be exhausted by the effort and be of little help—and that does not take into consideration the likelihood of being hit by a storm on the way.

Getting caught on the difficult trek into Chechnya during a winter storm would be disastrous.

He entered the radio room. "You may go," he told the radio operator. He picked up the headset, adjusted it, and clicked his microphone.

"*As-Salamu Alaykum*, General Sayed," he said with appropriate respect.

"*Wa alaykumu s-salam*, General Labazanov. We live in great times, my brother." Sayed's words were measured, but beneath them, they betrayed his ebullience.

Cossack's thoughts darted into a higher gear. *All Glorious for Allah must have overcome the last logistical obstacles standing in the way of the New Year's Eve attacks.*

He thought of what he'd entrusted to the woman's casket and hoped it would be enough for Wolfe's people to uncover and thwart the schemes.

Keeping his response light, he said, "Did you receive much snow where you are?"

"Come and see, my brother."

Cossack laughed with good nature. "I would have to dig my way out of the mountains, General. My scouts tell me our route into Chechnya gained more than a foot of snow from yesterday's storm."

"I would not ask you to endure such an inconvenience if it were not important. Important, and perhaps even earthshaking."

An *inconvenience?* Sayed, like all narcissists, downplayed real objections when they countermanded his wishes.

Wariness stole over Cossack, even as he set himself to play Sayed's game. "You have whetted my appetite, General. Can you not give me a clue regarding this earthshaking news?"

"I can do better than a clue, brother. We have captured an American agent—and not just *any* agent, the very agent who defeated our plan to assassinate that Russian pig, Petroff."

Cossack felt the room whirl around him. He called upon all his discipline not to react but to respond as Sayed expected. "Even so? *Allahu Akbar!* What will you do with him?" He switched from "her" to "him" at the last possible moment and began to sweat at how nearly he had blundered.

"Not a man, General, but a woman, a deceptive infidel woman. She is quite valuable to us and to our plans, so when my American operative told us she was being sent to Tbilisi, I sent my men to capture her. What is even better? The Americans believe their agent to be dead."

Cossack's stomach lurched. He felt its contents rise as Sayed continued.

"I have not yet seen her, but my people have her. At my command, they hid her for a week in Tbilisi as a precaution—in case the Americans were to see through my ruse and use their influence to have the authorities set up roadblocks and begin searching vehicles for her. However, she is on her way to me now, and I expect my men to deliver her to me later today or tomorrow."

Cossack was instantly wary. *He has other reasons for delaying the woman's arrival, but as is his custom, he will hold those cards close to his vest.*

He answered enthusiastically. "*Subhan Allah!* Is this true? I must hear how you have managed this great feat."

While he spoke aloud, he thought, *There is no cell service in the mountains. I have no means of contacting Wolfe, no means of telling him that his operative is alive except through this radio, and I dare not use it lest it give me away.*

"I will tell you how we arranged her capture—and much more—when you arrive."

"Ah. And yet, because of the snow, General, I fear I must decline your invitation."

"Yes, yes, I know the snow will make the journey long and difficult. But I must have you with us, Arzu, for this glorious event. Come as soon as you can, but please arrive no later than the thirtieth of the month. The generals of our other militias are also coming. We will celebrate this great victory together, and afterward, I will brief you on the follow-on attack. Then we will plan our spring offensive—to take back Chechnya and Dagestan."

"Will not the many Russian troops stationed in Chechnya and Dagestan respond to another offensive?"

"After the follow-on attack, Russian command will soon be entirely too preoccupied with the Americans to think of us. I expect the Russians to move their troops out of Chechnya and Dagestan and reposition them along Russia's western border. They will be too busy with the Americans to swat the little flies stinging their backside."

Sayed laughed. "Little flies? From Ukraine to the borders of China, we will join with other like-minded jihadi militias. We will take all of southern Russia and its former satellites and unify them under one flag, the flag of Islam!"

Cossack was accustomed to Sayed's bravado and his arrogant, boastful plans. But today he heard a note of calm assurance in Sayed's voice that had sometimes been lacking in the past.

I know that, in addition to the string of New Year's Eve attacks, Sayed has some grander scheme planned. But what could he have planned—so audacious and destructive and so obviously a Russian *attack on America—that it would spark a war between the two superpowers?*

He made a split-second decision. "Of course, I will come, Sayed. I cannot miss such a celebration. The crossing could take up to five days, depending on the snow depth, so I will leave early. That way, if we are delayed, we will not be late. However, should the weather be amenable for the crossing, I hope you will not mind if I arrive a few days ahead of the thirtieth? I will radio when we leave and when you may expect us, should our trek go as planned."

"Good, good! I will provide a rendezvous point and have a delegation meet you—and then you will finally see our stronghold, eh?"

Cossack laughed along with Sayed and added, "I must see your trophy, too, eh? The American operative?"

"Yes, you shall certainly see her. Perhaps by then I will be willing to share her with you."

LAYNIE COULD TELL BY the noises bouncing off the walls on either side that they were in a tunnel. The mining cars rolled slowly onward, sometimes swaying side to side as the track made a wide turn. There was little light in the tunnel. She would have seen a glow through the fabric of the bag over her head had there been.

From the moment the cars had started forward, Laynie had given herself to calculating the time they were in transit. She silently counted off the seconds—*one thousand one, one thousand two, one thousand three*—until she reached *one thousand sixty.* One minute. Her hands were still bound together, but she was able to press and hold her thumb down on the back of her hand to signify the first minute, changing to her index finger when she hit the second minute.

She took her best guess at their speed. *We cannot be doing more than a whopping ten miles per hour.*

Speed and time. Speed multiplied by time equaled distance.

While she kept her count of seconds and minutes, she also tried to catalog the several noises she heard. The bag over her head made it difficult for her to distinguish the origin or distance of some sounds. The echoing bits of conversation between her captors combined with the *scree* and reverberating *clank* of the mining cars' wheels on the old track increased that difficulty.

It was more problematic to discern the track's trajectory. Was it level as opposed to up or down? Was it angling downward? After a few minutes, she decided they were steadily descending, if only by a couple of degrees.

Laynie kept counting. Far away, however, she caught the faint rumble of a motor or an engine. Before long, the engine's throb seemed closer. Then she heard something new. A heavy ratcheting noise, a ponderous but regular *chunk, chunk, chunk.*

Like a chain. Fed onto a sprocket. A gear with teeth. Taking up the links in the chain, the chain pulling the train of mining cars into the mountain.

Keep counting.

Keep counting.

When the car squealed to a slow, grinding halt at the end of the track, Laynie had counted off nine minutes. Nine minutes into an old mine shaft.

Nine minutes. Ten miles an hour. A mile and a half, give or take, but . . . a mile and a half into a mountain is pretty far.

Her keeper stood and growled a command in a language she didn't know. It may have been Chechen, but it could just as well have been a dialect from Georgia, Dagestan, or Azerbaijan. Any of a hundred tribal tongues.

Her keeper jerked her arm, and she could not mistake its meaning. *Get up.*

She attempted to rise, but her body, dehydrated and weak from inactivity, would not support her. Muttering under his breath, her keeper hauled her to her feet.

The moment she put weight on both legs, her calf muscles knotted. It was all she could do not to scream. As it was, she moaned and sagged and would have fallen if her keeper hadn't slid his hand under her arm.

Why? Why am I so weak and helpless?

The epiphany, when it struck her, explained her deep lethargy, mind fog, and inability to stand. The sudden, sharp insight terrified her.

I've been kept sedated longer than just two or three days. Much longer. Long enough for my muscles to lose their tone.

The man holding her up grumbled a complaint under his breath. He climbed from the car and dragged her out after him. He lifted her up in his arms and started walking. Not long after, he stopped, shifted her weight, then threw her over his shoulder—then Laynie understood why he'd done so.

Steps. He was trudging up steps inside the mine. *Steps too narrow to carry me without slinging me over his shoulders like a bag of potatoes.*

They arrived at the top of the stairs and what Laynie thought was a guarded checkpoint. Her captor was greeted and allowed to pass, for then they left the darkness of the mine behind. Through the bag over her head, Laynie could tell they had stepped into a lighted passageway. She thought the temperature had changed subtly, too. The farther her captor walked, the more certain she was that the temperature was warming.

Warm air? In a cave? Perhaps not merely a cave but a substantial system of caves.

Laynie was still cold to the bone, but the air around them was nearing a comfortable, livable temperature.

Livable. Yes, a cave system. Heated somehow to provide living quarters . . . a winter stronghold for Chechen freedom fighters.

The man carrying her kept walking, but now other men's voices greeted him, some in Russian, others in the dialect she did not recognize. Still others in Arabic.

"*As-Salamu Alaykum*, Bula!"

"*Wa alaykumu s-salam*, brother."

All the clues came together in a rush.

Not merely Chechen freedom fighters—Islamic militants. Jihadists.

Her keeper came to a stop. He grunted as he unslung her from his shoulder. Dumped her onto . . . a carpeted floor? Tugged the bag from her head.

Soft, pervasive light assaulted Laynie's senses. She ducked her face toward her chest and squeezed her eyelids together as hard as she could. Her eyes began to stream tears, the body's response to the shock and pain.

Her keeper's hands gripped her hair from behind and snapped her head up, hauling her up to her knees. Her wounded foot folded under her and stretched the healing incision. Laynie bit back a cry of pain. Instead, she worked to crack one eye, but the light's onslaught was too much.

A well-modulated voice in accented Russian asked, "This is the woman? Director Wolfe's prized agent?"

"Yes, Sayed."

"She stinks."

"Indeed, Sayed. Her long journey . . . she is not presentable. I apologize."

Laynie cataloged the new voice, the man her keeper called Sayed. She heard authority and pride in Sayed's words, in his tone. She also heard how her keeper responded to Sayed. His replies carried reverence. Even a touch of fear.

She sensed a form squatting before her. Her keeper's grasp jerked her head farther back.

I'm being inspected.

She commanded her eyes to open—she *demanded* that they obey her. In response, one eyelid cracked. She peered through the narrow slit and saw . . . a black beard. A thin face. A man, perhaps in his early forties. A slight build. She knew immediately who he was, this "Sayed."

You are the head man, aren't you? The leader of AGFA.

We have been looking for you.

His mouth curved into a smile as he observed her appraisal.

She tracked from the man's mouth up his face and stopped where her gaze should have encountered his eyes. Where the windows to his soul should have been.

Should have been.

Instead, hard, dead, glittering stones stared out at her.

She forced both eyes open and met those lifeless orbs.

"Ah, there you are," he murmured. "Much older than the *kafir* women I usually choose but defiant and godless as I presumed. Good. I shall enjoy breaking you—once you are cleaned up."

He stood and the grip on her hair let go. Laynie's head immediately rolled forward. Her stinging, fatigued eyes again sought refuge behind her eyelids. Her scalp tingled and ached where her hair had been yanked and pulled. Her injured foot throbbed.

"I congratulate you on your successful mission, Bula. Snatching her as you did was audacious. Worthy of great respect!"

"They will be looking for me." The words jumped from Laynie's mouth.

Sayed laughed. "No, they believe you are dead. In fact, I hear from our source that Wolfe and his so-called task force are in deep mourning. They haven't an inkling their agent is alive. Yes, well done, Bula."

"Thank you, General."

They believe you are dead. Sayed's words gutted Laynie.

They believe you are dead. Fatigue clawed at every joint in her body.

They believe you are dead. She swayed on her knees.

Her keeper grabbed her shoulder, held her upright. "What are your orders, Sayed?"

"You took many precautions and more time than necessary in bringing her here, Bula—but that was at my direction, and you followed my wishes exactly. However, I was told she is quite a beauty and am saddened to see she has not fared well."

He thought a moment. "Have two *kafir* women bathe and clothe her. Feed her and care for her needs. I will see her again after the recovery period, say, four mornings from now."

"Yes, General."

"Take care, Bula. I do not wish to see her in this weakened state when she comes to me. Do whatever must be done to restore her to health and vigor—particularly vigor. She will give me no pleasure if she is feeble when I take her."

"It shall be as you command, General."

Sayed thought of something else. "You carried her, Bula?"

"Yes, General. She had no shoes and was unable to walk even if she had."

"Yes, I understand. Since you have gotten her stench on yourself from touching her filth, please bathe yourself and put on clean clothes."

"I will, my General."

Laynie's keeper, the man Sayed called Bula, pulled her up and into his arms. Cursing her under his breath in Russian—but leaving the bag he'd pulled from her head behind—he carried Laynie from Sayed's presence, through a curtain, and back into the tunnels.

Laynie stared at the rock walls. A string of dim, widely placed, electric bulbs hung near the tunnel's ceiling, just enough light to illuminate their way. The low light was a welcome change. Her eyes began to adjust, and she tried to pay attention to what she saw and where Bula was taking her.

Then the tunnel took an abrupt right turn into a junction where tunnels branched in two directions, right and left. Bula took neither branch. He crossed the junction and entered a wide, spacious cavern with a high roof overhead. Laynie smelled more than felt moisture in the "room."

This space formed naturally, There must be a water source nearby that used to drip from the walls and ceiling. They probably diverted the water to dry the cavern.

Laynie saw lines of tables that would seat perhaps two hundred and a partition of rough wood built across the left side of the cavern. The partition had windows and counters for passing food into the open cavern—to the tables.

Kitchen and dining hall. Common area.

A massive old coal-burning furnace occupied the farthest reach of the room. The farther into the room and closer to the furnace Bula carried her, the warmer the air became.

Bula sat her at a table and bellowed for someone, but Laynie had eyes only for the furnace. It blazed away, pumping out merciful heat, its sprawling "octopus" ductwork pipes feeding its warmth—Laynie presumed—to other parts of the cave system. She noted a great bin of coal two or three yards from the furnace. She wanted to lie down in front of the furnace's belly and fall asleep in its warm embrace.

The person Bula had called emerged from the doorway leading into the kitchen—an old woman, hunched over, wearing a worn, full-length gown. Over it she wore a contrived niqab—two veils, one that bound her head and covered her hair, the other across her nose and mouth and tied behind her head so that nothing of her face was visible except her eyes. Her hands and shriveled face were the only parts of her body visible.

Bula spoke to the woman, gesturing toward Laynie.

The woman protested. She pointed to the coal bin, then the furnace.

She's the night caretaker, Laynie deduced. *Her job is to feed the furnace and keep it going all night.*

Right then, the pounding in Laynie's head reconvened.

I'm so thirsty. Dehydrated.

Bula said something else, and the woman nodded and half-bowed to Bula, then fixed her weary eyes on Laynie.

Bula turned to leave. Took several steps.

"Wait," Laynie called to him in Russian.

He returned but kept his distance and stared down at her.

Laynie experienced a moment's discomfiture as she visualized what she must look like. The only clothing she wore—as Bula had to have known—was a thin blanket over a soiled, reeking hospital gown. Her hair, too, was filthy and greasy.

Now that her body was warming, she caught a whiff of herself.

Ugh.

Bula's nose, too, wrinkled in disgust. "You speak Russian?"

"Yes."

"Why did you call to me?"

"What day is it, please?"

He snorted. "The day or date can mean nothing to you . . . here."

"As you say. However, since the day I was abducted, I have had nothing to eat or drink." Forming the words and ushering them to her lips cost Laynie. They scraped like broken glass across her throat, each syllable rougher and "croakier" than the previous.

He studied her. "Breakfast is in two hours. I will arrange food and water for you then—after you bathe."

"Thank you, but . . ."

He flicked an angry brow at her.

"May I have a drink of water now? I am parched and can hardly move."

He barked a command at the old woman. She shuffled through the kitchen door and returned with a ceramic bottle. The sight of water dribbling from the bottle's mouth and down its glazed sides fused Laynie's tongue to the roof of her mouth. She began to tremble.

Bula drew a knife from the scabbard on his belt and sliced through the tape binding Laynie's wrists together. Her hands fell to her side, fingers numb and cold, temporarily useless.

Bula chuckled softly. Laynie ignored him. Her attention was on the water.

The woman tried to hand off the bottle to Laynie, but her weak fingers couldn't even hold the bottle to her lips. Bula said something, and the old woman tipped the bottle into Laynie's mouth. The scent of minerals hit her nose at the same moment the ice-cold water triggered her gag reflex. She choked on that first sip, and the old woman drew the bottle back until Laynie recovered and could swallow again.

Laynie managed a second sip without coughing, then gulped down several mouthfuls.

"Thank you," she said to Bula.

A glimmer of something—curiosity? Pity?—lit his eyes. For an instant. Then he turned on his heel and left.

As soon as he was gone, the old woman left the bottle on the table near Laynie and stationed herself between Laynie and the entrance to the tunnel.

But Laynie's thirst had awakened. It clawed at her, greedy, voracious, demanding.

Drink it all. You don't know when they will give you more.

She told her brain to send a signal to her arms and was able to lift her weakened hands to the bottle. Cradling it between stiff fingers, she tipped it to her mouth and took slow, easy sips, carefully returning it to the table between drinks. When she had emptied the bottle, Laynie turned her head to her "guard."

"More?" she asked, indicating the bottle.

The old woman shook her head no. Her guileless expression alternated between fierce attention to duty and flickering worry.

Aren't you the cutest little jailer ever, Laynie thought to herself. *Don't worry 'bout li'l ol' me. Right now, I couldn't punch my way out of a wet paper bag.*

Bula was gone only a short while. He returned with a second man, much younger than him, and two women on a leash.

A leash.

That was the only way Laynie could describe it. The women's wrists were tied to a length of rope. Bula held the rope's end. When he jerked the rope, the slip knots around the women's wrists tightened.

The women wore black abayas—full-length outer garments—and niqabs. They kept their faces toward the floor, seeing nothing but what was in front of their feet.

The young guard, however, studied Laynie with unabashed interest. Laynie studied him back. He frowned and put his hand to the knife sheathed at his side. Laynie looked away.

No sense antagonizing my captors . . . not at this stage of the game.

Bula spoke to the old woman, who shuffled away toward a curtain off the near side of the kitchen. Then he spoke to the two bound women and the guard accompanying them. The guard began to loosen the ties around the women's wrists. Whatever orders Bula had given, Laynie did not know the language to understand them.

Finally, Bula spoke to Laynie in Russian. "These women will prepare a bath for you and help you bathe, wash your hair, and dress properly. This man—" he pointed to the younger guard, "will supervise."

Bula fixed Laynie with a cold stare. "You will be wise to follow his orders."

She nodded. *You are leaving me with a single guard—an inexperienced boy—because you know I am in no fit condition to try to run off.*

Bula reached for Laynie and pulled her up in his arms. Walked toward the curtain next to the kitchen. The young guard held the curtain aside, revealing an improvised bath house—two ancient tubs, nonslip rubber mats on the stone floor, and benches alongside the tubs. The two women followed Bula through the curtain.

The old woman was running water into one of the tubs. Bula sat Laynie on a bench beside the old cast-iron thing and said something else to the woman. Then he motioned to the guard. The boy ran his curious eyes over Laynie a last time before following Bula. Laynie heard Bula's footsteps fade as he left. The boy, however, remained just outside the curtain.

Laynie's attention was on the steaming water pouring into the tub. Its mineral scent filled the air.

They definitely have access to a natural water source, and they must use the furnace to heat a tank of it. Clever. They have all they need to shelter their entire militia here for the winter.

The old woman placed a stack of clothes on the bench next to Laynie. She kept her eyes averted, as though Laynie were something evil to be avoided. She shuffled to a cabinet and returned with towel, washcloths, and soap.

One of the women tended the bath water as it filled the tub. The other, while keeping her eyes on Laynie, absentmindedly rubbed her wrists. Laynie noticed the lines of chapped skin around them. She glanced at the other woman's hands and glimpsed the same red, calloused lines.

They are tied to a leash on a regular basis for those marks to be semi-permanent. Then she remembered Sayed's exact words, "*Have two kafir women bathe and clothe her.*"

Laynie had learned a few Arabic words and phrases from Jubaila and what they signified in Islam. *Kafir* meant "one who denies or opposes the truth."

An unbeliever or infidel.

Sayed had used *kafir* to refer to her, too.

"Sayed thinks I am a godless infidel," Laynie whispered aloud.

The three women turned toward her. They seemed upset.

"Is it because I used his name?" Laynie murmured, soft enough that the young guard wouldn't hear her. "Because I said, 'Sayed'?"

The old woman wrung her hands and glanced with apprehension toward the curtain and the guard. The woman who had been rubbing her wrists shook her head and raised a finger to her lips.

Laynie nodded her understanding. After a few more worried looks aimed at the guard on the other side of the curtain, the women seemed to relax.

They gestured for Laynie to get into the steaming bath. The one tending the water reminded Laynie of a much younger version of her former maid, Alyona. *Alyona*, the vigilant and sour Belarus woman who had served as Petroff's first line of surveillance over his "property," Linnéa Olander.

She spoke to Laynie, again gesturing her to the steaming tub.

Ironic. They have no idea how much I want to get in that tub, Laynie laughed to herself. *And if they knew how weak I am, they'd be less concerned about my running off and very worried that I might fall and crack my head open trying to get in.*

Laynie slowly stripped off the thin blanket and soiled hospital gown. She reached a hand toward the woman nearest her. After a moment's hesitation, she took Laynie's hand and helped her up.

Laynie tried to stand, but her strength wasn't enough. "Alyona" saw and came to help. With the two women supporting her, Laynie reached the tub. She sat on the side and put her right foot into the water. Her cold foot registered the warmth, and Laynie sighed.

Oh, such bliss!

The women helped her drag her left leg over the edge. All was fine—until Laynie's left foot registered hot water on its tender, not-quite-healed wound. It stung like fire. She hissed and lifted it out.

She hadn't had an opportunity to examine the gash. Now that she saw it, she grimaced. The women, too, saw the wound. The old woman peered closely and clucked over it. She said something and motioned to the other women.

Leaving her injured foot hanging over the outside edge of the tub, the three women eased Laynie down into the water. The remainder of her body she surrendered to the water's soothing heat.

They let her relax for a minute before coming at her with soapy rags. Laynie tried to take a rag, but they insisted on scrubbing her, going at her like a plucked turkey in the sink on Thanksgiving morning.

When they got to her hair, it was a different story. Laynie's last trip to a salon had restored her natural blond look, and all three of the women wanted to wash it or just touch it, whispering excitedly to each other.

After they had washed her hair twice, they assisted her from the tub, dried her off, and helped her don a shapeless shift. They pulled a faded abaya over that, then socks and sandal-like shoes.

The old woman, who seemed to have some authority over the two younger ones, insisted they sit Laynie in front of the furnace to dry her hair. Their guard, a frown perpetually creasing his face, apparently didn't like the idea and said so. The old woman, shaking her finger under his nose, told him differently.

Interesting. Apparently, this old gal isn't kafir. She has some pull and isn't afraid to use it on this young man.

A minute later, Laynie was ensconced on a chair before the roaring iron beast while "Alyona" and "Not Alyona" bickered over who got to brush her hair while it dried. It was then Laynie realized that the two women were quite young.

Why, they are no more than girls. Perhaps only fourteen or fifteen years old.

The old woman dispensed a cranky order, and "Alyona" ran to obey. She returned with a towel and a folded garment that she placed beside Laynie. She then worked the towel over half of Laynie's hair while "Not Alyona" brushed the other side. After a few minutes, they switched off, all the while whispering or giggling under their breath so as not to attract the young guard's attention.

Just girls. Barely teenagers.

Laynie was facing away from the furnace, toward the entrance to the cavern, when three additional women arrived. When they saw Laynie, they came to inspect her.

Breakfast crew?

Laynie's stomach lurched. Her belly was so hollow that, for an instant, she thought she might be sick. To distract herself, she studied the new arrivals. They, too, were young, possibly in their late teens, but obviously better kept and better dressed than "Alyona" and "Not Alyona."

While the new arrivals chattered, giggled, and fingered Laynie's hair, they gave no notice to the girls who had been drying her hair.

Not a nod or a word. Nothing.

In fact, at the appearance of the new arrivals, "Alyona" and "Not Alyona" had clammed up. They let go of Laynie's hair and stepped back, their heads tipped toward the floor.

The old woman entered. She shouted at the new arrivals. With a last glance at Laynie, they hurried to obey the summons.

Laynie suddenly got it.

Like the old woman, these must be "virtuous" *and acceptable women. Most likely soldiers' wives. The other women didn't acknowledge these girls because* "*Alyona*" *and* "*Not Alyona*" *are* kafir *women—tainted unbelievers.*

The image of the two girls being led in on a leash crystallized. Their eyes downcast. Their body language passive.

Oh, dear Jesus. These girls are slaves.

CHAPTER 16

WOLFE, SERAPHIM, TOBIN, and Jaz met with the FBI Hostage Rescue Team commander to plan and coordinate the rescue of Sherman's family. After discussion, they agreed to the commander's decision that his team would breach the house where the kidnappers held Sherman's family just before dawn the following day.

Moments prior to HRT's "go" order, Jaz would turn off the kidnappers' burner phone, removing the kidnappers' ability to call and alert Rosenberg. When the hostages were safely in hand, she would send the spoofed text to Rosenberg's Burner Two.

After the team commander left, they worked on the wording of the text. Agreement wasn't easy to reach. They argued over it, parsing it back and forth, until they reached a consensus. Then they hit a real impasse.

Seraphim watched the battle of wills between Wolfe and Jaz and chewed the inside of her mouth to keep from laughing aloud.

Wolfe frowned. "Not to say that your suggestion lacks, er, color or merit, Miss Jessup—"

"Then what's the problem?"

"You expect me to tell our FBI counterparts that we're calling our joint venture 'Operation Whack-a-Mole'? That's not a problem to you? Really?"

Jaz crossed her arms and sat back in her chair. "Nope."

"It's undignified."

"It *fits* like a glove. Frankly, *the team* feels it's inspired."

Wolfe rubbed his jaw. "Why am I not surprised."

Seraphim studied Jaz, seeing something new in her. The woman had come to the task force as a valued but one-dimensional resource. In the gap left first by Seraphim's injury, then by Bella's abduction, Jaz had demonstrated leadership abilities even she had not known she possessed. But the rough edges of her personality, the subtle (and not-so-subtle) lack of deference and proper respect for authority, and her stubbornness when she was determined to have her way were . . . problematic.

Seraphim found herself asking, *Is that such a bad thing?*

The "old" Seraphim, the career intelligence officer who demanded strict discipline and professionalism from her people had died in the hospital parking lot when shrapnel from the car bomb struck her. The woman had suffered a near-fatal brain injury and had lived to tell the tale, but the experience had changed her. Her former expectations didn't matter nearly as much as the people around her did. People like Jaz and Tobin and the rest of the team who got results despite their unorthodox methods, and who had a binding, unfaltering loyalty that Seraphim envied.

She cleared her throat. "Operation Whack-a-Mole is a go for me . . . sir."

Jaz cracked her gum and lifted one brow in Wolfe's direction.

"I'm sending you on sabbatical when this is over, Patrice," Wolfe sniped.

Seraphim lifted her chin. "Perhaps, sir. So, are we settled on operation name and the wording of the text?"

"Yah," Jaz said around the wad in her mouth.

"I'm good," Tobin replied.

Wolfe threw up his hands.

Jaz grinned and Seraphim had to grin back.

Tobin, as was his custom, kept his expression carefully *un*expressive . . . but perhaps one side of his mouth twitched.

Just a little.

BULA RETURNED TO THE cavern and shouted for the old woman. Rattled off orders and pointed at the young kafir women. They hurried to finish their work to Bula's satisfaction. "Alyona" stood in front of Laynie to scrutinize her, while "Not Alyona" waited close by, fidgeting and blocking the young guard's view.

Laynie took that opportunity to reach for "Alyona's" hand. The girl jerked away, fearful. Laynie was weak, and the effort cost her, but she reached for her hand again. Gently squeezed it.

"Thank you for your kindness." She spoke the words in soft, scarcely audible Russian. It had been both a sincere gesture and a test—did the girls speak or understand Russian?

Laynie saw no sign of comprehension in the girl's eyes, only a confused frown. Laynie decided neither of the girls spoke Russian . . . until she glanced at "Not Alyona." She stared at Laynie, her dark lashes unblinking.

Laynie lifted her brows a fraction. A question.

The girl dipped her chin. Once.

Laynie did the same, then turned her focus elsewhere.

A moment later, Bula waved the girls away and called to the young guard. Laynie thought he called the boy Doku.

Doku it is, Laynie decided.

While Bula examined Laynie, Doku strung the girls to the leash and led them away.

"You will cover yourself," Bula ordered Laynie.

"I'm sorry. I don't understand."

Bula pointed to the two folded garments near her. She picked the first up and unfolded it. A veil of old, threadbare cloth. Another, the same. She was to use them to make a niqab, the head and face covering the girls wore. She put them on as best she could.

"Can you stand?"

"With help, perhaps. May I have more water?"

"Someone will bring you food and water later. Stand up now."

Laynie tried. She shook from the effort.

"Get up, I said."

"I want to. I am trying."

She couldn't do it. Bula lost patience with her and jerked her to her feet. Laynie's legs collapsed under her. Fuming, Bula again swept her up in his arms, carried her out of the cavern, and at the junction turned left, down the other branch of the tunnel. The branch narrowed and darkened—the weak bulbs illuminating the passage were fewer and farther apart than in the cavern or the previous part of the tunnel.

Bula stopped, kicked open a tall, barred gate, and carried Laynie into a narrow, niche-like room. He dropped her on a slatted wooden bench.

Her landing was rough, and Laynie struggled not to topple onto her side. When she got her balance, she took quick stock of where she was. A cell, chiseled into the passageway wall. Cold, bare rock walls, floor, and ceiling. A gate of vertical bars—the cell's entrance and only view into the tunnel. No light except from the dim bulbs in the passageway.

"You will receive food and water after the men have eaten."

Bula locked the cell gate behind him.

Laynie looked around the cell, shivering, already missing the comforting warmth of the furnace. She saw a wadded blanket on the other end of the bench. The slatted bench itself—the only furniture in the room—looked to have been made from shipping pallets. The wood was unfinished and rough to the touch, but at least it was off the floor.

The floor? Laynie caught the outline of dark, dried stains on the stone floor, but the light was too low to determine what they were. They could have been blood or vomit or both. A covered bucket in the corner was the last item in the cell. Its reek announced its purpose.

Laynie slowly pulled herself toward the blanket until she could reach it without falling over. It was dirty and stank, but that didn't matter. She spread its folds around her shoulders and felt her body warm beneath it. A small laugh left her mouth. She was suddenly and inexplicably grateful for the full-length abaya and the veils that covered her head and face—as shabby as they were.

"One veil to warm my head, the other to serve as a pillow, a place to sit or lie down rather than the stone floor? Lord, I am blessed. Thank you."

She tightened the blanket around her shoulder and leaned against the rock behind her bed, surprised that the cell wasn't as cold as she expected. A random factoid about caves floated up from her memory, something about how the temperature in a cave was usually close to the average annual temperature for the region where it was located. Depth mattered, too. Deeper caves could be colder than those closer to the surface, cool in summer and warm—relatively—in winter.

Can't be too far underground. Feels like 64-66° in here. If I die in this cell, it won't be because I froze to death.

Even so, away from the wonderful warmth of the furnace in the communal area, Laynie's body began to announce little problems she hadn't yet acknowledged. Like the aching of her right hand. She peered at the top of it in the little light she had and thought a patch of skin was dark. Bruised. It was certainly tender.

Oh, right. The doctor removed an IV from this hand. For however long I have been missing, whoever was caring for me must have used an IV to feed me fluids and keep me sedated. No wonder my hand is bruised.

A spot on her left buttock was sore. Raw to the touch. Her hips hurt, too, over her hip bones.

I have bruises on my hips?

Sayed's voice played in her mind. "*You took many precautions and more time than necessary in bringing her here, Bula . . .*"

"How much time? How long have they had me?"

Not knowing the date, not knowing where she was or how long she'd been kept unconscious, and a million other unknowns assaulted her—until reason asserted itself.

Stop that. You know enough for now. You know you were sedated—and if you were unconscious, you would have lain in the same prone position for hours . . . until someone turned you. Like a bird on a spit.

"So," she whispered, "long enough that these tender spots are the beginnings of bedsores. I must be careful to let the deep tissues heal, not worsen. An open wound in a place like this . . ."

Would likely be deadly.

"*I was told she is quite a beauty and am saddened to see that she has not fared well. Have two kafir women bathe and clothe her. Feed her and care for her needs. I will see her again after the recovery period, say, four mornings from now.*"

"Four mornings from today, huh? Guess I'll lounge about and enjoy the five-star accommodations until then."

I need my strength back, but I will have to work for it.

She had three days to prepare.

Laynie relaxed against the rock wall behind her bed. Let herself doze off.

SHE ROUSED WHEN THE rusty barred gate creaked open. The young guard Bula had called Doku stood in the doorway holding a platter and a corked jug. When he set the jug on the bench, she heard its contents slosh inside—and Laynie's thirst roared back to life.

Doku placed the platter on the bench next to the jug and considered Laynie, sizing her up. She knew the look—oh, how she knew it! She stared back at him, daring him to make a move. He flushed and twitched his trousers in an obscene gesture.

Young and already sadistic.

Laynie pretended not to notice his vulgar threat. Instead, she kept her eyes on his and spoke a single word. Said it loud enough that Doku knew exactly what she meant. "Sayed."

He jumped back and glanced behind him, his reaction guilty and afraid.

Laynie laughed softly. *You know full well that the big boss has already "claimed" me. Do you have a death wish?*

Doku scowled and reddened. He retreated, slammed the cell gate behind him, and locked it. Laynie listened for the sound of the key after it left the lock. Would he pocket it? Or . . . no, she wasn't certain, but she thought she heard a metallic clink against the passageway rock wall.

Did he just hang the key outside my cell?

Her question was derailed when she smelled warm food. She half-lifted, half-dragged the platter onto her lap. Stared at the little covered pot and a fist-sized lump wrapped in a faded cloth. She lifted the lid on the pot. *Soup!* Unwrapped the lump. *And bread.*

Laynie took a worn spoon in hand and dug it into the pot. Brought it, shaking and trembling, to her lips. The broth she sucked into her mouth was nectar. Every taste bud in her body sang for joy. She looked at what remained on the spoon after sucking off the broth. Barley. Meager, limp vegetables. A scrap of some kind of meat. Her stomach twisted.

Careful, Laynie. You need every one of these calories. You cannot afford to throw up what you've eaten, so go easy.

Laynie put the spoon back into the bowl and broke off a bite of bread. She dipped it into the bowl and let it absorb the broth, then brought it to her mouth. Nibbled on it.

Wonderful . . .

But she felt the caution her body spoke. She finished the bite of bread, then rewrapped the small loaf and put the lid on the pot. Reached for the jug. She estimated it held close to two liters of water—and she didn't know if or when they would refill it. She also could not remember the last time she'd urinated.

If I don't get fluids moving, my kidneys will shut down, but I also need to be wise. Restrict myself.

She managed to uncork and lift the heavy jug to her mouth. Took three sips, lowered it to her lap, then waited a full minute. She repeated her disciplined actions—Three sips. A full minute's wait. Again. And again.

When she shook the jug, she figured she'd downed ten to twelve ounces—and she was exhausted. She set the jug aside, wrapped herself in the blanket, and leaned back.

Instantly asleep.

She spent the next hours following the same routine. A few bites of bread soaked in broth, a cup or more of water. Sleep.

THE CREAK OF THE CELL gate dragged her from sleep—but not as quickly as before. She'd been deep into a REM cycle when the noise set off her internal alarms. It took her a minute to clear her mind.

What woke me?

Doku again stood in her cell, staring. Glowering and resolute.

Laynie was in no shape to repel him.

Her hand crept out from under her blanket and slithered toward the water jug. Doku did not notice. His attention was fixed on her face. The blanket. What he imagined lay beneath the blanket and the abaya.

This is going to hurt me more than it hurts you, little boy. Laynie was neither proud of nor happy with her next move. She was taking a risk, but she figured it was the soundest play . . . for her long-term safety.

Mustering her strength and sending it down her arm, she pushed the jug. It slid off the bench, fell to the stone floor. Cracked open. Her precious water poured out. Doku's eyes jerked toward his wet shoes and the pieces of the jug, first surprised, then angered. He reached for the blanket to rip it from her—

Laynie held on to the fabric and called aloud, "I belong to Jesus." She spoke in English. She said it again—not screaming, not protesting, not fearfully, but a simple declaration.

"Listen to me," she said, staring him down. "I said, *I belong to Jesus.*"

Her volume increased. "I belong to Jesus. I belong to Jesus. I belong to Jesus! *I belong to Jesus!*"

Doku let go of the blanket tug-of-war. He seemed confused. He cast a wary look over his shoulders at the gate.

Laynie leaned toward him. "I. Belong. To. Jesus."

She smiled. "I rebuke you in his mighty name, the name that is above every name, the name at which *every knee will bow*. THE NAME OF JESUS."

Doku's eyes went wide. He stepped back. Onto a piece of broken pottery. It crackled under his foot. Jumping like he'd been bit, he ran out, slammed the gate shut, and locked it.

This time Laynie was certain she heard the key scrape on the rock wall outside her cell. She sighed and leaned back, closing her eyes. The confrontation had sapped what little strength she had.

"Thank you, Lord. I belong to you. I love you, and I trust you. Whatever comes, I will always love you."

When Laynie opened her eyes, she looked down at the shattered jug. She almost sighed with regret until she remembered why she had sacrificed it—and that she had soup left in the little pot.

"So what if the soup is cold? My stomach feels stable. Maybe I could try a bite or two of the barley and meat."

She was right—the soup had cooled and congealed. She scooped out a small bite, smeared it on her bread, and nibbled at it. Finished it and ate more. When she felt she couldn't eat another bite, she put the remains aside. The food seemed to settle in her stomach, and she felt some strength return.

Her thirst returned, too.

I must ignore it. Eventually, they will give me more water.

Calling on the bit of energy and strength the food had produced, Laynie worked her right leg and foot. She stretched her foot, starting with her toes, working her way up to her cramping and sore calf and thigh muscles. She switched to her left leg and foot and did the same.

The wound on the outside of her leg above her ankle pulled as she stretched. It looked healthy enough, but the skin around it was tight and puckered. She gently massaged and worked the tight skin. Then, from her sitting position on the bench, she attempted some simple leg lifts.

"Eight, nine, ten. Switch. One, two, three," she counted.

Two sets of ten lifts for each leg winded her—but she wasn't done. After counting off three minutes of rest, she scooted forward, tenuously placed her weight on her legs, and levered herself up to standing.

The cell whirled around her. She came close to falling, but she had fixed her eyes on the wall across from her. She stared at a point on the wall until the world righted itself. Her equilibrium steadied, and she exhaled in relief.

"Whew. Thank you, Lord. I'd rather not become closely acquainted with whatever that is puddled and dried on the floor."

Some hours later, another guard appeared at her cell gate. By then, Laynie had finished the food from breakfast and repeated her leg stretches and lifts twice. Although she'd napped once between the sets, she was still fatigued and, by then, craving water. She was also stronger than she'd been that morning.

The guard frowned at the pieces of the ruined jug on the floor, but he said nothing. He put a plate on the bed and left, removing the platter with its empty soup pot.

Laynie examined the plate. Two slices of bread spread with honey. She didn't try to regulate how she ate this time. She devoured the bread, one slice following the other, savoring each bite.

Then she walked. From one end of her cell to the other, sticking close to the wall in case she faltered. She made six crossings before sitting down to rest. Before nodding off yet again.

THE GATE TO HER CELL crashed open. Bula appeared, and he was angry. Apparently, the last guard had reported on the broken jug—as Laynie had hoped he would.

"What is this?" he shouted, pointing to the shattered jug on the floor. "You think you can defy General Sayed's orders? You think you can waste what costs the blood of our martyrs? What is the meaning of this?"

Laynie stayed calm and answered as she'd rehearsed. "You should ask the boy Doku what happened to the jug—and the water I was supposed to drink."

Suspicion bloomed on Bula's face. He studied her and said nothing for a long moment. "What is it you accuse him of?"

"The boy you call Doku tried to assault me. He forced me to defend my honor. When I did, he broke the jug. Out of spite." It was partly truth and partly lie, but she didn't flinch under Bula's scrutiny or at his mirthless laugh.

"You defended your *honor?*"

It had been months since Laynie had conversed in Russian, but the language and all its subtleties and inferences flowed from her with ease. "I am a woman of the Book. A follower of Isa, the Christ. I am a new believer with much to learn, but of two things I am certain: Isa has washed me clean of all my sins and has removed the guilt and shame of my former life."

Thank you Jubaila and Soraya for your many insights into Islam, including the name of Jesus in Arabic, Laynie said within herself.

Bula's gaze never left Laynie's face. Finally, and without another word, he left her. Minutes later the guard who had brought her lunch returned. He bore another jug of water, which he set on the bench. He said nothing and kept his eyes averted.

I see Bula has warned his underlings not to harass me—as I had hoped would happen. I wonder what sort of chastisement Bula laid on Doku?

Laynie spent the afternoon consuming half the water in the jug. She swallowed careful, measured amounts between a steady regimen of leg exercises and walking up and down the length of her cell. She also massaged her leg muscles to work out their painful knots and spasms.

Following the small meal provided for dinner, Laynie drank all but perhaps a cup of what remained in the jug. She saved the last little bit for first thing in the morning.

That evening, before she lay down to sleep, Laynie pulled her legs up on the bench and spent thirty minutes stretching. When she'd completed sitting stretches, she stood and worked on her calves and the front and backs of her thighs. She did three slow and careful sets of squats before moving on to her arms, chest, neck, and back.

Gonna be really sore tomorrow. Doesn't matter.

Sayed's words rang in her head. "*Feed her and care for her needs . . . I will see her again after the recovery period, say, four mornings from now.*"

"Lord Jesus, my Savior. I have two days more to regain my strength. Thank you for helping me, my Lord."

Two more days to prepare herself physically and mentally for what came next. To prepare spiritually.

"*Ah, there you are. Much older than the kafir women I usually choose, but defiant and godless, as I presumed. Good. I shall enjoy breaking you—once you are cleaned up.*"

"Sayed believes I am godless, but whatever it costs, I won't submit to him without a fight," Laynie whispered aloud.

Whatever it costs? That declaration, dredged from her training days, the genesis of her sordid past, rang with new meaning. Holy meaning.

"Yes, Sayed believes I am *kafir*, a godless woman. I pray, Lord God, that I might show him otherwise . . . before I die."

The seed had taken root in her heart—the notion that she would die in this place. The seed had put down roots and sprung up, and had already sprouted, flowered, and borne fruit. Armed with that conviction, every apprehension, every dread and worry perished with it.

After all, if one is already dead, what is there to fear?

LAYNIE TRIED TO CURL UP on the bench to sleep that night, but the bruises over her hip bones were too tender. She wrapped up in the blanket and again leaned against the wall to sleep sitting up. Before she gave herself to slumber, she finally allowed herself to think. About Mama and Dad. About Kari. About Shannon and Robbie. About her friends on the task force.

About Tobin . . . and the heavy weight of pain and grief he must be carrying.

Oh, Quincy, I promised that I would come back to you, God willing. I guess my situation isn't looking good for that. I don't understand the "why" of his plan, but I know that it is *his will that I, by his grace and the leading of the Holy Spirit, glorify the Lord in all I do and say, whichever way this goes—by my life or by my death.*

She sighed. *That is my goal, to acquit myself well on behalf of the Gospel. Doesn't mean I don't long to be back at Broadsword with you and with our team, but I accept that this may be "my time." And so . . .*

Words and phrases from the book of Philippians dropped easily from her lips. "I thank my God every time I remember you, Quincy Tobin. In all my prayers for you, I always pray with joy . . . being confident of this, that he who began a good work in you will carry it on to completion until the day of Christ Jesus. The Lord will carry it on to completion in you, and he will carry it on to completion in me . . . just not us together."

Laynie's breath hitched. "Yes, Lord. You will finish the work you've begun in Tobin and in me, too, because I know . . . I know *you.* And I know that you are faithful."

She choked down the lump in her throat, but she could not hold back the tears. "And this is my prayer for you, Quincy, that your love for our God may abound more and more . . . and that both of us will be found pure and blameless on the day of Christ, filled with the fruit of righteousness that comes only through him—to the glory and praise of God."

Chapter 17

WOLFE, SERAPHIM, AND THE task force assembled in the bullpen at 5:00 a.m. the following morning. Official sunrise wasn't until 7:18 a.m., but HRT planned to breach the house at 5:48 a.m., an hour and a half before sunrise.

Richard joined them in the bullpen after he'd arranged a table laden with pastries and coffee. Task force members stood in line for a turn at the coffee urn. Despite having worked around the clock for two days with little rest, few on the team had slept well the past night.

They were nervous.

Keyed up.

Anxious.

Too much rode on the outcome of the morning's actions.

Some of their angst was due to not being read into HRT's plan. With the exception of Wolfe, Seraphim, and Tobin, the task force members were largely unfamiliar with HRT's weapons and tactics. All the team knew was that Sherman's wife and young son were being kept prisoner in a house guarded by an unknown number of hostiles and that HRT would strike with the intention of taking down the hostiles while saving the hostages.

Tobin knew full well how easily things could go wrong. With one hand cradling his coffee mug, the other laid across his eyes, he leaned back in his chair and prayed.

Lord, I'm calling on you. In the mighty name of your Son, Jesus, I am asking for your help and your protection for the Hostage Rescue Team and for Sherman's family. Lord, I'm even asking for mercy for the men holding them captive. They are blind, my God. Please open their eyes and show them Jesus before it is too late.

And Lord? I acknowledge what your word says—that you are mindful of your people, that your eyes roam back and forth across the earth, that you bend low to listen to us. O Lord God! You have also said that you are faithful to a thousand generations of those who love you.

So Lord? You know that I love you. You know that my Marta loves you.

He laughed aloud softly. *Marta. Bella. Elaine. Laynie—whatever name she goes by, you already know her by it, my God. You also know that her family loves you and has served you faithfully for generations. Generations!*

You are Lord of all the earth, so I call upon you, Father, to show yourself faithful to my Marta and lead us to the place where she is hidden from us. Amen.

Tobin watched the clock. Its forward motion was slow and tiresome, while tensions in the bullpen ratcheted higher. Finally, at 5:25, Wolfe received a call.

When he closed his phone, he addressed the assembled team. "Listen. I know we're all on edge this morning, and I fully understand—the stakes are high. What I can tell you is that the Hostage Rescue Team, using thermal imaging from the air, completed its final reconnaissance of the target a few minutes ago. They know how many hostiles are in the house and where they are positioned. And because of the smaller size of Sherman's son, they were able to determine the room where he and his mother are together sleeping."

Wolfe paused a moment before continuing. "At 5:48, when the kidnappers are judged to be in their least watchful state, HRT will breach both entrances to the house. Sherman's wife and son are alone, sleeping in a back bedroom. If all goes well, HRT will neutralize the hostiles without harm to the hostages."

Hopeful murmurs wafted around the bullpen.

Lord, I am asking you to help the rescue team, Tobin whispered within himself. *Guide them in this operation and keep them safe*.

Wolfe concluded, "Let's gather around now and listen in while HRT does what it is best in the world at doing."

Bo and Harris had placed two chairs and a small table in the center of the bullpen. Wolfe and Seraphim, both of them somber, took the seats closest to the table. On the table sat a military-grade field radio—their line to the HRT's command center. Bo switched on the radio and tuned it to the proper channel. Adjusted the volume.

Tobin observed as task force members inched their chairs closer to the radio, every ear intent on the drama about to unfold. Except Jaz.

JAZ REMAINED AT HER DESK and had only one ear attuned to the radio chatter. She was busy on her laptop, working on her part in the operation. She glanced at Sherman's phone, Burner Zero, lying on her desk beside her keyboard. She had wormed her way into the company that provided cell service to Rosenberg's four burner phones and uploaded a software program of her own design to the provider's system.

At 5:30 a.m. she opened a command prompt and called up her program. She typed in a command and pressed Enter.

Done.

She had altered or "spoofed" Burner Zero's outgoing number. From this moment on, any phone receiving a call or text from Burner Zero would see Burner Three's number—the kidnappers' number—on the caller ID screen instead of Burner Zero's. It meant that when she texted Rosenberg from Sherman's phone, the incoming message would appear to have come from the kidnappers' phone—not from Sherman's.

Next, she prepared to shut down service to Burner Three, the kidnappers' phone. She would lock it down just as the Hostage Rescue Team's vehicle entered the kidnappers' neighborhood.

At 5:35 a.m. the HRT team leader keyed his mic. "Command, Team Leader. Approaching drop."

"Acknowledged, Team Leader."

Jaz killed service to Burner Three. The kidnappers' phone could no longer make or receive calls. She had severed their connection to Rosenberg and inserted Sherman's phone in its place.

Tense minutes passed until, at 5:45 a.m., a voice from the radio said, "Command, Team Leader. HRT in position. Perimeter secure."

"Roger that, Team Leader. Stand by for go."

"Copy, Command. Standing by for go."

Jaz watched the clock on her laptop count down the minutes and seconds to 5:48 a.m.

"Team Leader, this is Command. Execute, execute, execute."

"Command, Team Leader. Execute acknowledged. Go! Go! Go!"

Until now, the only sound over the radio had been the murmured exchange between the command center and the Hostage Rescue Team leader. Now they heard team members' heavy breathing and the launch of flash-bang grenades followed by doors splintering, shouted commands, and the *pop-pop-pop* of semiauto weapons.

Then, silence.

No one in the bullpen spoke. Jaz stared at the radio as they all waited, holding their collective breath.

"Command, this is Team Leader. Three hostiles in custody—one casualty. Two hostages safely recovered. No team injuries."

"Acknowledged, Team Leader. Congratulations. Sending backup."

A shout rose in the bullpen, rising and rising as the team whooped and hollered, danced and hugged. No one was exempt.

It was a breathtaking moment, one that caught Jaz blinking back tears—even as Tobin plucked her from her chair and swung her around in a crushing bear hug.

"One step closer to finding Bella," he shouted in her ear.

Jaz pulled away. "Yeah, thanks for that. I'm gonna need that ear, you dork."

She and Tobin grinned with mutual joy.

Then Wolfe calmed them down. His eyes shone with satisfaction as he spoke. "This team, each of you, are the reason we're here. Your hard work has brought us to this morning's victory. You should be very proud. I know I am—but we're not done, are we?"

He found Jaz with his eyes. "Miss Jessup, you are authorized to execute the next step in Operation Whack-a-Mole."

Wolfe's words elicited another shout of laughter and more congratulations.

"One last announcement before I let you get to it," Wolfe added. "I'm taking Seraphim with me into DC. I have a few tasks for her. She will be back, but Miss Jessup and Marshal Tobin will keep things running on this end for the time being."

The gathering broke up. Jaz and Tobin returned to Jaz's desk. It was time to send the text message that would, they hoped, set Rosenberg's hair ablaze.

Wish I could see your face when your house of cards starts to collapse, Jaz grinned to herself. She looked to Tobin.

He was grinning, too, but it was a disconcerting and scary grin. "Time for Operation Flush-a-Mole. Let's do it."

As Jaz prepared to key in the contents of the text, she first unwrapped three fresh sticks of Black Jack and stuffed them into her mouth—one-handed. As she chewed and keyed in the message, she smirked.

Oh, you can run, you ugly little varmint—and we really, really *want you to. The thing is? Wherever you go, we'll be on you like stink on a skunk.*

Jaz reread her text. She'd sprinkled in a few typos that she, Tobin, and Seraphim believed would inject a sense of panic into the message.

Caught armed individ
cheking out house
looking in window
Advise pleze

The response came three minutes later.

ID?

Jaz waited five minutes before typing.

FBI

Jaz closed her eyes. Imagined the shock on Rosenberg's face. Sighed with satisfaction. The reply was instantaneous.

OPTION B

Option B, according to Rosenberg's text log, meant "kill the hostages, kill the phone, then get the heck outta Dodge." It was an all-around bad-news text for the phone—not to mention the hostages. Rosenberg didn't want the phone telling tales any more than they wanted the hostages identifying the people who took them—or their boss. Jaz was relieved Sherman's wife and son were safe.

"Why do people always think that breaking a phone's SIM card will erase their call and text logs?" Jaz snickered to herself.

She checked her laptop. She was watching Rosenberg's phone ping off a DC cell tower, hoping it would soon start to move. Not that her oversight was necessary. Wolfe had a team of two watching Rosenberg's home and vehicle, and they had already planted a tracker on the vehicle. Two other operatives, based out of Italy, were already *en route* to Grozny, Chechnya, Rosenberg's destination—if Rosenberg's travel arrangements were to be believed.

"Any movement?" Tobin asked.

"Nothing yet. Wish I were a fly on the wall watching Rosenberg's perfectly ordered life exploding into itty bitty pieces."

"I feel ya."

"But you don't have the same vengeful bloodlust I have, do you?"

Tobin smiled, and Jaz saw the sadness behind the smile.

"Guess I don't. I have to work at it, but I try to keep my heart from . . . going there. It's kind of a one-way trip, y'know?"

Jaz's jaws slowed. "Not sure I agree. I mean, I understand the whole 'vengeance is mine, says the Lord' bit you follow because you're a Christian, but I don't get the 'one-way trip' part."

When Tobin glanced up and his eyes locked on to hers, Jaz was shocked by the depth of pain in them. She was more shocked when he answered her.

"Vengeance and bloodlust are *easy*, Jaz. Easy to give into, easy to follow, easy to justify. Getting out? That's the hard part, and most people who go there don't ever escape. Because once revenge gets its hooks in *you*, you aren't running the show any longer. It's running you. You have to ask yourself a tough question: Do I want the rest of my life consumed with making someone pay for what they can never give back or fix? Because that's the deal."

He put his ham-sized palm on her shoulder. "I wouldn't wish that for me, and I wouldn't wish that for you."

WHEN THE TEAM'S CELEBRATORY mood tapered off, Tobin walked across to the house and headed for the library where Sherman was being kept under the watchful eye of a Broadsword guard. Tobin knocked.

The guard opened the door. "Marshal Tobin."

"Hey, Manny. May I have a minute with the prisoner?"

The guard stepped out of the room and left Tobin and Sherman alone.

"I have good news for you, Sherman."

Hope ignited the man's weary face. "News about my family?"

"Yes. HRT has them. They are safe. Since we are still operational and need to keep a lid on their rescue, they are being taken to a military hospital where they will be evaluated and kept under wraps."

"Will I . . . will I be able to see them?"

"That's up to Director Wolfe and the powers that be. You have a lot to answer for, including the lives of the guards who died protecting us when the Ukrainian assassins hit us at our apartments."

Sherman bowed his head. "I know. Right now, I'm just grateful that my wife and son are alive and safe. It . . . it means a lot."

Tobin put his hand on Sherman's shoulder. "I'm glad, too. Listen, I figure you have a heaping plateful right now and it's gotta be overwhelming—and this is a total jump to another topic—but would you like me to pray with you?"

Sherman glanced up, surprised and . . . touched. "I'm not religious, man."

Tobin smiled. "Neither am I. I am, however, a believer in Jesus. He'd like you to know who he is, that he loves you, and that he's willing to help. So. Want me to pray?"

"Yeah. I think I would. Thank you."

CHAPTER 18

LAYNIE WAS READY ON that fourth morning when Bula appeared. She'd worked hard to rebuild the strength and muscle tone she'd lost. She wasn't fully recovered by any means, but she could walk under her own steam now.

More importantly, she was "prayed up," as prepared inside as she could be for whatever the day held.

Bula unlocked her cell an hour after breakfast and walked her to the common room again, to the improvised bathhouse behind the curtain. The old woman had run another bath. "Alyona" and "Not Alyona," eyes down, waited nearby. This time, Bula stationed two guards outside the curtain, neither of whom were Doku.

Laynie kept her expression studiously blank. *Sayed has ordered that I appear before him appropriately "clean," yet he is snared by his own blindness. He fails to see the irony of insisting that* I *be clean while his own lusts rise as a stench before the throne of God in heaven.*

Bula handed her into the old woman's care and left. Laynie removed her veil. She offered the old woman a small smile and a soft greeting.

"*As-Salamu Alaykum.*"

The old woman's mouth dropped open—and Laynie saw that she did not have many teeth left. Laynie turned to "Alyona" and "Not Alyona" and nodded. "Thank you," she murmured, first in Arabic, then in Russian.

Laynie didn't wait for the women to respond. She was not attempting to garner a reply but to earn the minimum measure of goodwill, perhaps even build simple relationships—if she were around that long. She disrobed and tested the water. It was quite warm, but not excessively so. She stepped into the tub on her right foot and eased her left one in to see how it fared. The wound stung briefly, then adapted to the water. Laynie slid down into the water, grateful again for the soothing relief on her sore muscles and tender spots.

This time, when the women came at her with soap and washcloths, Laynie shook her head. She gestured for them to give one to her. The old woman shrugged and handed over her cloth.

Laynie bathed herself, washed her own hair, and—reluctantly—left the tub, then toweled herself off. "Alyona" and "Not Alyona" held up extra towels. When Laynie nodded, they worked the water out of her wet hair.

Then the old woman patted a stack of clean clothes on the bench. Laynie sat and started to dress herself. Slowly.

She sighed. *The heat took more out of me than I thought.*

The old woman must have motioned to "Alyona" and "Not Alyona," because they began to help her.

"Thank you," Laynie whispered again.

Laynie thought "Not Alyona" smiled beneath her veil. The movement flashed across the visible part of her face like the sweep of a bird's wing. There and gone.

The old woman waved them into the common area where the two girls dried her hair, brushing it to a shimmering sheen.

Bula returned, and the three women hastened to finish whatever preparations they'd been ordered to make. "Alyona" fetched the folded veils from the bench, but Bula gestured her away and motioned Laynie to him, her head uncovered.

Laynie summoned all her strength and rose from the chair. With her chin held high, her eyes straight ahead, she walked to Bula.

Lord, if I'm going to die today, let me die as a daughter of the King of Kings—full of your grace and righteousness.

TWO GUARDS SNAPPED TO attention and one held the curtain aside for Bula, who pulled Laynie into Sayed's salon after him. Some memory of the room must have remained with her from her first encounter with Sayed, because she recognized the air of formal opulence of the room, if not the actual surroundings.

"Ah, Bula. Good. I am anxious to see her," Sayed called from the U-shaped seating area. Although the couches and cushions were of the same style, Sayed's seat was noticeably larger. Larger and more . . .

Regal, Laynie thought as Bula led her forward. *Elegant and regal. Sayed's ego requires a throne to signify his importance.*

Bula pulled on her arm and led her to a low table in the center of the seating area. He pushed her down onto her knees, Sayed directly across from her. Laynie didn't sit back on her feet. She kept herself erect on her knees. Tall.

Amused, Sayed smiled. He ran his eyes over her. "Yes, you are much improved today. And your hair—it is as beautiful as I was told. Not a single color but a kaleidoscope of many. It reminds me of wheat fields near harvest. A rippling of white and gold and every shade in between. I look forward to running my fingers through it."

He wants to talk first. He hopes to interrogate me, but what is he after?

In addition, Laynie wondered why Sayed spoke English to her. It was not a language known by many of his soldiers, including Bula. Maybe he felt that a conversation in English with her would give him a modicum of privacy.

More likely he wants to impress me, Laynie thought. The illustrious AGFA general—a great tactician and cultured, intellectual leader—a Renaissance Man. Instead, it put her in mind of Petroff. Laynie nodded to herself. *A powerful man with an inflated sense of self and a fragile ego.*

When Laynie failed to respond to Sayed's compliments one way or another, he snapped his fingers. A servant who had been waiting off to the side of the room unfolded an intricately embroidered cloth and spread it across the table. The cloth was so beautiful that Laynie reached out and stroked one perfectly smooth blossom and a fringed tassel attached to the cloth's corner.

Sayed's man placed a small plate of dates and figs in the center of the table. Laynie's stomach lurched. She was so hungry that she tasted stomach acid at the back of her throat.

The servant then brought a tea service to the table and poured two glasses of steaming tea. He carefully stirred sugar into one glass that he set before Laynie. The other he placed before Sayed.

While he worked, Laynie's eyes were busy, but not noticeably. They roamed across the servant and took in minor but important details—such as the way his teeth pulled nervously on his bottom lip as he spooned sugar into her glass for her and how he avoided looking at her. She slid her gaze to Sayed, captured a picture of him, and waited to dissect it until her eyes had returned to the steaming glass in front of her.

Sayed gestured to Laynie. "Please. Partake of my hospitality."

Laynie had cataloged the microexpressions on the servant's face, had watched the flicker around Sayed's eyes. She left the glass sitting where the servant had placed it on the table.

Sayed picked up his own glass and blew across its steaming surface. "Surely you would not deny yourself a bit of refreshment?"

"No, thank you."

Sayed's smile dropped. "You refuse my hospitality? Your behavior borders on offensive."

"So does ordering your servant to drug me. Do you deny it?"

Sayed flushed, then mastered himself. He spread his hands in a placating manner. "Perhaps I simply wished to have a productive conversation with you. I have questions you would answer with more candor were you . . . relaxed."

And I think that although you enjoy taking a woman against her will, getting off on her screams and protests, you prefer to blunt her strength while you rape her.

"Ask away," Laynie said. "I promise to be candid."

He snorted. "Tell me, then, why you were in Tbilisi."

It was Laynie's turn to smile. "It is a beautiful city with much to see. I particularly enjoyed visiting the cathedral."

"And the market?"

"A unique and pleasurable experience."

"You entered a car with two men as you left the market. Who were they?"

A fractured memory flickered behind her eyes. *I left the Tbilisi bazaar with two men? Oh, yes. I remember now. Rode in a car with them and a driver. Two men in the front. One in the rear with me.*

"Everyday tour guides. Did you kill them?"

A truck careening off course—going to hit us!

Sayed shrugged. "People die in war."

Horrible pain—my ankle. The coppery smell of blood mixed with that of spilled gasoline. Someone prying open the car door and pulling me out . . .

Then nothing.

"I wasn't aware that the Republic of Georgia was at war."

Sayed sipped at his glass. "Universally, the followers of the Prophet are always engaged in a holy struggle."

Laynie fiddled with the tassel hanging from one corner of the ornate tablecloth. "Your struggle cannot be very holy if it requires you to murder innocent people. Of course, religious fanatics often excuse their own evil acts as obedience to their god."

Sayed's lips thinned. He switched directions. "You are American, are you not? It explains why you are so outspoken."

"My passport says I'm American—and you have my passport, do you not? It was in my bag when the truck you hired rammed us."

Ignoring her question, Sayed murmured, "And yet Bula tells me you speak Russian like a Russian native. A Muscovite. How curious."

"Yes, I'm fluent in Russian. However, I'm most comfortable in English."

"You mean American English."

"If you say so."

Sayed leaned toward her. "I have visited America. I love many things about your country. Its wide-open spaces, its cars, and its entertainments. A country's entertainments can reveal a lot about a culture . . . particularly its indulgences. Its weaknesses."

He's bragging now. Showing me how worldly he is. Trying to elevate himself in my eyes.

"America is only truly great when its people are faithful to the God of the Bible, when they repent of their sins and return to him—of their own free will, not at the prodding of a sword."

Again Sayed ignored her. Laynie figured he had an agenda, a script he wanted to follow that would take him to his real questions.

He sat back. "As for American books, I have many favorites. For example, I have enjoyed all of Tom Clancy's novels. *Debt of Honor* and *Executive Orders* are my favorites. I found them pleasantly prophetic—particularly the plane in *Debt of Honor* that flew into the US Capitol building, killing the president, most of Congress, and all the justices of the Supreme Court."

His servant presented him with a box of cigarettes. Sayed took a moment to light one and draw on it, pulling the smoke deep into his lungs. "They are presently filming the movie version of Clancy's *Sum of All Fears*. I've heard it won't be released until this coming May, but I arranged to receive a copy of the script. It was positively inspirational."

"I'm not much of a moviegoer," Laynie murmured. "I prefer not to immerse myself in fantasy."

She was exaggerating, but it allowed her to administer a dig that would not go unnoticed.

"*Touché*, but you miss my point," he answered. The smoke curled from his mouth.

"I'm sure you'll enlighten me."

"The enlightenment comes not from me but from one of the movie's characters, a German named Dressler—a visionary. The script quotes him as saying, 'Let no man call us crazy. They called Hitler crazy. But Hitler was not crazy. He was stupid.'"

Laynie's attention sharpened. "Hitler could very well have been both crazy and stupid—he did lose because he elected to fight a war on two fronts."

"Perhaps. But I have not yet reached the meat of the quotation, the essence that our movement has ingested and made our own. Here it is. 'You don't try to fight Russia and America. You get Russia and America to fight each other . . . and destroy each other.' If such a feat were successful, it would leave the world open to so many possibilities, would it not?"

Laynie shrugged and tipped her chin toward her chest—to hide the shock that Sayed would surely have seen written in her expression.

That is exactly what Rusty suggested! Lord God, his theory was spot on.

She played back his passionate "what if" in her mind.

"I keep hearing your voice in my head, Bella, asking for AGFA's real objective—and what got me was that it has to be something so significant that it requires pitting the US and Russia against each other. And then I thought, what if that objective means they want more than another cold war between the two nations. What if they want to start a real conflict, a shooting war? A conflict that would remove these two 'superpowers' from the picture?

"And I asked myself, 'What objective could warrant taking such a risk? What goal would inspire AGFA to attack the West like al-Qaeda did?' Certainly not mere Chechen independence. So, I told myself, 'Think globally, Rusty!'

"What if these radical Chechens are more closely aligned with al-Qaeda and like-minded Islamists than we thought? What if they are part of a global strategy *to raise up a Salafi–Wahhabi caliphate?"*

Her perceived nonchalance seemed to anger Sayed. "You do not seem concerned for your precious America, Miss Garineau."

In control of herself again, she glanced up, eyes innocent. "Sorry. Did I miss something?"

She knew it would anger him, push him harder than she'd already pushed him, but she did it anyway. The slap, when he lunged across the table and delivered it, stole her breath away. Made her nose and eyes run.

Sayed was out of patience. "You are an American operative named Anabelle Garineau—which is not your real name. You lead a team, a task force, whose mission is to thwart the plans of All Glorious for Allah.

"If you say so."

Sayed studied her. "What about your task force?"

"What about it?"

"I would very much like to know more about it—for example where your little troupe is hiding."

Laynie smiled to herself. *Interesting—and revealing, Sayed. I thought the Ukrainian mob wanted our location because they were trying to track down Jaz. Why would you want to know our location unless . . . unless you are working with them?*

She answered Sayed, "We gave the mob the slip when we up and left Germantown all together."

Sayed's lips thinned. "Mob? What mob?"

He wasn't as smooth as he thought he was.

"The Ukrainians. Your partners in America, I surmise."

"Nonsense. I wish you to tell me where your task force is."

"I wished for a pony once. Never got one."

Sayed ignored her flippant response. "Tell me, what has your task force uncovered? What do the Americans know of our upcoming attacks?"

"We have no knowledge of upcoming attacks."

True. The task force had no operational knowledge of the attacks, only Cossack's word that they were imminent. *Cossack.* She hoped he had found another route to securely pass the attack details to Wolfe.

"You are lying, and I *know* you are lying."

"Am I lying? Now, how would you know that? Is it because your operatives have wormed their way inside our ranks?"

Sayed did not rise to the bait. "You may have played at being a secret agent for many years. You may have even taken pride in your work, but it all ends now. This day I will chain you to my bed. I will take your body and use it to satisfy my desires. Again and again and again. You will remain chained to my bed until I have broken your spirit."

An irrational picture popped into Laynie's mind. Princess Leia chained to a slimy, slobbery Jabba the Hutt—and Leia strangling him with the very chain he used to keep her tied to him.

Sayed laughed to himself. "I will use you as I wish, and you will beg me to stop, but I will not until I have properly humbled you. Then and only then will I give you to my men to use as often as they like, and—"

"You cannot humble me, Sayed."

A look of puzzlement strobed over his face. Before he could exert his own better judgment, he asked, "How do you mean, Miss Garineau? *You* are not in control here."

"No, but my God is. You should know that I am a woman of the Book—a follower of Jesus Christ. Jesus is the Son of God, God himself born in human likeness to become the Savior of the world. I have submitted my life to Jesus and have *already humbled myself* under his mighty hand."

Sayed barked an incredulous laugh. "And will your precious Jesus save you from me?"

"He already has. Jesus gave me everything I need to live as a woman of God, both in this life and the next, when he said, *I give you eternal life, and you shall never perish.* So you see, Sayed, nothing you can do to me matters."

Sayed first gaped, then he raged. "Isa is but a third-rate prophet who failed the purposes of Allah by dying an ignoble, barbaric death! *He is nothing*, and he cannot protect you. Only Allah is God—"

"Allah is not my god, nor is he the god of the Bible. The God and Father of our Lord Jesus Christ is the Eternal One, the Ancient of Days, the maker of heaven and earth—and Jesus is his only begotten Son, the Son who is both fully God and fully man. As Muslims are fond of saying, *Allah has no son*—therefore, Allah is *not* the god of the Bible.

"Jesus also said, *My Father, who has given you to me, is greater than all, and* no one *can snatch you out of my Father's hand.* Jesus is greater than Allah and 'no one' includes you."

"You speak blasphemies!"

"Says every false leader who hides behind phony piety while violating the chastity of virtuous women *and little girls*—in order to satisfy their own sinful lusts while puffing up their sinful egos."

This time Laynie was ready and waiting. When Sayed's right hand flashed out to slap her a second time, Laynie's left hand was faster—faster than Sayed expected, faster than Bula or the guards could react. She grabbed, twisted hard, and felt the satisfying *snap* of Sayed's fingers—his index and middle fingers—before she let go.

To top it off, she wanted to leave him with a memorable and visible token of their encounter—something all his men would see and remark on. No sooner had the audible *snap* echoed around Sayed's salon than Laynie delivered a right hook.

He gasped as Laynie's knuckles connected with his left eye and kept going to crack the nasal bridge—ensuring copious amounts of bleeding and a wicked shiner.

Seconds later, Laynie was on her back on the floor, Bula's boot on her throat. She couldn't breathe, and the torque on her neck told her that even an incremental transfer of his weight would shatter her cervical spine.

Sayed's servant and his soldiers crowded around him until Sayed screamed for them to get out. Everyone but Bula and Sayed's personal servant fled the salon. Laynie couldn't see much with Bula's boot and leg in the way, but she caught a glimpse.

Sayed's left eye was quickly swelling closed. He held a towel and some ice to his streaming nose while his servant had his right hand in his, applying ice to it, attempting to straighten the broken digits.

Sayed cursed and spit, his rage enough to terrify the hapless soul who might unintentionally get in his way.

Too bad his focus is on me, huh?

Laynie quivered and choked as Bula waited Sayed's instructions. Any moment, she expected Sayed to give the word for the swift thrust of Bula's boot to sever her spinal cord—or an even quicker bullet. And . . . she was strangely all right with either prospect.

Lord Jesus, thank you, Laynie prayed with wide-open eyes, her soul at peace. *Thank you that I won't die with that man's hands around my throat after he's abused me. I belong to you, Jesus, and I thank you for saving me from Sayed's plans.*

A shadow hovered over her. Sayed, burning with red-hot hatred, his eye swelling closed. Blood from his broken nose dribbled through the towel and fell on Laynie's face and hair.

Intentionally.

Sayed slowly pronounced, "You have interfered in the holy work we have undertaken for Allah, Anabelle Garineau. For that you will never leave this mountain alive. But before I allow you to die, you and I have much to discuss. You will suffer greatly at my hands as I extract what I need from you, and you will beg for death. So you see, you may count yourself already dead."

He dabbed at his nose. "Take her back to her cell until I determine how I wish to proceed," he ordered.

As an afterthought he added, "And douse her with water."

Bula hauled Laynie to her feet. She hadn't regretted her actions until now. Douse her with water? The temperature in the caves, while not freezing, was uncomfortable. Soaking her would create real hardship—but first it made Laynie mad.

"You are a bitter, *little* man, Sayed," she said to him. Loudly. She used Russian because it was better known in Sayed's militia than English. Her words would be heard in the passageway outside his salon and repeated among his soldiers a thousand times.

"You are a sniveling coward. Only spineless men torture defenseless women."

Sayed shook with fury. He would have killed Laynie himself, then and there, if he'd had both hands to do it—but Laynie had effectively deprived him of the ability to strangle her.

For now.

"Strip her before you pour on the water," he shouted. "Let her suffer and freeze!"

Laynie's taunts echoed down the passageway as Bula and two other soldiers dragged her away. "Spineless coward! Weakling! You are not a real man, Sayed—you are pathetic!"

She shouted until Bula shook her so hard that her teeth cracked together.

HOURS LATER, SAYED CODDLED his fingers and waited for his servant to bring him the satellite phone. His militia's medic had set the digits and bound them together to stabilize them, but Sayed's hand had swelled and purpled, and it ached. His mottled face, too, bore testament to the Garineau woman's fisted hand.

When his servant delivered the phone, Sayed scowled at the brick-shaped device. He was not in the mood for the call scheduled minutes from now. Nevertheless, he would handle it. Needed to handle it.

A cable attached to the phone snaked across the floor to a tapestry hanging beside his bookshelves and an alcove cleverly hidden behind the tapestry. From the alcove, the cable ran one hundred thirty feet up a narrow stone "chimney" and emerged into the open air from under the metal plate that capped the chimney, sheltering it from rain. Close by the chimney, the cable attached to a directional antenna.

Buried as he and his militia were in the mountain, the satphone was an invaluable tool. Setting it up had been a feat of incredibly dedicated work.

His men, led by a jihadi geologist and Sayed's technical advisor, had settled on a protruding "shoulder" of the mountain to drill. They had bored straight down, sculpting a chimney six inches in diameter to a point not far from the large cavern where Sayed's militia had initially lived. His men had carved a tunnel from the cavern in the direction of the chimney and, at the point where the tunnel broke through to the chimney, had hewn Sayed's living quarters around it.

At Sayed's direction, they had completed a second challenging and labor-intensive task—the construction of an escape shaft. The narrow shaft, designed to accommodate a single man, entered through the alcove, then straight up. His men had bolted a ladder inside the shaft. Where the ladder ended, the tunnel took a sharp turn and wended gradually downward, ending on a slope above the valley. A metal plate covered the shaft's opening, and a small pile of rocks hid the plate itself.

Allah most certainly blessed our efforts, Sayed told himself.

To reach a handful of his less-accessible generals, including General Arzu Labazanov, Sayed used an HF radio he also kept hidden in the alcove. It, too, had required an antenna. It had been but a simple matter to attach an HF antenna to the rock near the satphone's antenna and feed a second cable down the chimney to the radio.

Sayed needed the HF radio, but it was the satphone that was his true lifeline to the outside world—to his stateside commander, Khasurt, to his arms dealers, to a handful of his generals, to his contacts in other jihadi networks, and to the Ukrainian mob whose cooperation was so vital to Sayed's plans.

It was, of course, important to maintain a harmonious, symbiotic relationship with the Ukrainians while simultaneously disguising AGFA's true objectives. A piece of that complicated dance was hiding the timeline of AGFA's attacks in the US without raising the godless Ukrainians' suspicions. He could not, for example, give the Ukrainians what they wanted *most* too soon.

The fact that they are desperate for the information favors us—as long as every delay is convincing.

Sayed composed himself. "Good morning," he answered in Russian, one of two languages they held in common.

"And good afternoon to you, General Sayed," the elderly head of the US Ukrainian crime syndicate answered. "Have you news to report?"

"Yes, we have received the woman. She arrived in a fragile, dehydrated state, I am sad to report. However, it is nothing a week of food and water will not cure."

Sayed purposely inflated the recovery period.

"A week you say?" The old man's disappointment was clear.

"You know how doctors are. They are concerned. When she is recovered, we will interrogate her. I doubt it will take much to break her, but the doctor did caution me to wait. We wouldn't want her to expire before we extract the information you need, would we?"

"No. We would not want that—as long as we receive the information *before* your next shipment is due."

Sayed smiled to himself. "Very good. In that case, I do not foresee a problem. Until then?"

"Yes. Goodbye."

BULA DRAGGED LAYNIE INTO her cell and ordered her to strip off her abaya, the shift she wore under it, her stockings, and her sandals. He tossed the items of clothing into the passageway one by one. She was surprised that he kept his eyes averted as she undressed.

"Stand with your back against that wall," he said, pointing to the end of her cell, just past the end of her bed. A guard outside the cell handed him a bucket. Bula looked only at Laynie's feet when he tossed the bucket's contents on her.

The water was so cold that it knocked the breath out of her chest.

"Turn and face the wall."

Laynie turned, and Bula poured the contents of a second bucket over her head. He said not another word, but Laynie heard the key turn in the lock—and the tiniest of clinks as the key was left hanging from the passageway wall.

Bula had left her the blanket from her "bed" but nothing else. Maybe he felt it indecent to leave her naked before the eyes of anyone peering through the bars into her cell. Regardless of the reason, she was grateful.

She grabbed up the filthy blanket and rubbed herself as dry as possible, lessons from her survival training shouting at her, warning her of the trouble she was in.

When you are wet, heat flows from your body into the water on your skin. Water is a higher heat conductor than air, thus your body will lose heat more rapidly when it is wet.

Dry. I must get dry, or I'll freeze to death.

Her hair was her worst problem. No matter what she did, it would not dry for hours. At the cave's temperature, perhaps days.

Unheeding of the blanket's filth, Laynie chewed through its selvage and tore off a strip a foot wide. She wrapped the strip around her head, and tied the ends around her neck. She twisted the wet ends of her hair together and tucked them up into her utilitarian head covering. Then she huddled on the bench, knees pulled up to her chest, the remainder of the blanket wrapped as tightly around her as she could manage.

She had to preserve whatever heat her body made inside the folds of the blanket. She shook from the cold and from Sayed's words clanging within her.

"*You have interfered in the holy work we have undertaken for Allah, Anabelle Garineau. For that you will never leave this mountain alive. But before I allow you to die, you and I have much to discuss. You will suffer greatly at my hands as I extract what I need from you, and you will beg for death. So you see, you may count yourself already dead.*"

Some bit of Sayed's boast sounded familiar.

"Lord God?"

In the same way, count yourselves dead to sin but alive to God in Christ Jesus.

"Oh. Y-yes. I-I-I c-can do that. I can do all things through Christ who s-s-strengthens me . . ."

I give you eternal life, and you shall never perish; no one will snatch you out of my hand.

"Yes, Lord. Whatever h-h-happens, I w-will conduct myself in a manner worthy of the gospel of Christ."

Laynie shivered and shook.

"Dear God, I'm so c-c-cold."

CHAPTER 19

GROZNY, CHECHNYA, WAS ONLY a middling city of less than a quarter million, but it did have one of the few commercial airports in the south of Russia. Wolfe's agents had arrived from Italy two nights before. They now awaited Rosenberg's arrival.

The flight from Sheremetyevo Airport in Moscow via the Russian airline, Aeroflot, landed. When it had taxied to its gate, the passengers began to disembark, flowing into the airport proper, making their way to baggage claim.

"I'm not seeing her."

"Patience, Jeff. Patience."

The last passengers trickled through the door. They knew the men were the last passengers when the gate agent closed the door and locked it.

"We've been played, Stu."

His partner cursed. "Phone it in, Jeff."

"*You* phone it in. I'm not gonna be the one who tells Wolfe we blew our assignment."

WOLFE WAS IN HIS DC OFFICES holding a staff meeting when the call was routed to him. When he picked it up, he sensed immediately that it was bad news. Asking his deputy to finish, Wolfe shut himself up in his office.

"She wasn't on the plane, Director."

"You're sure?"

"Yes, sir."

Wolfe hung up and called Jaz. "Rosenberg switched flights on us. This was *your idea*, Jaz. It's probably too late to do anything about it, but figure it out anyway."

"Yes, sir."

JAZ RELUCTANTLY MET HER teammates' questioning eyes as they turned toward her. She swallowed.

"Seems our traitor switched flights mid-route. Did a runner."

"Probably made the switch in Toronto," Brian suggested.

Jaz nodded, bent her face to her laptop's screen, and hacked into the airline where Rosenberg had tickets from Toronto to Moscow. It took her far longer than it should have to uncover Rosenberg's new route—Toronto to Kiev, Kiev to Baku—but only because Rosenberg had swapped out identities, too.

She told the team and then called Wolfe back. "Sir. Rosenberg arrived in Baku, Azerbaijan, thirty minutes ago."

"Baku. The backdoor to Dagestan and Chechnya. Long gone by now."

"Yes, sir. I . . . I'm sorry, sir."

Wolfe's reply was tight. Cold. "I am, too, Miss Jessup."

"Yes, sir."

He's right. I got distracted. Didn't follow through. What is wrong with me?

Jaz was unaccustomed to failure. As its weight settled on her, she threw her phone down and hung her head over her keyboard. She knuckled her eyes hard, then harder, but it didn't help. Sorrow and an aching fear collided with guilt and shame. When she tried to inhale, she shuddered instead. Then the tears she'd fought hard to contain . . . let go. Exploded. She buried her face in her arms to muffle her sobs, but it didn't work.

Chairs rolled away from desks. Careful footsteps approached. Hands came to rest on her shoulders, back, and neck. Simple, soft pats or awkward but gentle little rubs.

Her team. Her friends. Wanting to console her. Doing their best to take her pain and make it their own. Their care undid the little restraint she had left.

It's my fault—it was my idea!

It was my idea, and now I've lost our only lead.

Not just a lead. I've lost her.

I've lost Bella.

She shuddered. And broke inside.

She wept until she had nothing left.

ROSENBERG LEFT THE AIRPORT terminal and hailed a taxi. Ordered the taxi to drive to the Teze Bazaar, one of Baku's most famous open-air markets. After wandering for half an hour, constantly checking for a tail, Rosenberg located a pay phone and placed a call. She had chucked all her burner phones before she left the US.

"Baku Produce Delivery."

Rosenberg, who did not speak Azerbaijani, replied in broken Russian.

"To whom am I speaking?"

"This is Emil. I am the owner."

"Very good. This is Archangel. I request the transport of a shipment of pears and apricots."

Emil sucked in a breath—the request was code. "I must check our delivery schedule."

"I am calling from a pay phone. Here is the number. I will wait here until you call back."

"It may take an hour or more."

"Understood."

Emil disconnected and dialed a memorized number. "I have a delivery for the general."

"Oh? None was scheduled."

"The request was properly worded."

"Who was the requestor?"

"Someone named Archangel."

"Stay near your phone. I will get back to you."

The man disconnected. He unlocked a cupboard, removed a phone reserved for this purpose, and dialed. The satphone on the other end rang fifteen times before it was picked up.

"Yes?"

"General, we have received a properly coded request from Archangel for transport to your location."

Sayed stilled. Too soon by at least two weeks. Nothing, however, could stop the New Year's Eve operation from going forward.

"Very well. Request granted."

LAYNIE FOUND IT IMPOSSIBLE to count the passing of time. No one came. No one peered into her cell. The passageway was utterly silent. But she didn't wait passively. She made herself get up and walk. When her bare feet couldn't stand the cold rock floor any longer, she walked back and forth on top of her bench, stopping to do squats at each turn. She exercised her arms and legs to keep the cold from stiffening her muscles. She rubbed her feet, the coldest parts of her body.

She kept up a continual conversation with God by talking aloud, singing, humming, repeating scriptures. Praying for her family members by name. Praying for her friends at Broadsword. Praying for Tobin. When she was tired, she huddled on the bench and slept.

As far as she could estimate, three days had passed. During that time, she'd received no food or water. She'd grown so thirsty that she searched out the little puddles remaining from Bula dousing her. She licked the water off the filthy, uneven stone floor and thanked God for it.

The lack of nourishment only heightened the exquisite pain the damp cold produced in her muscles, her fingers, her feet. She began to wonder if this was how Sayed would end her. A slow, painful freezing death. Alone.

He doesn't know that I'm not alone. He doesn't know that I have you, Jesus.

Laynie sat on the slatted bench, blanket clasped around her, counting off leg lifts and singing aloud to herself.

She didn't hear the key rattle in her cell's lock or the gate swing open. She looked up, and there was Bula. Observing. Listening.

The half-smile she offered him was part relief and part ironic humor. "Hello, Bula."

He stared around the empty cell. Perplexed.

Did you think I'd be dead? Perhaps you expected to find a gibbering idiot. Think again.

It was obvious he had not expected singing.

Laynie's voice was ragged and dry from lack of water, but she had sung and then whispered the same songs again and again—surprised when her mind defaulted to old hymns, more surprised that many of the verses to the church songs she'd learned as a child came back so easily.

She had sung until her voice gave out. Then, each time she thought her voice was completely gone, she would rest it for a while and it would come back, still rough, but functional.

Bula gestured behind him, and "Not Alyona" crept into the cell. She clutched a bundle of clothing in her shaking arms. Her soft brown eyes, the only exposed part of her face, were wide and fearful. Perhaps she, too, had expected to find Laynie dead or close to it.

Unexpectedly, Bula withdrew from the cell, leaving the girl with Laynie. The girl offered the bundle of clothes and mimed that Laynie should dress herself.

Laynie would have, but her fingers were stiff from the cold, dehydration, and lack of nourishment.

Since she knew the girl understood at least a little Russian, she asked, "Please. Will you help me?"

Glancing over her shoulder toward the barred entrance, she nodded and then whispered through the veil's fabric, "*Da*."

She held up a stocking and gestured for Laynie to lift her left foot. When she picked up Laynie's foot, she muttered something disapproving under her breath. She began to rub Laynie's foot between her hands.

"Ohhh . . ." The warmth radiating from the girl's hands was marvelous—until her gentle massage revived feeling in Laynie's toes. As blood rushed to them, Laynie flinched and moaned.

With a little grunt of understanding, the girl stopped rubbing and drew on the clean stocking, then pulled the sandal onto Laynie's foot. She repeated the same with Laynie's right foot—gently massaging it first until Laynie could stand it no longer. Then she helped Laynie don a clean shift and an abaya. Although she still shivered, Laynie immediately felt warmth coming back into her limbs.

Her hair, however, was a matted mess. The girl sniffed it and shook her head.

"Yeah, not much I can do about that," Laynie muttered in English.

The girl jerked at the sound of the unfamiliar words.

Laynie switched back to Russian. "Thank you for your kindness to me. May I . . . may I ask your name?"

She again glanced toward the cell gate. Softly, she answered, "I am Ksenia."

"Ksenia. It is a beautiful name."

Ksenia's eyes filled with tears.

"I-I am sorry," Laynie whispered.

Ksenia shook her head. She wiped her face on her sleeve and turned away.

"Wait." Laynie touched her hand. "Ksenia, thank you again for your kindness to me. My name . . . my name is Laynie. I want you to know . . . you are not alone."

Ksenia stared at Laynie's hand on hers. She wiped away more tears.

Then she was gone.

Bula returned. He studied Laynie for several minutes. Laynie, in turn, studied him back.

"You broke General Sayed's fingers," Bula said.

"He tried to drug me. Then he slapped me."

"He will kill you for embarrassing him."

"I understand."

"But first, he will debase you in ways you cannot imagine."

"Not until his fingers heal, he won't."

Bula grunted. Laynie wasn't certain, but she thought—imagined?—that the ghost of a smile touched his mouth.

The truth was, Laynie recognized the numerous and unimaginable horrors Sayed could inflict on her, either personally or at his command. Hadn't she witnessed his ugly, volatile temper? But she sensed that, for some hidden reason, he had curbed his normal inclinations.

The brute should have killed me for humiliating him publicly, but he held back. His restraint has to mean something. I must provide some strategic benefit to him, something I know nothing about. Whatever it is, Lord? I am grateful.

Laynie added, "I would rather die knowing I had done all I could to preserve my dignity and honor before God and man."

She saw a tiny, reluctant nod.

"I must agree. The honor of a man and his family rests upon a woman's virtue, and so she should fight to preserve it—although, once her virtue has been taken, there is no restoring it."

"With respect, as a woman loved by God, I know differently. The Lord my God *has* restored my virtue."

Bula laughed under his breath. "You are a strange one."

He left Laynie, locking the gate behind him.

LATER, A GUARD DELIVERED a plate of food and a jug of water to her. She devoured everything on the plate, all of it. She sipped water between bites, trying to slow down and make the food last but failing at it.

The guard returned to take away the plate. He also removed the bucket in the corner and replaced it with an empty one. The empty one didn't smell any better than the full one. In fact, because it and the residue within it were warmer than the temperature in her cell, the stink was noticeable.

As Laynie relieved herself in the bucket, the smell started to get to her, and the food in her stomach lurched. She held her breath until she finished, then returned to the bench. When she was certain she would keep the food she'd downed, she began to warm up her muscles.

You have to ignore the smell. Keep the food in your stomach. It's time for another set of exercises and stretches.

She told herself that the odor of the bucket would lessen as its temperature cooled, but the niggle of a complaint lifted its head in Laynie's heart. *Why do I—*

No. Don't do it. Don't go there. Don't allow that thought even the smallest toehold, Laynie.

Laynie lay on her back on the bench and counted sit-ups. She reached inside her heart and retrieved a passage of scripture. Recited it aloud.

But we have this treasure in jars of clay
to show that this all-surpassing power
is from God and not from us.
We are hard pressed
on every side, but not crushed;
perplexed, but not in despair;
persecuted, but not abandoned;
struck down, but not destroyed.
We always carry around in our body
the death of Jesus,
so that the life of Jesus
may also be revealed in our body.
For we who are alive are always
being given over to death for Jesus' sake,
so that his life may also be revealed
in our mortal body.

"Jars of clay, Lord. Jars of clay." She managed twenty-five sit-ups before she rested, repeating the same lines out loud, over and over.

"Lord Jesus, I pray that your life in me will be revealed through my body, this vessel of breakable clay . . . even while it is being given over to death for your sake."

CHAPTER 20

SAYED VIEWED HIS NEWLY arrived guest from under hooded eyes. "I did not expect you until well after the New Year. Until after the Hammer of Allah had fallen upon the Americans' heads."

His guest nodded, properly respectful. "I apologize. However, I had reason to believe that my cover was blown. I could have run and hidden for a time, but if I had been captured, I may have been forced to give up valuable information. I deemed it better to come a little early than risk capture."

He grunted. "You may be right—and perhaps you will be of assistance to me concerning the American operative."

"I wish to serve, Sayed. How may I help?"

Sayed sat back and stroked his chin with his uninjured hand. "The woman is strong. She has both a strong body and an obstinate and recalcitrant spirit."

His guest laughed softly. "I assume you did not blacken your own eyes."

Sayed shot a withering glare across the table. "She had the temerity to say I could not humble her. Some nonsense about having already humbled herself before her God and, therefore, I could not. It . . . momentarily distracted me and, in that moment of distraction, she broke two fingers and my nose. I would have had Bula snap her neck on the spot, but as she is the key to our final attack, I am temporarily constrained.

"I cannot kill her until my use for her is at an end—nor can I damage her so much that I cannot retrieve the information I need. Unfortunately, having witnessed her strength of will, I believe we would need to bring her to the point of death before she breaks—and even then, she might choose death rather than give me what I need. I must find a more effective means of obtaining the information."

"Ah. I see. You planned to debase her sexually until you'd crushed her spirit." His guest offered a cunning smile. "Would you be open to suggestions?"

Sayed seemed hopeful for the first time since his guest had joined him. "Suggestions? Indeed I would."

IN THE SPACE OF ONLY a few days, the task force had risen to victory and crashed in defeat. With Rosenberg's escape, the celebration for saving

Sherman's wife and son and ridding Wolfe's organization of its two moles now tasted like ashes.

Tobin stationed himself by the gym door as the team dragged themselves inside the next morning and helped themselves to coffee or tea. He was watching for Jaz. By 8:30, it was starting to look like she wasn't going to show.

"Anyone see Jaz?"

Vincent said, "Not since yesterday when . . . you know."

"And she skipped dinner. What about last night?"

Gwyneth, Jaz's roommate, said softly, "She never came to bed. I figured . . . I figured she just needed to be alone for a while, except . . ."

"Except what?"

"When I woke up this morning, she wasn't there and she hadn't slept in her bed."

Tobin grimaced. "All right, I'll go look for her. In the meantime? We, as a team, have a choice to make. Do we fold up? Give in to despair and quit? Or do we soldier on? Don't forget, there's a whole lot of hurt headed down the pipeline for New Year's Eve—exactly two weeks from today."

He put his hands on his hips and addressed six members of the task force who'd showed up to work. "None of us dreamed we'd ever see Jaz crack, but it goes to prove that even the toughest of us can break. That's why *a team* is so important, why the strength of the team is *not* in any individual, but in the whole. That 'gestalt' business Bella laid on us."

He lifted his chin toward Vincent. "You're doing a bang-up job of organizing the task force's findings, keeping us centered and focused on the holes in the data, so this is what I'd like the six of you to do. Walk through every assumption to date. Look at each bullet point like it's the first time you've seen it. Talk through how you got there—make certain you haven't glossed over anything and jumped to an unsubstantiated conclusion. Poke holes and then plug them. Can you do that?"

Vincent looked around, uncertain of his teammates. "Guys? Ladies?"

A dispirited Rusty shrugged. "Sure, Marshal Tobin. We can do that."

"Good. Get to it. I'll hunt down Jaz."

TOBIN LEFT THE GYM AND headed for the house. He'd gone through all the possible hiding places on the grounds. Unless Jaz had bedded down with the horses, that left only one place where she might be.

He took the stairs to the second floor bedrooms and stopped in front of Bella's room. Seraphim had taken the second bed until she left Broadsword with Wolfe. That left the room empty. He tried the door handle.

Locked.

"Hey Jaz? It's Tobin. Open up, please."

"Go away."

"Nope. We have work to do."

No response.

"Jaz, the task force is assembled in the bullpen. They are working. You don't have any right to sit on your butt up here while they are carrying on."

He heard a rustle. Then the door cracked open. A bleary, black-smeared eye peered out.

"For your information, I haven't been sitting on my butt."

"Have you been working?"

"No, but—"

"No, *but?* Point carried. No sitting on your big 'buts.' Everybody has them. No one gets to rest on them. *You* don't get to give up because of them. Wash your face, change your clothes, and get cracking, missy. People are counting on you."

That one bloodshot eye blinked back a tear.

"I blew it, Tobin."

"And you're not used to 'blowing it,' right?"

"Well . . ."

"How *fortunate* for you that you lead such a perfect life. The rest of us slugs blow it on a regular basis—and we still get up in the morning and push on. Stop feeling sorry for yourself. Think of someone other than yourself for a change."

"I—"

But Tobin had stomped off and was halfway down the stairs.

WHEN JAZ SLUNK INTO THE gym an hour later, the team was debating another of Rusty's impassioned theories. When they looked her way, she waved at Rusty to continue.

"That's what I'm telling you—I've changed my mind. I don't think AGFA is manufacturing fentanyl," he insisted.

"But you were the one who said they were in the first place!" It was Brian, the volume of his retort rising with each word.

"Well, like Tobin asked, I've been punching holes in my own assumptions, and a bunch of stuff doesn't quite add up."

"What doesn't add up?" Jaz asked. She plunked herself into her seat, her face a careful mask.

"Gee. Glad you could make it, Jaz," Brian sneered.

"Yeah, sorry about that. Had to look up the meaning of the word 'loser.' I was unfamiliar with it."

Jubaila snickered. "Unfamiliar territory, you mean."

Soraya deadpanned, "And it took you twenty-four hours, did it?"

"Yah. Had to slog through pages and pages of Brian's face popping up under the definition."

"Hey!"

Jaz finally cracked a smile. It was a sad and tired little smile, but sincere. "Just kidding, Brian. What I really mean to say—to all of you—is I'm sorry. Had me . . . a humbling moment. I . . . apologize for bailing on the team."

"Are you back, then? Are you with us?" Vincent asked.

"Yup. I'm all here. Heart and soul. Now, what about the fentanyl, Rusty?"

"I don't think AGFA is manufacturing it."

"That was pretty much our whole underlying assumption, Rusty. And didn't Cossack affirm our assumption?"

"Yes, he did. And if AGFA isn't making the stuff, how are they paying the mob?" Soraya asked.

"Didn't say they aren't paying the mob with fentanyl. I said I don't think they are *making it* themselves. And for the record? Cossack didn't say AGFA was making fentanyl for the mob. He said they were *providing* it to the mob—as well as using it in their New Year's Eve attacks."

"Explain the difference," Jaz asked. "And start at the beginning for us slow learners."

Rusty chuckled. "Right. Okay. At the beginning, when we infiltrated the jihadi chatrooms in Kazakhstan and started monitoring them, we picked up significant chatter about lab equipment. Based on the type of equipment, we deduced it could be used to manufacture drugs. From there, we developed the assumption that AGFA had recruited some unemployed former Soviet chemical scientists and was standing up a fentanyl lab. Cossack's intel, smuggled to us inside not-Bella's casket, confirmed the use of fentanyl."

"With you so far. What's changed?"

"Well, my thinking has. See, fentanyl is much more potent than heroin. If I were a drug dealer, I'd buy a bunch of fentanyl, mix it with the heroin and, *voilà*—instant increase in profit.

"But then I kept coming back to fentanyl's lethality. I mean, I'd have to be super careful how I mix it with the heroin, right? Because, *gee whiz*, I don't want to kill my customers, right? Bad for business.

"So, I figured that, in order to double my profits, I'd have to first cut the heroin with some harmless powder that doesn't change the heroin's appearance or the size of the dose I'm selling. The ratios would look like this."

Rusty went to a white board and wrote, *1 kilo heroin + 1 kilo HP = 2 kilos street product.* "HP means harmless powder."

Brian sniped at him. "Glad, you can add, Rusty. I'm impressed."

"Shut it, Brain Dead. I'm making a point."

"And we'd all like you to get there sometime *today*," Tobin said from the sidelines. He was on his feet, pacing back and forth behind the bullpen.

"All right. Then, say *you* are the dealer. How much fentanyl will you add to two kilos of this street product to give it the same kick as one kilo of pure heroin—*without* killing anyone?

As one, the team's eyes turned to another board where Rusty had previously taken a penny from his pocket, taped it to the board, and touched the tip of an erasable marker three times to the board next to the penny.

The penny was still taped to the board, three dots signifying a lethal dose of fentanyl adjacent to it.

"Not very blessed much," Brian breathed.

"You're right. The entire two kilos of street product would require only one grain of fentanyl per dose on the street."

"That makes the margin of error really, really small," Jubaila whispered.

"Yeah, I've crunched the numbers, but I won't bore you with the math. Bottom line? Twenty kilos of fentanyl carefully added to heroin cut with an equal amount of harmless filler totals *twenty million* doses on the street. Twenty million hits *doubling* the profits of the entire American branch of the Ukrainian mob from New York down to Florida and wherever else they have their hooks into the heroin trade."

Tobin had jumped ahead to Rusty's conclusion. "We get how easily someone could OD on a fentanyl-heroin mix, but that's not what you're getting at, Rusty, is it?"

"No, it isn't. What I'm saying is that twenty kilos of fentanyl would satisfy the mob's needs for six months, maybe a year." He looked at the team. "So why would AGFA set up an entire lab just to make a mere twenty kilos of fentanyl?"

"Don't forget the fentanyl they need for the New Year's Eve attacks," Brian said, his doubt still evident.

Rusty shook his head. "Still can't imagine them manufacturing their own."

"They wouldn't." That was Tobin. "Wouldn't be anywhere close to cost effective. They could buy as much as they need for thousands less—if they had a supplier."

Rusty jumped back in. "That's exactly what I'm saying. AGFA needs *some* fentanyl, but they don't need so much that they would go into the business of making it."

"Then what's the lab equipment for?" Soraya asked.

Tobin left off prowling the back of the bullpen and joined Rusty and Vincent at the front.

"I haven't been a contributor to the team like the rest of you have been, but I do know a little bit about the drug trade from my years with the US Marshals. That said, because AGFA has purchased equipment consistent with manufacturing drugs, we can assume that they are manufacturing *something*.

"However, Rusty's calculations have convinced me that it's unlikely the 'something' is fentanyl—meaning our first assumption has changed."

Heads slowly nodded.

"Since our first assumption is now 'AGFA is procuring fentanyl' rather than making it, I suggest that we validate that assumption by *proving* that they're buying it."

Vincent grabbed a marker and started a bullet point. "Got it. Find the point of sale?"

"Yes. Then we need to ask ourselves, what *are* they manufacturing in that lab? Because whatever it is? In my book, it has to tie to their next attack, has to be essential to it. And if we figure out what they're making, we can extrapolate the nature of the attack."

"Well, they can't make whatever 'it' is from nothing. They would need chemicals—the right chemicals," Gwyneth said, "and they'd have to buy them on the black market."

Amid excited chatter, Vincent added another bullet. "Identify chemicals bought."

Jaz brought the team to order. "Okay, everyone. We have new lines of investigation, and we know what we need to do. Soraya, Jubaila, Gwyneth? We need the list of chemicals AGFA has bought. If we have a list, we should be able to extrapolate what witches' brew AGFA is concocting.

"Brian and Rusty? You're with me. If AGFA bought fentanyl, they had a supplier. The list of fentanyl manufacturers open to selling in bulk is a short one, and the Chinese manufacture it on the cheap, so I'm betting on them. Unfortunately for us, their cybersecurity is as vicious and paranoid as a junkyard dog—meaning we need to be extra careful and extra sneaky."

"Wait." It was Brian.

"What?"

He wrestled with an emerging thought. "Just . . . if the Chinese manufacture cheap fentanyl, why do the Ukrainians need AGFA? Why doesn't the mob buy it direct from the Chinese?"

All eyes turned to Jaz.

"Good question with a simple answer—competition. The US Russian and Ukrainian mobs are locked in mortal competition with the Chinese for the North American drug market. The Hong Kong triads have most of Canada and the US west coast sewn up and are encroaching on Russian and Ukrainian mob territory. The Chinese won't knowingly provide an edge to the Ukrainians by selling them fentanyl."

"But they'll sell to AGFA?"

"As long as they don't know that AGFA is passing it on to the US Ukrainian mob."

"Got it. We need to find AGFA's Chinese supplier."

"And once we've identified the supplier, finding AGFA's order should be relatively easy. She ended on a note of determination. "When we have their order, we'll follow the money right to them."

CHAPTER 21

WITH FOOD IN HER STOMACH, Laynie slept well that night. When she woke, she was hungry again and hoped one of the soldiers would bring her another meal soon. When the gate clanged open, the rumble in Laynie's belly became a demanding roar.

It wasn't one of the soldiers. It was Bula, and the cold look on his face told Laynie breakfast wasn't on today's menu. She noted how he kept one hand behind his back.

"Get up."

Laynie stood. Bula pulled his hand from behind his back. In it was a rope.

No. A leash.

"Do not fight me on this," he warned her. "I will not hesitate to break your arm."

Laynie looked down, indecision fogging her sight. Then the stones beneath her feet came into focus.

I have licked water from these filthy stones—and it does not matter. My standing before you, God Almighty, has not changed. Lord, I humble myself under your mighty hand. In due season you will lift me up.

But she was tired. Cold and hungry.

In due season? Lord, when is "due season?"

The answer hummed in her spirit.

It is when I declare it to be, my daughter.

"All right," Laynie murmured. "Due season it is."

She straightened. "Whatever happens, I have determined to conduct myself in a manner worthy of the gospel of Christ."

Bula cocked his head. "What are you saying?"

"Oh. Sorry. I was not talking to you."

She held out her hands. Bula slipped a knotted loop over them, crossed her wrists and snugged the loop to bind them together. Then he unwound the veils from her head and tossed them aside.

"If you do not wish to be jerked off your feet and dragged, you will keep up with me."

He set off, tugging her through the narrow passageway. The passageway curved, and the number of electric bulbs increased. The light grew brighter. Then they reached the junction where the tunnel widened, and she recognized it, the domed cavern on her right, the long tunnel straight ahead eventually reaching the mine cars.

But Bula jerked the leash and pulled her down the passageway to the left. To Sayed's quarters. The same guards stood at the entrance to Sayed's lavish salon and swept the heavy curtain aside. Eyed her as she passed. She stood tall and held her chin up. Stared straight ahead.

Sayed's salon was empty except for Sayed, his servant in the far corner, and a figure shrouded in glistening veils seated next to Sayed. Bula led Laynie to the low table. He again forced her to kneel across the table from Sayed.

Laynie sank to her knees, keeping her expression a perfect mask but her eyes fixed on Sayed. His nose was swollen and distorted, the skin around both eyes a vivid kaleidoscope of blues and purples. Two fingers of his right hand were splinted and taped together.

The sight of her handiwork sparked a thrill of gratification in her flesh.

Sorry, Lord.

She glanced down at the table. On it were the remains of a sumptuous breakfast—figs, almonds and pistachios, breads, creamy butter, scrambled eggs, fresh chopped tomatoes, pickled herring. At the sight, her body trembled with hunger.

Out of her peripheral vision, she inventoried the woman seated to the left of Sayed. Laynie took in the beautiful kaftan of blue shot with silver thread and a hijab of expensive, shimmering blue fabric. The woman had drawn the tail of her headscarf across the lower part of her face. All Laynie's once-over told her was that the woman was short and dark skinned.

Sayed spoke. "You have information I want—the location of your so-called task force."

A short laugh slipped from Laynie's mouth. "I thought we'd covered this topic."

Bula slapped her from behind, and Laynie's ears rang.

"I will ask you again. I warn you—if you do not give me a credible response, you will live to regret it. *Give me the location of the task force.*"

"No."

Laynie waited for Sayed to speak—to rant or rage at her. Instead the woman greeted her.

"It does my heart good to see you again at last . . . *Magda.*"

Laynie kept her expression passive and did not flinch. But inside? Her heart ached and throbbed, each pounding beat threatening to burst from her chest. She could not swallow. Could not breathe.

And then sweat broke out on her brow and dribbled into her eyes, down her nose, onto her upper lip.

Gupta.

LAYNIE COULDN'T CALM HER mind, make it grasp what she was seeing. "You. You were the mole in Wolfe's organization. All along, it was you?"

Gupta tugged the scarf aside from her face so Laynie could see her triumphant smile. "Why yes, of course it was me, and I did play a superb game, didn't I? Had you and Wolfe chasing your tail for months?"

She chuckled. "It is amazing the level of clearance given to me, a trusted in-house psychiatrist, and the depth of confidential information I was granted when I requested it—all in order to better understand and treat my Marstead patients, those whose minds hold vast operational secrets."

Laynie's thoughts raced through every event and problem since she was introduced to the task force, plugging Gupta into the blanks and question marks—Gupta's behind-the-scene machinations to have herself assigned as Laynie's counselor. Her subtle attempts to coax Laynie into talking about the task force and their assignment. The "bugs" planted in the hotel suite after Ruth took over Laynie's counseling. The Ukrainian mob's assassination team and their hit on the apartments—their attempts to execute Tobin and Laynie and take Jaz. The car bomb in the hospital parking lot that had nearly killed Seraphim, had almost cost Tobin a kidney.

Yet the only reason we were in that parking lot in the first place was to visit Gupta after she was . . .

"You had your own men beat you to a pulp. You acted the role of victim to remove yourself from suspicion."

Gupta couldn't restrain her smirking pleasure. "What is a little transient pain when compared to our future great gain?"

"What future great gain might that be?"

"Nice try, Magda."

Laynie watched Gupta smile on Sayed and his nod of amiable agreement.

"It was you who laid the ambush for us in that hospital parking lot. To draw us into a kill box."

"Well, there was *that*." She giggled a little, and Sayed smiled indulgently.

"I am confused by one thing."

Gupta, enjoying herself immensely, played along. "Are you? Oh, let me see if I can guess. Is it how I could be a follower of the Prophet? Blessed be his name."

Her smirk widened. "Dear me. How shortsighted, parochial, and utterly unimaginative you are—and always have been, Magda. Am I the only woman of Indian and Hindi extraction to convert to Islam? Not at all. I proclaimed *shahada* decades ago—and served Allah inside of Wolfe's organization even before he rose to the directorship. But neither he nor you, with your narrow, biased mindset, could see what was right before your eyes."

Gupta placed something on the table, but Laynie didn't look away from the woman. She couldn't keep herself from staring at Gupta's raw evil and marveling at how effectively she'd masked it . . . for years.

"I did so try to warn you, Magda. Remember? *We are all the products of our choices—some are, admittedly, considerations made for the good of the many. There's no shame in that.* I told you what I was, that I had chosen the good of Allah's will, but you did not listen."

Something in the woman shifted. "And how did you reward me?" Gupta's eyes narrowed. Her swarthy complexion flushed red with hatred. "You struck me. Knocked me over—and everyone heard of it. *You humiliated me.*"

Laynie mimicked Gupta. "Awww, what's a little transient pain when compared to your future great gain?"

Bula was standing close behind Laynie. When Sayed lifted his chin, Bula slapped Laynie across the back of her head. Laynie swayed. Her ears rang. She slowly shook her head. Blinked her dripping eyes to clear them.

Gupta smiled her thanks on Sayed, then returned her attention to Laynie.

"What an impudent, prideful mouth you have, Magda. So full of yourself! But at this point we should concentrate on satisfying General Sayed's interests. Why, just yesterday, he confided in me how very much he wished to see you humbled. I told him I would dearly like the opportunity to do so. After all, you humiliated me. Shouldn't I repay the debt?"

She giggled again, and Sayed laughed aloud.

"Wait," Laynie interjected. "I . . . Gupta, I see how you look at Sayed. You are infatuated with him, with his leadership and importance, aren't you? You have visions of a happily-ever-after ending? A high position in his council? Perhaps something more intimate? But it's not going to happen. He doesn't see you the way you see him, because women have no value in his worldview. To him you are merely a useful tool. That is all."

Gupta frowned and slanted an uncertain look in Sayed's direction. He, too, frowned but was quick to pat Gupta's hand.

"Pay her no mind, Halima."

At Sayed's signal, Bula moved—quicker than Laynie could react. He jerked the rope binding Laynie's wrists up to her chest and looped it around her shoulders. Startled, Laynie resisted, but Bula had already pinned her arms to her sides. She tried to launch herself to her feet—he slammed her back onto her knees. He wound the rope around her torso once more, threw his knee into Laynie's back as leverage to cinch the rope tighter, then twined the rope around Laynie's feet and tied it off.

Abruptly, Laynie stopped struggling.

Whatever was coming, she could not stop it. Could not prevent it.

Laynie, my daughter. I am here.

"Thank you, Lord," she whispered. "Now and forever, I am yours."

Gupta picked up the item she'd placed on the table. It gleamed.

"I told General Sayed that humbling a woman such as you required another woman's insight and touch. Your hair? It's been your glory all your life. Let it now be your shame."

Gupta stood. "Drag her into the middle of the room, please. Yes. Just there, on the drop cloth. Too bad her hair is such a ratted mess. I would have liked it to shine and look its best. Ah, well. Is the video camera ready? Yes? Excellent."

Sayed's servant trained a camcorder on Laynie. Gupta stood to Laynie's side . . . with a large pair of scissors.

"I am Halima bint Abra, Halima, daughter of Abra Gupta. We humble this *kafir* woman, this blasphemer of the Prophet—blessed be his name—this filthy woman who has played the harlot with many men in her service to the Great Satan. She has plotted to thwart the will of Allah and the establishment of his caliphate across this land. At the appropriate time, when her use in Allah's work is ended, we will end *her*. In the manner she deserves.

"Today, however, we make this statement to the world: Those who oppose the will of Allah will suffer defeat and humiliation as she does—this woman who has spied upon the Great Satan's enemies as the imposter, *Linnéa Olander*, and, more recently, in another false identity, *Anabelle Garineau*."

Gupta opened the shears wide. Slowly, so slowly, Gupta drew the length of the outer blade across Laynie's cheek, letting her feel the weight of the cold steel, allowing the cutting edge to lightly score her cheek. Gupta ran the blade diagonally across her lips, drawing a fine line of blood. Then Gupta grasped a thick hank of Laynie's hair from the crown of her head and held it high to demonstrate its length. At Laynie's hairline, Gupta began to saw through the hair.

Lord, even my hair? I must surrender that?

Did I hold anything back, my daughter?

Laynie sighed. *No, Lord.*

When long strands began to float to the floor, Laynie said aloud, "I proclaim that Jesus is the Christ, my Lord and Savior."

"No! Stop the camera. I want that edited out." Gupta moved in front of Laynie and slapped her across the mouth. "Do not speak again."

Gupta returned to Laynie's side. "Resume recording." She didn't pick up another strand, She simply began at Laynie's forehead and cut at the root line whatever hair the points of the scissors fed into their blades, letting the tips stab and dig at Laynie's scalp first.

Laynie shouted. "For God so loved the world, that he gave his only begotten Son, Jesus!"

Gupta slapped her twice and continued cutting.

Hair fell down Laynie's face and onto the floor. She saw it lying on the drop cloth in chunks, strands, and chopped bits.

Whatever happens, I have determined to conduct myself in a manner worthy of the gospel of Christ.

Laynie licked blood from her lips. Took a breath. Stared into the camera. "At the name of Jesus every knee will bow, in heaven and on earth and under the earth, and every tongue will acknowledge that Jesus Christ is Lord, to the glory of God—"

As soon as Laynie began speaking, Gupta walked to the table and returned with a stone ashtray. Making certain the camera would capture her actions, she slammed the ashtray into Laynie's mouth.

Laynie's head snapped back.

When she came to herself, Bula was holding her upright, and Gupta was cutting her hair. Laynie blinked against the pain in her mouth. Her eyes strayed to the large mound of matted blond hair now piled on the drop cloth.

Must have been out . . . a while.

Laynie spit out the blood pooling in her mouth. A tooth dropped into the pile of hair along with blood and saliva. Her mouth ached and throbbed.

For it has been granted to me on behalf of Christ not only to believe in him, but also to suffer for him . .

If Bula were to let her go, Laynie would have fallen over.

Thank you for Bula, Lord, that I might make my declaration for you.

Laynie looked directly into the camera.

"My name is . . . Beloved of God. I am the daughter of Yahweh, Creator and King of the Universe, the Ancient of Days, God Almighty.

"There is no God but Yahweh and Jesus his only begotten Son. I—"

AT GUPTA'S DIRECTION, Bula continued to hold Laynie's unconscious form upright. Gupta tipped Laynie's lolling head forward to cut the hair from the nape of her neck. It was the work of a few minutes more to shear the remainder of Laynie's hair from her head.

Gupta stood back and surveyed her work. Laynie's scalp was scored with little cuts and jabs, all bleeding. The ugly, uneven stubble left behind was the artistry of a madwoman.

"Very good. I see no need to shave her scalp and tidy things up," Gupta decided. "What I have left behind will further her disgrace."

She nodded to Sayed's servant. "You may stop recording."

Sayed stood. "I applaud you, Halima."

Gupta beamed under his praise.

Sayed said to Bula. "I wish her placed with the other *kafir* women now—but she is not to have a veil. Let the women see the punishment for rejecting Allah. It will be a good lesson to them all."

He had an idea and added, "I wish my soldiers to see her as she is. It is near the midday meal. Take her to the men. Parade her before them. Tell them that in a few days I will let them have her. In fact, let us hold a lottery for her. It will boost morale."

To Gupta he said, "Halima, you have done well, and I wish you to oversee editing of the video. Please accompany my servant to his work area. Send word when you are ready to show the final cut to me."

Gupta's face fell. "I . . ."

"Yes?"

"I had hoped to spend more time with you."

Sayed smiled. "Ah, but we must all do our part to see in the caliphate, mustn't we? When the video is ready for release, I will bestow a rich reward upon you. Do not worry. I have chosen an honor befitting your loyal service."

Gupta revived a little. "Thank you, Sayed. I will make certain the video is all you could wish for."

WHEN LAYNIE'S CONSCIOUSNESS finished its long climb up and out of darkness, Bula was dragging her through the tunnel junction on the leash. The rope tore at her wrists and strained her arms, pulling at her shoulder sockets. Her shoulder blades bumped painfully over sharp stone points and edges. When Bula slowed, her head struck rock.

Her head. She felt its cold nakedness.

Bula dragged her into the cavern and up and down between the tables where Sayed's soldiers were eating. Stolid expressions studied her. When Bula had their attention, he yanked on the leash, hauling Laynie up to sitting, stretching her arms over her head.

Letting them see the wares, Laynie thought. For a second time, she was grateful for the shapeless black abaya that covered her.

In that Chechen dialect Laynie did not know, Bula addressed the men. He emphasized a point by shaking her wrists, and the men cheered.

When he finished addressing the men, he dragged her away, down the narrow tunnel toward her cell . . . except he took an abrupt left-hand turn long before they reached it. The side tunnel did not go far. It widened dramatically and ended at a heavy, barred grate bolted across the width of the tunnel, from one wall to the other. Whatever lay beyond the bars disappeared into shadows. Bula lifted a key from a peg in the wall. He jerked Laynie over to the grate, unlocked a gate in it, and dragged her through.

Laynie heard rustling from the cave's darkness to her right, far into its depths. Bodies shifting away from Bula. From her.

Her nose twitched at the mingled odors of mildew and raw sewage. And campfire smoke?

Bula sat her up and held her hands in his while he teased open the loop around her wrists. He grunted as the loop loosened. He released her hands, and Laynie slumped sideways onto the floor.

"Do not move."

He need not have bothered with the warning. Laynie was too tired, worn, and damaged to move.

Bula stepped out of the cell. With the barred gate still open, he turned and stared at her. "In a few days, when you have healed, you will be given to the men. Sayed has decreed it. I have announced it."

She lifted her eyes to him. "Is this how godly men treat women of the Book?"

He didn't answer right away. When he did, it was with a pragmatic sigh. "No, but Halima bint Abra has testified that you are a whore for the Americans, a spy who seduces men. One cannot be both a whore and a woman of the Book."

"I *was* a whore," Laynie answered calmly. "I was like the woman in the Bible who wiped Jesus' feet with her tears—not merely a flawed, fallen individual, but a notorious sinner."

"I have not read about this woman."

Something in Laynie's throat made her gag. She brought up a wad of blood and spit it out. She ran her tongue around her mouth, found where Gupta's scissors had scored her lips, where the stone ashtray had struck her mouth and split it open. Felt the raw, empty socket where a canine was missing.

"That sinful woman came to Jesus—you call him Isa—in front of everyone. She came weeping and using her long hair to wipe his feet. The religious teachers knew who she was. What she was. They were upset when Jesus allowed her to touch him, that he didn't immediately send her away. They thought that if Jesus couldn't discern what kind of woman she was, then he surely wasn't the Messiah the people hoped him to be."

She looked up at Bula. "Of course he knew what she was—he is the Son of God! But because the woman approached him with penitent sorrow, he said to her, 'Your sins are forgiven.'"

Bula shook his head. "No. Such stains cannot be removed. They remain to this day."

"Perhaps in your eyes they do, but you are not God. You do not get to decide what he forgives. Only he does. This is how God's nature differs from ours—it is higher than ours. Jesus also said that day, 'Her sins, which are many, are forgiven, for she loved much. But whoever has been forgiven little, *loves little*.'"

Laynie swallowed a groan of pain. "I know what it means to be forgiven much, Bula. I was that woman, but I am not her any longer."

"One cannot become someone else simply by wishing or choosing it."

"You are right. *I* did not change who I am. Jesus did. He said I could be born again by the Holy Spirit. In that moment when I was born of the Spirit, the woman I once was died. She was buried, never to rise again. I am a new woman, a new creation made clean in Christ. All my sins are gone—as far as the east is from the west. I stand before God pure and holy, with no stain from my past upon me."

He considered what she said and shrugged. "Then I am sorry for you, because you will be well used in the coming days. I doubt your God will be able to look upon you after that."

"Jesus said he would never leave me. He said he would never forsake me."

"And yet it seems he has. Do not your circumstances prove how powerless your Jesus is?"

Laynie shivered. The chillier air of the cell was working its way into her body. She lifted her hand, confused that her head seemed so cold . . . startled when her fingers encountered its rough, barren landscape.

Bula couldn't resist goading her. "If Isa loved you as you say he does, if he were who you say he is, would he have allowed you to suffer this indignity, this shame?"

An aching wave rippled across her body, and she laughed softly through gritted teeth. "A servant is not above his master, Bula. My Jesus suffered a greater indignity than this, and he did it willingly, *purposely*, knowing that his blood and only his blood could cleanse away my filth. *That* is real love. I am not afraid to suffer the indignities others do to me, because Jesus comforts me in my fear."

She looked up at him again. "Tell me something, Bula. Is Allah pleased with the sexual immorality practiced in these caves and tunnels? Is he pleased with men who have intercourse outside of marriage?"

Bula frowned and looked aside. "The men have needs."

"Oh? Does that excuse their sin? Where is 'the men have needs so it's all right if they fornicate' found in the Quran?"

Bula's mouth hardened in anger. "Do not presume to lecture me on morality!"

"Very well, but I offer you a warning instead: You should think before defiling a woman who belongs to Jesus. You should consider well what Jesus thinks of the man who harms one of his own—what he will do to that man."

Bula snorted with derision. "Oh, and are you one of his own? If you are, it seems he cares very little for you."

Laynie locked eyes with Bula. "I am sorry for you, Bula. Not long from now, you will stand before Jesus and give an account for what you have done in this place."

Laynie Portland
SPY RESURRECTED

PART 3:
I AM NOT ASHAMED

LP

Chapter 22

AT FIRST LIGHT, COSSACK and two hardy soldiers, experienced mountaineers and guides, both a decade or two younger than their revered general, departed the militia's stronghold. The three men wore webbed snowshoes in the shape of teardrops.

They carried packs containing food, water, and shelter, and they traveled single file, one of the guides always a few yards in the lead. The other guide took up the rear, which put Cossack in the safest position—between the two men. The lead guide broke trail for the others, dangerous and laborious work that compelled the guides to trade places every hour.

The grueling, punishing trek led upward into increasingly rugged terrain and deeper snow. Fatigue, physical and mental, was their greatest enemy. Fatigue tempted a man to be less observant and less careful—more apt to commit a fatal mistake. The guides knew all this and more. It was their duty to navigate Cossack through the mountain passage and all its perils. It was their responsibility to deliver him safely to the rendezvous point on the other side.

They did not speak of it—it was understood: Should one of the guides put a foot wrong or step into a hole and break a foot or leg, the other guide would lead Cossack on, leaving the injured guide to make his own way out of the mountains . . . or die trying. It was a brutal custom, but a necessary one if Cossack were to survive the crossing.

AFTER BULA LEFT HER, Laynie stretched out on the cold stone and let her head fall onto her arms to pillow it. Her mouth and face throbbed. Her scalp ached where her hair had been yanked and where scissor jabs stung and bled. Her wrists, shoulders, back, and the heels of her feet were scraped and bruised from being dragged through the tunnels. Blood clotted on her cheeks, lips, and inside her wounded mouth.

She couldn't process the pain without groaning.

"Lord, please help me."

I don't want to have run in vain. Please help me finish my race, Lord.

The book of Philippians opened to her, the four chapters she had devoured and memorized the weekend she'd been under house arrest . . . back in her apartment, right before the Ukrainian hit squad had tried to kill her and Tobin and abduct Jaz. As much as it hurt to form the words, Laynie forced her lips to speak aloud, to make her personal profession of faith, again and again until the separating line between the verses and her prayers faded, then merged.

"Oh my Jesus! I consider everything in my life loss because of the surpassing worth of knowing you. For your sake I willingly surrender it all. But I have actually lost nothing, Lord, because before I knew you, I *had* nothing.

"And I know my suffering is transient—that my true citizenship is in heaven—so I eagerly await you, my Savior, my Lord Jesus Christ, who, by the power that enables you to bring everything under your control, will transform my lowly body so that it will, in that day, be like your glorious body. All these things done to me will pass away. Someday soon, you will transform my lowly body into one like yours, Lord Jesus!"

She shivered and shook, the cold seeping into her bones, making every injured part throb, wracking her with pain. Tears flowed from her eyes, soaked her arms, ran onto the stones.

"O Lord, I love you. Please help me."

She vaguely heard rustling in the shadows behind her, footsteps that came near. A form stooped over her. Got on its knees and leaned toward her.

"Lay-nee. Oh, Lay-nee. What have they done to you?" A young woman's voice, a girl's voice, speaking broken Russian.

The compassionate words reached into Laynie's hurting heart. She sobbed once and opened her eyes. "Ksenia?"

The scarf Ksenia wore across her mouth before men was pulled down around her neck. Although the second scarf still bound her hair, Laynie saw all of Ksenia's face for the first time. A young face twisted in sorrow.

"What have they done to you? They cut off your beautiful hair, Lay-nee."

"I know, but I . . . cannot think on it, Ksenia. I mustn't."

Ksenia sniffed and wiped at her eyes. "Come, then. I have a mattress and blankets against the far wall. A fire of my own away from the others."

"Others?"

"The other *kafir* women. Come, Lay-nee."

Ksenia helped Laynie get up. With her help, Laynie hobbled away from the grate and into the recesses of the cave. It was far deeper than she'd realized. Although she could see little into its depths, she heard whispers, a few, then more, followed by shuffling feet moving toward them.

"What are they saying?"

"They want to know who you are. Where you come from."

"Oh."

She was soon confronted by other young women, all clad in abayas and niqabs, "Alyona" among them. While they studied Laynie, she studied them back—appalled.

These are the kafir *women? What these men consider women are mere girls! I don't see even one who could be older than sixteen or seventeen.*

Several of the girls pointed at her bare head. They clucked and hissed.

To be uncovered in this culture must be bad enough. To be shorn? Far worse.

One of the girls jabbed her finger toward Laynie and spoke roughly to Ksenia. Laynie might not have understood her words, but her tone and body language spoke well enough.

Others joined in.

It was clear that they didn't want Laynie near them—and their demands were increasing.

Ksenia stomped her foot and shouted back at them. Waved her fist at them. She pulled the scarf from around her neck and, gently, lifted it over Laynie's bare head where it settled.

To hide my shame from these women.

Laynie's eyes watered. She told herself it was because of the girl's selfless action. She wouldn't allow herself to think about the loss of her hair.

Oh, my hair!

No. I cannot allow myself to mourn it.

I count all things as loss, Lord.

Laynie wiped away her tears as Ksenia helped Laynie navigate the dark cave, heading farther back and to the left.

"Here. Sit here, Lay-nee."

Laynie sank down on a thin, mildewed mattress. She leaned back against the rock wall.

Ksenia added a few sticks to the fire in front of her mattress. She felt around and found a jug of water and held it to Laynie's lips.

Laynie took a sip—it stung her mouth and lips. "What is it?"

"Only water with a little vinegar mixed in. It is what they give us."

Ksenia moistened the tail of her scarf, then urged the jug again on Laynie. "Drink more while I wash the wounds on your head."

Laynie took a mouthful. Gritting her teeth against the sting, she swished the liquid around until the raw places calmed. She was able to drink again after her mouth had adjusted to it.

While Laynie sipped, Ksenia lifted her veil from Laynie's head and dabbed the vinegar water over her wounded scalp. She then tucked a blanket over Laynie's legs and feet.

"Ksenia, why are you over here by yourself and not with the others?"

"Oh. They are mostly Kurdish girls stolen from their homes in Iran, except the two from Azerbaijan. I am Yazidi. My family lived in the hills of Turkey, near Iraq."

"Why does this matter?"

Laynie felt rather than saw Ksenia shrug. “Except for myself, the others are Kurds, Muslims who are not of a sect the soldiers approve. I am of *Melek Taus*. The Kurds call the Yazidi devil worshippers. They will not associate with me unless the soldiers make them.”

Laynie was careful. “And . . . are you a devil worshipper?”

Ksenia shrugged again. “We have one god, but his name is not Allah. I do not think either god sees us. Or why would we be here?”

Softly, she added, “The others, they do not speak Russian as I do. I am the only one. I heard what you said to Bula.”

“What I said about Jesus?”

“Yes. He is your God?”

“He is.”

“I think Bula is right, Lay-nee. Jesus does not see you—any more than Allah or my God sees us.”

“He lives in me,” Laynie whispered. “I feel his presence. Hear him speak to me.”

“Maybe you are just crazy,” Ksenia suggested.

Laynie had to laugh, as much as it hurt her to. “I don’t think I’m crazy, but then again, do crazy people know they are crazy?”

Ksenia did not reply.

Laynie leaned against the wall, exhaustion overtaking her pain. She was drifting away when something roused her . . . Ksenia, keening softly. Seated beside Laynie, her hips against Laynie’s hips. Weeping. Holding her veil over Laynie’s bare head.

She is mourning for me. Over the shame of being shorn.

Laynie slept again.

IN THE PAST FORTY-EIGHT hours, Rusty, Brian, and Jaz had hacked every Chinese pharmaceutical and medical supply company they could identify, and they had failed to find any suspicious fentanyl orders. The orders they did find were well under six ounces and had been shipped legally through hazardous material carriers to various heart clinics or research institutes worldwide.

Frustrated, the three of them peeled off in separate directions, trying one line of investigation after another, in an attempt to find the source of AGFA’s fentanyl.

Late that afternoon, her face wearing a tight, triumphant smile, Jaz called out to the team. “Listen up, me hearties. I be the bringer o’ fine booty. Two things. First, I’ve found AGFA’s supplier.”

“Arrr! I could stand some good news, Cap’n,” Brian grumbled, “and I’m likin’ to savvy how you scored your booty—seeing as we had already scrubbed the records of every Chicom pharmaceutical and medical supply company out there.”

"Yah, this one's sneaky, I'll give them that. Here's how I did it. First, I wrote a special little worm that, when released into a company's inventory and order program, would sort orders for every given product in the past year—you know, all crutches in one pile, all hydrocodone in another, inhalers in a third.

"Once all orders were sorted by product, the program would compile and analyze the quantities of those orders and return a min, max, and mean. It would also return orders that exceeded the product's usual quantity parameters, flagging outliers on the high end. Well, I ran that program through the networks of every Chinese company on our list."

"And that got you AGFA's fentanyl purchase *how?*"

Jaz bestowed an arch look on Brian. "See, I wasn't focused only on fentanyl, was I? And if I were just a touch jaded, I'd say the employee who wrote up the order fabricated it. I mean, *really*, does a small animal clinic out in the boonies of Azerbaijan actually *need* fifteen thousand dollars' worth of x-ray film? Particularly when, after investigation, that clinic doesn't exist?"

"They hid the fentanyl purchase under another product name!"

"On the nose, Brain Pan. So then I found the payment for the so-called x-ray film and traced it. Electronic funds transferred *to* a bank in Hong Kong *from* a bank in Baku—and multiple points in between—in an attempt to hide the transaction's point of origin. A *vain* attempt, I might add."

Rusty jumped up. "You found AGFA's bank account? You tracked the money back to them?"

"Indeed I—"

Rusty swooped down on Jaz, yanked her from her chair, and spun her around, whooping it up as he did. Instantly, task force members were on their feet, laughing, shouting, dancing. Rusty pulled them into one huddled, bouncing group hug.

"You did it! You did it!" Gwyneth celebrated, grinning madly.

She stopped bouncing and pulled Jaz away from the hug fest. "Wait. You said you had two things. *First*, you found AGFA's supplier and the money trail."

Jaz slumped into her chair and answered, "Whew. Yah. First, the money trail—but I have more."

Rusty's bellow cut through the bedlam. "Everybody SHUT UP!"

The celebratory dance hit a wall and fell apart.

Soraya gasped, "What? What is it?"

"Jaz found more."

The team members regained their usual businesslike manners and turned to Jaz.

"Thank you, Gwynnie. First, the money trail. Second? The originating bank account in Baku—is registered to none other than one Mohammed Eldar Sayed."

"*Sayed?* No way," Rusty breathed.

Brian shook his head. "You telling me he used his real name to open that account? The daring leader of AGFA? What a dufus!"

"Yup. Stupid Criminals 101: Don't use your own name, Bonzo. Guess Sayed skipped that class or thought he could bury the payment in anonymizers. Anyway, as long as AGFA doesn't catch us at it, we can keep following the money into and out of the account, wherever it comes from and wherever it goes.

"Third, speaking of *into* the account, how does a hefty deposit of seventy-five thousand dollars from an account in the Cayman Islands just this week sound? An account, I might add, that belongs to a shell company, owned by another shell company, that's part of a consortium whose majority owner is an attorney for the US Ukrainian mob?"

Rusty lifted a hand.

"You don't have to raise your hand, Rusty. Remember?"

"Yeah, yeah, but something you said hit me like a brick to the head. The mob paid AGFA seventy-five thousand dollars? For what? A couple kilos of fentanyl AGFA bought for fifteen grand? Even with a stiff markup, that can't be right."

Jaz mused aloud to herself. "What, besides the fentanyl, would the mob pay AGFA for? What do the jihadis have that the mob needs?"

Task force members furrowed their brows and sat down. Gwyneth and others put their heads together, whispering, seeking an answer that fit.

Jaz was mulling the same questions when she became aware of the silence growing around her. She glanced up to find her teammates' attention studiously fixed elsewhere.

Anywhere but at her.

"What? What's going on?"

"*Think*, Gwyneth whispered. "The mob overpaid AGFA for the fentanyl, right? Well, what else do the jihadis have? They have *Bella*. That's what the rest of the money was for. The mole told AGFA that Bella was headed to Tbilisi. AGFA called the mob and cut a deal with them. To snatch her. *To make it look like she died*."

"Why? What does she know that the mob would pay—" Jaz's protests died in her mouth. "She knows me. Where I am, and . . ."

"And that you arranged for the feds to confiscate the mob's financial records," Tobin finished. "*You*. You're what the mob paid for in return for the rest of the money, and Bella can tell them where to find you."

Jaz's gorge rose in her throat. "But that would mean . . ."

"That if AGFA is torturing Bella, it's to get your location? I'm sorry, Jaz, but that's what it means."

He hustled toward the door, then stopped. "It also means we need to warn Richard. If AGFA has gotten what they want from Bella and conveyed it to the Ukrainians, an attack on Broadsword could be imminent."

LAYNIE WOKE A WHILE later to a stirring in the cave. Voices. Footsteps. Moments later, Ksenia sat down beside her. She had two jugs of water and two plates.

"Lay-nee. Here is food and your own jug of water."

The plate Ksenia handed to her held a fat slice of bread and a serving of warm rice topped with gravy of some kind. Laynie again rinsed her mouth with vinegar water to disinfect it and soothe its sting. Then she used her fingers to shovel rice and gravy into her mouth. The gravy, she thought, had bits of lamb or goat in it. It hurt to chew the warm food, but Laynie's stomach rejoiced.

"Soon," Ksenia said between bites, "they will take us to the soldiers. We will be gone until late tonight."

"Will I go, also?"

"Not yet. The men who bring our food said in two nights. They said . . ." her words trailed off.

"They said what?" Laynie prompted Ksenia.

"They said . . . the soldiers are picking numbers for you. To be first on the list. Even though your hair . . . is gone."

"I see."

They finished eating in silence. Ksenia took their empty plates to the grate. When she returned, she helped Laynie to her feet.

"Come. I will show you where to relieve yourself."

They walked toward the grate. By the light shining from the other side, Ksenia pointed to the wall on the right. They walked to the wall, passing a large bundle of sticks for the women's fires. They followed the wall away from the grate, into the shadows to a pair of foul-smelling five-gallon buckets.

Laynie saw that a branch of the cave meandered from the buckets into the dark. With her hand on the wall to guide her, she began to walk that way to stretch her legs. To learn the boundaries of her new cell.

She had gone several yards when Ksenia grabbed her abaya and stopped her mid-stride. "No. Do not go back there."

"What is there?"

"A deep hole. An empty cistern. If you fall into it, you may break your legs." While they walked back to Ksenia's mattress, she added, "If one of us does not submit herself to a soldier, if she persists in displeasing him, Bula will have the soldiers drop her into the cistern."

Laynie swallowed. "I see. And . . . what becomes of the woman?"

"It depends. If she repents and begs them to pull her out, they do. Sometimes. If they do not pull her out, they let her die there."

"Are there bodies in the cistern now?"

"No. After a week or so, Bula makes them remove the dead woman. He does not want disease, you see. We are not very clean here. Neither are the soldiers. Disease in this place would spread very rapidly."

They reached Ksenia's mattress, and Laynie asked, "Is it all right if I sleep on your mattress while you are gone?"

"Yes, certainly. I . . . I am glad you are here, Lay-nee—not that I wish you to be in this awful place. But . . . the day you spoke to me, you said, 'I want you to know you are not alone, Ksenia.' You did not know how long I have been here. Alone."

She coughed to hide her emotions. "I am glad, you see, to have someone to talk to. Someone who is . . . kind."

"I am glad I can be here with you, Ksenia."

Laynie reached her hand toward Ksenia. The girl grabbed it and held it to her cheek, sobbing softly.

LATER, LAYNIE HEARD A stirring from the girls on the other side of the cave. "It is time," Ksenia said, releasing Laynie's hand. "We will return in four or five hours."

Laynie touched the girl. "Ksenia. Can you . . . can you ask one of the men what day it is?"

"Does it matter?"

"To me it does."

"For you, I will ask." Ksenia got up and went to the front of the cave where the others had gathered.

Laynie crept forward to watch, staying in the shadows. She counted eleven girls total. Three soldiers had arrived. They brought two steaming kettles to the bars.

Each girl had a rag she pushed through the bars and dipped into one kettle, wringing it out, washing her face, hands, and arms. They rinsed the rags in the second kettle, wrung them, then dipped them again in the first kettle, turning their backs on the soldiers to lift their abayas and wash their bodies, rinsing and replenishing their rags with hot water as often as they needed. When they were finished, they again rinsed their rags then dipped them in the "clean" hot water for a final rinse before hanging the rags on the bars to dry.

Laynie shuddered as she considered how rampant venereal disease had to be within the soldiers' ranks . . . and the girls'. As they filed from the cell and were tied onto three leashes, Laynie prayed.

O Lord God, I promised you that I was done with sexual sin. Please help me to hear and follow your voice when I am led with them from this place—for I will never again submit myself to a man outside of marriage.

She returned to Ksenia's mattress and laid herself down. When she could not sleep, she prayed aloud. When sleep did not come, she sang.

Blessed assurance, Jesus is mine!
O what a foretaste of glory divine!
Heir of salvation, purchase of God,
Born of His Spirit, washed in His blood.

This is my story, this is my song,
Praising my Savior, all the day long;
This is my story, this is my song,
Praising my Savior, all the day long.

"Yes, Lord. I will praise you all this day long." Without thought, Laynie scratched at an itch on her head. Her fingers encountered a crusted smear of blood. The reminder that her hair was gone jarred her yet again.

"I count all things as loss for you, Jesus."

A different sensation . . . a quiver of uneasy guilt crept over her. No, not *guilt*, but something much more insidious. It took her several moments to identify it.

Shame.

Laynie blinked her eyes against sudden tears. "Lord?"

She didn't know where the passage came from. It welled up inside her of its own volition.

So do not be ashamed
of the testimony about our Lord
or of me, his prisoner.
Rather, join me in suffering for the gospel,
by the power of God.

"Oh! *Do not be ashamed.* Yes. Lord." She turned the verse over in her mind, and mouthed the words aloud.

Then she declared, "I will gladly suffer for the gospel—by the power of God. And I will not be ashamed, nor will I be shamed by any man."

Peace washed over her.

She murmured to herself, "I am not ashamed."

She saw the stick Ksenia used to poke the fire. Fished it out. Pulled up the sleeve of her abaya. Carefully scrawled on the inside of her forearm with the stick's charcoaled tip.

Chapter 23

LAYNIE WOKE UP WHEN the girls returned to the cell. Ksenia shuffled to her bed and sat down next to Laynie.

"Lay-nee, the soldiers say this past day was December 19. Is that what you wanted to know?"

"Yes. Thank you."

Far later in the month than I thought! She began to calculate backward the time she'd been in Sayed's stronghold and the date she'd arrived in Tbilisi. More than a week. Eight or nine days.

Did they really keep me unconscious for so long?

Ksenia hadn't replied to Laynie's thanks. She sat quietly. Subdued. Her head on her knees.

I have been self-absorbed, Laynie chided herself. *Not thinking of what these innocents suffer every evening. For weeks. Months. Perhaps longer.*

She grieved for Ksenia and the other young women.

How many? she wondered. *How many men were you forced to endure in just the past several hours?*

Laynie groped for the girl's hand. "You are not alone, Ksenia."

Ksenia sobbed, and Laynie drew her into her embrace. Softly, in English, Laynie murmured into Ksenia's hair, praying over the girl from Ephesians.

"Lord God! I pray that out of your glorious riches you would strengthen Ksenia with power through your Holy Spirit in her inner being. I ask that you help me share the gospel with this precious girl."

She sensed the Holy Spirit moving, quickening within her, stirring her to action. Felt his presence hovering over her and over Ksenia.

"Father, I ask that you open Ksenia's heart to receive the Good News. I ask that you would reveal Jesus to her and that she would ask him to dwell in her heart by faith."

Laynie opened her mouth to continue her prayer . . . but strange words, words that made absolutely no sense to her, rushed out. Her prayer stumbled to a stop.

What?

She tried again, spoke a string of words—and halted when they were just as unintelligible.

Ksenia pulled away from her. "Lay-nee. How do you know my people's tongue?"

"I-I don't. I don't know your language."

"But you were speaking it to me. Speaking Kurmanji, the language of the Kurds and Yazidi."

Laynie didn't answer. *Lord? What in the world?*

She was half-afraid to say anything else.

"Lay-nee, is it true, what you said?"

Laynie shivered. *Lord?* She ran her tongue over the splits and cuts on her lips. "Ksenia . . ."

Okay, that came out right. Oh, sure—because Ksenia is Ksenia in all languages!

"Um, Ksenia, what did I say when I spoke . . . Kurmanji?"

Whew.

"You do not know?"

"No, I don't. Can you tell me what I said?"

"But you clearly said, 'Dear little woman, if you ask me to be your Lord and your Savior, I will come into your heart, and you will never again be alone.'"

"Ohhhh . . ."

The glory of God fell.

Like a holy blanket, the presence of the Holy Spirit was so heavy that Laynie felt it in the air, soaking into her clothes, permeating her skin.

She wanted to fall on her face before God.

Ksenia shook. Her voice trembled. "I wanted . . . I needed to ask you what you meant, who was speaking to me when you said, 'ask me,' but before I could ask, you said, 'I am Jesus.'"

"O Lord God!" Laynie took a deep breath. "Ksenia, I speak the Russian that you and I share. I also speak English, Swedish, a little German, and some French. I promise you that I do not speak Kurmanji."

"Is it Jesus then, who I feel? Who makes me tremble? Is it him?"

"Yes. Oh, yes, it is."

They were both quiet, and Laynie prayed silently.

Dear Lord, what have you done here? It is marvelous in my eyes! Now, please open Ksenia's heart to hear the Good News.

Ksenia leaned toward Laynie and whispered in her ear. "Lay-nee. Please tell me of Jesus. Please. You say he lives inside of you. I do not want to be alone . . . ever again."

Laynie gathered Ksenia into her arms. Her own aches and pains forgotten, Laynie held Ksenia like the daughter she would never have.

"Ksenia, many, many years ago, God looked down on humanity's sinful, hopeless state and had compassion on us. At just the right time, because of his great love for us, God the Father's Spirit hovered over a virgin girl and placed the Father's seed within her. In this way, God sent his Word into the world to be born of a woman.

"They named the baby boy born to her *the Lord's Salvation*. They named him Jesus."

TOBIN AND JAZ WERE in the conference room, on speakerphone with Wolfe and Seraphim. Jaz had presented their recent findings.

"Sir, although we knew that AGFA had built themselves a lab, we now know that they weren't using the lab to make fentanyl. Instead, they bought enough fentanyl from the Chinese for both their own purposes and the Ukrainian mob's.

"We need to understand what they *are* manufacturing. The product of that lab will give us the basis of their third attack. To that end, we are monitoring AGFA's bank account, tracing every dollar moving in or out of it. Their finances and the private radicalized chat rooms we watch are our best avenues for figuring things out."

"Miss Jessup, I agree we need to be looking ahead to AGFA's third attack, but we can't forget that we have a more immediate threat before us. New Year's Eve is exactly twelve days off. Yes, we know AGFA will use fentanyl in the attack, and Cossack tells us the attack will come against ten major cities on the east coast, but none of that information is actionable.

"The task force has to uncover their plans—the exact where and the exact how. My ability to convince the FBI, other law enforcement agencies, the federal government, and applicable state and municipal governments *to act* depends upon hard, specific evidence—actionable evidence—of the impending attack.

"All your work will be in vain if we are unable to stop AGFA from pulling off another terrorist action as devastating as 9/11. I'm being blunt because the facts are blunt. *Find the where. Find the how*. This is your immediate mission."

Inside, Jaz scowled, but all she said was a clipped, "Yes, sir."

As Wolfe ended the call, Jaz threw her pen across the room. Threw her notebook.

Tobin tried to put a calming hand on her shoulder.

Jaz threw it off, too, and shouted, "This is why *I don't* *bleeping* *do management.*"

"And that's why I'm sharing the load with you, *Vyper*. Come on. We have work to do."

"This is not the gig I signed up for."

Tobin yanked her by the arm. Made her face him. "It's the gig you have. You think Bella would be pitching a fit like this? No. No, she wouldn't. AGFA has her. We have no idea what they're doing to her, but my nightmares have come up with some pretty creative ideas of their own. Do you think she's caved to that psychopath Sayed?"

She set her face like stone.

He shook her. "*Do you?*"

Jaz looked down. Shook her head. "No. But . . ."

"But what?"

"But she . . . she's got religion. You know."

"I know she has Jesus, Jaz. Not religion. And I know that the same Jesus Bella has is waiting for you to ask him for help."

"Whatever."

"*Whatever* doesn't cut it, Jaz. You already bailed on us once. You don't get to do it again."

ANOTHER DAY AND NIGHT passed for Laynie in the cell with the *kafir* girls. Over breakfast, Laynie retold the story of Jesus' birth to Ksenia, then moved on to his ministry, his arrest and crucifixion. His triumphant resurrection. His coming return.

Laynie led Ksenia in a prayer to repent of her sins—but had to stop and explain to her that her treatment at the hands of the soldiers and what she was made to do against her will was *not* sin. It was abuse.

After they had talked through it several times, Laynie was able to lead Ksenia to repent of her sins as she understood them, profess Jesus as her Lord and Savior, and receive his forgiveness.

"You are no longer to think of yourself as a *kafir* woman, because you are neither unbelieving nor unclean in God's eyes. Because of Jesus, you are pure and holy, a royal daughter of the King."

Ksenia hung on every word. Her hunger for God and for his word exhausted Laynie's recent memorization, and she found herself drawing on verses she'd learned as a child. Laynie told Ksenia about heaven, the dwelling place of God on his throne. Laynie also taught Ksenia how to pray . . . and how to worship.

She sang *Amazing Grace* for Ksenia in English, then translated the verses as best she could into Russian. All afternoon, she and Ksenia sang the same song, and every time they reached the last verse, Ksenia would weep with joy.

When we've been there ten thousand years
Bright shining as the sun,
We've no less days to sing God's praise
Than when we'd first begun.

"Will it be like that, Lay-nee? Will we see heaven where God sits upon his throne? Will we live with him ten thousand years?"

Laynie brushed a kiss over Ksenia's cheek. "Ten thousand years upon ten thousand years, my little daughter."

Ksenia sobered. "They, the jihadis. They killed my family. My mother, my father, my brothers. All dead. I can never go back to my people, Lay-nee. There is no one left there for me. No one. Would you . . . would you let me think of myself as your daughter, Lay-nee? Might I call you *Mader?*"

Laynie turned inward. *Neither of us will leave this place alive. What will it matter if I say yes? Shouldn't I comfort Ksenia with the love she needs today?*

She sighed over Ksenia's broken heart . . . and gave herself a stiff talking-to.

You cannot make empty promises to this child, Laynie Portland. She is not a mark you can lie to and walk away from. That is no longer your way of life.

She remembered the sense of Jesus' presence, how it overjoyed and comforted her, and what it meant when he whispered in her heart, *I am here, Laynie, my daughter.*

O Jesus! You didn't comfort me with lies. And you never held my past against me. Instead, you received me as your daughter. I should . . . I should do the same. Share the love you poured into me by receiving this motherless child as my own.

She stroked Ksenia's hair and waited until the tightness in her throat eased.

"I would be honored to have you call me *Mader*, my little daughter."

MIDMORNING ON LAYNIE'S THIRD day with the *kafir* girls, Bula called for her from the grate. She straightened her abaya and walked to him. Bula had unlocked the gate and placed a small pot of water and a rag inside the cell.

"Clean yourself. You will go to Sayed before you go to any of the men."

"Are you sure he's up to it?" Laynie regretted the snide words as soon as they slipped from her mouth.

Sorry, Lord. My heart is nowhere near perfect yet. Lots of junk hiding in there. Please cleanse my heart right now as I wash. I want to please you in every way—even how I respond to Sayed.

Laynie had no sense of what she was going to do when Sayed laid his hands on her. All she could manage was to murmur to herself over and over, "I count all things as loss for you, Jesus. I am not ashamed of the gospel. It is the power of God to salvation. No man can shame what you have made holy—nor, as much as it is within my power, will I allow a man to dishonor my body."

Bula led her on the leash through the tunnels to Sayed's salon. The guard stared at Laynie's bare head as he held the curtain aside. Bula led Laynie to where Sayed was waiting.

He offered her a gleeful smile. "Oh, yes. You look as if you may be feeling better, Anabelle."

He lit a cigarette and added, "News that I will be giving you to the men has raised quite a stir. But I wished to see you first to assure myself that, at last, you had been properly humbled."

Laynie said nothing with her mouth. Her eyes, on the other hand, radiated mocking defiance.

Sayed sighed. "It seems that Halima's efforts were not as effective as I wished. Very well. I will undertake the task myself."

To Bula he said, "Remove her abaya."

"Do not resist," Bula warned Laynie.

She held out her arms and let him lift the garment from her, leaving her in the sleeveless shift.

Sayed sat forward and frowned. He got up and came closer. "What is this dirt on your arm? I gave orders for you to wash yourself."

Laynie glanced at her forearm. She saw the words she'd scrawled there in charcoal and had left untouched when she washed.

"It is my declaration. Nothing you do can or will humble or shame me before Jesus, my Savior. He has removed all guilt and shame from me."

Sayed shook with cold anger. "Very well. You wish to wear those words? So you shall."

He shouted to his servant, who fetched him a cigarette lighter and a long, thin stiletto. At Sayed's command, Bula pushed Laynie onto her knees in front of the low table, then bent her over it. Sayed's servant held Laynie facedown to the table while Bula put his booted foot across her extended elbow.

Sayed heated the stiletto's tip over the lighter's flame and brought it close to her skin.

"If you attempt to move, Anabelle Garineau, Bula will snap your arm like a twig."

Laynie felt the heat before Sayed touched the blade to her tender skin, but it hurt beyond belief as he began to trace, then sear, the charcoal letters into her arm.

She didn't want to—she clenched her teeth and tried very hard not to—but she screamed anyway.

THE SENSE THAT TIME was getting away from them, leaving them without answers, hung over the task force. Team members began to arrive earlier each morning, working until dinner. By unspoken consensus, they returned to work following the evening meal and stayed until their eyes were too bleary to read what was on their screens.

Jaz had parceled out assignments, all of them focused on the impending New Year's Eve attacks. All except Brian. Brian she took aside.

"Listen, Brian. I have a separate assignment for you. I've chosen you to do one thing and one thing only, what the girls came up empty on—find me the list of chemicals AGFA ordered. Can you do that?"

"Wow. Uh, yeah, I-I can. Thanks for trusting me with this."

He'd gone away from their short convo with renewed determination.

What I need is a different approach, another angle.

He leaned back in his chair, fingers twined behind his head, staring at the updated notes Vincent had so carefully scribed on the boards. All the notes were about the New Year's Eve attacks with the exception of one bullet reading, "What is AGFA making in its lab?"

He doodled on a scrap of paper, an itch of an idea making him back up. Rethink. Ask himself what Jaz would do with the same idea. Or Rusty.

Brian got online and began to dig.

WHEN BULA RETURNED LAYNIE to the cell, she was shaking all over and hoarse from screaming. Without a word, she sat down beside Ksenia, pulled up her abaya, and reached for the shift she wore. She tore into its hem and ripped it off in a long strip. She soaked the fabric strip in vinegar water from her jug.

When she lifted her sleeve, Ksenia saw words burned into Laynie's flesh, *I Am Not Ashamed.* She did not know how to read them or what they meant, only that they were seared into Laynie's skin, and she would bear them forever.

"Oh, *Mader!*"

"Wrap. Help me."

After the initial sting, the cool, moist cloth soothed the pain of the burns.

The relief is temporary. I will need to keep it moist for a time.

"I will be all right, Ksenia. The Lord will help me through this. In one way, it is a blessing. After Sayed had expended his energy and hatred doing this to me, he no longer wanted to rape me."

"But this evening, when the soldiers will come for us, they will come for you also," Ksenia whispered to Laynie. "Many men have put their names on the list. They will do a drawing for you tonight."

Laynie bowed her head to pray silently. She stopped. Lifted her chin.

"Then let us beseech the Father in Jesus' name to deliver us both from their evil intentions, Ksenia."

The girl was eager. "Yes! Let us pray in Jesus' name."

Joining hands, Laynie murmured, "Lord God, Ksenia and I come to you in the name of your Son, Jesus. We call upon you to move this mountain before us. Lord, we are asking that you save us from degradation and abuse. O God, I am willing to suffer and die for you and the cross, and I promised you I would never willingly give my body to sinful use again. However, unlike me, Ksenia doesn't have the training and experience I have to refuse a man. O Lord, we need your deliverance here. Please help us. Amen."

"Amen," Ksenia breathed. She looked at Laynie curiously. "What did you mean, when you said I didn't have the training or experience you have to refuse a man?"

Laynie nodded slowly and unconsciously rubbed at her stomach before she answered.

"I am trained to fight, Ksenia. The second time I saw Sayed, when he tried to drug and rape me, I broke two of his fingers and punched him in the face. Broke his nose."

Even through the gloom, Laynie could see white all the way around Ksenia's dark eyes.

"You . . . you struck Sayed?"

"He slapped me. I probably shouldn't have hit him, but I'm trained to defend myself, so I did."

Laynie sensed Ksenia struggling, wanting to ask more questions. She preempted the girl's curiosity.

"Let me share something important with you, dear one. It is this. After we come to know Jesus, we begin to realize that our lives are now cut into two parts—the part before Jesus, without him, and the part after Jesus, with him. Two lives. An old, dead life, and a new and resurrected life."

Laynie's stomach cramped on her. She put her hand to it. Ignored the cramp until it went away.

"I was an ungodly woman in my old life, Ksenia. I did many questionable and wrong things . . . and many terrible things. I learned to fight, to lie, to deceive and steal. Even to kill."

Ksenia's eyes betrayed her. She was frightened.

Frightened of me.

"That was my old life, child. Jesus forgave me my sins, just as he forgave you. Now I tell everyone I know how Jesus has saved me from my former wretched, sinful life. Sometimes, though, habits from my old life—"

Laynie's stomach cramped again. She felt its contents roll around uneasily.

"I—" Nausea rose in her throat. "Oh, dear. I . . . I-I'm going to be sick."

Laynie lurched from Ksenia's mattress. She ran across the cave to the waste buckets and heaved into them. Almost immediately, her bowels tuned to liquid and released. She remained near the foul receptacles, alternately throwing up and hugging her middle against vicious cramps followed by diarrhea. In between, she leaned against the stone walls, seeking their coolness.

She remained near the foul buckets, alternately throwing up and hugging her middle against horrible bowel cramps followed by diarrhea. In between, she leaned against the stone walls, seeking their coolness.

Ksenia brought Laynie's water jug to her, but every sip she took exited as fast as she swallowed.

The girl felt Laynie's forehead. "You are hot to the touch. Like a griddle, *Mader*."

Laynie shivered violently and vomited again.

The other girls in the cell shouted for the guards until they came.

"They are afraid you will make them sick," Ksenia translated. "They want the guards to bring them different buckets so they don't come into contact with your refuse. They are saying I am contaminated, too. We must stay away from them."

Laynie only groaned. She panted through another round of cramps.

"Oh, dear God, please help me."

I am answering your prayer, Laynie, my daughter.

It took more than a moment for the words to sink down into her spirit, for her to understand. For a small smile to rise to her lips.

Before she again vomited.

CHAPTER 24

TO COMBAT MUSCLE FATIGUE and the energy-sapping cold, Cossack and his guides halted regularly. When they stopped, they gulped water and devoured nuts, dried meat, and fruit—even chunks of butter.

The three men reached the summit of the pass an hour before dark on the third day. They hiked a short distance down the other side until they reached a rock outcropping that would help shelter them from the wind. They made camp there under an overhang, erecting their tent and firing up the tiny gas stove to heat water for tea. Huddled around the little stove, they ate as many calories as they could swallow, drank down two cups of hot, sweetened tea each, then burrowed into their sleeping bags for the night.

They woke to a blinding sun glancing off two inches of fresh snow.

"Our hike is downhill now," the lead guide said. "We will make better time today and should reach the rendezvous tomorrow."

Cossack only nodded. He was feeling the fifteen or more years he had on the guides. He struggled onward, mostly in silence. He was near the point of exhaustion when they crossed the timberline and made camp in the trees.

IT WAS CHRISTMAS EVE. Somehow, the date had snuck up on everyone in the task force. When Jaz announced they would quit early that afternoon and Richard would serve a special Christmas dinner the following day, the members of the task force shrugged and received her news without enthusiasm.

The only meaning Christmas Eve held for them was to herald the one-week mark before AGFA's attack on New Year's Eve. They had nothing with which to stop the terrorists. Nothing to give Wolfe, nothing he could take to his superiors.

"I will never think of New Year's Eve the same after this," Gwyneth mumbled.

"Nor Christmas Eve," Soraya responded.

No one was certain Brian had heard Jaz's announcements about dismissing early Christmas Eve. He skipped lunch and kept at it through the afternoon. When he didn't break for dinner that evening, the rest of the task force began to hope that Brian was onto something concrete.

"Could really use some good news," Rusty said. "Maybe we can give him a hand."

In agreement, the team, minus Tobin and Jaz, returned to the bullpen and converged on Brian's desk.

Rusty took charge. "Brian."

Nothing.

"Brian."

Still no response.

"*Brian!*"

"What?"

"Need to get your hearing checked, bro. That's the third time I've said your name."

Brian tore his eyes away from his monitor. Saw the team crowded around his desk. "Huh. What do you guys want?"

"Can we help?"

"Thanks, but nope. Got it covered." He hit print. "Hang on, though. I'm about to blow you clowns away." He tilted his chair back and announced, "I've got the list of chemicals AGFA ordered for the third attack."

JAZ AND TOBIN JOINED the other team members in the bullpen. Jaz said, "Okay, Brian. Tell us what you've got and how you got there."

"Roger that. Well, since we scoured what was coming into and going out of AGFA and made no progress there, I decided to work the problem from the other end. I started with the same Chinese pharmaceutical and medical supply company they ordered fentanyl from. I dug down into the company's files to learn more about them. The more I dug, the more obvious it appeared."

"What's that?"

"I was getting to it. Seems the company is a front for *Tai Huen Chai*, the 'Big Circle Boys,' a Hong Kong-based Chinese triad. Tai Huen Chai is a transnational organized crime syndicate with a significant foothold in Canada. The Big Circle Boys conduct legit business through this pharmaceutical and medical supply house, but they also distribute drugs and launder a lot of their drug money through it."

"Wow," Rusty said, eyes wide.

"Yeah. Super tangled mess. Took me days to find what I was looking for—not another connection to AGFA, but a connection to their friends, al-Qaeda."

"You found a link between this company and al-Qaeda?"

"Yup. Once I was in their files, I had to employ a dictionary's worth of key word filters before the right records popped—I looked into orders sent to Pakistan, Afghanistan, Iran, Iraq, Syria, Lebanon, even Saudi Arabia before I found the commonalities that led me to al-Qaeda's pass-through companies."

"Look, Brian," Tobin interjected. "We will all sign an affidavit attesting to your stellar international hacking abilities if you will just tell us you found AGFA's chemical order."

"Actually, I'm learning from him," Rusty said. "Kinda in awe, if you need to know."

"Me, too," the girls echoed.

Tobin grumped. "Fine. Get on with it."

"I don't need to get deeper into the weeds. The short version is this. AGFA has ties to al-Qaeda. Al-Qaeda had a preexisting 'business' relationship with Tai Huen Chai. Al-Qaeda placed the order for AGFA through one of their shell companies, but had the order shipped to Baku where AGFA picked it up. AGFA paid for the order on the installment plan—a recurring monthly payment of five thousand dollars over three months. Then—"

"This is the short version? Not getting deeper into the weeds?" Tobin's grump was more pronounced. "Do you have the list or not? And have you deduced what AGFA is making in their lab?"

Brian had Vincent hand around a printout. "Here's the list."

While the members of the task force scanned it, Brian sighed. "Hope one of you is better at chemistry than I am, because I'm stumped. Phenethylpiperidone? Hexamethylphosphoric triamide? Ammonium hydroxide? Danged if I can tell what they're cooking up."

BECAUSE THE CHILDREN wanted to honor their usual holiday traditions, Kari and Søren had packed up the household, including Gene and Polly, and flown to New Orleans. They planned to spend the week before Christmas through New Year's Day at Kari's house on Marlow Avenue.

It wasn't easy for Kari to join in the customary baking and decorating. She forced herself to do it for Max, Shannon, and Robbie's sakes.

Polly and Gene understood her feelings. They, more than her, were grieving the uncertainty of Laynie's absence.

Lord, you know where Laynie is. Please bring her home to us, Kari prayed.

The children, Max, too—who wasn't a child any longer—gathered in the kitchen during the week leading up to Christmas. Under the tutelage of Kari's housekeeper, Azalea Bodeen, they cooked, made candies, and baked up a storm.

Gene and Polly weren't left out. Gene manned the kitchen sinks, washing mixing bowls, spoons, measuring utensils, pots, pans, and cookie sheets as fast as they were dirtied. Polly, from memory, recalled her favorite Christmas recipes, and called out ingredients and instructions that Azalea oversaw. Kari and Søren made at least one trip to the grocery store each day to supply whatever was lacking—and something was always lacking, usually at the last minute. That evening, while everyone was watching *It's a Wonderful Life* on television, Kari's cell phone buzzed. She'd turned the ringer off for the week, telling her staff not to call her unless their offices were afire.

She picked up the phone, grumbling to herself. Saw the caller ID. Moved into the kitchen to take the call.

Lord, if it's bad news . . .

She calmed herself. "Kari Thoresen."

"Ms. Thoresen, it's Quincy Tobin calling."

"Yes, Marshal. How . . . do you have any news?"

"No, ma'am. We are a touch closer to finding the group who took Marta. Elaine. No, Bella. I mean *Laynie*. Sorry. I apologize."

"No need to, Marshal. I understand."

"I called to wish you and your family a blessed Christmas. I hope it isn't an intrusion."

"No, Marshal. I'm glad you called. And thank you. We wish you the same—a blessed Christmas."

The lull in the conversation caused Kari's heart to quicken. "Was there something else you called to say, Marshal Tobin?"

He huffed a sigh. "A prayer request, actually."

"A prayer request? You called the right place. We'd be happy to pray with and for you." She listened to the laughter from the living room and smiled. "Actually, we've got a pretty strong prayer team assembled here."

"Good. We need you. It's, ah, well the details are classified. I can only offer the suggestion of it. Let me just ask that you pray for us, the task force and . . . whatever is in the works for New Year's Eve."

"Whatever is in the works? As in . . ."

"Ma'am, I can neither confirm nor deny."

Kari stilled. "I think I understand. Go on."

"We know *it*—the thing I cannot divulge—is arranged and we know who's behind it. We know what they intend to use and that it involves more than one . . . location. The thing is, what we know is not enough to stop it. Not enough for authorities to alert the public."

"And it's the task force's mandate to find those missing pieces?"

"Yes, ma'am, meaning we're under some heavy pressure. Morale is thin, and we're worked to the bone."

"A lot of cities have New Year's Eve celebrations."

Tobin didn't answer.

Kari understood his silence. "We are grateful that you called on us to pray for you and the task force, Marshal. You may count on us to pray this through."

"Thank you. And please don't give up on Laynie. I haven't."

"That's the best word you could have delivered to me, Marshal."

"Quincy, ma'am. M'friends call me Quincy."

"I'm honored to be your friend, Quincy. A blessed Christmas to you and all your friends on the task force."

CHAPTER 25

EARLY THE FOLLOWING AFTERNOON, the three men reached the narrow, secluded valley where they were to meet Sayed's men. They had hiked four punishing days to reach the rendezvous, a journey that in snowless circumstances would have taken only twelve to sixteen hours.

Cossack's limbs were shaking with fatigue when they spotted the two trucks waiting for them at the base of the mountain on the opposite side of the valley. He gathered himself for the formalities ahead.

"*As-Salamu Alaykum*, General Labazanov," one of Sayed's lieutenants said. "I am Usama."

"*Wa alaykumu s-salam.* It is good to see a friendly face," Cossack replied.

"We are glad you made the trek safely. We have been waiting since yesterday for you to appear. General Sayed sends his greetings. If you will come with us?"

Usama gestured Cossack to the cab of one of the trucks, Cossack's men to the bed of the other truck.

"Your men will not be coming with us, General. My people will take them to a place of safety and comfort where they can recover from their journey."

"No. I wish my men to remain with me."

Sayed's lieutenant ignored Cossack's objection. "General Sayed's apologies, but they will remain here. Do not worry. They will rejoin you for the journey back."

A black bag appeared in Usama's hand. "Please put this over your head, General."

"This is impertinence. I will not submit to it," Cossack said evenly.

"I mean you no disrespect, General Labazanov. General Sayed's instructions are the same for all visitors, regardless of rank. No one outside our militia is permitted to know the approach to our stronghold."

Cossack shrugged. "I shall speak to General Sayed about this when I see him. I hope for your sake that what you say is true."

Cossack endured the blind and jostling forty-minute drive across a rocky and pitted landscape. When the truck stopped, Cossack realized the wind had died away. At the same time, he recognized the signature ambiance of a tunnel—the shift in sound, temperature, and humidity.

This truck drove directly into the entrance to Sayed's stronghold?

"I will lead you from here, General Labazanov. You may rely upon me."

Cossack had no choice but to tolerate being led like a child. Then he heard something else. A clang, deep and metallic, and its echo reverberating down a tunnel.

"General Labazanov, sir, place your hands here."

Cossack felt the cold shape of metal under his gloved hands and recognized it. A mining car. His toe stubbed against something unyielding.

"We have placed two steps before you, General, for your convenience. I will climb up and you will climb up after me. I will help you into the car."

Soon Cossack was seated, the cold, unyielding metal chilling his backside, the car running into the depths of a mountain.

An easy drive through a valley to a cave entrance, followed by a ride in a mining car, Cossack thought. *No treacherous hikes through mountain passes for Sayed. His stronghold is likely deep within this mountain! I marvel that he discovered such a place—and I see now why the Russians have never been able to ferret him out.*

Another thought occurred to him. *If the Russians could not find him here, how will I ever convey its location to Wolfe?*

USAMA LED COSSACK FROM the mining cars up a stairway carved out of rock and removed the bag from Cossack's head. Cossack looked beyond the lieutenant leading them and squinted at an iron door apparently locked on the other side. The lieutenant pounded twice on the door, then twice again. A peephole slid open, then the door's bolt on the other side grated and the door swung open. They walked past two guards, who bolted the door behind them.

Cossack's guides turned right into a tunnel. Straight ahead, the tunnel widened into a sophisticated system that boggled Cossack's mind. Because it had once been the home of a successful mining operation, the tunnels had lights to illuminate their way, strings of electric bulbs fastened near the tunnel's ceiling.

Off the wide main tunnel were many short side tunnels. Cossack glimpsed niches carved into the branch walls—various-sized rooms furnished with simple wooden sleeping benches. The niches were designed to accommodate two to four soldiers, and each was as good as or better than the one Cossack occupied back in his own stronghold.

One by one, the men guarding Cossack peeled off, leaving only Sayed's lieutenant as Cossack's guide. And with every step, the temperature in the wide tunnel rose a little until it was as comfortable as any home.

They came to a branching passageway, a junction, and to their left, the entrance to a cavern—the heart of Sayed's stronghold. The cavern alone was larger than the two combined caverns that comprised the bulk of Cossack's entire compound.

Cossack stopped and took three steps into the cavern to satisfy his own curiosity. Usama was patient and respectful and did not interrupt as Cossack viewed what was certainly a communal dining hall arranged like a cafeteria set with rows of long tables and chairs. A kitchen was built onto one wall of the cavern. The source of the tunnels' warmth, an old coal-burning furnace, presided over the rear of the cavern, its sprawling ductwork feeding heat to various parts of the cave system.

Compared to Sayed's stronghold, Cossack's winter retreat was as primitive as a caveman's. Envy crept up Cossack's neck until he reminded himself, *Sayed has occupied these tunnels for some years now. He has had time to refine them, to make them fit for his militia's needs.*

Cossack returned to his guide who nodded and led him down a dim side tunnel. Not far into the side tunnel, his guide motioned Cossack into a niche with a bed, a chair, and other furnishings.

"Your quarters while you are here, General."

A servant stood and bowed.

"This man will care for your needs," Usama said. "He will prepare a bath for you so you might clean up from your journey. I will return in an hour and take you to dinner with General Sayed."

When his guide departed, Cossack placed his pack on the bed and opened it to retrieve his only fresh clothes. They were crumpled from being stored in the pack. They were worn because Cossack owned only three sets of clothing.

"General," the servant murmured, "we have taken the liberty of providing you with a wardrobe while you are here." He pointed to trousers, shirt, and tunic laid out on the chair.

"I see."

I see that I am to be treated as an honored guest while, at the same time, Sayed makes certain I know he is above me, that he is condescending to my level. Typical of him.

"This way, General."

The servant led him back to the cavern and into a curtained bathing area not far from the furnace. Minutes later, having sent the servant away, Cossack reclined in a tub of steaming water. It was an indulgence he'd not enjoyed for close to a year, having used a basin of warm water to wash in each day, just as his men did.

He laid his head back and sighed.

"I KNOW AUNT LAYNIE can't be here for Christmas," Shannon sobbed, "but I keep thinking she'll find a way, that she'll ring the doorbell, and I'll answer it. And-and-and Christmas just isn't the same this year because she *said* she would come. Her boss *promised*."

"You aren't the only one missing her, Shannon. Please believe me that if Aunt Laynie could get here? Nothing in this world would keep her from us."

They felt a vacuum at Laynie's absence, in their dashed expectations. The past four weeks had dropped their family into deep mourning then pulled them only halfway out. Knowing Laynie hadn't died in the car fire was a relief. Not knowing where she was or if she was alive was every bit as hard.

And Gene fretted over Polly. "She doesn't complain, Kari, but with not knowing if Laynie is alive? Polly has gone as quiet as the snow falling back in RiverBend. She's praying, but she's too quiet. Perhaps it would have been better for us to stay home this year."

Kari sought out Søren and Max. "I'm wondering if we should just pack up and go back to Nebraska tomorrow."

Max surprised Kari when he nodded his agreement. "Let's. It's like we're here for Aunt Laynie's funeral all over again. And Shannon's a mess. I don't like to see her like that."

Søren had a slightly different outlook. "Instead of going home, what do you think of this idea? Leave tomorrow and fly to Seattle. Stay in a big ol' hotel suite, use the pool and hot tub, send Gene and Polly to visit their other grandkids and maybe do some skiing while they're gone. All of us take a drive over Stevens Pass to that little Bavarian village, Leavenworth. See all the lights there. How's that sound?"

"Yes!" Max was all in.

"I love it all, Søren. All right then. Let's talk it over with Gene and Polly, Shannon and Robbie. If they're for it, I'll make the arrangements."

"Your pilot won't mind flying the day after Christmas?"

"I hope the bonus I plan to offer him takes the sting right out of it. He'll make enough to take his kids to Disney World."

BRIAN, RUSTY, AND JAZ had walked away from Richard's fabulous Christmas dinner when Tobin caught up to them.

"Hey, guys, can I talk to you for a minute?"

Rusty answered, "Sure, Tobin. We're just walking off that pecan pie."

Brian elbowed Rusty. "You'll need an hour on the elliptical machine, dude. I saw you eat two slices of apple with ice cream *and* a piece of pecan."

Rusty patted his belly. "Man's gotta eat, Brain Pan. Man's gotta eat."

As they walked the path around the perimeter, two abreast, Tobin pointed back at Brian. "See, I've been thinking about the list of chemicals you handed off to us yesterday, Brian."

"Yeah, okay," he said. "Make any sense of it?"

"No, but I have a friend in the DEA. He's quite the science geek. On a whim, I grabbed a copy of that list of chemicals and faxed it to him last night. Got a call from him just before dinner."

"The guy works on Christmas Day?"

"No, but I sent the fax to his home office. Apparently the list, coupled with a short explanation as to why I was asking, was enough to make him take a break from hosting his in-laws for Christmas dinner to check some things and then call me. What he said about those chemicals soured my dessert but good. Turns out that the list has all the major ingredients for making carfentanil, a drug used to tranquilize elephants."

They halted in the path and stood in a little knot facing each other.

"What, AGFA's in the zoo business now?"

"Ha ha. Good one, Rusty. No, what he said is that carfentanil is an analog of fentanyl."

"Hold up," Jaz said. "I know what analog means relative to digital. What does analog mean when you say carfentanil is an analog of fentanyl?"

"I had to ask, too. It can mean that two drugs are either structurally similar *or*, as in this case, that they have similar effects. Fentanyl and carfentanil have similar pain-relieving and sedative effects, only—*get this*—you know how fentanyl is fifty times more powerful than heroin and a hundred times more potent than morphine? Turns out carfentanil is a hundred times more powerful than fentanyl—meaning it packs a punch a thousand times harder than morphine."

Rusty's whistle was mirrored in Brian and Jaz's expressions.

Tobin added, "You can overdose and die just by *handling* carfentanil without the right kind of protective gear. Get it on your skin? The skin absorbs it and you die. Lick your finger or pick your nose? You die."

The shock on his companions' faces told Tobin that they were processing the information and coming up with the same questions he had.

Rusty spoke first. "So . . . we've got to ask ourselves why AGFA is in the business of manufacturing carfentanil."

"We know the reason. It makes total, twisted sense."

"What makes sense?" Jaz asked.

"AGFA plans to use fentanyl to attack us on New Year's Eve. The follow-on attack? They're gonna use carfentanil."

CHAPTER 26

LAYNIE'S DYSENTERY LASTED for days. Days of fever, painful cramps, and endless trips to the latrine. She was vaguely aware that Ksenia had brought a bucket closer to their mattress so Laynie didn't have as far to go. And she was aware of praying, although in her fevered state her prayers were a peculiar mixture of verses from Philippians . . . and Tobin.

Over and over Laynie muttered, "I want you to know and remember, Quincy, that what has happened to me—whatever comes—has served to advance the gospel. It has become clear to these girls who do not yet know Jesus—well, one of them at least—that I share their chains for his sake."

Laynie considered every indignity and punishment she'd suffered since arriving in Tbilisi well worth it—knowing she'd led Ksenia to Jesus. And during the time Laynie was sick, God answered the prayer she and Ksenia had prayed together, for the guards did not take any of the girls to the soldiers. Instead, they brought additional latrine buckets for the others and extra jugs of water for Laynie and Ksenia. They even supplied hot water and rags to clean their bodies in an attempt to keep the sickness from spreading.

Their precautions did not work.

On Laynie's third day of illness, Ksenia took sick with the same symptoms. As weak as Laynie was and as best as she could, she tended Ksenia. She tore the hem from Ksenia's shift, dipped it in water, and swabbed the girl's feverish face, arms, and legs in an attempt to bring her temperature down.

It was only as she was beginning to feel better that Laynie understood how much time she had lost track of. That she had missed Christmas Day.

Christmas? Laynie exhaled in surprise and dismay.

I was supposed to spend Christmas with my family in New Orleans. An entire week with Mama, Dad, and Kari's family.

Seraphim promised me.

Wolfe promised me.

Laynie caressed Ksenia's flushed cheek. *So what? It's just a date. Christmas isn't about the date. It's the celebration of Jesus' birth—and he transcends mere dates.*

Missing out on Christmas bothered her less than she had expected it to.

She half-smiled. *If we were to ever escape from this place, I would have a daughter to bring home for Christmas.* She even laughed a little. *I wonder what Tobin would think if I were to show up with a ready-made family?*

Ksenia fussed and moved in discomfort. Laynie freshened her rag and sponged Ksenia's face. She began to croon over the girl.

What child is this, who, laid to rest
On Mary's lap is sleeping?
Whom angels greet with anthems sweet,
While shepherds watch are keeping?
This, this is Christ the King,
Whom shepherds guard and angels sing;
Haste, haste to bring Him laud,
The babe, the son of Mary.

LAYNIE SANG EVERY COMFORTING Christmas carol she could conjure from her childhood memories. When she stopped, Ksenia moaned and begged her to keep going. Laynie did, humming or singing the same songs over and over. Later, Ksenia was well enough to sit up and keep a little food down. She clung to Laynie's hand and asked Laynie to sing to her again.

Singing really isn't my forte, Lord, Laynie thought, but she sang anyway—because she was available and no one else was. And because she had an audience. A shuffle from the shadows had caught Laynie's attention an hour ago. She kept singing, and the shuffle came a little closer, squatting just yards from their fire. When her features came into view, Laynie recognized her, one of the other girls.

Good heavens! She can't be more than thirteen or fourteen.

Laynie nodded to the girl, acknowledging her presence, letting her know she was welcome. The girl hung her head and glanced toward the other campfire, but she did not leave.

Laynie didn't want to infect her, so she didn't beckon her closer, and the girl was satisfied just to listen. Laynie wasn't certain, but she sensed the presence of at least one other girl farther back in the shadows.

So she sang an old, familiar carol.

Away in a manger, no crib for a bed
The little Lord Jesus lay down his sweet head
The stars in the bright sky looked down where he lay
The little Lord Jesus asleep on the hay.

Laynie sang on, just the slow, sweet hymns of Christmas to a captive audience who understood nothing of what she sang, but maybe, just maybe, sensed the holiness of what Laynie caroled.

What a way to spend Christmas, Lord, even if we're late. Right now, I wouldn't trade this for anything. In fact, today, I feel like Paul. I know what it is to be in need, and I know what it is to have plenty. I have learned the secret of being content in any and every situation, whether well fed or hungry, whether living in plenty or in want. I can do all this through you, Lord Jesus, because you give me strength.

Will you also give me these girls?

Her communion with the Lord was interrupted by someone running to the *kafir* girls' separate latrine. Laynie heard retching, vomiting.

The sickness had taken hold on the other side of the cell despite the guards' precautions.

IT HAD TAKEN GUPTA and Sayed's servant six days to produce the final cut of the video. The video editing process had been painstakingly tedious, made worse by the less-than-state-of-the-art equipment available to them.

First they had to capture the taped video recording on computer. That had taken more than two days, days in which the capture process had glitched twice, forcing them to start over.

Had taken *them?* Hardly! Sayed's servant had demonstrated the capture process to Gupta, then left *her* alone in a dingy room carved from rock—the same room he obviously slept in—while *he* attended Sayed.

Gupta ground her teeth. Her meals were delivered to her, and she ate alone. She had to ask the guard outside the room to escort her to the latrine. Late, at the end of the day, Sayed's servant showed her to her quarters and told her, "You must remain here until I return to fetch you. You may not go about unaccompanied."

This is not what I gave up my whole life for.

"I wish to see Sayed."

"*General* Sayed. You will show proper respect. I will convey your wishes to the general. However, you must realize, he has said he will see you when the video is complete. It would not be wise to appear before him without the finished product. Do you understand?"

Gupta sank down on her bed. *I understand I am trapped here.*

After the video capture was done, Gupta had to cut the audio of Laynie's outbursts from the tape and overlay her own voice either narrating what she was doing or quoting from the Quran. When she had completed the process and saved the project, she had to "render" the file into a compressed, smaller file format that could be uploaded to websites and jihadi chat rooms.

Rendering the final file took an unbelievable amount of time, so after six hours, Gupta let the process run overnight, only to find in the morning that the process had "hung up." She had to force a program stop, reboot the computer, and restart the rendering process.

Adding to her frustration and the time to completion, Sayed's servant took issue with parts of her narration in the final file and insisted that she make corrections. The changes to the overall project required that she again render the video—another overnight process.

Gupta was irritable and short with Sayed's servant when, after the six days, the final product—a twelve-minute video—was loaded onto Sayed's laptop for him to preview.

Gupta sat in silence as Sayed watched the film. Twice he nodded. At the end, he sat back with a satisfied sigh.

"Excellent! We will share this video across our network. It will bolster our credibility and, in turn, our numbers."

He turned luminous eyes on Gupta. "I am well pleased with your work, Halima, and I will honor you."

Gupta's eyes teared, and she swallowed. "Then may I . . . may I now leave my quarters? Does that mean I may spend time with you?"

Instead of answering, Sayed's smile stretched wider. He called to the guard on station just inside the curtain to his salon. The guard returned with one of Sayed's soldiers. Gupta thought the soldier looked sixty-five years old or older. More than a few years older than her.

The man saluted Sayed, and Sayed motioned for him to sit opposite Gupta.

"Halima, this is Maskhadan ibn Musa, a proven warrior in the jihad and a trusted lieutenant. He has given thirty years of his life in pursuit of the caliphate. Two years ago he lost his two sons and his wife to the Russians."

Gupta glanced at the old man. He nodded at her. Uncertain how to respond, she simply nodded back.

"Good, good. Maskhadan, too, has agreed to this marriage."

Gupta choked on her own saliva. "I—what?"

"I have bestowed this great honor upon you, Halima, in recognition of your service to Allah and the jihad. Maskhadan will make you a fine husband, and you will care well for his needs. It is a good match."

Sayed stood and offered Gupta his hand. Slowly, she placed hers in his. He led her out of the conversation area. When the old man followed, Sayed reached for his hand and placed Gupta's hand in his.

"You are new to our ways, Halima, but you must learn them quickly. Your husband requires you to behave in a manner that honors him. You will respect his wishes in all things and obey his commands at all times. If he expects you to help cook and clean for our soldiers, you will do so and your service to others will honor him. And, of course, you will surrender your body to him as well as your will. In all things, he is your master."

Sayed smiled. Gupta perceived—too late, now that her blind devotion was stripped away—the patronizing smirk in that smile.

Anabelle was right.

Gupta was mute as she followed Maskhadan from the salon into the tunnel, but the voice inside her head was not.

"I see how you look at Sayed. You are infatuated with him, with his leadership and importance, aren't you? You have visions of a happily-ever-after ending? A high position in his council? Perhaps something more intimate? But it's not going to happen. He doesn't see you the way you see him, because women have no value in his worldview. To him you are merely a useful tool. That is all."

She snarled in impotent rage. As she blindly followed her "husband," she collided with a man approaching from the other direction.

He, however, did not so much as look at her.

Is this to be the remainder of my life? Will I—

She hesitated. Something about the man she'd run into snagged her attention. She looked back, but he'd already gone through the curtain.

She shook herself.

What was it?

THE HEAT HAD BEEN intoxicating and healing. When he could scarcely keep his eyes open any longer, Cossack scrubbed himself with soap, rinsed, and—reluctantly—climbed out.

At the end of the hour, dressed in the clothes Sayed had provided, Cossack was ready. His guide, Usama, appeared to escort him.

They returned to the junction not far from the entrance to the cavern. Cossack, with a clear sense of how to return to his quarters from the junction, paid attention to their next steps.

Usama strode about ten yards down the well-lighted tunnel opposite the cavern. Where the tunnel ended, they encountered two guards in front of a curtain. One of them swept the curtain aside.

Cossack's guide motioned him into what was obviously the first room of Sayed's personal quarters—a long, formal salon carved from the mountain. It may have been hewn from rock, but costly carpets covered the floors and hung from the walls. Soft lights illuminated a U-shaped conversation area formed by two divans and a chair for Sayed. A stove burned at one end of the salon, providing abundant warmth.

Beyond the conversation area, Cossack's examination took in a vintage desk and credenza flanked by tall bookcases. In the corner he saw curtains pulled to one side of a doorway leading, he presumed, to Sayed's sleeping chamber.

If Cossack's mountain hideaway was primitive in comparison to the tunnels and common area of Sayed's stronghold, Sayed's salon, by contrast and by far, eclipsed both.

But there was also something about Sayed's quarters that, to Cossack, was discomfiting. Sayed's rooms and furnishings were blatantly inharmonious with that of his men's. They were too different and too much. They smacked of arrogance and ego.

Can a true leader live in such opulence while the men who fight and die for him have so little?

"Ah! You have come at last. Welcome to my humble home, General Labazanov."

Sayed was ensconced in his chair, the crosspiece of the conversation area. His seat, raised above the divans on either side, was the focal point of the room. He did not stand at Cossack's entrance but waited for Cossack to present himself.

Cossack bowed his head once. "Thank you for your invitation, General Sayed. I look forward to my stay with you."

"As do I, Arzu. I have much to show you, and we have a great deal to discuss."

"As you say, General—particularly if you, as you suggested you might, allow me to bed your enemy operative." Cossack made himself chuckle in a crass manner. "You are certain she is an American, are you not? As I said when we spoke of her, I have never had an American woman. I wish to be confident—for bragging purposes."

Cossack's pretense disgusted him, but he was not above using such a ruse to meet face-to-face with Wolfe's operative. At least they would be assured of privacy.

The sudden turndown of Sayed's mouth made Cossack wonder if the man had bitten into something unexpectedly sour.

"I am sorry to disappoint you, Arzu, but I wish . . . for more time with her. As you suggest, she is an . . . exotic commodity."

Sayed's words rang just shy of true, but Cossack would not dare push the topic. Whatever Sayed's character flaws, he was keenly intuitive and rabidly suspicious.

"Of course, General."

"Shall we eat?" Sayed motioned to the cushioned divans and the low table. His servant began laying out a veritable feast—a variety of foods Cossack and his men had not tasted for months.

"When we finish our meal, Usama will show you back to your quarters. Rest yourself from your journey. Tomorrow, after breakfast, I will show you my manufacturing operation."

After the meal, Usama escorted Cossack to his room. Although the room was fitted with carpets, a chair, a lamp, and a warm bed, there was no door or even a curtain for privacy. One of the soldiers stood post with his back against the wall outside the doorway.

I am more a prisoner here than a guest. Perhaps tomorrow I will learn something further.

IN THE MORNING, Usama accompanied Cossack to the dining cavern for breakfast. Many soldiers greeted Cossack with earnest respect, coming to embrace him and express their happiness at seeing him. Although Usama tried to steer him to the officers' table, Cossack first went from table to table, asking Sayed's men about their wives and children and about their health or injuries and whether they had healed.

When he joined Sayed's lieutenants and commanders at their table, they welcomed him. He ate with them, sharing bits of how his own militia was faring through the winter, painting a contented picture while his own thoughts were not as certain.

I can only hope Rasul is following my orders.

"Come," Usama told him after breakfast. "I am to show you our manufacturing operation."

Cossack was mildly annoyed. "Will not General Sayed join us?"

Something flitted across Usama's face. "Unfortunately, other business detains him. I will do my best to entertain you."

They left the domed cavern, taking the main tunnel back toward the mining cars. When they reached the checkpoint that led down to the cars, Usama made a sharp right. A ways down the new tunnel, they encountered yet another checkpoint and a heavy wall built across the tunnel with a strong door set in it.

"On the other side, General, we will be required to put on special clothing to avoid contamination."

Cossack wondered what they might be contaminating. It did not immediately dawn on him that Usama meant *they* would be contaminated—not until he had changed into what reminded him of a space suit, completely enclosed and with its own oxygen supply. They had to go through yet another room that had overhead sprinklers, although they did not use them, before they entered the laboratory itself.

Cossack marveled at the setup—two long aisles of stainless steel countertops and functioning lab equipment. Four men, dressed as he and Usama were, ran the production line. Usama walked him from the first complicated and timely step to the last, pointing out the batch farthest along in process.

"The finished product is delivered to the next room where it is packaged. We were in full production up to three weeks ago. Now that the primary shipment is away, we have slowed down. Of course, when Sayed identifies another use for it, we will ramp up production yet again."

"What, exactly, is the product, Usama?"

"Oh, a very potent drug, indeed. The process is, sadly, hard on our packaging area."

Cossack frowned, wondering at Usama's meaning.

In the packaging area, he found out. The workers in the processing area were protected the same as he and Usama were, but the equipment was used. Worn. Tears and cracks in the face shields were taped with ordinary duct tape. The workers glanced up, fear showing through those face shields.

"Who are your workers?"

Usama grunted. "Infidels we rounded up here and there. We use them until they die—not usually so very long. Constant exposure, even protected exposure, eventually gets them."

He led Cossack across the packaging room to a deep niche carved from the rock wall. He gestured, and Cossack peered inside . . . not understanding at first what he saw.

Long bundles wrapped in ordinary cotton fabric and tied at both ends, reminiscent of five- or six-foot-long logs, stacked one atop another and piled like cordwood, filling the room.

Bodies.

Shocked, Cossack took a step back and bumped Usama.

"I apologize, General Labazanov. I should have warned you. We will clear this out in late spring when the roads are clear and have firmed up after the runoff. We have a pit where we dispose of them."

Cossack composed himself quickly. "I've seen enough, Usama. Thank you."

On their way out, they stopped in the shower area. Usama turned on the water and stood under the spray. "Be sure to rinse every part of your suit. We've had accidents where workers going out were not thorough."

Cossack, recalling the room of bodies, shuddered.

USAMA DELIVERED COSSACK back to Sayed's salon. "Well, Arzu! What did you think of our laboratory?"

Cossack was careful not to allow a hint of how much the drug lab had disturbed him seep into his reply. "I thank you for the tour of your stronghold, General Sayed. All of it, laboratory included, is impressive—far greater than what my men and I can boast."

"It is my pleasure to show you the spine that undergirds our victory."

"As you say! Very good, indeed. Well, now that I have seen your stronghold, it makes me wish to return to my own sanctuary and set my men to work. We have occupied our residence only months, and it is not nearly as sustainable or easily reached as yours is. We have many improvements to make—and I am filled with ideas from your stronghold I might incorporate into our humble quarters.

"Of course, there is idleness, too. During the long winter months, the men, if not kept busy, begin to quarrel and discipline suffers. It takes a strong hand to keep them occupied and rewarded with simple amusements when they do well. If you would, please summon my soldiers so that we may be off."

Sayed slowly twirled an unlit cigarette. "Rasul is an adequate leader, is he not? Surely you trust him to command during your absence?"

"That is hardly the point. Please allow me to depart in peace."

Sayed stretched out in his chair. Sighed. "Arzu, I must insist that you remain with us for the time being—until after the New Year."

"That is nearly a week off!"

"I apologize, but I must insist."

"I have been your trusted ally for years," Cossack growled through his teeth, "and you disrespect me so in front of your men?"

"An ally, yes, certainly. However, this close to certain victory, I cannot take any risk that might jeopardize our plans. Rasul will follow your orders while I keep you close, Arzu. As for your soldiers? Your men will be well treated. You need not worry on that account.

"And as the Americans' New Year's Eve celebrations near? We shall be receiving many visitors here, many friends and comrades in arms. Let us eat, drink, and enjoy ourselves while we await this triumph, eh?"

Cossack saw it all in Sayed's eyes. The paranoia. The suspicions. Couched in pleasantries that did not mask the "velvet chains" by which Cossack found himself bound.

I can do nothing except capitulate. I must assuage Sayed's mistrustful nature and wait for a viable opportunity to leave this place.

He sat back and relaxed. "Then I shall settle in to enjoy a much-needed respite, General Sayed. Thank you for your gracious hospitality."

CHAPTER 27

USAMA ESCORTED COSSACK TO breakfast as he had many days in a row, for nearly a week now. Cossack played his usual part in the charade. He offered cordial greetings to Sayed's lieutenants, joined them in prayer, and treated them as faithful but lesser officers.

In return, Sayed's lieutenants were uniformly polite—and uniformly restrained. They liked Cossack, that was plain, but they must have received orders to remain aloof. To put nothing more than superficial trust in him.

Cossack understood their dilemma. He took his meals apart from them—as a general should—and in every way conducted himself with the discipline and deportment befitting his status. He employed every opportunity to show himself a devoted follower of the Prophet and a loyal ally to the cause.

Day by day, he waited for Sayed to call him, but only three times did Sayed's men usher him into Sayed's presence to share the midday meal. They ate and Sayed alluded to his grand schemes but, when Cossack asked for details, Sayed politely refused.

"All in good time, Arzu," Sayed promised.

The routine continued in the same manner with no change. Until today. This morning following breakfast, instead of returning Cossack to his room, Usama escorted him to Sayed's salon.

Sayed sat on a cushion before the low table at the center of the conversation area. His servant and two guards stood nearby. Sayed was absorbed with the contents of a wide bowl, while his servant eyed Cossack and gestured to the sofa across from Sayed.

It wasn't a suggestion.

Cossack lowered himself to the sofa. He watched Sayed dig his hand into the bowl, fill it, and let the small, cellophane-wrapped bits fall through his fingers. He held the last one up to the light and studied it.

"I thought white ones stamped with a crescent moon most appropriate," Sayed murmured. He slid his gaze to Cossack and tossed the object to him.

Cossack caught it. Held it in his hand. The tablet was small, round, fairly flat, and very light. He noted the distinctive crescent Sayed had remarked on.

The other side was stamped with a stylized "x." A candy, perhaps? The clear wrapper was fused at both ends similar to a peppermint or an individual Life Saver.

He smiled to himself. *When was the last time I thought of Life Savers?*

"What is it?" he asked.

"Our gift to America on New Year's Eve."

Cossack's eyes jumped back to the innocent-looking thing, but he said nothing.

"You want to ask me, Arzu. It is written on your face."

Cossack shrugged. "As you have not trusted me with details before today, I will not ask you to extend an explanation that you feel you must refuse."

Sayed laughed softly. He looked to his servant and the two guards, and they laughed with him. Sayed turned back to Cossack. "Do you know what the date is today, Arzu?"

"I confess that I have found it difficult to keep track of the date since I arrived."

"Yes, I suppose I take your point. Well, it is December 30, *General*. We are eight hours ahead of America on their east coast, so it is already December 30 there also, but earlier in the day. Tomorrow is New Year's Eve, and the Americans set great store by their New Year's Eve celebrations. Very large, very public celebrations."

Cossack tossed the candy back to Sayed. "All right. What are these?"

Sayed grinned. "Since the plan is now in motion, I can trust you with the details, Arzu."

He scooted to the edge of his seat and leaned forward. Dropped the candy into the bowl with the rest. Reached his hand into the bowl and filled it. "Ecstasy is a popular recreational drug in America. A party drug—and what bigger party is there than New Year's Eve?"

"Drugs? You packaged drugs to look like candy? What if a child were to—" Cossack stopped himself. Sayed cared little for the children of his enemies.

"Calm yourself, Arzu. I suppose it is possible, but children are unlikely to eat these. If they did?" He shrugged again.

Cossack wanted to kill him. Right there, he wanted to strangle the man and see the darkness in his cold, unfeeling eyes go out.

Sayed smiled. "Put another way, children are not my target. No, it will be adults, mostly young adults, who benefit most from these beauties. Some may mistake them for candy, but anyone acquainted with the drug ecstasy will recognize it."

"I am not familiar with it."

"No? I hear it gives the user boundless energy, a sense of well-being or euphoria. American youth love to take it when dancing. The drug allows them to dance and enjoy themselves for hours."

Cossack was somewhat confused. "How is this a weapon?"

Sayed chuckled. "The tablets are made to disguise our most special gift. You see, each of these 'hits,' as I believe they call them, also contain a potent dose of fentanyl."

Cossack's thoughts moved at lightning speed. "Your weapon lacks an effective delivery system. You said the New Year's attacks would be devastating and point to the Russians. That they would "soften up" the Americans for the follow-on blow."

He laughed at Cossack. "My dear General! We won't be walking the streets of New York's Times Square, handing them out. Of *course*, we have a delivery system."

At Sayed's nod, one of his men handed him a tube-like device. He held it up for Cossack's inspection. "We tested a number of these and settled on the 80cm model for power and range."

Cossack nodded but said nothing. Sayed laughed again.

"It is harmless, I assure you. It is called a confetti cannon. We have, of course, required our manufacturer to make improvements. Each cannon must be able to not only shoot the confetti high into the air, but also three hundred of our ecstasy tablets. As I said earlier, anyone acquainted with ecstasy will recognize it for what it is. And are they not all individually wrapped to ensure their cleanliness?"

"You're going to shoot a few hundred of these into the air at midnight and expect devastating results?"

"Not a few hundred. To be precise, *six hundred thousand*—three hundred 'hits' shot from two thousand cannons. During their public celebrations, ten cities on the east coast of the United States will each be the beneficiaries of two hundred of these cannons and sixty thousand tablets."

Sayed giggled. "We will salt Allah's faithful among the unholy celebrants. At the stroke of midnight, they will discharge the cannons as instruments of celebration. What could be more innocent?"

"You'll have these loaded confetti cannons at big, outdoor New Year's celebrations and, at midnight, your people will shoot the cannons, launching the ecstasy tabs into the air. You think people will pick up the tabs from off the street—and swallow them?"

"Our studies show that half-inebriated partygoers are not the most discriminating consumers. However, the outdoor celebrations will not be the only places we sow our gifts. We have positioned squads of willing helpers, both men and women, in these same ten cities. They are all young and zealous for the jihad, eager to serve Allah. They have targeted the largest, most popular dance parties of the night and will attend them, dancing the evening away until the countdown to the new year.

"At midnight, they, too, will shoot confetti cannons into the air above the partiers. Trust me when I say that scores of partygoers belonging to America's up-and-coming generation will enthusiastically catch the tabs as they fall and partake of them. Why should they not? We've taken pains with our packaging to assuage their qualms."

Sayed stood to pace, his excitement growing. "I have heard infidels say that the followers of Islam across the world comprise a very large number and that we jihadis are only a tiny fraction of that number." He laughed. "The intelligent ones—not that there are many—warn that even a small fraction of a very large number is still a really *big* number. What they do not perceive is that this axiom applies in many situations."

He stopped pacing and faced Cossack. "The first collapse of the night will occur within fifteen minutes of the new year. Death within another five minutes or so. Of course, when the first victims succumb, no one will suspect the ecstasy. The pounding, deafening music will play on, the strobing lights will dazzle and mesmerize, the crowds will continue to dance, drink, and flaunt themselves, and more partiers will indulge in a little harmless 'molly,' as they call it.

"By thirty minutes past midnight, party organizers will realize they have a problem on their hands. Minutes later they will see death all around them. Some of the partiers may even wonder if the ecstasy they've blindly swallowed might be the problem. Soon after, their concerns won't matter.

"You see, fentanyl binds to certain receptors in the brain and switches them off. Without those receptors, the brain doesn't know that the body is low on oxygen. The confused brain will forget to tell the lungs to breathe—and so the victim will stop breathing. Death soon follows.

"In the cities we've targeted, calls to 911 will overwhelm the system. Not enough ambulances, police, or firemen—not enough time and not enough Narcan. Narcan can pause a fentanyl overdose, buy the victim a little time, but only if administered quickly enough.

"Did I say, 'pause a fentanyl overdose'? Yes. Narcan—naloxone—bumps the fentanyl off those vital receptors in the brain, but only for about thirty minutes. Without additional treatment, the fentanyl will reattach itself to the receptors and continue marching the brain to its own death."

Sayed said with wonder, "Did you know that only two milligrams of fentanyl is lethal? Two milligrams! *Subhan Allah!* Comparable to a few grains of table salt."

Cossack was like a spring stretched to its breaking point. His shoulders and neck were so tight he was afraid the rigidity of his posture would give him away. He wagged his head slowly side to side to mimic Sayed's mad awe. "I did not know this! Indeed, this is a powerful weapon, General."

Sayed grinned and laughed for joy. "But can we expect the devastating results I promised?" Breathing hard, he said, "Let me reassure you. Three hundred tabs per cannon multiplied by two thousand cannons? That's six hundred thousand lethal doses spread across ten cities. We've run the numbers through various computer models, using our lowest casualty estimates.

"If only *two percent* of the tablets are ingested? Twelve thousand deaths will result. Twelve thousand! The noble jihadi acts of September 11 resulted in less than four thousand deaths. At the very least, we will kill many times that number. What do you think of that, eh, Arzu?"

Cossack was frozen to his seat, unable to speak. When he could answer he murmured, "You were not exaggerating when you said your plan would outstrip 9/11."

"Your enthusiasm is less than expected, less than desirable, my friend."

Cossack snorted. "Not at all! I am . . . I am overcome by the beauty and sheer audacity of your plan." *Dear God or whatever high power exists in this craven universe, please help me play along*. "I am trying to wrap my feeble mind around the sweeping scope of your plan."

Cossack pursed his lips thoughtfully. "However . . ."

"However?" The corners of Sayed's mouth turned down, declaring that he did not wish to hear anything but praise.

"My General, I am merely wondering why the Americans will attribute this act to Russia. That is your objective, is it not? That the Americans will blame Russia and condemn it as an act of war? And when they do, Russia will shift its attention away from *us*, from the rise of the new Islamic caliphate?"

Sayed's good humor returned. He sat down beside Cossack and slapped him on the back. Then he removed one of the candy-like pills from the bowl and took up a small penknife. He sliced down the middle of the wrapper. He laid the pill on the table and used his fingers to carefully tease one of the fused ends apart. He laid a portion of the clear wrapper on the table and reached for a magnifying glass.

He handed the glass to Cossack and motioned to the wrapper on the table. "What do you see, eh?"

Cossack took the glass, held it over the tail of the clear wrapper, and leaned closer. The tiniest Cyrillic print appeared. Translated to English it would read *Bogolyubsky Confectionery Concern*.

Wholly owned by the Russian Federation.

"*Ya lahwy!* This wrapper was made in a Russian government factory?"

"Yes—as were the confetti cannons. We paid dearly for their 'under-the-table' production, but the wrappers and confetti cannons appear innocuous enough, no? That is, until the American FBI inspects them."

Cossack smiled. "You have thought of everything, Sayed."

Sayed lifted his head with pride. "Thank you. I have shared all this with you so that you will enjoy and appreciate the celebration."

"Ah, I see." Cossack had no idea what Sayed meant, but he tagged along, an eager audience to Sayed's madness.

"Tomorrow we will host a party—my own officers and a few intimate outside friends, our fellow fighters in the holy struggle. These friends will begin arriving later today. In less than forty-eight hours, when it is the midnight of New Year's Eve in America, it will be the first morning of the new year here. On that morning we will feast together and celebrate the glory of the attack as it is actually happening.

"A few hours after, we will hear from my commander in America, and he will report on the details of our victory, including casualty numbers as they are reported by the dumbstruck American media.

"Our fist—the fentanyl attacks—will fall upon the east coast of America, and when the evidence is collected, it will point to Russia as the malefactor. Perhaps, given enough time, the Americans will come to suspect that the clues we have provided for them are a bit obvious. However, within but a few weeks—before they can verify the Russian Federation's innocence? They will experience the crushing weight of the 'Hammer of Allah' *upon their heads*. And when the 'Hammer of Allah' strikes them, there will be no doubt in the Americans' minds who has attacked them. I promise you—there will be war between the Americans and the Russians."

Cossack did not have to pretend his eagerness. "Tell me, Sayed. Tell me of this 'Hammer of Allah.' What is the plan?"

Sayed's excitement cooled. "Not today, Arzu, but soon, I think."

He nodded to the soldiers who had brought Cossack to him. "Show him to his quarters."

Cossack lurched to his feet. "You brought me to your stronghold only to tease me?"

"No, I brought you here to prepare you to witness our greatest moments. Also, to keep you under watch. You see, even now I am not entirely confident of you, Arzu."

Cossack's expression was a mixture of confusion and indignation. "I have fought for Chechen independence for two decades and served with you half that long! What do you mean?"

"Perhaps nothing, but if I err, I err on the side of caution."

Usama approached Cossack, his meaning clear. Cossack nodded his compliance but threw Sayed a bone to stroke the man's ego. "You have the courage of a tiger, General. I hope to prove myself trustworthy to you."

"We shall see, Arzu. We shall see."

Usama returned Cossack to his "room," and he sat on the edge of his bed, the details of Sayed's plans consuming his thoughts.

I knew Sayed planned to hit ten cities on New Year's Eve. I had even learned he would use fentanyl as his weapon. However, I did not know how he intended to deliver the fentanyl.

I cannot hope that Wolfe's people will untangle the complexities of Sayed's plans enough to stop them. I gave them only what I had, and it was not enough!

Moreover, as grotesque and inhumane as Sayed's "fist" may be, I fear it will be overshadowed by this "Hammer of Allah."

WOLFE STOOD BEFORE THE task force. It was December 30, and he was staring the greatest intelligence failure of his lifetime in the face. He usually wore his responsibility well, but the weight of it lately had carved new lines around his eyes and mouth.

"People, the east coast of the United States will ring in a new year less than thirty-six hours from now. Please tell me you have actionable intel we can pass to our partners in the FBI, concrete information that will help them prevent the disaster looming over us."

When eyes skittered away from him and no one answered, he turned to his team leader—and was struck by the decline in her appearance. Patrice Seraphim was not the woman she'd been only two months ago. The lingering injuries from the car bomb, Bella's abduction, and the task force's inability to prevent the impending terrorist attack had beaten her down. She appeared mentally and emotionally demoralized.

I shouldn't have asked Seraphim to return before she was fully recovered—just as I should never have sent Bella to Tbilisi. These ill-advised decisions fall on me and me alone.

Jaz, the *de facto* team lead, reluctantly replied for Seraphim. "Director, knowing that ten cities are at risk, we've run the variables we believe would compel AGFA's target selection—a given city's population density, the popularity of its public New Year's Eve celebrations, the venue and its security's strengths and vulnerabilities. With a moderate degree of confidence, we can list twenty cities that fit the criteria. We believe the ten cities AGFA has targeted will be among those twenty."

"That's it? Ten cities out of twenty you 'believe' are the targets—with only a moderate degree of confidence?"

"We also know their chosen weapon, fentanyl. What we don't know is the delivery mechanism—although the most likely scenario tells us that street drugs will be laced with lethal doses of fentanyl."

Wolfe's voice rose. "And, therefore, FBI strike teams should just descend *en masse* on these public celebrations, guns at the ready? To what? Spread the word about the likelihood of deadly street drugs?"

"No, sir." Jaz took a breath. "However, with our deductions in hand and the high probability of mass casualties, someone could issue a public alert. Maybe the president?"

"Issue an imminent terrorist alert based on dodgy, piecemeal intel? Not bloody happening," Seraphim said quietly from where she sat.

Wolfe sighed. "Seraphim's right on that count. The President of the United States may be many things, but the poster child for political suicide he is not."

Jaz slogged on with dogged determination. "But we *do know* people are going to die from fentanyl overdoses—we have intel to back that up. We could call on the CDC to issue a repeating public health alert, a warning against buying drugs at these celebrations. It might not stop every overdose, but it could save hundreds, perhaps thousands of lives!"

"Stop wasting your breath," Rusty growled. "Don't you get it? As far as the bureaucrats are concerned, the task force and all our work has produced a big, fat *nothingburger*. Sure, we've got bits and pieces, but when stacked up, they don't prove a thing."

He snorted. "It's like a bad Western, us standing on a plateau and watching through binoculars while the innocent heroine is tied to the train tracks—and hearing the whistle of an approaching train grow louder and louder as it bears down on her. We're too far away to mount a rescue and there isn't a blessed thing we can do to stop or even slow the momentum of the oncoming locomotive."

Grumbles ran through the team, attesting to Rusty's morbid outlook. With a jerk of his head, Wolfe called Seraphim to him and they left the gym together.

There isn't a blessed thing we can do to stop or even slow the momentum of the oncoming locomotive.

Jaz swallowed hard and ground her knuckles into her eyes.

"Has to be something we can do. Has to be."

CHAPTER 28

BY MORNING, TASK FORCE morale had sunk even lower. The team gathered in the bullpen at the usual time, but no one had the will to work. They sat in knots of two or three, slamming down coffee, eying the various lines of inquiry on the boards, and halfheartedly discussing the unresolved questions posed in Vincent's orderly handwriting.

Faking it.

As they talked among themselves, they carefully avoided bringing up the possibility—the very real probability—that the task force was officially "done." Finished. After an unproductive morning, they gave up even the pretense of working.

In a corner of the gym, Tobin and Rusty let Bo run them through a demanding workout, a workout intended to make them forget everything except surviving Bo's demands.

The rest of the team—Brian, Vincent, Gwyneth, Jubaila, and Soraya—retired to the cabin's library to dull their pain on a *Die Hard* video trifecta.

Jaz alone remained in the bullpen, thinking, scheming, planning.

That evening, Bo brought a TV down from the dormitory above the gym and wired it to the dorm's antenna. He added a VCR and showed Vincent how to record from TV to VHS tape. Then Bo, Harris, Tobin, and Rusty hauled in a couple of sofas and some beanbag chairs.

"Why all the fuss?" Soraya asked. "You think we're in the mood for a party? Or that we want to witness what's coming?"

Tobin replied, "For no other purpose than to document the actual events and learn from them? Yes. We should watch and record what happens. Might need it later—you know, working on AGFA's next attack."

Brian snorted. "Riiiight. 'Cause the task force will still be around, and we'll all still have jobs after tonight."

"Shut the **blank** up, Brian," Vincent shot back.

In an attempt to lift the task force out of their morbid, leaderless funk, Richard laid a table of finger foods, snacks, and sodas, to which he added a half-dozen bottles of champagne.

The team largely ignored them. The idea of a New Year's Eve party was a joke—and a bad one. Brian's acid wit again best captured the team's mood.

"It's not actually a New Year's watch party. It's more of a death watch party, kind of a 'wake waiting to happen.'"

"Way to call it, Brian," Rusty whispered. "We're not counting down to the ball drop in Times Square. We're counting down to a people drop—people dropping like flies in the streets. And what are we doing about it? Why, we're kicking back like nothing's wrong—and y'know what that makes us? Officially disgusting."

Throughout the day, the team had seen little of Jaz. Even now, as the evening grew later, she kept plinking away at her laptop.

"What are you doing?"

She flicked one eyebrow at Rusty. Returned her attention to her screen.

"Seriously, what are you doing, Jaz?"

"*Seriously*, leave me alone. I'm busy."

Instead, Rusty rolled his chair to her.

"Is this your version of leaving me alone, Rust Bucket?"

"I'm going to ignore that undeserved barb—*for now*—because I know you're up to something. Might as well tell me. I'm not going away until you do."

Jaz huffed her exasperation. "Fine. We'd all like to stop the worst one-night mass murder in the history of the world, but since stopping it altogether isn't feasible, I'm hoping to limit the carnage."

"Yeah? Can I help?"

"Thanks, but not necessary. I already have an army at work."

Rusty frowned and leaned toward her screen. "An army? Show me what's going on."

Jaz tipped her head down, inviting Rusty to lean closer. "Spent a couple hours early this morning establishing the route for my posts."

"You're using anonymizers?"

"Duh. Fifteen of them—from Romania to Rajasthan, Belarus to Bolivia, Egypt to Ecuador, and nine places in between. The upshot is that anyone attempting to trace me will run smack into an inglorious dead end, a public computer sitting in a lowly Internet café in Jersey City."

"You hacked the Internet café's computer, then established a route through fifteen anonymizer sites?"

"Actually, I hacked the Harbor branch of Fleet Bank first, then hacked the Internet café's network from there. After that, on through the anonymizer sites."

She snickered. "Should an exceptionally good hacker—a miracle worker—manage to trace my posts back to that café and that particular computer? He will encounter the little gift I've left for him—my own special brew of malware—the cash cow of all computer contaminants, a cornucopia of caustic crimeware. After my pretty little viruses and worms chew through his system, there won't be enough of his hard drive left to even boot up."

"Brilliant, as always. So, what's your plan?"

"Already in motion."

Jaz scrolled down and pointed to her screen. On the public page of a popular bulletin board Rusty spied a call to arms.

WARNING | DANGER
Terrorist attack New Year's Eve.
Terrorists will release street drugs
cut with deadly FENTANYL
at NYE celebrations, US east coast states.
STOP TERRORISTS | SAVE LIVES
FORWARD THIS WARNING

Rusty appropriated Jaz's mouse and clicked on the word FENTANYL. It took him to an article on the lethality of fentanyl. He clicked back. Re-read the warning. Studied the profile of the individual who had posted the warning. Noted the profile's tiny icon—a fanged serpent's head.

He gaped at the 486 comments and exchanges below the post. Make that 489. The number of comments ticked up as he watched. He scanned the first comment, saw that its profile icon sported a trident, and the reply bore the fanged serpent's head icon.

Vyper, that you? Where you been?

Yes, me, Poseidon. Spread warning please.

Hear Ukrain. mob looking for you.

Those losers? What a joke. Spread warning please.

Done. Posted to seventeen boards and texted to rave organizers in NYC, Atlanta, and Miami. Forwarded to friends who will do same.

Good work, Poseidon.

Anything for the Venom Queen.

"Venom Queen? Holy moly!"

Jaz grabbed her mouse from Rusty and toggled to another screen, another message board. The same warning posted there boasted 542 comments or replies.

Jaz sighed. "Like I said, Rusty, already in motion. I hope it will be enough."

Almost as an afterthought, she muttered, "I'd *pray* it will be enough, but I don't do prayer."

THE DROPPING OF THE BALL at the stroke of midnight in Times Square went uncelebrated at Broadsword. Instead, it served as the final bell in what seemed like a twelve-round match. An unsuccessful fight. The team collapsed in on itself, beaten to a collective pulp.

Tensions rose higher as Seraphim, Tobin, Richard, Bo, and all off-duty guards gathered around the television to watch the wild celebration in the streets of New York following the countdown. Jaz sat cross-legged off to one side of the TV, her nose practically pressed up against its screen.

The cameras panned across the crowds of kissing couples and screaming partiers. Streamers, confetti, and fireworks filled the air.

The team, frustrated with her, began to pelt Jaz with popcorn. She didn't even notice.

"Down in front!" Brian shouted.

"Hey! Did you see that?" Jaz pointed, but the camera had already moved on.

"No! All we can see is your oversized head—or is that your bloated ego?" Brian heckled.

"Did we see what?" Tobin asked.

"That tube thing, that confetti-throwing gizmo. It—"

"Confetti cannon?" Rusty asked.

"Whatever. It lobbed more than confetti. Looked like candy raining down with the confetti."

"So? People like candy."

"Not if it kills you or your kids they don't."

All eyes shifted back to the TV, trying to spot what Jaz had seen.

"We can play it back later, if we need to," Tobin reminded the team.

"There!" Brian shouted. "That guy dressed like a stuffed bear. He *is* tossing candy into the crowd."

"I saw him. For maybe half a second," Jubaila said.

"I wonder . . ." Jaz got up, paced up and down, stepping in front of the television with each pass. She halted. Addressed anyone who cared to listen. "Do you suppose the terrorists might have devised multiple delivery mechanisms? Drugs from a confetti cannon, Fentanyl-laced candy from a man in a cartoon bear costume?"

Harris spoke up. "Smart military tacticians never rely on only one weapon or strategy."

"Right." Jaz frowned in concentration. "It's just that I was thinking it's great if you catch candy while it's still in the air, but not everyone is going to pick up something edible once it hits the ground. I mean, tossing it in the air isn't the most foolproof way to delivering candy, is it?"

She thought for a moment. "Where do people go when they leave the ball drop?"

"That's easy," Gwyneth said. "Dancing. Pretty soon all these channels will switch to the 'after parties.' But you knew that, right?"

Chewing the inside of her cheek, Jaz muttered, "I don't do dancing."

"Good grief, Jaz. Do you live under a rock?"

But Jaz didn't hear her. She ran to her laptop, entered a web-to-text site, pasted a long list of recipients into the "To" fields, and began furiously pounding out a message to the network of hackers with whom she'd been messaging most of the day.

Second FENTANYL warning
fwd to parties, raves, clubs
BEWARE FREE DRUGS

For emphasis, Jaz tacked on the word *LETHAL* at the end of the message and sent it. Almost immediately, the web-to-text site began receiving short, pithy responses—*OK*, *roger*, *yes*, *NP*, *on it*, and a plethora of ASCII characters affirming that Jaz's message had reached its intended audience and was being forwarded to nearby phones.

After that, there was nothing to do but wait for the media to announce the first deaths.

Seraphim stated she was going to bed. Everyone said goodnight, but no one doubted she needed the rest. The guards left for their shift. Richard returned to the house. Tobin, Bo, and Harris retreated to the other side of the gym to talk.

The remainder of the team didn't say much. They sipped beverages. Nibbled on the snacks Richard had laid out. Watched the muted television. Nervously anticipated the appearance of a Breaking News banner crawling across the bottom of the screen.

The first inklings of trouble, however, came through Jaz's web-to-text message, a reply from a fellow hacker.

Warehouse rave Phila
9 down near simultaneous
Suspect OD

"It's started," Jaz announced, her voice low and emotionless. She hadn't shared her last-ditch efforts with anyone on the team but Rusty. He nodded and sat down next to her to watch her screen.

Another text from the same hacker arrived.

23 now down,
blaming bad x
big panic

"This guy in Philly says they figure the fentanyl is in ecstasy tabs."

Rusty shook his head. "Party drugs? Not the hardcore stuff like heroin? Strange we didn't think of that possibility and put more emphasis on it, considering New Year's Eve is the biggest party of the year."

When the "Breaking News" finally hit the television, the time was approaching 2:00 a.m. The anchor, her expression professionally concerned, reported that 911 call centers were experiencing an overwhelming amount of traffic and that overtaxed emergency services were slow to respond. Other accounts trickling into the newsroom stated that paramedics were arriving only to find victims already dead or unresponsive. They also stated that no aid they rendered to the unconscious victims seemed to help them. The death toll, from multiple cities, was estimated at 273.

While still speaking, the anchor received a sheet of paper. She scanned it quickly, went back to the top, and read aloud, "Ladies and gentlemen, this is an emergency notification to the public at large from the director of the FBI, Dillon Patterson. Again, this is an emergency notification to the public at large from the director of the FBI."

Reading from the sheet, she announced, "The cities of Boston, New York, Philadelphia, Atlantic City, Newport News, Baltimore, Charlotte, Atlanta, Tampa, and Miami are reporting unusually high numbers of New Year's Eve fatalities, cause of death unknown at this time. However, accounts of these fatalities began shortly after midnight among New Year's Eve revelers attending public celebrations and at New Year's 'after parties.'

"Police and paramedics on the scene report that the afflicted partygoers collapsed then died within ten to fifteen minutes, often before medical help arrived. While the specific cause of death cannot be immediately confirmed, first responders suggest tainted recreational drugs may be at the heart of the outbreak.

"First responders also report that the use of Narcan—known by its generic name naloxone—is initially effective in treating victims on scene. However, the treatment's effect is temporary and does not halt the deterioration of the patient's condition for long. Patients who are guardedly stable when transported to the hospital are dying before receiving further medical treatment.

"The FBI Director has, therefore, issued a strong warning to the public at large, and I quote, 'Until the source of these deaths can be determined, the FBI urges citizens to trust no food or drink they have not personally prepared and avoid recreational drugs at all costs.'"

The news anchor looked straight into the camera's eye to deliver her last lines. "The FBI states that, at last count, the combined death toll across these cities stands at 617. The agency expects that number to increase. We will keep you updated as new information comes in."

When someone turned the volume down, the task force members began to throw out comments.

"No mention of a terrorist connection yet."

"Ten cities simultaneously? The feds have to know it's an attack."

"Right. They just haven't found the nerve to say so publicly yet."

"Too soon after 9/11. Think of the panic . . ."

"It's gonna get bad."

Another hour passed. At 3:15 a.m., the anchor updated the number of deaths to 753.

Vincent stepped in front of the team. "Uh, guys, I have something to say. See, I did some online research the other day. Afterward, I ran some numbers."

Jubaila asked, "What kind of numbers?"

"Um, morbidity numbers. Like, with a viral or other biological weapon attack, the epidemiologists look at replication rate as a factor in projecting the number of casualties. Replication rate means how fast the bug doubles and, thus, how fast it overwhelms a body's system—how fast an infected person dies."

"This ain't no bio weapon, my boy. Replication rates don't apply." Brian's drawled reply dripped with his usual sarcasm.

"Didn't say it did—I was drawing a contrast when you interrupted me."

Laughter and the welcome release of it went around the room. The laughing and banter increased when Rusty pointed at Brian. "He got you, man."

"Yeah, yeah. Whatever."

Vincent picked up where he'd left off. "With an infectious biological, we'd be calculating replication rates and infection vectors. A model built on those factors would show a slow but exponentially increasing number of infected individuals—a line gradually sloping upward, the slope increasing as the number of infected doubles.

"Then they'd take the number of casualties and divide it by number of infected to produce a mortality rate. The mortality rate would further aid in projecting the disease's path. Ebola, for example, depending upon which strain it is, can yield a mortality rate of fifty percent to nearly ninety percent. Think of it—out of 1,000 infected, 500 to 900 dead. A *lot* of deaths.

"In contrast, the use of a nonbiological such as poison gases, mass shootings, and bombings are large-scale attacks where the greatest numbers of casualties occur *immediately*. I am, of course, excluding nuclear attack in this comparison where radiation sickness adds another layer of casualties, usually at the end of the model.

"But back to a nonbiological mass attack? A graph of those casualties would show a sharp, horrendous uptick followed by a short plateau and an equally sharp decline."

Jaz squinted her tired eyes. "You've lost me. What in the world are you getting at, Vincent?"

"Just this. We knew AGFA would attack ten cities simultaneously. Given the lethality of fentanyl and the terrorists' certainty of their success, we projected very high casualties from each city within the first two hours, even thousands—that's thousands multiplied by ten."

"The FBI said the body count was at 753."

"Right."

"You're saying it should have been much higher."

"Exactly. What I'm getting at is that the first numbers of a nonbiological attack are indicative of how high the casualty totals will go. All things considered, the overall number should *right now* be in the thousands."

Gwyneth squeezed her eyes closed. Hard. "The terrorists' plan didn't work as they intended. We're not going to see thousands of casualties, because *something went wrong*."

Vincent, a sheen of tears glistening in his eyes, nodded. "Yeah, that's what I think it means. We've already seen the 'sharp, horrendous uptick' and it was *not* as advertised. Yes, we'll likely see more deaths over the next six hours, either at the same level or below, but we're not going to see a *rate* increase. If we graphed the number of deaths from midnight through tomorrow noon? We'd see that we've already passed the apex of the curve. It's downhill from here."

Vincent tried to contain his relief, but it overflowed and ran down his face. "Consider this for a minute—AGFA's big attack? The one that was supposed to make 9/11 look like Tinkertoys? The attack they were going to pin on the Russians so the US government would blame them—putting further strain on America's already strained relationship with the Russkies? *It fizzled.* Bottom line? As awful as this night is, it was supposed to be a hundred times worse."

Across the room, Jaz and Rusty exchanged small, knowing smiles. Their smiles grew into grins. They got up, threw their arms around each other, and hugged. Hugged madly—in front of everyone.

"It worked, Rusty!" Jaz shouted.

"AGFA laid a goose egg!" Rusty shouted back.

Then they were laughing so hard that they couldn't stop. They laughed with such hilarity that soon the others were laughing with them. Little by little, as Rusty and Jaz were able to explain, and as the task force realized the implications, the morale of the team soared.

Tobin summed it up. "You and your hacker network saved thousands of lives today, Jaz. In addition, because AGFA's attack did not accomplish its goal, you've set back their 'grand plan.' The US and Russia won't be going to war any time soon—especially after Wolfe presents the evidence of what AGFA was attempting to do."

"Evidence? Yikes!" Jaz shouted. "We need to call Wolfe. He needs to have every bit of the debris in Time Square collected and analyzed. Bet you a donut, something in the debris was supposed to pin the attack on Russia—and we need that evidence."

The team gathered around as Vincent put a conference call through to Wolfe's home. Not surprisingly, Wolfe was not asleep. He, too, had been monitoring the news.

Jaz nodded to Rusty, asked him to tell Wolfe about the hacker network. Then Vincent explained why the mortality rate from AGFA's attack had not and *would not* rise to the level of AGFA's expectations.

The explanation had to be repeated, and Vincent had to walk Wolfe through his reasoning as to why the attack, bad as it was, had actually failed. Wolfe was an astute listener. Even with half the team chiming in, he caught the gist of the call inside of five minutes.

"Got it, thank you. I need to get off the phone with you and call the Director of the FBI. Explain it to him and have that evidence collected."

Wolfe paused a beat too long. Despite his best efforts, the team heard him trying to get a grip on his emotions.

"You people. I am . . . very proud—" His voice cracked. What he could manage after that was only a simple, "Well done," before he hung up.

With the dial tone humming on speakerphone, the task force members stared at each other.

"I know we averted a bloodbath," Brian commented soberly, "But still . . ."

"Hard to celebrate what *didn't* happen when a lot of parents will be burying their children in the next few days," Soraya finished.

Tobin stood up. "Right. This is not the time to celebrate, and we can't afford to lose our focus. We have a job to finish. Stop AGFA's third attack."

"And find Bella," Jaz said softly. "No days off for us."

"Find Bella," the others echoed.

THE NEXT MORNING, the task force members returned to their desks and settled back into their work. Only minutes later, Brian pushed his chair away from his computer. Slammed a notebook onto his work surface. Screamed in disbelief and rage.

"No! Oh, no! Make it stop!" Brian's protests dissolved into tears.

The team rushed to his workstation and crowded behind him. He was logged into a jihadist recruitment website. Watching a video.

A monstrous creation.

A woman kneeling, bound hand and foot. Another woman in a blue kaftan wielding a pair of scissors, hacking away at the kneeling woman's hair.

The kneeling woman licking blood from her lips, staring with defiance into the camera. Shouting, "At the name of Jesus every knee will bow, in heaven and on earth and under the earth, and every tongue will acknowledge that Jesus Christ is Lord, to the glory of God—"

Bella's voice.

Bella's face . . . marred by blood and bruises.

Bella's hair falling in chunks to the floor.

The woman in blue hefting a stone ashtray. Making certain the camera would capture her actions. Slamming the ashtray into Bella's mouth.

Tobin sank to his knees. "Lord God! Oh, Lord God! Please! Please have mercy . . ."

CHAPTER 29

LP

COSSACK WAS OBLIGED TO attend Sayed's high-spirited festivities The first party, a day-long celebration on the thirty-first, included Sayed's top officers and the generals and lieutenants from five militias—prongs of the Chechen freedom movement as radical as Sayed.

During the second party, while the actual attack was happening, close to thirty men gathered in Sayed's salon to await word of the success of their operation in the US. Since Chechnya was eight hours ahead of US eastern standard time, the second party convened at the unusual time of eight in the morning—midnight on the east coast, the exact time Sayed's people would launch their operation.

Four hours later, at noon Chechen time, Sayed's top man in the US would report in with the first accounting of casualty numbers. Until then? Sayed would entertain his guests and bask in their congratulations and honor.

The morning began with a splendid breakfast. Sayed's servants plied his guests with fresh fruits and vegetables, a whole sheep roasted over an open fire, broiled fish, fresh breads, and a number of tantalizing side dishes. Breakfast was followed by platters of sweets along with two kegs of beer and a case of a vodka hauled to Sayed's stronghold especially for the celebration. Then Sayed himself revealed a liquor cabinet stocked with mixers and tonic water.

Cossack had not noticed the cabinet before. How could he have? The cabinet was cleverly hidden, built into Sayed's bookcase.

Cossack watched Sayed's guests flock to the alcohol while he nursed the single glass of beer Usama had pressed into his hand. The visitors toasted each other, toasted Sayed's visionary planning, and toasted the Islamic caliphate so close at hand. Relaxed and jovial, each salute grew more verbose and boisterous than the previous.

How interesting that Sayed and his "holy" jihadis have dedicated their lives to proclaim Allah's rule over all nations and yet, with such ease, indulge in what is haram. *The Quran clearly labels intoxication and drunkenness as abominations of Satan's handiwork.*

Cossack snorted into his glass. Sayed also kept a stable of kidnapped women to satisfy his men's sexual needs—and that wasn't sanctioned by the Quran either. He frowned a little as he thought of Wolfe's operative languishing in captivity, much the same as Sayed's sex slaves.

He shook himself and got up. *Time to mingle, my boy.*

Cossack was well known to the visiting generals. He chatted casually with Sayed's guests, keeping his interactions pleasant, moving around the room, never staying too long in any conversation. As the men relaxed into the party atmosphere, so did their conversation.

The alcohol loosened men's tongues and relaxed their vigilance. By careful listening, Cossack picked up bits of useful information, storing them away in his mind for later reference. The most interesting information concerned the next attack, the so-called "Hammer of Allah" as Sayed had named it. Everyone agreed—the New Year's Eve attack would destabilize the already tenuous US and Russian relations, and Sayed promised that his "Hammer of Allah" would shatter any hope of peace between the two superpowers.

I could have thwarted Sayed's New Year's Eve attack if I'd had the means to convey what I knew of the attack to Wolfe. It is too late for that, but not too late to foil the next one, this ludicrously titled "Hammer of Allah." No matter the consequences, I must uncover the plans and convey them to Wolfe.

Something final and resolute shifted in Cossack's belly. *No matter the consequences. It is why I am here.*

At eleven o'clock, Sayed's servants delivered fresh platters of food and carafes of thick Turkish coffee. Cossack watched as the servants tidied up and discreetly removed the last of the beer and vodka.

He smiled to himself. *Ah. I see. Sayed wishes his guests to enjoy themselves, but he doesn't want them insensible when his US commander reports the success of the New Year's Eve attacks. The generals' congratulations for his great victory must be lucid if they are to stroke Sayed's ego with the proper weight of respect and honor due him. Hardly possible if his sycophantic guests are falling-down drunk.*

Forty-five minutes later, the food and coffee had done its work. Sayed's guests had sobered enough to turn their anticipation toward the upcoming report. As for Cossack, he continued his passing conversations while keeping his attention focused on Sayed himself and watching for the means by which this great, vaunted report would arrive.

At five minutes to noon, Sayed assumed the seat of honor in his salon and waved his hand to an owlish young man hovering in a corner. The bespectacled twenty-something acknowledged Sayed with a smart salute—and stepped away from the small table he'd been guarding. He and another man picked up the table, carried it to Sayed, and placed it before him.

The guests immediately sought the best seats or places to stand around Sayed. They quieted, and Sayed smiled an indulgent acknowledgement of their fawning submission.

Cossack was more interested in stationing himself where he could best observe the object on the table—a brick-like satellite phone.

A satphone? Here?

Curiosity warmed him and ignited a spark of hope. No mobile phone had yet been invented—cellular or satellite—whose signal was strong enough to penetrate the rock between Sayed's salon and the sky far above. Sayed had not even bothered to remove Cossack's own mobile phone from his person because it was nothing but useless bits of plastic and electronics within the mountain—or without the mountain, for that matter. Their location was miles from any functioning cell tower.

What Sayed did not know is that Cossack's mobile phone had been heavily modified to disguise a different type of electronics, one that had not come standard with any phone. *A personal locator beacon.* In fact, one could make the argument that his actual phone had been grafted onto a PLB transmitter, his phone being the lesser of the two technologies.

Switched on in the open air, the distress alert would be received and processed by the International Cospas-Sarsat Programme. COSPAS was the acronym of a Russian phrase meaning Space System for the Search of Vessels in Distress. SARSAT was the acronym for Search And Rescue Satellite Aided Tracking. Together, they formed the international satellite system for search and rescue.

It was Cossack's means of signaling his handlers that he needed immediate extraction, and it was a foolproof one. Once his personal signal was identified, his GPS coordinates would be forwarded with all speed directly to his agency and handlers.

Not that it does me any good inside these impenetrable rock walls. But if I were ever able to get the beacon to the surface and switch it on?

The immediate question was, how did Sayed expect to receive his commander's report mere minutes from now? Even with a satphone, how could an orbiting satellite pick up his phone's signal from inside this mountain?

Cossack sidled up to a certain affable lieutenant and murmured something in passing to him, solely for the sake of his ever-present "companion," Usama, who was watching him and keeping tabs on his interactions. Cossack pretended to sip from his tiny cup of coffee. His attention to the coffee, however, was a diversion. His objective was to discover how Sayed's technicians would connect the phone's signal to an orbiting satellite.

He thought of his own stronghold and its simple radio room, the brave soldier who had scaled the face of the ravine above the stronghold's main entrance in order to bolt an antenna to the rock face and attach a cable to the antenna.

Ah! A cable. Sayed must have a cable leading up to the surface. A cable attached to an antenna. But to string cable from the antenna to a phone this far underground? How did they manage it? The cable must be hundreds of feet long, as must be the shaft to accommodate the cable—a shaft bored through solid rock.

He shook his head. *An impossible engineering feat.*

Impossible? If Sayed had accomplished such an undertaking, then it was not impossible.

He had his answer when Sayed's young technician attached a coaxial cable to the phone and, with a nod, placed the phone in front of Sayed. Alongside the phone was a conference call hub. Another line ran from the phone to the hub.

A murmur of anticipation rippled through the room as Sayed switched on the hub, then the phone. He waited until the screen on his phone indicated a network connection, then dialed a long string of numbers. Through the hub's speaker, everyone heard the phone's warbling ringtone, the uplink to the satellite, and the subsequent transfer to the phone on the other end. The crowd of guests leaned forward, anxious for Sayed's American commander to pick up.

Cossack leaned forward, too, but his eyes were not fixed on the phone but on the coaxial cable. Without moving his head, he shifted his peripheral vision and traced the cable down the table and onto the floor—where it disappeared between the legs of Sayed's tech man and then under the ornate robes of Sayed's top two lieutenants.

They are blocking my view. I need another vantage point.

But now was not the time. Shifting to another standing place at this juncture, while Sayed's guests were holding their collective breath waiting for the phone to be answered, would only draw undesirable attention to himself.

After. During the celebration after the call.

The call picked up. A voice answered with appropriate respect.

"*As-Salamu Alaykum*, General Sayed."

"*Wa alaykumu s-salam*, Commander Khasurt," Sayed replied. "My lieutenants and many important guests are assembled in my salon. We have been celebrating our victory over the Americans, this important milestone in our quest to enmesh the Americans and Russians in war, a war that will open the door to our Islamic Republic."

"Sir? General Sayed—"

Sayed rolled over his commander. "I have you on speakerphone, Commander Khasurt. We are all anxious to hear your report. Tell us the good news. Include as many details as you like, please."

But Cossack had heard the reticence in Khasurt's voice, and he stopped breathing for a moment. Something was wrong. Others around him stilled also, sensing something amiss in Khasurt's voice.

Had Wolfe's people been able to stop the attack after all?

"General Sayed. Sir, perhaps . . . perhaps you would allow me to report to you in private, first?"

Sayed's temper flared. "You will report to me now."

"Yes, General Sayed, sir. However . . . I am sorry to report that the operation has not been as successful as we hoped it would be."

Sayed paled. "Repeat that? How many deaths so far? How many?"

"Media reports say 996 deaths."

"Yes, yes. In Philadelphia where you are. What about the other targets? What about New York?"

"General, sir, the number covers all ten of the cities we targeted."

"You are saying only 996 deaths from all ten cities?"

"Yes, General. We . . . we expect that number to grow. But only a little."

Sayed's jaw hardened. "What went wrong? *What did you do wrong?*"

"Sir, nothing went wrong. Our operatives did everything as planned. We had no problems, no mistakes. No one was discovered, no one was arrested. However . . ."

"What?" Sayed shouted, forgetting his audience. "However, *what?*"

"I-I have received word that a warning went out in the hours before midnight."

"My people here have been monitoring the news channels since yesterday. They heard no such warning! You are lying, Khasurt—and I will have your head for it!"

Khasurt was offended at being called a liar in such a public venue. His tone hardened. "General Sayed, there was a warning, but it did not come from the government or through the news media. It came across various Internet bulletin boards and chat rooms. It was picked up and passed from one user to another to other boards and chat sites. It was sent by text message to various party organizers and attendees."

"Who? Who started it? I will tear out their fingernails and gouge out their eyes!"

"I . . . we . . . that is, it is the nature of these boards and chat rooms that communications are often anonymous. Discovering the post's author was not the problem. We know *which* online profile started the posts. But tracing that profile to an actual person and their location after they have logged off would be—no, *is*—impossible."

Sayed's protests ground to a halt. Abruptly, he switched off the conference hub and put the satphone to his ear. "Who, Khasurt? Whose online profile?"

Cossack watched Sayed's expression as he listened. He asked a few more questions, then ended the call and turned in on himself. The man was dangerous at any time, but when crossed? He was pernicious and vindictive.

Unpredictable.

Volatile.

Cossack eased back a step and maneuvered himself out of Sayed's direct line of sight. A few other astute individuals did the same. The visiting generals and their seconds who could not hide themselves schooled their features and dropped their eyes. The technician who had set up the call froze in place, afraid movement would draw attention to himself.

Minutes crawled by and no one spoke.

Then Sayed, as if nothing were wrong, stood and said, "My honored guests. I am grateful to have you here. Please. Let us enjoy ourselves, shall we?"

He clapped his hands and shouted to his servants. "More food! Bring fresh coffee and tea! Break out wine and beer. Let us be merry."

It was both a suggestion and a warning.

His servants jumped to do his bidding. His lieutenants rushed to mingle with the guests, their conversations constructed to defuse the situation's discomfort. The technician and his helper quickly removed the table with the satphone and speakerphone hub.

Cossack, from behind Sayed, kept an eye on the two men. Noted where they stowed the phone and the hub.

I now have the wherewithal. What I need next is opportunity.

His gaze did not linger on the men or the equipment. He took a plate and heaped fruit on it, then joined a visiting general.

The man slid a knowing eye over Cossack. "General Labazanov. How long, do you think, before Sayed's anger and blame falls on some hapless soul?"

It was a backhanded mockery of Sayed and a forecast Cossack shared. It was also a pit Cossack would not willingly step into—particularly since Usama was never far from earshot.

Cossack selected a grape and considered it. His response was noncommittal. "*Inshallah*, General Isamov." If Allah wills it.

The general chuckled. "Well spoken. You are ever the cautious one, Arzu."

Cossack allowed himself to return the smile with good humor. They were in accord without saying anything further.

A LOT HAD HAPPENED behind the grate since Laynie came down with dysentery. She'd suffered for three days and slowly recovered. Then Ksenia had caught what Laynie had—and so had all the other girls in the cell with them.

But not all at once. No, the eleven others who'd refused to have anything to do with Ksenia and Laynie and had segregated themselves at the far side of the cave should have been fine. Instead, they fell victim to the illness like dominoes in sequence. With near-precision accuracy, they sickened in rotation, one or two women becoming ill just as the previous ones were recovering.

And as long as the guards heard groans and vomiting coming from behind the grate, Bula ordered them to keep their distance lest the entire stronghold succumb to the illness. The guards brought food and water regularly. They brought Laynie her own mattress. They even brought hot water and fresh rags for the women to clean themselves after being sick. But they refused to empty the slop buckets . . . and they did not come in the evenings to take the girls to the soldiers.

Thank you, Lord! I thank you for this dysentery that keeps Bula from ordering us out of the cell to service the soldiers. Thank you for extending your covering of grace over us for a season.

Most importantly during the sickness, God moved.

While Laynie tended and sang to Ksenia, the girl from the other campfire drew near to listen when Laynie sang. She watched and listened like a little bird but kept far enough away, Laynie believed, not to catch the bug.

Not so. As soon as Ksenia was on the mend, their little sparrow fell ill . . . and the girls of the other group, with shouts of fear and disgust, cast her and her contaminated mattress and blankets out. Laynie and Ksenia dragged her things to their fire and tended the girl through her fever and all the unpleasant distress that accompanied it.

"What is her name?" Laynie asked Ksenia.

"She is Asmeen."

While Laynie bathed Asmeen's face, arms, and chest, she whispered, "Asmeen, Jesus loves you," repeating the words even though Asmeen understood nothing she said.

It didn't matter. Laynie's gentle words and ministrations spoke the language of love to Asmeen—and she understood *that* dialect perfectly. While Laynie stroked her cheeks, tears leaked from under the girl's lashes. When Laynie held her hand and sang, Asmeen and Ksenia closed their eyes and let the melody wash over them.

I hear the Savior say,
"Thy strength indeed is small;
Child of weakness, watch and pray,
Find in Me thine all in all."

Jesus paid it all, All to Him I owe;
Sin had left a crimson stain,
He washed it white as snow.

Laynie sang the same song so often that Ksenia and Asmeen sang the choruses with her, not knowing the meaning of the words they mimicked.

When the infection caught hold at the other campfire and a girl threw up, the remaining "unsick" females would push her and her mattress away from them, and Laynie and Ksenia would bring the outcast into their circle. The first had been Asmeen. The second was Mariam. Others followed.

It was then that Laynie, between songs, began talking about Jesus, beginning with Adam and Eve's sin and the promise of a Savior. While they cared for the sick girls, Laynie talked about Jesus, pulling from every Sunday school lesson she'd ever heard. Ksenia, as enthralled as the other girls in their little clan, translated.

What must Miss Laurel think of all this, peering down from heaven? Laynie reflected. *Most of what I share I learned in her classes. The last time I saw her, she gave me a word from God, a correction that could have saved me from the unholy life I chose had I heeded it. In my ignorance and arrogance, I sneered inside and blew her off—and she knew it.*

Laynie bent her head and whispered, "I am truly sorry, Miss Laurel. I hope Jesus gave you a great golden crown set with lots of jewels when he welcomed you into his presence. Thank you for instilling so much of God's word in me when I was a child. It did not return void."

While she nursed the Muslim women, they listened to Ksenia's translations of Jesus' life. They mourned his death, they exclaimed with wonder at his resurrection and considered Jesus' promises of eternal life. Asmeen and Mariam prayed to receive Jesus as their Lord. They chose to remain with Laynie and Ksenia, even after the sickness left them.

The other girls, however, returned to "their side" of the cave after they recovered, although . . . when Laynie sang, she would sometimes hear the soft echoes of voices from the other campfire, singing with her.

Jesus paid it all, All to Him I owe;
Sin had left a crimson stain,
He washed it white as snow.

"Your word is not fruitless, O God," Laynie murmured. "It is alive, active, and working in our hearts. I planted the seed. Someone else will water it. Your word will not return void."

She looked around their meager campfire at the three young faces turned to her in hope, turned to her for love. She led them in worship and in prayer. She taught them about Jesus. And she gave them what love and care she could.

They told her their stories—Ksenia, from the hill country of Turkey, who watched her family be murdered. Asmeen and Mariam, who were stolen from their families in rural Azerbaijan—*not* from Muslim families, Laynie discovered to her surprise, but from an Armenian Orthodox village.

"We knew about Jesus," they told Ksenia, who then told Laynie, "but we did not know him as you do. Now he lives in our hearts, too. This is why we have hope!"

For twelve days the sickness protected the girls within the grate from being taken to the soldiers. It hid them inside a fragile and transient bubble of peace and safety.

On the thirteenth day, Bula stood at the grate and shouted for Laynie. And took her away.

THE SERVANTS LOADED THE tables with yet more food and drink. The alcohol Sayed had cut off earlier flowed again, and the gathering regained its party-like atmosphere—even if the attack's failure left a bitter taste in everyone's mouth.

Sayed had withdrawn for a while to his sleeping chamber, taking his satellite phone with him. When he returned, he whispered orders to his servant, who scurried from the salon to obey him.

His anger chilled, some of his usual bluster restored, Sayed held court in the center of the salon. He told jokes, recounted successful battles, and occasionally clapped a guest on the shoulder, regaling his listeners with some anecdote that flattered the guest. It was Sayed's way of bestowing attention and favor on an individual, thus binding a naive man to him with cords of appreciation and obligation. The more astute individual received the honor but committed nothing of himself to Sayed.

Cossack, passing from one knot of conversation to another, noticed Sayed's eyes flick to the doorway of his salon. They were fierce and cold, not at all in keeping with his jocular mood.

What is he up to?

A moment later, Cossack saw Sayed again glance toward the entry.

What is he waiting for?

General Isamov's warning jangled in Cossack's head. Something terrible was about to take place. Cossack stepped behind a group of men and pressed himself against a wall, removing himself from Sayed's sight.

Bula appeared in the doorway, his hand gripping a woman's arm. Sayed spotted him and smiled. Bula pulled the woman into the center of the salon.

Laughter and conversation died away. Everyone stared at the woman and wondered why she was there. She was appropriately dressed—a fresh niqab over a soiled abaya. The veil covered her head, hair, and all of her face but her eyes, which were suitably downcast.

All very proper.

Sayed turned to his guests. "A while ago, I inquired further of my American commander concerning the failure of our attack—this vital piece of our overall plan. You heard Khasurt speak of the warning that went out to bulletin boards and chat rooms across the Internet. This warning was the cause of our failure. And you are, no doubt, wondering who released the warning and who is to blame?"

Cossack stiffened. Steeled himself. Whatever was coming, it would be brutal.

Sayed smiled at his listeners. "We are partners of a sort with a crime syndicate in New York, both sides benefitting from the arrangement. They agreed to provide us with cash and certain favors necessary to our cause.

"In return, they asked us to supply them with a drug called fentanyl. We did so. They also asked for something more—the location of a certain woman, a computer hacker of some repute, whose icon is a fanged asp and whose 'handle' is Vyper.

"You see, this Vyper person who works for an American intelligence organization caused the syndicate's electronic files to fall into the hands of the FBI. The syndicate, understandably, wishes very much to get their hands on this woman. Through our eyes and ears in America, we were able to provide the syndicate with her location.

"It was detrimental to us that our syndicate friends' attempt to capture this wicked woman did not succeed. I say it was detrimental to us because, as it turns out, this same Vyper is believed to be the individual who started the Internet warning yesterday—the warning that caused our plan to fall far shy of its needed objective."

Sayed nodded to himself. His smile widened in a manner that chilled Cossack.

Then Sayed pointed at the still, garbed form. "*This* woman is the leader of the hacker's team. She is an agent of the Great Satan's government who was sent into Tbilisi some weeks back to meet a local contact. But we knew she was coming, you see, because we had our own people embedded in the Great Satan's government. And so, we captured her. Perhaps you have even seen her featured on many jihadi websites?"

Sayed drew near the woman. "If you wish to know who is responsible for foiling our plans? Look no further."

Sayed yanked the niqab from the woman's head, and his guests, as one, gasped. The woman's hair, all of it, had been shorn at the scalp leaving a bare, scabbed terrain behind.

A knife flashed in Sayed's hand. He grabbed the front of the woman's abaya and slit it from the neck down to her breasts. While Bula held the woman, Sayed ripped the garment to its hem. Bula released the woman's arm and the gown fell away.

She wore nothing but a ragged shift under the outer gown. She was filthy, disheveled, and nearly naked, but she stood uncowed and did not cringe or grovel. She lifted her chin and confronted Sayed's guests. In perfect Russian she addressed not Sayed but his guests and his officers.

"Did my team defeat a cowardly attack on innocent men, women, even children? Although this is the first I have heard of my team's success, I celebrate it.

"And I ask you, why do you follow such a man—" she lifted her chin toward Sayed, "if he *is* a man? He is no man who shames a devout woman of the Book as he has tried to shame me. Yes, I am such a woman—a Christian, a follower of Isa—Jesus the Christ. And does not the Quran say, *Do not kill a soul that God has made sacrosanct?*

"You seek to raise a new caliphate for Allah, but did not the first Caliph instruct you, *Do not kill women, children, the old, or the infirm; do not cut down fruit-bearing trees; do not destroy any town?*"

She stared her contempt at Sayed. "This man has made you odious in the sight of your god. He has—"

Bula grabbed her by her neck. Sayed struck the woman in her mouth, ending her proclamation. With clenched fist, Sayed struck her again. A third and fourth time. Blood flew from her nose and mouth.

Cossack felt his heart stutter and seize.

She was older. She was thin and ill-looking. Her head was shaved—all her beautiful, long blond hair gone.

But he *knew* her—and he knew that voice.

He staggered against a wall, undone.

His mouth breathed a name only he could hear, a familiar name but *old*, a name from another life, years before he was Arzu Labazanov, the *Dark Destroyer*.

When he had been but a young, impetuous man . . . in a different life.

"Magda."

FROM SOMEWHERE OUTSIDE himself, Cossack heard General Isamov shout a protest. Other visitors also grumbled against Sayed, their protests gaining strength and volume.

"General Sayed! Stop this at once!"

"Filthy *kafir* whore!" Sayed let go, and the woman dropped to the floor, senseless. When her head struck the carpeted rock, it made the sound a ripe melon makes when thumped.

Isamov spoke above the protests. "If the woman is a spy deserving of death, General Sayed, then put her against a wall, shoot her, and be done with it. But to strike her in the face with your fist again and again? This is not right."

The atmosphere in Sayed's salon swayed under Isamov's commanding presence. Sayed himself was intimidated for a moment. But only a moment.

He drew himself up and squared his shoulders. "Take her away," he ordered Bula. "As for the rest of you? You have come into my home as my guests, and I have lavished my hospitality on you. Calm yourselves. Perhaps we did not achieve everything we hoped for in last night's attack, but we will not be thwarted in our next effort—I promise you."

"You promise many things, General Sayed," Isamov said quietly.

Sayed stared at Isamov. "If any of you wish to leave our gathering early before I share the details of the next attack, I will bid you safe travels."

Isamov nodded. "Very good. Thank you, General Sayed, for your gracious hospitality. I and my men will gather our things and depart. The blessings of Allah be upon this place."

Others followed Isamov's example, queuing up to thank Sayed and say their goodbyes—a lengthy process in Islamic culture.

Cossack shook himself free of his shock and dismay. As soon as the exodus began, he stepped back, keeping one eye on Sayed and the other on Sayed's confounded servant lingering at his master's elbow. It was the work of but a moment to reach one hand behind the heavy tapestry curtain beside the bookshelves.

He was nonplussed when his hand encountered nothing—no wall, no door, nothing but open air . . . and the hint of a breeze.

A shaft for the satphone's cable? Or an escape tunnel?

He didn't think it through—there was no time for that. He stepped behind the curtain and stilled its movement behind him.

Idiot! It's too dark in here to see anything.

He felt for a wall, found one, and followed it. About two feet along, it curved left. Almost immediately he encountered a dead end, and his hands brushed up against a cable. He followed the cable up until it disappeared into a shaft only inches in diameter.

As I thought, this cable leads up to the surface, to an antenna. No exit here.

He continued to "walk" one hand along the wall, thinking to make a complete circumference of the alcove and return to the curtain—until his hand fell through an opening in the wall and he nearly fell in after it.

An opening in the wall, three feet off the rock floor.

Cossack felt around the opening's edge then spanned the opening with his arm, estimating the tunnel a little more than two feet across. A tight squeeze, except . . . He reached his arm inside and felt for the "roof." He stretched himself, following the roof and then encountered a vertical shaft. It, too, was roughly the same distance across.

Cossack laid on his back, scooted into the tunnel opening until he reached the shaft. He raised his arm and encountered a metal handhold or step pounded into the shaft's rock wall. He also found the source of the slight breeze.

This is Sayed's exit. It goes up to the surface. I can leave right now.

He began climbing, the handholds and footholds alternating right and left. It was utterly dark in the shaft, and he wondered how far he had to climb. When he tired, he leaned back into the opposite wall to rest. It was during his first rest that he began to reconsider.

If I leave now, how long will it be before my beacon results in a rescue? Will my rescuers know to bring troops? Doubtful. Will they walk into an ambush? Possibly. And will Sayed have killed her before I return?

I might never have the opportunity . . .

He was already climbing down.

He reached the bottom of the shaft and slid out into the alcove. He listened at the curtain and heard the murmurs of Sayed's guests, a sizable number still lingering over the food and drink. He slipped out from behind the tapestry and walked directly to a table without looking around. After helping himself from the platters of fruit, he turned, scanning as he did.

Sayed was still engaged with his departing guests.

Timed that just under the wire, Cossack realized.

He was already making plans to find her, break her out, and flee Sayed's stronghold via the escape shaft. All three objectives would prove difficult, perhaps impossible. Getting caught would confirm Sayed's suspicions about him. Would certainly get him killed.

He no longer cared.

CHAPTER 30

THAT NIGHT IN HIS SLEEPING niche, Cossack put out his light and pretended to go to sleep. He prepared to wait for the night guard Usama had posted outside his sleeping niche to go relieve himself. Instead, he discovered something useful—the guard had become lax since Cossack's arrival. Once the guard felt assured that Cossack had retired for the night and was asleep, he left Cossack's doorway.

As the guard's steps shuffled away, Cossack drew back the curtain. Several moments later, he heard the soft greetings of two other guards far down the tunnel, toward the exit to the mining cars. Cossack slipped from his niche and turned in the opposite direction. He thought he knew, generally, where the *kafir* women were kept. To get there, he'd have to pass through the intersection of tunnels at the cavern without encountering anyone.

The farther from his niche Cossack got, the more authoritatively he carried himself. If someone challenged him at this point, he would need to bluff his way through.

He crossed the intersection, passed the cavern, and kept walking straight ahead. He hadn't gone far when he noticed that the tunnel had narrowed and the lighting had dimmed. Then he hit the first branch off the tunnel, a left. He turned into the branch and stopped to listen.

He heard no sounds.

When he had waited five minutes and nothing had caught his attention, Cossack advanced slowly, taking his time. He was surprised when the tunnel abruptly widened and ended. The lighting increased some here, enough to make out a barred grate across the tunnel and, behind the grate, what looked like a natural cave, stretching away into darkness.

Checking carefully to ensure he hadn't overlooked a guard curled up and sleeping in a corner, he went up to the grate. Far back within the cave, he spotted the banked embers of a campfire. Farther to the right, he saw the coals of a second fire.

If anyone behind the grate had noticed him, they remained quiet.

This has to be the place, but they are all sleeping. I need . . . I need to be careful.

He rolled a few ideas around and chose one.

He called out softly, "Magda."

No answer. No reaction or response.

He called out again. "Magda. Magda!"

LAYNIE STIRRED. HER FACE hurt so abominably! And her arm ached where Sayed had burned her days before. She found it impossible to lay in any position long before the blood pooling around her injuries pounded her to wakefulness, forcing her to turn over. After she shifted position she snatched bits of sleep, but her unconscious mind troubled her with fretful dreams and kept her from the healing sleep she needed.

Far away, she thought she heard a voice calling to her.

No . . . not me. That's not my name . . . not anymore.

Ksenia jiggled her. "*Mader*, a man is standing at the bars. I do not know what he says. The same thing, over and over."

Laynie groaned as she sat up. She reached for her jug of water, took a sip, and swished it through her sore, raw mouth.

"Magda. Do you hear me?"

The voice spoke English.

Laynie shot from her mattress, disturbing the slumbering girls clustered around her. She struggled to catch her bearings in the dark and stumbled on unbelieving feet to the bars.

The man, a Chechen like the other soldiers, saw her. Stopped calling and waited for her.

She drew near him and took in what she could see in the low light—black, untrimmed beard and hair shot with gray, a face weathered by a life spent outdoors, one cheek horribly scarred, and glowing amber eyes that peered out from under hooded eyelids.

"Magda."

At first Laynie couldn't "see" him. She stared and stared—until he reached his hand through the bars to touch hers.

She knew then.

"Black?"

"Yes, Mags."

"The scars on your cheek?"

"The result of being too close to an exploding Russian mortar."

She watched as the man considered her, too. She was calm as he inventoried her bruised, beaten features, the scabs on her bald scalp, her thin, shivering body, the absence of any clothing except for her shift and a pair of socks. The severe lines around her eyes and mouth scored by pain.

She watched him struggle with fury.

"Sayed, that sadist pig! How long has he had you?"

Laynie tried to remember. "Maybe . . . three weeks? I was kept somewhere else for at least a week before being brought here."

"What is that on your arm?" The days-old declaration burned into Laynie's arm was an angry red, the swollen letters running together.

She met his outraged eyes. "You could say I've had a change of heart about many things. Mainly about God. It says, 'I am not ashamed.'"

He looked away, trying to get a grip on his emotions.

"All right. We can talk about that later. First, we need to get out of this place, and I've found a way. Do you know where they keep the key to this cell?"

"It's hanging on the nail over there. Wait—" she said as he turned to fetch it. "We're in the mountains, in the middle of nowhere. Winter. Snow on the ground. I don't have boots . . . or clothes."

"My cell phone has a personal locator beacon. As soon as we reach open air, I'll activate it. Within an hour, my handler will receive my exact location. We'll grab a few things on our way out to keep you warm until they arrive."

"The way out. Can we take the other women, too?"

Cossack swore under his breath. "I didn't come here to get them out. I came to get *you*, Mags."

She pulled back from the grate. "I see. Perhaps, then, we should reconsider. You go and activate the beacon. When you're picked up, contact Director Jack Wolfe. He'll send an assault team for me and blow this evil place to kingdom come."

Cossack drew back, startled. "You work directly for Wolfe?"

She nodded once. "And I'm guessing he's your handler, too, right, *Cossack?* I'm not surprised. Wolfe holds his secrets closer than a poker pro holds his cards. Never mind. Can you tell me how you plan to get out?"

"Sayed has a personal escape route in his salon. It starts behind a tapestry hanging on the wall next to his bookshelves. The problem is getting into his salon. One or two soldiers guard the doorway around the clock."

Laynie shuddered. "Not particularly looking forward to another visit to Sayed's suite."

"And I can't guarantee that the escape route will be viable a second time if I were to use it."

"Right. I . . . um, the thing is? I can't leave without at least three of the girls coming with us."

"You've formed attachments, is that it?"

"Yes."

"Doesn't sound like the professional I knew."

"Like I said. I've . . . changed."

Silence stretched between them for several long minutes until Black broke it. "I cannot tell you how much regret I have lived with over the years. I have always wondered—what if we had left Marstead back then? What if we'd run together? Gotten away to live a normal life?"

Laynie reached her fingers through the bars and stroked his scarred cheek. "I would never have recognized you, but your voice—I will remember it forever."

Slowly she pulled her fingers back and answered him. "But you left without giving me that option, without letting me choose to run away with you. You turned yourself in to save my good standing with Marstead."

"I suppose you're right. I chose for you. After they had interrogated me for two weeks, I had them convinced that you'd broken off our relationship months before, but that I still loved you. That I had been, for lack of a better word, stalking you.

"When they finally believed I'd jeopardized my cover, your cover, and Marstead itself over 'a petty love affair,' they offered me an opportunity to redeem myself. It was a long-term, backwater assignment far from you. Somewhere my Russian proficiency would be useful.

"They sent me into Ukraine to integrate myself into the dissident tribal people, to become one of them and worm my way into the anti-Russian factions. To play the dissidents against Russia—except when helping Russia was *more* in Marstead's interests."

A phrase he'd used had shaken Laynie. *Was it only a petty love affair, Black? It wasn't to me.*

He had to have heard her thoughts, and his voice roughened with emotion. "I told them what they needed to hear, but it was never a petty affair, Maggie. You were the love of my life."

She sniffed and looked down. "I made myself forget you. I killed my love for you."

"You had to. I understand. It's in the past for both of us."

She again nodded.

He asked, tentatively, "Do you . . . have anyone? Someone who loves you?"

"Yes. Quincy Tobin."

Laynie closed her eyes. *Oh, Quincy! I want to come back to you, I do!*

He was quiet before murmuring, "Then I'm glad for you, Mags. You deserve to be happy."

He didn't speak again for another moment. When he did, his words were undergirded with steel. "We've got Sayed's escape route. Let's get out of here, shall we?"

Laynie sucked up her turbulent emotions. Let her game face slip into place.

"Listen. The key to this cell is hanging on the wall just over there, but I want you to do something for me." She gave him directions to her old cell. "There's another key hanging on the wall outside that cell. From what I've glimpsed of the keys, they aren't sophisticated. I think the same key may work in all the locks. If that cell is still unoccupied—"

"I will get the key from the unoccupied cell but leave the key to *this* cell where it is. They expect to see it hanging where it belongs. It's presence will delay the guards finding out you're gone."

"Yes." They still had that instant understanding between them, and she smiled.

"Right, then. I'll return shortly."

She stepped back from the grate until she was hidden in the shadows—in case Black was caught and the guards came to check on the women.

He returned safely after a few minutes.

"Take it, but we have to delay our plans. I need to go—right now. They're looking for me. I'll be back as soon as possible."

He shoved the key through the bars into her fingers.

"Black? I'll be praying for you."

Surprise, consternation, confusion flickered over his face. "Thank you—I guess."

Then he was gone. Laynie slid her hand through the bars in the gate and angled the key into the lock. It turned easily. She relocked the gate and withdrew the key. Took it back to her mattress.

She forgot the pain of her injuries and began to hope.

Laynie Portland
SPY RESURRECTED

PART 4:
LAZARUS, COME FORTH

LP

CHAPTER 31

"LISTEN UP, PEOPLE." Jaz had given them enough time to grab their coffee before she called them to order. "Listen up. We eked out a win two nights ago. Yes, we lost a terrible number of people, but not nearly as many as we could have."

"That was you, Jaz," Rusty pointed out.

"Yes, it was," Vincent agreed. "Take a bow, Jaz. You got the warning out when the feds didn't take us seriously."

Amid the subdued cheers and whistles, she bowed. Then she reminded them, "Gestalt, remember? A win by one of us is a win for the team. And that wasn't the extent of our win. Because we had warned the FBI prior to the attacks that AGFA was trying to drive a wedge between America and Russia, AGFA couldn't pawn off their failure as an act of Russian aggression.

"New Year's Eve was supposed to be *big*, remember? *So big* that it should have pushed US and Russian relations to a dangerous place. Well, they fumbled their strategic objective. As Rusty put it, AGFA laid a great big goose egg. That, me hearties, is the real win."

A few half-hearted cheers and high fives.

Jaz laughed with them—but only for a moment. "Settle down, you scurvy crew. We still have AGFA's third plan to scuttle."

"Arrr, Captain," Brian growled. "The Secret Treasure of the Carfentanil Ghost Ship be our mission."

Soraya folded her arms. "Really? Are we really stuck with pirate talk all day? We're talking serious stuff here."

"We could go back to clowns," Jubaila laughed.

"*Gah!*"

"Soraya's right. Carfentanil is nasty. From what Tobin's friend told him, anywhere AGFA dumps or disperses the carfentanil, people will die—and if the amount of chemicals tells us anything, it's that AGFA made a *lot* of carfentanil."

Tobin cleared his throat, signaling he was joining the conversation. "One thing my DEA geek friend said really stuck with me. He said that carfentanil dissolves easily in water."

The team went silent as they considered Tobin's revelation.

"That's super bad news," Rusty said first, "worse than the HF scenarios we ran because so little carfentanil can kill you. I mean, the possibilities? They might bottle and distribute it. Put it in soft drinks, juices, just about anything."

"Or," Tobin said softly, "Just dump a ton of it into a city's water supply. Remember, it's easily absorbed through the skin. Wash your hands, take a shower, swim a couple of laps in the local pool? Dead in under five minutes.

"What if they dropped it into DC's water supply? Or Seattle's? Or Denver's? They have thousands of cities to choose from. We have millions of lives at stake."

He let his eyes drift over to Jaz, then addressed the team. "Let's take a vote. Who here, rather than guess how and where AGFA plans to use the carfentanil, would rather ID the shipment and stop it from ever reaching port?"

All hands shot into the air.

"How do we do that, Tobin?" Jaz asked.

He nodded, a smile growing on his face. "Well, who, besides AGFA, knows where the shipment will land?"

"The mob," Vincent declared.

"Yup. I wonder if they know how complicit they'll be in what could be the largest terror attack the world has ever seen. Personally? I think it's time Wolfe drops the hammer on them."

Jaz jumped up. "C'mon. Let's make the call, Tobin. The rest of you? It's time we get serious about finding Bella. Get to it."

By consensus, the task force members refused to talk about the jihadist video, but they couldn't get the images out of their minds—Bella's beaten, bruised face. Her defiant proclamation of faith. The heavy ashtray slamming into her jaw. Her unconscious body toppling to the floor.

Jaz didn't add what they were all thinking—*Find Bella. Before it's too late.*

WHEN TOBIN AND JAZ left the gym, the air sort of left with them. The remainder of the team watched Vincent record the latest developments as bullet points on the board, then opened their computers. And exhaled on a collective sigh.

"Man, it's like one giant haystack after another," Brian sighed, "with another buried needle to locate. *Find Bella*, she says."

"We can't give up," Gwyneth murmured, "but I'm with you. I don't know where to go next."

"Doesn't help that Rosenberg hasn't used Burner Two to call anyone, let alone AGFA's satphone."

Rusty wasn't sitting. He did his best thinking on his feet. At the moment he paced up and down the gym, fretting, pulling at invisible threads, trying to tease out any kind of new lead.

He stopped and mumbled, "What if . . . what if Rosenberg's burner isn't the only phone that's called AGFA's satphone?"

"Who else would call them?" Brian asked.

Rusty concentrated. "Well, who initiated business discussions between the Ukrainians and AGFA? And wouldn't the arrangements have had to, at some point, percolate up the ranks? The Ukrainians paid AGFA seventy-five thousand dollars for some fentanyl and for Jaz's location, requiring high-level approval.

"Then AGFA delivered Jaz's apartment address to the mob, and the mob sent a hit squad to get her, first taking out Tobin and Bella. Except their op didn't work out as planned, did it? And it wasn't AGFA's fault, so the Ukrainians couldn't exactly ask for a refund.

"Nevertheless," Rusty theorized, "when AGFA learned that Bella was flying into Tbilisi—compliments of Sherman and Rosenberg—they told the mob that they would squeeze Jaz's location from *her*—and *oh*, would you please sneak our shipment of carfentanil into the US for us, thank you very kindly. Thing is, they had to coordinate all those arrangements, right?"

Rusty had his audience's attention, now.

Vincent said, "You're suggesting that Ukrainian leadership had to have spoken directly to AGFA leadership in Chechnya."

Rusty stopped pacing. "Huh. I guess I am."

"And?"

"Oh. Well, *how* would mob leadership have spoken to AGFA leadership? Had to be via AGFA's satphone, right? The satphone Rosenberg called."

"Jaz and Tobin left a few minutes ago to convince Wolfe that he needs to set up a meet with the mob," Soraya said. "So—"

"So, *we* can't just give AGFA a call. What would we say if we did? 'Hey there, AGFA. This is the task force. We know about the carfentanil shipment and we know you have Bella.' How's that gonna play out? I'll tell you—shortest call on record."

"Right," Brian agreed. "Not enough time to get a lock on their location."

"You got it, Brian. What we need is for Wolfe to pressure the mob into giving us the carfentanil shipment *and* convince them to call AGFA, keeping both parties on the line long enough for the tech-weenies to triangulate the call. With satellite positioning, they can tell us the location within twenty feet."

"Gee," Gwyneth snarked. "That's all? Get Wolfe to pressure the mob into giving us the carfentanil shipment *and* convince them to call AGFA, keeping them on the line long enough for the tech-weenies to triangulate the call? Sure, pal. We'll be lucky if Wolfe gets the shipment info out of the mob. He's got leverage for that. All the rest is highly unlikely."

Soraya folded her arms. "Well, we need to try, don't we?"

CHAPTER 32

JANUARY IN NEW YORK City can be brutal, the average temperature hovering between a low of 27° and a whopping high of 38°. Add some breeze to those temps, and you get a couple million people, bundled from foot to face, exiting their cabs, buses, or trains and striding the streets of Manhattan Island with purpose, bent on reaching their destinations and ignoring everything else.

In Central Park, a gentleman of indeterminate age, his slight body bent into the wind, crept down the walk. Two women trudged as fast as they could manage on the sidewalk's slippery surface, no doubt cutting through the park in order to reach their workplace a few minutes sooner.

No mothers with children had ventured into the park this gusty morning. Sure, a few zealous joggers made their rounds, but no one just sat around in the cold wind. Waiting.

No one except Jack Wolfe.

He perched on the edge of a stone bench, within sight of the bumper-to-bumper traffic of Central Park South. He wished his Burberry overcoat and cashmere scarf were heavier, but he was grateful that his team had insisted he don a thick watch cap to protect his head and ears from the frigid wind. He wondered if his toes—or the back of his head, for that matter—would survive the approaching meet. Wolfe had a sniper positioned to take a shot if ordered. The mob probably did, too.

He held two steaming cups of coffee in his gloved hands. At present, the cups acted more as hand warmers than beverages.

Wolfe's earwig clicked on. "Heads up, boss. Your three o'clock."

Out of the corner of his eye, Wolfe watched a woman approach from his right. She was tall and long-legged, but her entire body, down to mid-calf, was draped in a beautiful red fox fur coat. The coat's fur hood, thick and heavy, was pulled up and over her head so that only her face and a few tendrils of auburn hair showed. Her feet and legs were wrapped in high-heeled boots of golden-red leather, and she wore matching gloves.

She stopped at the bench. "Hello. You are Director Wolfe?"

"I am. Please join me."

She sat down next to Wolfe, and he offered her one of the coffees. She used the coffee as he did—to warm her hands.

"Thank you. I have heard a lot about you, Director Wolfe. You may call me Svitlanya."

Pure American. No hint of accent.

He took a moment to study her. From a distance, he'd thought her young. Up close, he saw that she wasn't. With the slight sag of her jaw and the deep lines at the corners of her mouth and between her eyes, he judged her age to be around fifty-five. But a fit and well-preserved fifty-five.

"I'm always pleased to see women promoted to senior roles these days. The mob's sensitivity training must be paying off."

She replied with a knowing smile. "I enjoy a man with a good sense of humor. No, in my organization it is second of all who one *knows* . . . but first of all who one is related to."

He didn't need the voices in his ear to fill him in. Svitlanya Davydenko, daughter and youngest child of Semion Davydenko, crime boss of the Odessa *mafiya* or mafia. The Ukrainian crime syndicate, based out of Brighton Beach in Brooklyn, was often called Odessa after the port city on the Black Sea of the same name.

Svitlanya's father had sired two sons before Svitlanya was born. The older—and heir to his father's throne—was killed five years ago in an argument with a disloyal underling. The next in line was now serving fifteen to twenty in federal lockup for securities fraud, mail fraud, and RICO—racketeer influenced and corrupt organizations—charges.

Semion, pushing eighty-five, had been left with two options. Either choose and groom Svitlanya to take his place or pick from among his trusted *pakhans*—bosses or captains. In his view, promoting one of his many bosses above the others would risk jealousy and rebellion in the ranks.

Svitlanya had been the safer, if less conventional, choice.

Wolfe smiled back. "Thank you for meeting me, Svitlanya."

She nodded. "You are welcome. However, one must wonder what is so important that a man of your rank would ask for a meeting with us rather than communicate through . . . channels."

"You know who I am—what I am. Because the matter is critical, we asked to meet with someone in your organization of equal stature. Can you tell me you are that person?"

"I admit to nothing—except a great deal of curiosity. I suppose I would also admit that our organization insists on a certain level of respect in such situations. You have extended such respect to us and may rely upon our returning the same."

He liked how she'd replied. Carefully but clearly.

In other words, you've answered my question with a yes.

He said, "I'm glad to hear that. Shall we begin?"

"Please. It is colder today than I care for."

Wolfe smiled again. "That it is, and I will get straight to the point. Your organization has business dealings with the leaders of a Chechen separatist group. You believe the relationship to be mutually beneficial—fentanyl from them to increase your heroin profits, money and small favors in return to help them continue their fight."

"Heroin profits? I would never acknowledge that our organization deals in such things, Director. We are a business, not a criminal organization."

"You are recording our conversation, are you not? You have people not that far from us listening in? As I do?"

Her brows lifted. "My, you are blunt. And if I said yes?"

"Then let us agree to drop pretense, today only, in favor of preventing a heinous crime against America. I am not here regarding your organization's 'businesses.' This is not a trap or a sting. I asked you here so I might offer you a warning."

"What warning?"

"That the separatists are playing you for fools."

The woman flushed and her jaw hardened. "The Russian military soundly defeated the Chechen rebels last summer. Of course, the rebels are a determined bunch and will continue their efforts using guerrilla tactics, but they cannot achieve independence through these paltry methods."

"Granted, but what if I told you that the separatists with whom you have business dealings are actually Islamic fundamentalists, bent on forging a united Islamic caliphate extending from the steppes of Ukraine, across the Caucasus, to the Caspian and beyond? What if I said they are working hand in glove with al-Qaeda, the terrorist group that planned and executed the 9/11 attacks?"

She thought a moment. "*If* we had business dealings with Chechen separatists and *if* what you say is true, we would not welcome such news. It is, after all, our city they attacked in September."

"Then let me elaborate on these separatists. They call themselves All Glorious for Allah. We call them by their acronym, AGFA. You are right when you say AGFA cannot win against the Russian military, so their leader has undertaken an audacious plan, one that will pit America and Russia against each other. His people are working to goad and manipulate the two superpowers into a shooting war—and they are fully committed to achieving this goal.

"Why? Because they think that if America and Russia came to blows, Russia would recall their military from Chechnya and Dagestan and focus them on defending their borders against Western aggression. Then AGFA and its affiliated separatist militias could sweep through southern Russia and declare its caliphate rule. Moreover, al-Qaeda forces out of Iran, Pakistan, and Afghanistan would rush to reinforce them. Likeminded jihadis from Syria, Lebanon, and Saudi Arabia would join in. Together, they would subdue the Caucasus states, push into Ukraine and—"

She laughed. "That is preposterous!"

"Perhaps, but so was the idea of flying airliners into the Pentagon and the World Trade Center—until they actually did it. What we call preposterous, they celebrate as bold and worthy of praise. Trust me when I say that nothing will turn AGFA from the course they are on."

She fidgeted. "I do not say you have convinced me, Director, but as you insist you have a warning for us, I am willing to listen a little longer."

"Good. Here is what we know. AGFA devised a series of three terror attacks on US soil to escalate tension between the US and Russia. Two of the attacks have already been carried out. The first was the attempted assassination of Vassili Aleksandrovich Petroff. Our people—*my people*—foiled that attack."

Wolfe stared into the woman's hooded eyes. He noted the shrewdness in their depths as she considered his words. Semion Davydenko may have chosen well when he selected his successor.

"Of course we know who Petroff is. However, we understood that this attempt on his life came from an angry American woman. She said the Russian Federation had foreknowledge of the 9/11 attacks. She was angry because Russian politicians did nothing to warn us."

"Yes, a young American girl made the attempt. An unsophisticated girl who somehow managed to get her hands on a couple of gallons of hydrofluoric acid, a dangerous and controlled chemical. A girl whose brother did two years in prison, came out a radicalized Muslim convert, then converted her."

The two creases between her eyes deepened. "We did not hear that part."

"We kept it quiet."

"You spoke of two attacks already carried out?"

"Yes. The second occurred on New Year's Eve. We could not prevent that one, but we blunted its impact by spreading a warning through the Internet. AGFA arranged for somewhere in the neighborhood of five or six hundred thousand ecstasy tablets laced with fentanyl to be given away at public New Year's Eve celebrations and dance parties. Tens of thousands of Americans were supposed to die that night. Instead, less than twelve hundred succumbed."

Her mouth tightened. "Still . . . a horrific number."

"Yes, a horrific number. The final death toll was 1,123, although a few more may follow. The FBI picked up all the tabs they could find after the fact, but some people may have pocketed one or more and saved them for later use."

He waited a beat. "I'm sorry to be the one to tell you, but your organization was complicit in those deaths."

"Nonsense! We would not partner in such madness."

"Oh, but you did. Your people took delivery of the cargo when it arrived and passed it on to AGFA's people—as you well know."

Svitlanya stood to her feet. "This conversation is over."

Wolfe fought the urge to grab her arm and pull her back—convinced it might earn him a sniper's bullet. Instead he said quietly, "Sit down, Svitlanya. We aren't finished, and you *need* to hear my warning."

BULA APPEARED AT THE grate that morning and called to the girls. When enough of them had responded, he asked, "The guards tell me they no longer hear the sound of retching and vomiting. Are you well again, or is anyone among you still sick?"

No one replied, but several of them hung their heads and shook them slowly side to side.

"Tell me now if anyone is running a fever," Bula demanded.

The same girls shook their heads.

"Very well. I will have the guards clean out the refuse. When they finish, they will bring you clean clothes and double the amount of bathing water. Be ready this evening to resume your duties to the soldiers."

Ksenia had crept forward to listen. She returned to Laynie, Asmeen, and Mariam and repeated his message to them. The three girls turned glum faces away from Laynie while she digested the news, but Asmeen began to weep silently.

Their hopeless state pierced Laynie's heart.

Lord, you know how much I thank you for the season of peace you provided. Through the dysentery I was able to minister to these young, sorely abused lives and bring them to Jesus. But that season is closing, Lord, and I have no means of protecting them. O God! Please tell me what to do. Please!

Laynie considered the key Black had slipped to her—now hidden behind a large rock against the cave wall.

If I could reach Sayed's salon undetected, I would take them out of here. I don't care if I freeze, Lord, if it means they have a chance to escape.

But she couldn't reach Sayed's salon without being caught, particularly with three girls in tow. Black had assured her that one or two guards were stationed at the salon's entrance, day and night.

She whispered her prayer, "Lord, what would you have me do?"

A conviction flowed over her, an action accompanied by certainty—for her and her alone.

"Lord, please let my sacrifice be holy and pleasing to you." She drew in a steadying breath. "And may my example give my daughter Ksenia courage."

THE SOLDIERS CAME, four of them, dragging a wagon across the uneven stone floor. Two soldiers kept watch while the other two, wearing rubber gloves and bearing soap and hot water, removed the loathsome containers, cleaned all around the area, and took the full buckets away.

An hour later, the soldiers returned with two wagons, one bearing clean buckets and a load of firewood and a bucket of coal. The other wagon carried soap, four kettles of hot water, and fresh rags and towels. They replaced the old refuse buckets with clean ones, dumped the fire fuel, and handed over stacks of worn but freshly laundered shifts, socks, abayas, and veils.

The girls jostled for position in line to access the clean water. Laynie observed as they used one kettle to dunk and soap their heads and another to rinse them. After three of them had washed their hair, the water in the two kettles was filthy.

At least I don't have to worry about putting my head in that polluted water.

She did, however, scrub herself as clean as possible, towel off, and dress in fresh clothing—with the soldiers staring, pointing, and leering. She didn't need Ksenia to interpret what they said. Instead of fretting, she turned inside.

"Thank you, Lord, for clean clothes." She truly was grateful for the clean clothes and a veil's warmth on her bare and wounded head.

Ksenia stayed close to Laynie and mimicked her simple prayers of thanks. Laynie smiled her approval.

Ksenia is like a young chick following my every move. Lord, please do not allow me to disappoint or discourage her.

Back at their campfire, Laynie helped the girls dry their hair. Ksenia tended to the burns on Laynie's forearm.

The girl pointed to the wounds. "This is not good, *Mader.*"

Laynie already knew that the burned skin was festering. She had soaped it well, hoping to allay infection. "Wipe it with vinegar water and wrap it, Ksenia. It will be all right."

When they received their noon meal, Ksenia put into words what she, Asmeen, and Mariam were wondering.

"*Mader*, when the soldiers come this evening . . ."

"Yes?"

"Jesus has made us clean inside and out, even from . . . you know. What would he wish us to do when the soldiers come?"

Laynie bowed her head, seeking the right words to answer. "You must do whatever you believe Jesus is speaking to you. What I do may be different than what you do—but only because Jesus has spoken something different to me. Above all, we should trust him and be brave."

Ksenia sniffed back tears. "I am not like you, *Mader*. I am not brave. I am afraid."

"Every person is afraid, my daughter. A brave one looks to Jesus and says, 'I will do what you ask of me, even when I am afraid, for you have promised never to leave me nor forsake me.' That is brave, Ksenia."

Ksenia's trembling hand crept into Laynie's. "Maybe I can do that."

Maybe I can too, my little daughter.

"A WARNING, DIRECTOR WOLFE?" Huffing with disdain, Svitlanya lowered herself again to the cold bench. "Make your point, please. I am freezing."

"As am I, but what I have to say is critical to both of us. We believe the third attack is poised to happen within the month, perhaps sooner."

"And what? My people will magically be implicated?"

Wolfe gentled his voice. Cajoled her. "While the victim of the first attack was supposed to be a high-level Russian official, the attack's purpose was to spread disinformation about Russia's role in 9/11. What did the girl shout when she splashed the acid on Petroff? It was 'Death to all Russian cowards!' to which she added, 'You knew about the 9/11 attacks ahead of time. You knew about them and you did nothing.'

"Word of Petroff's ugly, grotesque death would have spawned an international incident. The assassin's shouted manifesto should have been the headlines on every newspaper and the lead of every newscast in America. Her words and Petroff's death were intended to fuel suspicion in the minds of the American people and kindle animosity toward the Russian government."

He took a breath. "After all, we Americans didn't think our nation was vulnerable before 9/11. In its aftermath? Most of us want *someone* to blame. We want justice. Some in the government might even jump at the chance for payback. For revenge."

Svitlanya lifted her chin. "I understand those sentiments. We lost people that day. Friends and family members who were in the vicinity of the twin towers. I nearly lost someone quite dear to me who was on that other flight into New York—the hijacking stopped by the two air marshals."

"I . . ." Wolfe stumbled to a halt.

Marshal Quincy Tobin and Marta Forestier . . . Laynie.

The sense of someone higher than himself at work, of something much larger than what he could wrap his mind around, rolled like a wave down Wolfe's back and prickled the skin on his arms.

Svitlanya frowned. "Director Wolfe?"

Wolfe shook himself. Refocused. "AGFA's second attack was more blatant—it should have been devastating. Hundreds of thousands of poisoned pills were supposed to cause mass casualties—mostly young Americans. Who would America blame this time?"

Wolfe glanced up. "Please tell your people I'm going to retrieve a sample for you."

She turned her head and murmured something, then nodded to him.

He reached numb fingers into his Burberry's pocket and, courtesy of the FBI, pulled out one of the tabs. "The pills were manufactured in Russia, each one in its own individual transparent wrapper, the wrappers fused on both ends."

He offered the tab to her. "Have it analyzed if you doubt me—but be careful with it. Oh. And when you pull the wrapper apart? Look between the fused ends. Use a magnifying glass. I think you'll find the name *Bogolyubsky Confectionery Concern* in Russian. A wholly owned Russian Federation candy company."

Svitlanya slowly took the pill, stared at it, then slid it into the pocket of her fur coat. She unconsciously wiped her gloved fingers on her coat. "How does this involve us?"

"The pills and the confetti cannons used to distribute them arrived in the US on a Ukrainian ship, but the cargo originated in Russia. It was shipped down the Caspian, offloaded in Azerbaijan, trucked across Georgia, and loaded onto that Ukrainian ship in a Georgian port. Your organization, Svitlanya, *your people* took receipt of those pills on December 21."

"Y-you cannot prove we had knowledge of what they were!"

"And I told you we aren't interested in your crimes today. By agreement with the US Attorney General, we are going to let your unintentional involvement slide . . . for the moment."

"For the *moment*. You will now explain about the third attack? Will you ever get to your so-called warning?"

"Yes. However, let's recap. AGFA provided your organization with fentanyl to increase your heroin profits. In return, you did a few favors for the American arm of AGFA. Provided them with hydrofluoric acid and delivered a shipment of confetti cannons and more than half a million poison pills to them. Seems an equitable trade."

Svitlanya said nothing, but a nerve jumped at the corner of one finely creased eye.

Wolfe moved ahead. "On to the third attack. Having stirred animosity between America and Russia with the first attack, and having blamed tens of thousands of American deaths on the Russians with the second attack, AGFA would now be champing at the bit to deliver a follow-on blow so egregious as to guarantee an American retaliatory strike on Russia, a strike that would escalate into war—except for one little problem. *Neither the first nor the second attack performed as planned.*"

Svitlanya exhaled, and Wolfe realized she'd been holding her breath before she responded. "I see. Hardly the buildup an 'egregious' third attack requires, yes?"

"Yes, but do you recall my saying that nothing would turn AGFA from their course? My experience with their organization to date tells me that the hand on the switch isn't entirely stable. Do you follow?"

Svitlanya stared. Wolfe saw a slight tremor roll through her.

He said softly, "My people made additional calculations last week. The results caused them to rethink their previous conclusions. Turns out you don't need more than a few pounds of fentanyl to double the profits on a *ton* of heroin. Mix half the normal amount of heroin per hit with an equal amount of some harmless white powder, then drop in a single grain of fentanyl? You've just doubled your profits.

"With that in mind, we recalibrated our assumptions. We *had* assumed that AGFA was manufacturing fentanyl. That assumption had to go. Shoot, if they sent you twenty or thirty—even fifty kilos of fentanyl—that amount might last you a year or better.

"But see, we knew they had bought lab equipment. Our mistake was in presuming they were using the lab to manufacture the fentanyl they sold to you. All that cost and trouble for a mere twenty kilos of fentanyl? Once we realized our mistake, we had to wonder what they were really manufacturing."

"What indeed, Director?"

"Ah, I see I have your attention now. You're wondering—as we did—where they got the fentanyl they sold you. Without giving away our methods and means, let me just say that we uncovered AGFA's orders for the drug. Yes, orders. AGFA actually *bought* fentanyl from a Chinese source and shipped it to you *at significant cost*. Interesting, yes?"

She frowned. "Quite."

"Once we knew they were not making fentanyl, the lists of lab equipment they ordered no longer made sense. So, we went hunting for the chemicals they would be using in their lab. It took a while, but when we found them, it took a DEA chemist to tell us what we were looking at. Are you familiar with carfentanil?"

"No."

"I wasn't either. It's best known and used as an elephant tranquilizer. Carfentanil is so lethal that even rubbing your nose with a finger that has touched the drug will kill you."

"Again, what has all this to do with us?"

"We asked ourselves the same question. What in the world would incentivize the Brighton Beach bunch to take receipt of a shipment of carfentanil for AGFA? It couldn't be money, because AGFA has no money to spare. In fact, they have nothing at all to offer you. But then we figured it out. Do you know what we came up with?"

He watched Svitlanya's color fade and her eyes narrow.

"Seems that you lost copies of your financial records a few months back—the records your boy Syla had on his servers? The FBI swept up those servers when they raided Syla for marketing pornography. And how did they know about the porn in the first place? Someone tipped them off.

"To sum up, the FBI has your records—all the evidence they need against you. If they could open those files, your organization would be cooked. However, the files are so highly encrypted, that the FBI hasn't been able to crack them. Yet. Maybe they never will, but that's doubtful. And can you take that chance?"

Wolfe sighed. "*You* know and *I* know that your records were delivered to the FBI courtesy of a hacker whose handle is *Vyper*."

Svitlanya's face went from white to an angry red.

Wolfe kept going. "I'd like to make two points about Vyper. First, you know we have her. Frankly, you've bent over backwards trying to get at her. You even sent a hit squad to her apartment complex. People in my organization died, Svitlanya, because you want Vyper that badly."

She said nothing, but she watched him as warily as he watched her.

"My second point about Vyper? She might not be able to crack Syla's encryption either, but maybe she could do something just as good. See, we figure Vyper is the only hacker in this hemisphere who could breach the FBI's firewall and destroy your files—which, as long as the FBI no longer has them, is a win for you."

"You have a wild imagination, Director Wolfe."

"I don't need to add my imagination to the mix. This situation is already as complex and far-reaching as any novel on the *New York Times* Best Seller list. But back to my point? AGFA agreed to deliver Vyper to you in exchange for your organization smuggling a sealed sea can into the US. However, I can promise you right now, you will never get your hands on Vyper. But, let's just say if you did somehow manage to? I would personally hunt you down, Svitlanya, and make you pay—a life for a life."

Svitlanya stared back at him. "Perhaps we can come to some other kind of agreement regarding our data?"

"Perhaps we can. I'm open to discussing the situation later, depending upon the resolution of this crisis."

"Crisis? What crisis? I do not understand. AGFA's first and second attacks failed to sufficiently strain relations between America and Russia, did they not? Therefore, their plan to start a war between the two nations can no longer work, can it?"

"No, for those reasons it cannot. It also cannot work because we know their objective was to incite war between the US and Russia, yet regrettably, I don't believe the leader of AGFA has the good sense to pull back, do you? Not when he has an opportunity to hit America like the heavy hitters of al-Qaeda did on 9/11.

"AGFA's leader is a megalomaniac. To him, calling off the attack would be the same as admitting defeat—it would ruin his standing before his own men and other terrorist organizations. But to kill an entire city with one blow and strike terror in the hearts of Americans? Now that is a feat to elevate him in al-Qaeda's eyes and earn him a greater level of credibility."

"Kill an entire city? How? How does this carfentanil kill a city?"

"We had to wonder the same. What does AGFA intend to do with *an entire sea can* of carfentanil? A sea can you agreed to deliver to them."

"You keep angling for an admission from me, Director, one I will never provide. And where is this warning you spoke of earlier when you insisted the separatists were playing us for fools?"

Wolfe leaned toward Svitlanya. "Bet you also don't know that carfentanil is water soluble, so I need you to think on this. An entire sea can of carfentanil—several tons of it—dumped into a city's water supply. No purification system would detect it as it made its way into thousands, perhaps millions of homes, its unsuspecting citizens drinking it, bathing in it, *giving it to their children*."

Her face froze in horror. "Where? Which city—"

"We don't know which city or cities. Our worst-case scenario says Washington, DC, where the drug would kill thousands and would, for some time, render our seat of government a wasteland. We don't, however, have evidence that the target is DC. Since we cannot allow the same fate to befall *any* US city, we much prefer confiscating the shipment *before* it makes port.

"So, let's consider the facts, shall we? If you were to deliver the carfentanil to AGFA and they were to proceed with their attack as planned? With the Russians off the hook, on whom, exactly, would the blame fall?"

Wolfe sat back. "This, then, is our warning. If AGFA succeeds in their attack, they will also ensure that *your* people, Svitlanya, are implicated—in which case we will not hesitate to prosecute you and yours for an egregious act of domestic terrorism. Please do not doubt me."

Svitlanya bit back a curse. Staring at Wolfe, she said, "I must take a moment . . . to consider what you've said."

She turned away from Wolfe. Listened to the voice whispering in her ear. Answered a question, listened again, and muttered an agreement. Turned back.

"Director Wolfe, before we go further, I require assurances."

Wolfe nodded. "I'm going to reach into my breast pocket. Please order whoever has my head in their sights to take their finger off the trigger."

For the sake of all listening ears, Svitlanya growled, "Stand down. *Do it*."

A second later, she nodded to Wolfe. "You may proceed."

Wolfe slowly unbuttoned his Burberry and reached inside his suit's breast pocket. Pulled out an envelope. Handed it to her.

"Read it now but not aloud. If you agree, we need an immediate response."

She withdrew the folded sheet of paper and scanned it. "All right. We'll give you the ship, the number of the sea can, and our Chechen contact here in the US."

"No."

Svitlanya's chin jerked up. "What?"

"We have a different plan. First, give me your earwig."

"I—"

"You have your signed letter of immunity—nothing said here can blow back onto you or your organization. But we won't go any further down this road until you hand over your earwig, its transmitter, and the bug that's listening in on our conversation."

She thought for a moment. Listened to the voice in her ear. Made some monosyllabic comments. Nodded.

Wolfe had to believe old Semion Davydenko himself was speaking to Svitlanya.

She reached into her fur hood and removed a device from her ear. Pulled the wire from it.

"Now the transmitter and the bug."

She unbuttoned her coat and retrieved them.

Wolfe dropped them on the asphalt at their feet.

"Sorry about this." He used his heel to crush them, then reached into his pocket and flipped a switch.

"I just turned off my own listening device. Leveled the playing field."

"Now what?" she demanded. "I said we would give you the shipment information."

"Yes, and we will certainly take it, but I . . . we need a little something more."

"Oh?"

"You have spoken directly to AGFA's leader, haven't you? When I said he was unstable, you shuddered a little—because you knew *and agreed* with my assessment. Why? Because you have spoken to him or listened in on calls to him. Now I need to know *how* you talk to him, Svitlanya."

She sat taller and her eyes hardened. "You have gone beyond the scope of our agreement, Director Wolfe. We agreed to give you the carfentanil shipment in exchange for immunity—but now you want something more?"

"Call it a favor."

"No."

Wolfe nodded. He'd come back to it when the rest of the details were settled.

"All right. Then about your AGFA contact—we don't want him. We'd rather that you use him to identify all the members of AGFA's American branch."

She sneered. "Do the work for you and *then* give them to you?"

"No."

Wolfe wondered if she would understand what he was implying. She got it faster than he thought she would.

"I see."

"As I said, Americans want justice. Some of us want it sooner than the wheels of an overburdened system can deliver. And some of us believe sooner is safer for this nation."

She shrugged. "It may take a little time. When the shipment fails to reach them, they will hide as fast as cockroaches do when the lights come on. But, until then, I will have my people follow our contact and begin to identify his crew. I can promise that, eventually, they will all disappear . . . permanently."

"Thank you."

She gathered herself and started to stand. This time, Wolfe did place a hand on her arm, and she lowered herself to the bench with an angry toss of her head.

One last chance.

"Svitlanya, who was on the plane that was almost hijacked on 9/11? The person special to you?"

"What has that to do with any of this?"

"Humor me, please."

She lifted her chin higher. Studied him. "If you must know, it was my daughter. Returning from England."

"I am glad she survived."

"As am I. Losing her would have been an insurmountable blow."

Wolfe slowly nodded. "Our children are the purest part of the dirty world in which we live. They are the 'right' we cling to when what we do is often wrong."

She said nothing, but moisture sheened her eyes. "I must agree."

"Svitlanya, I need to tell you something."

Those lines between her eyes appeared. "What now?"

"The two marshals who saved your daughter's flight? Everyone assumed that both of them were sky marshals, but actually only one was. The other was my operative. Without hesitation, she jumped in to assist the marshal."

Svitlanya cocked her head. Listened intently.

"Five hijackers died before they could wrest control of the plane from the pilots. The marshal killed two of the five terrorists, but he was shot and wounded during the exchange. My operative killed the other three hijackers. Three of them.

"Without my agent on board, the sky marshal, by his own testimony, would have failed to save the plane. We found out that the hijackers had intended to fly the plane into a hospital. They wanted to kill a thousand sick people—and your daughter. "

The woman took it in then said softly, "My daughter was seated in business class. She witnessed some of what happened. She told me about the second marshal, the woman. Said she was the bravest woman she'd ever seen . . ."

"That she is. And she . . ."

Wolfe's chest had tightened. His words stuck in his throat.

He considered the paper cup of now-cold coffee sitting on the stone bench between them. In an abrupt and violent move, he swept the cup from the bench, hurling it onto the sidewalk. Its lid flew off. The contents splattered across the asphalt. The slurry froze on contact.

He regretted the outburst at once, but he'd momentarily reached the end of himself and his ability to tamp down his anger.

Frustration.

Impotence . . . and a sorrowful sense of inevitability choking him.

He felt something, looked down, and found Svitlanya's gloved fingers touching his arm. "What is it?"

He shook his head. Couldn't answer.

"What have you not told me, Director Wolfe?"

She waited. When he'd regained control, he murmured, "I sent her to Tbilisi. A simple meet with an informant, but AGFA found out. They took her. Have her."

Wolfe stared into Svitlanya's eyes. "AGFA took my operative because she knows where we've hidden Vyper. They have her for one reason—to extract Vyper's location from her so they can pay *you* the promised price for safely delivering the carfentanil."

He made certain she understood exactly what he said next. "She's only of use to AGFA as long as she ensures the delivery. Once they realize we've intercepted it . . ."

Svitlanya slowly nodded. "They will no longer keep her alive. It is why you wanted to know how we have spoken to their leader. So you might save her."

"That—and we'd love to deliver a slice of karma to AGFA."

Wolfe pushed Svitlanya. "Do you call a satellite phone to speak with him, their leader? Would you tell us the next time you are scheduled to speak to him? We can track a satphone while it is in use."

When she didn't move, he played his last card. "You said . . . you said that losing your daughter would have been an insurmountable blow. This operative. She is something like a daughter to me—and I sent her to Tbilisi. Whatever AGFA is doing to her? However they are torturing her to give up Vyper's location? *I sent her*."

The face she turned to him was lined with regret. "I am truly sorry, Director. I can tell you that at our last communication your operative was still alive. Beyond that? I cannot do what you are asking of me, even if I wished to . . . even though it seems I owe this woman a debt I can never repay. As I said earlier, position in our organization is, first of all, who you are related to."

Semion Davydenko. She may be his daughter, but he is still calling the shots. Svitlanya will never cross her father. Disloyalty has but one outcome, and that punishment would fall on her—and her daughter.

He pulled himself together, retrieved a business card from his pocket, wrote on it. "I'm glad we were able to come to the arrangement we did. Please forward the shipping info to this email address."

It was an email account Jaz had recently created for this express purpose.

Wolfe stood, careful of his cold, stiff muscles and the slick sidewalk. "As soon as we receive the information, we will intercept the carfentanil."

She stood, too, and shivered. "The shipment is eight days from port. The longer you wait to intercept the cargo, the more of AGFA's people we will be able to . . . identify."

"Eight days. Good to know."

As she took his card, Wolfe added, "If . . . if you should change your mind about the other, please call or send an email."

He walked away, Svitlanya's last words occupying his attention.

Eight days. Eight days to intercept the shipment. Eight days to find and save Laynie.

God, you know I have never asked you for anything. From a young age, I have derided the very idea of a higher being who gives a rip about human civilization, and I have treated those who believe in you with scorn.

Not for my sake, but for hers, God . . . if you are there? If you do actually care? Please save Laynie.

LAYNIE HEARD THE RHYTHMIC pounding of the three soldiers' boots on the tunnel stones as they drew near that evening. She slowly removed the veil from her head, twisted it tightly to form a rope, stood, and used the rope as a belt around her abaya, cinching the garment in, close to her body. Her second veil was bound around her burned arm.

She walked toward the grate, alone, leaving her little chicks huddled by the campfire in a nervous knot.

The other *kafir* girls, seeing a bareheaded Laynie facing the grate and sensing something amiss in her stance, whispered among themselves uneasily. They, too, hung back.

The three soldiers, with leashes in hand, unlocked and opened the gate. The soldier who appeared to be in charge motioned Laynie forward.

"I will not go," Laynie answered in Russian.

He bellowed a sharp command. Immediately, the girls from the other campfire hurried toward the gate. When Laynie held out her hand toward them in the universally understood signal to halt, they stopped. Their nervous eyes darted from Laynie to the soldiers and back, and they stayed well clear of both.

The soldier again gestured for Laynie to come to him.

"No. I belong to Jesus. I am a virtuous woman. I will not defile my body."

The *kafir* girls lifted mutters against Laynie, then shouts. She felt their fear and anger in the curses they called down on her. Between the soldiers and the angry women, the tension in the cell mounted until it was a palpable, pulsing thing Laynie forced herself to ignore.

The lead soldier carried a whip coiled around his waist. He made a show of unwinding its coils and flicking it, sending a resounding *crack* into the air. The girls scattered before the threat, but Laynie did not move or flinch. She focused on the man's hands. When he sent the lash snaking toward her, she reached out for it and let its stinging bite wrap around her wrist and forearm. As soon as it did, she grabbed its length with her hand and jerked the whip toward her.

It flew from the soldier's hand. Laynie gathered the whip's coils to herself, then tossed it aside, out of the soldier's reach.

"I belong to Jesus the Son of God. I am a virtuous woman. I will not defile my body."

Incensed and mortified, the man stormed the short distance between them, swinging his fists at Laynie's head. She sidestepped, grabbed his wrist, and rotated his entire arm.

The sharp snap of bone drained the cave of all other sound—until the man's shriek of agony filled it back up. When he fell, writhing, onto the stone floor, the other two soldiers acted. One rushed to pull the man away from the grate. The other slammed the gate closed behind them and locked it. The wounded soldier's screams of pain echoed and grew fainter as his friends retreated down the tunnel, dragging him with them.

Laynie remained where she was.

Inside the cell, the girls of the second campfire were beside themselves in an uproar, yelling at Laynie what she surmised were obscenities.

She did not move, not even to see how her girls fared.

Minutes later, the two soldiers reappeared. Bula and two other soldiers were close behind.

"What are you doing?" Bula asked her.

"Defending my honor."

"I cannot permit your bad example before the others."

"You should not be surprised by my actions. I told you I would defend my honor."

"And I told you Sayed would kill you."

"What you are doing is wrong. It is unholy and sinful, displeasing to God."

Bula motioned for one of the soldiers to unlock the gate.

Laynie dropped her chin to her chest, then lifted it again and said in a loud voice, "I declare that I am a disciple of Jesus Christ, the Savior of the world! I will defend my virtue as any Christian woman should. If I die, I die as a Christian, as a testimony to Jesus' saving grace."

Bula drew a stout club from his belt. The two men with him did the same. He shouted into the cell. "This woman is an enemy of Islam. Has another of you committed such apostasy? Does anyone else wish her fate?"

Laynie stared at Bula, unblinking, half-praying her chicks would remain silent.

One did not.

Ksenia peeked from behind Laynie's back. "I, too, love Jesus. I-I will stand with her." Her quavering voice spoke first in Russian. She repeated herself in the dialect the other women knew. Sobbing, she buried her face in the skirt of Laynie's abaya.

From a few yards behind her, Laynie heard Asmeen and Mariam's keening sobs. Bula and his men, clubs whirling, advanced on them. Laynie knew the danger of those weighted blows so she dodged them, looking for her opportunity to reach inside the arc of a swing. Meanwhile, Ksenia quailed before the advance and retreated. Laynie, unable to fend off all three men, gave ground—only to back into Ksenia, knocking her down. When Laynie tripped and sprawled over Ksenia's body, Bula and his men descended on her, beating her with their clubs and fists.

Bula shouted to the men to grab Laynie's arms. They dragged her, kicking and fighting, across the rocks, farther back in the cave where she hadn't gone—where Ksenia had warned her not to go.

"*What is there?*"

"*A deep hole. An empty cistern. If you fall into it, you may break your legs . . . If one of us does not submit herself to a soldier, if she persists in displeasing him, they will drop her into the cistern.*"

"*And . . . what becomes of the woman?*"

"*If she repents and begs them to pull her out, they do. Sometimes. If they do not pull her out, they let her die there.*"

Bula's soldiers flung her over the edge, and she felt herself falling. At the last moment, she pulled her arms and legs into a tuck. Then she struck the bottom, landing on her side. The air whooshed from her lungs.

Moments later, Ksenia's body fell on her, and Laynie lost consciousness.

BULA PEERED INTO THE CISTERN. He could not see into its depths—he could barely make out its treacherous edge.

One of his men asked him, "Shall we throw these two in as well?" He gestured to the two girls weeping in the hands of the other soldiers.

"I did not hear them declare themselves for the false Christian messiah. Besides, we have work for them this night. Get the women ready. All of them."

When the soldiers left to do his bidding, Bula stared down into the cistern's darkness.

"You defended your virtue well, Christian lady, and preserved your honor—such as it was—unto death."

Before he turned away, he nodded. "I salute your courage."

CHAPTER 33

WOLFE RETURNED FROM New York after meeting with Svitlanya and drove to Broadsword to brief the task force. It was evening when he called the task force together, posted Bo and Harris outside the gym, and shared the results of the meeting with the team.

"Settle down, everyone," Jaz ordered, then took her seat with them.

This had better be good, Wolfe.

"A reminder. Everything I'm about to tell you is classified at the highest levels. Although I won't disclose every detail of the meet, I can say that it was successful. I met with an individual from the Ukrainian mob whom I'll refer to as my counterpart. After we agreed that our conversation would be off the record, I laid out what we know about the mob's relationship with AGFA—money and favors in exchange for fentanyl, those favors including the mob taking delivery of certain shipments for AGFA.

"When I explained that the first shipment the mob smuggled into the US for AGFA had contained poisoned ecstasy and had killed close to two thousand Americans, my counterpart was suitably appalled. By the time I revealed that AGFA had bought the fentanyl from the Chinese instead of manufacturing it, I had their undivided attention.

"I told my counterpart that we believed the next shipment they had agreed to smuggle into port for AGFA contained carfentanil. I explained what carfentanil was, how we believed AGFA's American jihadis planned to use it in another terror attack on the United States—and that, since we knew the Russians were innocent of attacking us, AGFA was no longer attempting to instigate a war between the US and the Russians. Instead, AGFA's move was pure terrorism for terrorism's sake.

"I explained furthermore that, rather than risk the might of the United States coming down upon *their* heads, AGFA was happy to shift the blame onto the mob. These revelations gained us the candid cooperation we hoped for, and my counterpart verified that a sealed sea can was scheduled to arrive eight days from today.

"The meeting also resulted in another important bit of information. When I asked if they ever spoke directly with AGFA's leader, the answer was yes—but what they let slip was even more important. They confirmed that Bella *is alive* and being held at AGFA's headquarters—or rather, that at their last call, Bella was alive."

A murmur followed by a heavy exhale went around the bullpen.

Wolfe lifted a hand and the murmur died. "It's not all good news, I'm afraid. They also confirmed our theory that the only reason AGFA took Bella was to pry Jaz's location from her. As your team had already surmised, *Jaz* is the payment AGFA offered the mob for both money and for smuggling the sea can of carfentanil into the US. Of course, the mob doesn't want to be on the hook for enabling a terror attack, so my counterpart agreed to provide the shipping information."

Wolfe singled out Jaz. "I gave her the email address of that account you set up. You should receive the shipping info shortly. Let me know as soon as you do."

"Yes, sir."

Wolfe continued speaking to Jaz. "I made certain that the mob understood the stakes, should they come after you, Jaz. I was quite clear on that point. My only concession was an agreement to discuss the loss of their data at a later date—not that the FBI would ever consent to surrendering the files to the mob."

Jaz asked what was uppermost in the team's mind. "What about Bella? Did they tell you how they communicate with AGFA? Can we use their communications to find her?"

Wolfe looked away. "They call Sayed on his satphone. I asked if they would tell us when the next call was scheduled so we could track it, but my counterpart refused me."

Jaz couldn't let it go. "But did you . . . do the Ukrainians understand that AGFA is torturing Bella? To find *me?* To pay *them?* I mean, they have the power to make it stop, right? Can't you . . . can't you force them to do *something?*"

A shadow crossed Wolfe's face. "I tried. I did. Believe me . . . I did. As for making AGFA stop?"

He didn't finish the thought aloud.

Vincent did. "If . . . if the Ukrainians were to tell AGFA they no longer needed Jaz, then AGFA would have no reason to keep Bella alive."

Stunned, Jaz considered Vincent's logic, then looked to Tobin. He said nothing. He seemed to have pulled in on himself. Tobin's silence spoke louder than his words ever would.

"That's it for now," Wolfe said. As he stood, he said to Tobin, "No, not yet, Marshal Tobin."

Not yet, Marshal?

When the meeting broke up, she grabbed Tobin, dragged him outside. "Tobin. Are you . . . are you okay?"

What she saw in his eyes made her want to weep. It wasn't defeat. Exactly. It wasn't even resignation. It was brokenness—but not a "this person is injured and dying" brokenness. It was something else.

"What did Wolfe mean when he said, 'Not yet, Marshal Tobin'?"

"Oh. That. I . . . well, when we thought Bella was dead, I asked Wolfe why he was keeping me around. I don't really have a role on the task force. My job was to keep an eye on Bella back when he and Seraphim wanted to be sure she wasn't suffering from PTSD. With Bella gone . . ."

"Wait—you can't leave, Tobin."

"Didn't say I was. I said I asked him why I was still here."

"And he said what?"

"He asked, 'Marshal Tobin, is Bella still part of the task force?' That riled me up real big, which was what he'd intended. Then he said he still had hope for Bella—and until he no longer did, I was as much a part of the team as any of you clowns."

"There's *no way* he said, 'you clowns.'"

Tobin laughed a little. "You're right. He didn't."

"So the 'No, not yet, Marshal Tobin' back in the conference room? Wolfe was saying he hadn't lost hope for Bella?"

"Yeah. That's what he was saying. He did add, though, when I asked why I was still here, that I was a stabilizing force on the team."

"Well, he's not wrong. You can't leave, Tobin. We need you . . . and I'm a little worried about you, too."

"No need to worry about me, Jaz," he said. "I am praying and walking this through."

"Praying again! What **blanking** good does that do?"

"Thing is, Jaz, if you look for God's hand in any given situation, more often than not, you'll find it."

Jaz rounded on Tobin. "You know what praying is? It's **bleeping** double-talk. There's no God and no 'hand of God' to be seen *anywhere*."

Tobin smiled, his eyes weary, but something else flickered down deep in them. "Did you notice the mistake Wolfe made?"

"I—" Jaz frowned. "No. What mistake?"

"He used the phrase 'my counterpart' and non-specific pronouns throughout both briefings."

"Yeah. So?"

"Except the one time he said 'her.' He said, 'I gave *her* the email address of that account you set up.'"

"So?"

"We might be accustomed to women in leadership in the US, but how many female 'counterparts' at Wolfe's level do you think the Ukrainian mob has?"

Jaz frowned and stared down at the snow-packed path. Absentmindedly, she flipped a stick of gum out of the pack in her left hand. Unwrapped it. Folded it in half, then half again. Tossed it in her mouth.

"Dunno, but I think I'd like to find out."

Tobin motioned toward the gym. "Shall we?"

AN HOUR LATER, AFTER Jaz had done search after search trying to tease out the organizational structure of the Brighton Beach syndicate, she and Tobin had narrowed things down. Jaz toggled through the three screens open on her laptop.

"Would have been easier to hack the FBI's organized crime database," Jaz grumbled. "They probably have an org chart for the mob and know everything about them—right down to their underwear size."

She added a fresh stick of Black Jack to the five already in her mouth.

Tobin shrugged. "Maybe, but I think we have what we were looking for right here. Semion Davydenko is the Odessa mob's head honcho, right?"

"Yah, and his daughter Svitlanya looks to be the only female we came up with who's 'at that level.' Plus, her phone says she was in Manhattan not only when Wolfe was there, but pinging off the same towers as Wolfe's phone."

"Then it's her. Wolfe met with *her*."

"Okay, so now I do a deep dive on her. Find something we can use, some kind of leverage. It has to be big enough to manipulate her into calling their AGFA buddies over in Chechnya."

"No."

Jaz's jaws stopped. "What do you mean, *no?* The whole point of the search was to dig up dirt or a weakness we could use."

"No, the point of the search was to ID the person Wolfe talked to—not for you to make yourself an even bigger target for the Ukrainian mob."

"But what does figuring out who Wolfe talked to get us? How does that help at all?"

"It gives me the right person to pray for."

Jaz blinked once. And lost it.

Tobin hadn't seen Jaz totally lose it before. Neither had he been her target. But now that she was unloading on him, right then and there, *in his face*, cursing him up one side and down the other, one finger gouging a hole in his chest, while a great gobstopper of gray goop flew around in her mouth, he was certain he never wanted to see—or experience—such a tirade again.

Not to mention the mesmerized audience observing her meltdown.

Tobin grabbed the finger jabbing his chest. "I dare you, Jaz."

Tobin doubted Jaz heard him. Her tirade didn't stop—she didn't even let off the gas.

"Jaz, I dare you."

When she started poking him with her other finger, he picked her up. Two hands the size of east Texas lifted her up. Up. Over his head. Held her horizontal while she kicked and cursed. He carried her—dodging her boots and fists—through the bullpen and out the door.

"Put me down! PUT ME DOWN, you **bleeping** horse's rear end!"

The goggle-eyed task force followed Tobin out the door.

Rusty sucked in his breath. "Oh, man. He's gonna dump her in the snow," he pronounced.

"He wouldn't dare," Brian answered. "'Cause afterward? We still have to work with her."

"Five dollars says he does it anyway."

"You're on."

Tobin pointed Jaz's head toward a snowdrift.

She stopped cursing, but she didn't shut up. "Don't. Don't you dare, Quincy Tobin, or I swear—"

"Yeah, you swear all right. You swear a *lot*, and I'm tired of hearing it. Shut your pie hole, missy. And FYI? That wad you're flinging around in there is disgusting."

"I mean it, Tobin. Don't you dare drop me in the snow."

"Then listen up. I dared you first, Jaz. In front of all these people—" Tobin gestured with one hand, holding her overhead with only the other. "Now I *double-dog* dare you."

Jaz took the gob of gum out of her mouth and tossed it away. She sneered at him. "You dare me to what?"

"I dare you to pray for Svitlanya Davydenko."

Brian interjected, "Uh, Tobin? Who's Svitlanya Davydenko?"

Neither Tobin nor Jaz paid him any attention.

Brian leaned toward Rusty, "Who's Svitlanya Davydenko?"

"Dunno, but our bet is still on."

"Pray?" Jaz screamed at Tobin. "I told you, I don't *do* prayer!"

"Yeah, well I double-dog dared you."

"*And I don't care*."

"Do you care about landing in that drift?"

"You wouldn't—"

"Dare? I wouldn't *dare?* I dared you first, missy. Pony up or meet the snow head-on."

Jaz, staring at the snowdrift, whispered, "You want me to pray."

"Yes. But since you don't know how, I'll pray with you."

"Praying is pointless, Tobin. Just words. They don't mean a thing."

"Your words might not mean a thing, but mine do—and then you'll see God answer."

Tobin, holding Jaz aloft with both hands, "pumped" his arms, and tossed her into the air, rolling her like a log, before catching her. By the time Jaz's screech echoed into the mountains around them, Tobin had flipped her and set her feet on the ground.

In the snowdrift.

Up to her knees.

"You miserable—"

Tobin held out his hand. "Come on, Little Miss Swears-a-Lot."

Jaz weighed taking his hand against floundering through the drift. With a huff, she grabbed his hand. He jerked her onto the path—and wouldn't let go.

He motioned with his chin to their audience. "Y'all can get back to work."

With Jaz's hand in his catcher's mitt, he dragged her all the way to the conference room. Didn't let go until the door closed behind them. Leaned against the door and folded his arms.

Jaz dropped into a chair. "Do we have to kneel down for this-this-this *crap?*"

"Nope. I'll pray, and you say amen at the end. Amen means 'so be it,' or 'I agree.'"

"I agree? Whatever."

Tobin closed his eyes. "Lord God, in the name of Jesus, Jaz and I come before you. I first of all thank you for using Svitlanya Davydenko to tell us that, *yes*, Bella is still alive, and that, wherever AGFA's headquarters are, that's where they are holding her. We are grateful, Lord!

"Second, according to where you say in your word, *This is the confidence we have in approaching God, that if we ask anything according to your will, you hear us,* I ask that you move upon Svitlanya Davydenko's heart. Please change her mind. Please convince her to tell us when they next plan to call AGFA's headquarters.

"Father, I confess that tracing a call between the mob and AGFA seems like the only means of finding Bella, the only way we can save her and bring her back to us. However, it isn't the only way *you* can save her. After all you, Lord, *are* the Way, the Truth, and the Life. Jaz and I ask right now that you rescue Bella and return her safely to us.

"Thank you for hearing our prayer, Lord. Amen."

Tobin opened his eyes. "Well?"

She sniffed. "Sure. Right. *Amen*. Whatever."

JAZ STARED AT THE EMAIL account she'd set up at Wolfe's direction. Stared at the "1" that told her a new email had landed in the inbox. She clicked on it and read its brief contents.

"Brian!"

"Yo, Boss?"

"Sending you the ship's name and Ukrainian registry now. I want a location ASAP."

"On it."

The transliteration of the ship's name from Cyrillic to an English pronunciation was *Pluh Konya.* Loosely translated to English, it was *Plow Horse*.

Jaz made the call. "Director Wolfe? We have the shipping info."

"Copy the message contents into a new email from your task force account and send it to me. I'll forward it to my FBI counterpart."

Wolfe had shared everything they knew about the planned attack with the FBI—which wasn't much but certainly got their full attention. The FBI in turn had brought select members of the Drug Enforcement Administration and Environmental Protection Agency into a highly classified team.

No federal agency had, to date, dealt with a shipment as toxic as the incoming carfentanil. Within the team, hazmat response members were gearing up and scientists were crunching data to determine the best means of disposing of the carfentanil—or, should it be intentionally dumped overboard, how that amount of carfentanil would affect marine life.

The task force had done its part. When the FBI took over, they locked the task force out of the response.

Two can play at that little game, Jaz growled to herself.

Brian waved her over. "I have the *Pluh Konya's* usual route. Based on their thirteen-day average from the Republic of Georgia to New York, I estimate the ship is seven days out."

"That's what Wolfe said his mob counterpart told him."

She called Tobin and Rusty over.

"The carfentanil is a week from port. That means we have a week to find Bella before AGFA expects to receive its cargo. Before they know they've been had."

"You think the FBI would ask the mob to stall their AGFA contact? Put off delivery?" Rusty wondered aloud.

"I'm not counting on it," Jaz muttered. She was teasing out a few ideas of her own.

Tobin nodded. "I agree. We have a week before AGFA knows we've confiscated their carfentanil."

Tobin slid Jaz a look of concern, then motioned her back to her workstation. Tobin pulled a chair close to Jaz.

"I'm getting a vibe from you, Jaz."

"A 'vibe'? What's that supposed to mean?

"A vibe like when you decided to take matters into your own hands and sneak down to NOLA."

"And I was right, wasn't I?"

"Don't do it. Don't reach out to Svitlanya Davydenko. Don't meddle with the mob, Jaz."

"Sure, Tobin. You dared me to *pray* for that woman with you, but you won't dare to *act*. Has to be *all God*, huh?"

"If the Lord moves in that situation, Jaz, we'll know it."

"If the Lord 'moves'? What's he gonna do? Wave a red flag? Send up a flare?"

"However he chooses to act, it will be unmistakable. Until then? Keep your hands off."

THE WOMAN IN CHARGE of food preparation railed on her, punctuating her meaning with her hands. Apparently, she'd done something wrong, but Gupta—rather, Halima bint Abra and unwilling wife to Maskhadan—didn't understand a word the old hag shouted. Gupta swore under her breath, calling down upon the woman's head every vile epithet her vocabulary possessed.

Then she saw the man again, through the pass-through where they served the food, the one she'd noticed when leaving Sayed's salon after her "wedding." She had spent her long night of "wedding bliss" racking her brain, trying to evoke some memory of how she knew him. All she'd come up with had been the sense that he was much older than when she'd first seen him.

The hag kicked her, shoving her out of the way. Gupta moved over, but kept the man in her sight. He joined a table of soldiers who welcomed him warmly.

Huh. He fits right in. It would take someone decades to fool the natives. She frowned. *Decades. At least two. Where was I twenty years ago?*

It came to her. *Marstead's infernal training facility. Was he a trainee? Had to have been.*

Her thoughts reminded her that she had met Magda in the same place. *Oh, how I hate that woman! And—*

No. It couldn't be.

She picked up a pitcher of water and walked to his table. Began to refill water glasses, taking her time, using her imagination to strip away the damage of years. Of tens of years.

He handed her his glass and she filled it. Handed it back. His eyes strayed to her face, all but her eyes hidden beneath the hideous niqab. His glance swept over her eyes. Stopped.

Confusion bloomed and disappeared as quickly.

He's recognized me but is in the same boat as I. He can't place me.

But that glance had been enough to confirm her suspicions.

A trainee in the same class as Magda. I must tell Sayed that he is nurturing a spy in his bosom. Perhaps he will reward me for the information. Allow me to leave this place and my delightful "husband."

It would not be easy to obtain an audience with Sayed—but she knew where to reach his odious servant. She returned the pitcher to the kitchen and, ignoring the ranting abuse of her "keeper," she left the cavern.

Chapter 34

SVITLANYA KEPT A LIGHT on at night while she slept. The lamp in the bower window, close to her dressing table, worked best. And because her bed rested against the wall directly opposite the door to her room, she didn't sleep in it anymore, choosing the couch behind the door instead.

When she dialed down the lamp's dimmer switch to lower its light, the rest of her room lay in shadow—and she lay in wait, the Makarov loaded and ready under her pillow. Oh, she slept, but her ear was always listening, subconsciously attuned to the particular sounds the locks made when they slid open and the soft *ssss* her door made when it turned on its hinges.

Each morning, she went through the same routine. She removed the evidence of sleeping on the couch, mussed her bed as though she had slept there, and rearranged the pillows that had served as her "body" during the night.

Svitlanya had lived like this— fearful of an attempt on her life—for two years. Her precautions began the day her brother Symon had gone to prison and her father had announced that he would be grooming *her* to take over the entirety of the Ukrainian crime syndicate's US operations at his death.

Me. A woman, fear shrilled in her ear.

A competent woman, her outrage answered. *More than capable. A better businesswoman, in fact, than my father—better educated, better prepared for the future.*

Her father, Semion Davydenko, was old now, nearly eighty-five, and growing feeble. Fact or opinion as to her competence would matter little if certain men in the organization chose to decide the matter of Semion's replacement themselves.

She was aware of the danger surrounding her. Hadn't she lived with it in one form or another every day of her life? If it were only herself, she might have abdicated and gone far away to live out her days somewhere pleasant.

But it isn't only me. I have Zoya to think of.

Svitlanya had never married. It had been a blow to her parents when, at age thirty-nine, she announced her pregnancy. Her *intentional* pregnancy.

I wanted a child, but I didn't want the husband that went along with the usual way things are done—for who would have married me other than an ambitious man? A man who said he loved me but really wanted only to advance himself in the organization?

Eventually, her parents had accepted the news, and they had doted on Zoya. As Svitlanya had.

Wolfe was right. My daughter is the only pure thing in my life, the only thing I love—which is why I sent her away to school in Europe after Symon went to prison. To keep her safe and out of this ugly life entirely.

Svitlanya glanced at the clock again. Sighed.

Why can't I sleep?

When she checked the clock a third time, she gave up. Threw off the covers and sat up. Walked around her poorly lit room, restless. Concerned.

The meeting with Wolfe had been . . . eye-opening, particularly when he revealed that his operative had been instrumental in saving Zoya's plane. Svitlanya's heart pounded as it had on that day when the planes struck the twin towers and when Zoya's incoming flight had been rerouted to Canada. When the news had announced that two sky marshals had foiled one of the 9/11 hijackings. Had saved the plane. Had saved Zoya.

Wolfe's exact words came back to her. "*Without my agent on board, the sky marshal, by his own testimony, would have failed to save the plane. We found out that the hijackers had intended to fly the plane into a hospital. They wanted to kill a thousand sick people—and your daughter.*"

"I owe this woman for Zoya's life—and yet, I am forbidden to return the favor in kind."

Svitlanya knew little of this Sayed person, the man at the top of AGFA's hierarchy, only what Khasurt, Sayed's American commander, had unconsciously let slip. That and what Svitlanya herself had deduced during the negotiations between her father and Sayed. The negotiations had been held via Sayed's satellite phone with Svitlanya and Semion's two top pakhans present.

The image of Sayed she'd formed was of a self-obsessed, religious fanatic—a little man with a derisive and contemptuous view of women. "The kind of man," she was convinced her father's pakhans whispered to each other later, "who will never conduct business dealings with our organization if it is headed by a woman."

I must make a move, Svitlanya told herself, *and soon. Before my father dies and my Zoya and I follow him to the grave.*

She crept to her dressing table, retrieved her laptop, and took it back to the couch. She opened it and logged on to the new email account she'd created and used to send AGFA's shipping information to Wolfe.

Wolfe or his IT person had replied to the information on the carfentanil shipment with a succinct "Information received." Nothing more.

Svitlanya tapped the edge of the keyboard, thinking, weighing the few options open to her. Director Wolfe had been surprisingly candid about his operative. He had allowed Svitlanya to see his earnest feelings for the woman, the woman he said had saved Zoya's plane.

I regret that I was unable to give Wolfe what he needed to find and rescue his agent. If Papa had allowed it, I would have done as Director Wolfe asked and made a friend of this man. Friends in high places, even those on the other side, can sometimes render a favor in time of need. A personal *favor—that is a given—not a business favor.*

Something tinkered around beyond the edge of her conscious grasp. The glint of an idea in the making, not yet formed.

Our financial records in the hands of the FBI are a ticking time bomb. Someday, perhaps soon, they will crack the encryption on those files and have all the proof they need to ruin us.

Svitlanya didn't move as a suggestion crept around the corner and came into view.

If Papa agreed, I would attempt to trade his agent for our data.

It was an audacious proposal. Smart and simple.

If Papa allowed, I would exchange a conversation with Sayed for our records. No, not for the files themselves, but for their destruction.

But she knew Semion Davydenko too well. He would insist that she pitch the scheme to his pakhans. They, most certainly, would talk the idea to death and then slow-walk it to its grave.

Oh, the things I'd do if Papa's approval weren't needed.

Svitlanya mulled over the idea of sending Wolfe a second email. She stilled, barely breathing, as she considered how she might approach him. She even opened a file and slowly typed the initial gambit, the language she might use to put forward the suggestion.

Dear Director Wolfe,

Thank you for reaching out to us on a matter of grave concern on both sides—the safety and security of America from terrorism. I am glad we could come to a mutually beneficial resolution, now that you have received the requested shipping information.

Svitlanya thought through the next paragraph, then typed it out.

We also spoke of our other security needs, you of your agent's safe return, us of our data, presently held in other hands. How simply could both problems be solved if we were to, again, cooperate.

I propose we think on how to achieve such a solution. I await your timely reply.

Cordially,

S.D.

With the boldness she would need when her father passed, Svitlanya copied the text, pasted it into an email, and sent it to the address Wolfe had provided. As the message flew away, she did not allow herself to fear the repercussions.

If I wait until Papa is gone to be bold, it will be too late. I must be the leader now *that we will need* then.

Svitlanya returned to the couch, crawled under the covers, and slept at last.

JAZ SIGHED AND TURNED over again. It wasn't that she didn't need the rest. Plainly, she was exhausted. She couldn't sleep because she couldn't shut her brain off.

When she closed her eyes, her thoughts turned to finding wherever AGFA had stashed Bella and how Wolfe, with his many resources, would mount a rescue. The only things able to turn her thoughts in another direction were the problems assigned to the task force to solve.

Jaz was never far from her laptop, her ears attuned to its every sound. Even now, with the volume turned down low, the soft ping of an incoming email roused her.

She lifted the lid on her laptop and opened her email account. Nothing. She switched to the account she'd set up for communications between Wolfe and the Ukrainian mob.

Another email from Svitlanya Davydenko?

She read Svitlanya's email. Read it again.

"If the Lord moves in that situation, Jaz, we'll know it."

"If the Lord 'moves'? What's he gonna do? Wave a red flag? Send up a flare?"

"However he chooses to act, it will be unmistakable. Until then? Keep your hands off."

Jaz shivered. "Yah, this is pretty unmistakable."

Okay, I did what you asked, Tobin. I kept my hands off—until I got the unmistakable nod from your god.

SVITLANYA WAS TIRED WHEN she crawled from the couch to start her day. She had back-to-back meetings with her father and several pakhans all afternoon and would need her wits about her.

She showered, dressed, and called downstairs for the kitchen staff to bring her a breakfast tray. While she waited, she opened her laptop to review notes on the meetings. On a whim, she checked the email account she used to communicate with Wolfe.

Svitlanya was surprised to see an immediate response to her message of a few hours ago. Her surprise grew when she realized who had sent the response. *Not Wolfe.*

She read the message's content . . . and read it again. A viable path opened before her, the means to a successful transition as head of her father's organization. If she dared to step onto the path.

She chewed her bottom lip, gathering her courage. Then she replied to the email.

I accept. However, time is short. In a show of good faith, I will hasten to do my part. I expect you to complete your part of the exchange within the week following.

She set her laptop aside and thought through her next steps. The adrenaline racing through her blood had wiped out all traces of fatigue.

I can rest later. Now I must prepare myself to act decisively.

USAMA INTERRUPTED COSSACK'S conversation with the men in the cavern. "General Sayed wishes to see you." Something about Usama's demeanor and the tense set of his shoulders gave Cossack pause. As did the two flint-faced men who accompanied him.

"Of course." He murmured to the soldiers he had been sharing his lunch with, "Please excuse me." He tried to follow Usama, but the man insisted he go first.

"You know the way."

Not "You know the way, *General Labazanov*."

I am in trouble, and I don't know why or how. But after being found "wandering" around the coal-fired furnace in the cavern three nights past, he already knew he was walking on thin ice. He had explained that when he couldn't sleep, he had gone into the cavern to warm himself by the furnace, and had become interested in its workings.

"We need a dependable heat source in our stronghold, and I have been pondering how we might utilize such a device. I went behind it merely to explore and find where the ductwork came out of it."

"You weren't hiding from my men?"

Cossack had allowed his response burn hot. "Why would I need to hide myself, General Sayed?"

Sayed hadn't replied. He had flicked his fingers at Usama, dismissing them both.

Cossack arrived at the entrance to Sayed's rooms and waited for Usama. At Usama's signal, the guard pulled back the curtain and let them in.

Then Cossack saw the woman standing respectfully behind Sayed's seat. Even veiled, the intensity of her hatred reached out to him—as did the jangling alarms telling him that he should know her.

"Arzu, Arzu, Arzu. Halima bint Abra has the most incredible tale to relate. Honestly, I cannot give it credence . . . but she is quite persuasive. So, shall I let her tell the story?"

"As you wish, Sayed. I do not know the woman."

Sayed crooked a finger at her, and she spoke. *In English.*

At the sound of her voice, Cossack started to sweat.

"I was a medical doctor, a gynecologist, when I first laid eyes on you. And you? You were but a lowly trainee."

She removed her veils, and Cossack studied the woman's sallow skin, the pouches hanging below her dark eyes, trying to place her.

"You and she were quite close."

"I do not speak English as well as General Sayed. Please use Chechen or Russian."

"But you do know English—it is your first language. And I think you begin to remember me now? From Marstead's training camp? Yes. You knew me as Dr. Gupta back then, *Black*. You and Miss Green—or should I call her *Magda?*"

It took only seconds for Cossack's carefully crafted cover to come undone.

Sayed chuckled. "Oh, Halima! Yes, I see his guilt. It is written across his face. No wonder I have been suspicious of him all these years. You say he and the woman trained together to become spies?"

Gupta smiled her triumph. "That is precisely what I am saying. It was at least twenty-five years ago. I went on to other things later."

"What are you talking about?" Cossack roared, switching back to Russian. "I do not know this—this *liar*, this *deceiver!*"

"Oh, I believe it is you who is the liar and deceiver, Arzu—if that is your name. But no mind. We shall get the truth from you soon enough. I must know how many lies you have told and to whom you have whispered our secrets."

To Usama he said, "Give me his mobile phone then put him in a secure cell. I will use my own hand to pry the truth from him."

Usama shoved a gun into Cossack's side and pulled the phone from his pocket. "Do not resist me, *General*."

With Usama and his men following close behind, Cossack found himself being prodded down a tunnel, past the side tunnel where the *kafir* women were kept, to a cell carved into the side of the tunnel.

Usama stared at the peg pounded into the tunnel wall. "Where is the key?" he demanded of his men.

They looked at each other. One of them said, "I will fetch another key, Usama."

Minutes later, Cossack was alone in the cold cell, locked behind its barred gate.

THE HOUSE WAS QUIET. The kitchen servants were out doing the day's shopping. It was a good time to approach her father with a sensitive request. Svitlanya knocked on her father's door. Semion's office on the main floor of their family's home was spacious and grandiose—as befitting an American oligarch.

"Papa. I wish to speak to you."

"Come in, Svittie. Come in."

It struck Svitlanya almost daily how much bone and muscle mass her father was losing. He was, quite literally, shrinking before her eyes. In her mind's eye, Svitlanya could see her mother wringing her hands and hear her bemoaning her husband's fickle appetite—exactly as she would have done had she still been alive.

Her beloved mother had passed during the night six years ago, and Svitlanya could honestly say she was glad her mother had been spared her eldest son's death, her second son's trial and incarceration, and her husband's physical and mental decline.

"What is it, Svittie?"

Svitlanya sat before her father's desk like one of his pakhans. "I have received an email, Papa, from the hacker who stole our data, the woman called Vyper." She left the statement hanging in the air for her father to contemplate, for him to believe that the initial move had come from the other side.

"Is it a trick?"

"I cannot believe it is. The message came through the email account Director Wolfe provided. I think this Vyper must be under the director's personal supervision."

"And what does this woman want?"

"She wishes to make an exchange." Svitlanya laid out the offer. It wasn't long or complicated, but Svitlanya used simple, concise phrases. Her father's mind wasn't as agile as it had been in years past—and she wasn't the only one to have noticed.

As Semion Davydenko's mental acuity had slackened, the atmosphere in this room when his pakhans and their brigadiers were gathered, while calm on the surface, was often tense below, the cunning jockeying for position. And whenever Svitlanya joined them, the tension became a sticky, sucking quicksand, a subtle but ongoing group effort to run her down. Wear her down. Intimidate and repudiate.

But never directly. Never enough to catch her father's notice.

He sighed. "This woman. She has done us a great wrong, eh? But now she wishes us to trust her? And to set such a short deadline without allowing us proper consideration first? I don't know, Svittie." He shook his head wearily.

"I don't know."

"Perhaps we could consider the benefit versus the cost. The benefit? Our data could never be used against us. We would be safe from FBI prosecution. And the cost? It is little to us."

"Tell her I will think on it. Perhaps I will talk it over with Gregor. Yes, I will ask Gregor."

"Of course, Papa. Gregor is wise."

Gregor is a snake coiled in the grass, waiting for his moment to strike. But your eyes cannot see the danger, can they, Papa?

Svitlanya nodded to herself. She already knew the outcome of such a conversation. Gregor would pretend to ruminate on the situation, give it the serious consideration it deserved. Then he would denounce the suggestion—because it had come through Svitlanya to Semion.

But the window was too small to wait. Mere days. She would never have an opportunity like this one. Not before it was too late.

"Would you like a cup of tea, Papa?"

"Hmm?"

"Tea, Papa?"

"Oh. Oh, yes. Please."

In the kitchen, Svitlanya filled the kettle with fresh, cold water, and put it on to boil. While the water heated, she set a tray on the counter. Took down her father's favorite cup and saucer and carefully wiped them. Folded a snowy-white napkin and set it on the tray beside the cup.

She measured the loose tea blend he loved into a strainer. The tea filled her nostrils with the familiar mingled scents of orange, clove, white tea leaves, and nostalgia. Days long gone by, never to return.

She poured the boiling water into her father's cup and rearranged the napkin. Every little task an honor, each movement of her hands a loving tribute. When tears stung her eyes, she sniffed them back.

From her pocket, she withdrew a candy-like tab. She tore the wrapper's end and, taking care not to touch the tab, she squeezed it into the strainer then closed the strainer and placed it in his cup. She hummed a distracting tune to herself as the tea steeped exactly four minutes.

When she lifted the strainer from the cup, she dumped its contents into the garbage disposal, added the tab's wrapper, and flipped the switch that turned the disposal on. She ran water down the sink as the disposal worked, until nothing remained except the sweet scent of orange peel and cloves.

She poured a full tablespoon of honey into the cup and stirred.

Oh, Papa. The life you were born into didn't make you a good father, but you did love me . . . and I am grateful.

She carried the tray to his office and set the cup in front of him.

"Thank you, Svittie."

"I love you, Papa."

She kissed him on the forehead, picked up the tray, and closed his office door behind her.

CHAPTER 35

TOBIN WAS PICKING THROUGH the bagels in the bullpen when Brian sauntered in. Brian yawned and bellied up to his desk. Plunked his coffee down, sloshing it a little. Used a tissue to wipe the spill. Picked up the morning newspaper. Flipped it open.

"What the devil?"

Tobin turned, bagel in hand. "What's up, Brian?"

"Uh . . . that Svitlanya Davydenko chick you and Jaz were, um, *discussing* the other day? Part of the, um, you know, Ukrainian organized crime syndicate?"

"Yes, I know who she is. What about her?"

"Says here that her dad died."

"What? Are you sure?"

"Yeah. Article reads, 'Semion Davydenko, alleged head of the Ukrainian organized crime syndicate headquartered in Brighton Beach, Brooklyn, passed away suddenly yesterday morning.'"

Tobin was reaching for Brian's paper when his cell phone rang. "Hang on, Brian. Need to take this." He picked up.

"Marshal Tobin."

"Yes, Director?"

Wolfe's words were restrained but a hint of giddiness bled through his reserve. "Marshal, I just spoke with Svitlanya Davydenko. She has had a change of heart—and is going to call AGFA's headquarters later this morning, appropriating her father's death as the reason for the call and introducing herself to AGFA's leader.

"We're coordinating with the FBI, and they are taking lead on tracking the location of AGFA's satphone for us. I want you and Miss Jessup in DC for the call, so leave ASAP. Dress appropriately for high-level meetings."

Wolfe took a breath. "Marshal Tobin, this is what we've been hoping for. A real shot at pinpointing AGFA's headquarters."

Tobin hung up, a stunned expression on his face. "Lord. You did it. You changed her mind."

WORD OF SEMION DAVYDENKO'S passing had spread quickly, and the Davydenko's home was already burgeoning with flowers. Oversized wreaths with condolences spelled out on wide ribbons—Forever in Our Hearts, Resting in God's Arms, and other gratuitous sentiments. Great, impressive floral arrangements heavy with the cloying fragrances of lilies and roses.

Svitlanya, dressed in elegant black from head to toe, sat behind her father's imposing desk—*her* desk—receiving visitors. Overnight, she had cleared out the furnishings and bric-a-brac specific to Semion or too masculine for her tastes. She'd replaced the two chairs facing the desk with four from her previous office. The chairs were feminine, upholstered in bold, bohemian tapestry and intentionally an inch or two shorter than the ones they had replaced. The seats were presently occupied by old family friends, an elderly couple her father and mother had known all their married lives and their two daughters-in law. The couple's two sons, who had grown up with Svitlanya, stood behind their wives.

The sons had taken in the changes to Semion's office, Svitlanya's *de facto* assumption of power. They hadn't missed the large man serving as Svitlanya's aide standing respectfully inside her office doors. Behind them.

"I want to thank you for coming in person to offer your condolences at this difficult time," Svitlanya murmured at the conclusion of the visit. "I treasure the friendship our family shares with yours. Going forward, I won't forget your kindness."

Both sons understood her perfectly.

"You have our unconditional love and . . . support," one carefully answered.

The other nodded and said, "Yes. Unconditional."

"Thank you."

She arose from her chair and walked around the desk to receive their embraces. When she lifted a finger, her aide stepped forward to usher the visitors from the room and bring in the next group.

The aide, Nico, was armed and sworn to Svitlanya, one of four such allies, Svitlanya's newly chosen pakhans. He was, however, the only one of Svitlanya's pakhans visible to her guests. The other three captains were in the house, armed and discreetly out of view, but never far from Svitlanya's office and person.

Svitlanya had called the four men to her early yesterday afternoon . . . after the servants had found her father slumped over his desk, after the coroner and the police had come and eventually taken Semion's body away. She had called these four men and requested their immediate presence.

She had selected the men because they were steady, loyal members of the organization, but a tier below her father's pakhans. They had come to her, their eyes wary, well aware that her first moves would be swift and decisive—or they would be her last. They had come to take her measure, to judge whether she had the intelligence and brass to undercut and defeat her father's old guard.

"I require advisors and confidants, men I can trust," she had begun, "captains who will help ensure that this transition, per my father's decision, is a seamless one." She then told them of the agreement she'd made to rid the organization of the threat hanging over them.

"I have arranged that, within the week, our financial records presently in the hands of the FBI will no longer be a concern. However, should anything . . . unexpected happen to my leadership? I fear the deal I brokered would fall apart. And should that happen, the FBI would eventually find the means to decrypt the data."

Her eyes had rested on each man, assessing them as much as they were assessing her. She finished with, "It would break my heart should the FBI access those records and use them to systematically dismantle our organization . . . and its dedicated people."

On the one hand, the men understood the danger those records posed to them personally and the prison time they would face. On the other hand, they knew that they would never rise above their current stations in the organization on their own, certainly not to the level she dangled before them—*unless* they swore their allegiance to her.

One by one, they had done so, scribing the invisible battle lines for the war ahead.

This morning as Svitlanya received the condolences of friends and neighbors, her pakhans' trusted, armed soldiers—now *her* trusted, armed soldiers—guarded the grounds of Svitlanya's home, taking care to remain out of sight. Her pakhans had also salted a select few of their men—*her* men—among the mourners who had come to pay their respects. Two more posed as servants, two others acted as butlers.

"Nico." Svitlanya called the man to her. "I must make an important call. Please apologize to my guests for a short delay of no more than half an hour."

"Yes, ma'am."

Nico left and closed the door softly behind him.

Svitlanya spun the dial on her father's wall safe and ran it through the combination. She removed a burner phone from the safe, checked the phone's charge, and sat down at the desk. She placed the burner nearby.

A quick glance at the clock told her it was near 11:00 a.m. The time would almost be 7:00 p.m. where AGFA was. Svitlanya scribbled a few notes and paused to compose herself. She had listened in on her father's conversations with this man she would be calling, this "Sayed." She knew what he was.

But I think he does not know what I am.

She lifted the receiver on her desk phone and dialed the number Wolfe had given her.

"Wolfe here."

"Director Wolfe. Are you prepared on your end?"

"We are, Ms. Davydenko. Would you care to test your phone?"

Svitlanya reached for the burner and pressed the call key. The device attached to the phone—delivered to her house early that morning hidden within a floral arrangement—picked up the hiss of the phone's empty air and conveyed it to Wolfe through her desk phone.

Wolfe said, "Very good. Our people tell me we will be able to hear both sides of your conversation loud and clear. Please make the call at your convenience."

"Calling now." She set her desk phone aside and dialed the lone number stored in the burner.

NINE PEOPLE CIRCLED THE FBI conference table to listen in on Svitlanya Davydenko's call to AGFA. The FBI Special Agent hosting the surveillance, two of his agents, plus Wolfe, Seraphim, Tobin, and Jaz were intent on monitoring the call itself. Two FBI technicians—with Jaz intermittently lurking over their shoulders while snapping her gum—were focused on Svitlanya's call as it reached out to connect to the orbiting satellite and then the number on the other end.

The special agent said, "Here we go, people."

"We appreciate the assist this morning, Special Agent Marrs."

The man turned to Wolfe. "Our pleasure. What will you do with the location of the other satphone once we have it?"

Wolfe smiled. "I hope to meet this guy up close and personal."

Marrs seemed surprised. "You'll go into the field yourself, sir?"

"For this I will."

They stilled as the call was picked up.

"Da?" The man spoke in Russian.

The response was in English. "General Sayed? This is Svitlanya Davydenko calling."

Sayed switched to heavily accented English. "I see."

"Yes. General Sayed, I am calling to inform you that my father, Semion Davydenko, passed away yesterday morning."

"*Inshallah*. I am sorry to hear this."

"Thank you, General. Per my father's wishes, I have assumed the leadership of our organization. I also called to assure you that the agreements between our organizations are unaffected by the change in leadership. I will ensure that your American commander receives your incoming shipment as agreed upon."

Sayed was silent for several long moments, and Svitlanya did not interrupt the pause. Obviously, if Sayed, due to religious and cultural mores, was displeased with the idea of working with a woman, it stood to lose him the shipment she spoke of.

The shipment of carfentanil needed for his grand strike, Wolfe mused. *If it's a tossup between making nice with an uppity American female or losing the shipment, my money is on the shipment.*

"I see," Sayed said. A slight chill had attached to his voice.

Svitlanya pretended not to notice. "While we are on the subject of our agreements, may I inquire into your progress toward acquiring the location of the hacker named Vyper from the American woman?"

Sayed sounded irritated. Truculent. "Unfortunately, she arrived in less than optimal condition, after which she came down with dysentery. She is recovering, but these things have impeded our ability to properly interrogate her."

Svitlanya's tone sharpened. "Oh?"

The reaction on Wolfe's end was immediate. He, Seraphim, Tobin, and Jaz exchanged worried glances, first at the news of Bella's poor health, second that Svitlanya might, inadvertently, put pressure on Sayed to extract the information regardless of how it might harm Bella.

But it seemed Svitlanya had already thought through her role. "I would not wish the woman to die in your care, General, without her first delivering the hacker's location."

"Then more time is needed."

"In fact . . ." This time it was Svitlanya who paused before she spoke. "I believe I will wish the woman returned to me at a later date. She may have additional uses for us."

She added, "As you may understand, I am dealing with personal grief over my father's passing and am pressured by the preparations for his funeral—a much longer and more detailed affair in our traditions than in Islamic culture—as well as my other responsibilities. I will think on this situation and call you again say, just prior to the shipment's arrival? We will make the arrangements for the woman's return at that time."

It seemed to those listening that Sayed was reluctant to express his appreciation for the delay but he hardly had a choice. "Yes. Thank you."

"You are welcome. I look forward to our continued cordial relationship, General Sayed."

Wolfe exhaled his relief. Svitlanya had handled Sayed perfectly.

"Goodbye, Miss Davydenko."

"Goodbye, General."

Wolfe snapped his fingers to get the technicians' attention. Both of them were grinning. Jaz, hanging over them, was smiling, but also surreptitiously wiping the inner corners of her eyes.

Wolfe understood and swiped a hand across his own eyes.

Tobin, Seraphim, and Wolfe joined Jaz in peering over the techs' shoulders to their laptops.

One of them pointed to his screen. "Here you go. Latitude N 42°43'44.7", longitude E 45°48'07.2"."

Wolfe stepped back and spoke to his FBI counterpart. "Thank you, Special Agent Marrs, and thank you to your team. We appreciate the assist."

"And the rescue?"

"I'll be using a team under my command."

"It's *Russia*, Director."

"Oh, trust me, I know. Don't worry. We'll be coordinating with the appropriate authorities."

IT HAD BEEN ESSENTIAL to Svitlanya's plans to convey a sense of confusion and helplessness to her father's pakhans—Gregor, in particular. She had called Gregor yesterday, soon after the coroner had taken her father's body away, to give him the news.

"I-I'm in shock, Gregor."

"Of course. I am very sorry."

"I don't know how I will manage everything."

"I will come at once to help you, Svitlanya."

He hadn't been able to keep the thrill of victory out of his voice, Svitlanya sneered inwardly.

"How I thank you, Gregor! I am certain I will need to lean upon you many times in the coming weeks. However, at the moment, I am wearied and wound too tight at the same time, near to breaking. The doctor gave me a sedative and instructions to lie down, so I am going to take the pills and rest a while."

"I understand. I—"

"Could you come late tomorrow afternoon? I will be inundated with visitors all day and exhausted by then, so I will need help making decisions concerning the funeral arrangements. The priest is coming at six. If you and the others on my father's council could come an hour before then? We could discuss the service and you could help me through the meeting with the priest."

"We would all be honored to assist you, Svitlanya."

"Ah, Gregor. Thank you. I knew I could count on you. Until then."

Gregor had not waited until late in the afternoon, however, to send scouts into Svitlanya's home to spy out the land. What his scouts had observed and reported back to him were dozens of family, friends, and business partners from outside the organization, a handful of servants pressing refreshments upon the visitors—and not even a whiff of defenses.

Two of those "servants" had gently but firmly closed the door on new visitors at 4:00 p.m., had ushered the remaining visitors out before five o'clock, and then turned the door over to one of the Davydenkos' longtime maids.

By the time the maid showed Gregor and his companions into Semion's office, not another soul was in view.

Svitlanya was standing when they entered. She embraced each of Semion's pakhans and received their condolences. She invited them to sit, taking the seat behind Semion's desk herself.

Gregor smiled and spread his hands. "Svitlanya, we have been friends since we were children, yes?"

Svitlanya nodded and returned a wan smile. "Yes, I have known you my entire life, Gregor."

And have known what you are for almost as long.

"And we have been your father's counselors, his trusted pakhans, for more decades. We know the ins and outs of our organization's businesses. We recognize the great burden all this responsibility would be while you are grieving. Perhaps we should take the load from your shoulders for a little while, Svittie—just while you adjust."

Svitlanya studied her twined fingers for a moment, then spoke—but not in response to Gregor.

"You know that I met with a Director Wolfe earlier this week and agreed to give up the incoming shipment we were to deliver to our Chechen friends?"

"Yes. Of course."

"You will, however, be unaware that I struck a deal with the hacker whose actions resulted in our encrypted financial records ending up in the possession of the FBI. Within the week, she will either remove or destroy all copies of our data in FBI custody."

The man to the left of Gregor moved uneasily. Gregor's elbow between his ribs stilled him.

"You did this with Semion's permission?"

"No. I did it on my own authority as my father's successor."

It was then that her visitors began to sense a chill in the room.

"Svitlanya, how can you be confident that this *hacker* will follow through? What if she were to decrypt the files instead? Use them against us?"

"She and I have discussed what each of us hopes to obtain through this exchange. I wish our organization's data removed from the reach of the FBI, and she has the power to accomplish that. I possess things she values, including her own continued health and well-being and, uppermost to her, the well-being of a dear friend. She understands that her friend will be safe only as long as I decree it. Conversely, it is within my power to destroy her friend—so you see, I need not fear this hacker woman."

Svitlanya leaned forward slightly and tilted her chin toward the men. "You must realize that our organization has been threatened far too long by the FBI's attempts to decrypt our records. For that reason, I acted and removed *the obstacle* that kept us in this untenable position. I wish you all to understand that I will not tolerate anything or anyone who jeopardizes our businesses or our freedom."

Svitlanya watched Gregor's face turn red. She knew he was intuitive and conniving. He would have caught the essence of her statement—had he not been preoccupied by the sensation of power slipping through his fingers, eluding his grasp.

The expressions on the faces of Gregor's companions, however, told Svitlanya that they had heard, had *followed* the oblique reference Svitlanya had made. They understood what—or rather *who*—had been "the obstacle" she'd removed.

They grew utterly still, while Gregor, confident he could bully Svitlanya aside, barged ahead.

"Svitlanya, such a dangerous, unilateral decision was not yours to make. Why, it is plain that you are in no fit condition to lead our organization at this time. I must insist that you step aside and let us steer it forward." He smiled ingratiatingly. "We can, of course, revisit your participation when you have sufficiently . . . recovered from your grief."

One of Gregor's companions moved his head side to side, just enough for Svitlanya to notice. He placed his hands on his knees, palms up, in surrender and supplication. Pleading.

At Svitlanya's tiny nod, the man swallowed hard and dropped his head.

She returned Gregor's smile. "Yes, I was certain those would be your sentiments, Gregor."

She rang the little bell on her desk. Nico, with her other newly sworn pakhans, entered the room. Following them, a half-dozen of their soldiers—*her* soldiers—circled behind Gregor and his companions, their weapons trained on their heads.

"What is this?" Gregor hissed.

"Nico?"

"Six of Gregor's men attempted to approach from the rear of the house, ma'am. Three did not survive the encounter. Four more from the front—as you anticipated."

Svitlanya nodded to her new captains and the soldiers. "Well done. You have proven yourselves this day and may expect rewards for your loyalty."

She returned her attention to Gregor and said softly, "You asked what this is, Gregor? It is your curtain call—the last scene in the last act of my father's pakhans."

Pointing her chin at the man who had surrendered moments before, she added, "That one." She did not even use his name. "He has twenty-four hours to relocate his family to Australia or suffer the consequences."

She stood and walked to the door. Serene. Regal. Confident. Breathing the air of power and very much liking its scent.

"Their bodies are not to be found, Nico."

Nico's chest expanded. "You may be sure they will not, ma'am."

"Thank you, Nico."

"MADER! MADER, WAKE UP! Please!"

Laynie's head pounded. She struggled to breathe, to draw in enough air. Because of the pain, she resisted rising from the solace of unconsciousness.

But the voice calling to her was insistent. "*Mader*, please! Don't leave me here alone!"

Laynie needed to answer. *Love* compelled her to respond. To comfort.

"Ksenia."

"Oh, *Mader!* Thanks be to Jesus! I feared you were dead."

I feel like I should be, Laynie thought. She began to sort through her body's various conflicting signals.

My head. She tried to reach her hand to her head and the pounding source of pain. Ksenia restrained her.

"Do not touch, please, *Mader*. I have wrapped my niqab around the cut to stop the bleeding."

Hard to breathe. Laynie touched her side. Again, Ksenia gently clasped her hand between hers.

"I-I fell on you, *Mader*. I am sorry—I did not mean to."

Laynie groaned. "If you are all right, then I am not sorry. Help me sit up, please?"

Her vision dimmed, and she sagged briefly against Ksenia, then pushed herself to sitting. Tested her legs. Her arms. Flinched when her fingers encountered the burn on her left forearm. She could feel its heat even through her abaya.

Arms and legs undamaged. With the exception of a side of bruised ribs and a nasty headache, I am all right. That burn, though, is infected.

"Are you hurt, little daughter?"

"No, *Mader*, but . . ."

Laynie silently finished Ksenia's sentence. *But after a few days down here, our injuries won't matter.*

"We need to get out of here."

"How? There is no way out."

"Help me to stand. Now. Help me up." With reluctance, Ksenia assisted Laynie to her feet. Laynie put her back to the cistern wall, faced the wall opposite her and looked up. The faintest bit of light told her where the edge was. She measured the distance to the edge with her eyes.

Closer to twenty feet.

If it had been twelve or fifteen . . . But it wasn't.

She ran her hands around the walls, looking for purchase, for any protruding edge to give her a toehold.

Nothing.

After a while, her aching head and ribs forced her to sit down. Rest.

Ksenia crouched down beside her. She gently wrapped her arms around Laynie's torso and laid her head on Laynie's shoulder.

"Will you sing of God's amazing grace to me, *Mader?*"

Laynie knew Ksenia loved the song, so she did her best. The words and melody came in clipped, jerky phrases, because breathing was short and painful, but she sang anyway. And the song rose to heaven, not from her heart, but from a place far deeper within her.

When we've been there ten thousand years
Bright shining as the sun,
We've no less days to sing God's praise
Than when we'd first begun.

Ksenia added her voice to Laynie's on the last verse . . . and Laynie felt God's glory fill the deep hole where they were trapped.

O Father, even here, you are with us! And when I am surrounded by your very presence, my heart rests from its struggles and pain. In you, Lord, I need not fear. Thank you.

The last words of the song trailed off, and Laynie rested her cheek on Ksenia's head. "You were very brave today, dear one. I am so proud of you."

"No, I was afraid, but . . . I trusted Jesus anyway." Ksenia sighed. "I am glad we are together, *Mader*."

"I am, too, little daughter."

O Lord! The joy we feel now will last forever . . . when we are safely in your kingdom.

Chapter 36

WOLFE, TOBIN, AND JAZ returned to Wolfe's DC offices. Wolfe placed a call while Tobin and Jaz listened.

"Major? We have the location." He read off the coordinates. "Send reconnaissance now."

He glanced up at Tobin and Jaz as he added, "Yes, I'm headed your way. ETA nine hours. Please activate our partners. Put them on a twelve-hour standby. You should have a picture of what we're heading into by the time I arrive, yes?"

"Yes, sir. We'll have the operation mapped out with contingencies when you arrive."

Wolfe dropped the call and turned to Tobin and Jaz.

"I have called up a black ops assault team of my own, one pre-positioned at a US base in Turkey and authorized to operate anywhere except on American soil. Miss Jessup? You will return to Broadsword and apprise the task force. We may need the team to provide support. Marshal Tobin? I'm inviting you to accompany me."

"Thank you, Director. I accept. I would hate to have broken your arm to get a seat on that plane."

"Clever comeback, Marshal."

"Not a comeback. *Sir*."

At Wolfe's frown, Tobin shrugged. "Just the way it is, sir. I'ma going after Bella, an' ain't no force on earth gonna stop me."

Jaz looked from Wolfe to Tobin, her face a furious mask. "**Blank** your male chauvinism and patriarchy! Tobin goes, but I have to wait at Broadsword because I'm a woman?"

"Stand down, Miss Jessup. The reason you're not coming along is because we won't be sitting on our hands at the base in Turkey. Tobin and I are going with the assault team. You want us to armor you up and hand you a weapon? Say so."

Jaz's brows shot into her hairline. Her mouth shrank to a tiny "o."

"Didn't think so. I'll have a driver take you back to Broadsword. Tobin? You and I need to hustle. We have a plane to catch."

"YOU DID WHAT?" Sayed's rage was not unfamiliar to Bula, but he had never, before now, been its recipient.

"The woman led a rebellion in the *kafir* women's cell. She blasphemed against Allah and led others to do the same."

"I *need* that woman if we are to get our shipment delivered!"

Bula dropped his eyes. "She is likely not dead . . . yet. Perhaps she suffered a broken bone. If you order it, I will have her pulled out."

Sayed sat abruptly and considered his uneasy, shifting fortunes. That he was now forced to treat a *kafir* woman as his equal galled him to no end.

I will stall this Davydenko woman until it is too late. Even if Anabelle Garineau has perished, the Davydenko woman will not know until after Khasurt has the weapon in hand. Then it will no longer matter.

Afterward, as long as our attack on the Great Satan goes forward as planned, I can ignore the Ukrainian organization and its upstart leader.

"Leave her for now."

LAYNIE DIDN'T KNOW HOW long she and Ksenia had slept, but a shower of small pebbles woke them. Ksenia stood and looked up. Laynie was stiff and quite sore. It took her longer to get to her feet.

The faint outline of a head appeared at the cistern's edge. A voice called softly.

"It is Asmeen!" Ksenia relayed to Laynie. "She has our water jugs."

"Tell her to tie her scarves together, tie one end to a jug, and lower it to us."

We will at least have water until Black finds a way to get us out.

The jug slowly descended to where Laynie could reach it.

When they had both jugs, Laynie said, "Ask Asmeen if she and Mariam are all right."

A lengthy conversation ensued before Asmeen disappeared.

"Asmeen says the other girls were very cruel to her and Mariam when they came back to the cell last night. They slapped them and called them names and told them they were not welcome to return to their fire. Asmeen says that part is good, though, because our jugs were waiting next to our mattresses, and they could drop them to us."

Laynie could hear Ksenia's smile in the cistern's darkness. "After they slapped Mariam, she told them how much God loves them—so much that he sent his Son to die for them."

Tears sprang to Laynie's eyes. "They are brave, too."

"Yes, that is what I said to Asmeen. I told her that we are proud of them."

Laynie hugged Ksenia. "My good girl."

A moment later, Ksenia said, "I forgot. Asmeen also said the soldiers were talking about the man who came to see you. The one who said 'Magda, Magda.'"

"What did the soldiers say?"

"They said he has been found to be a spy for the Americans, that Halima bint Abra testified against him."

Gupta!

"The soldiers say Sayed will kill him, but he has put the man in a cell for now."

The last vestige of hope seeped from Laynie's body, and she sagged against the cistern wall.

Oh, Black. It seems that neither of us will leave this place.

JAZ REVIEWED HER PLANS on the ride back to Broadsword. *Think you're the only one with skills, Director? I may not know guns, but I played you and Tobin like a violin.*

When she entered the bullpen, the team was waiting. Waiting for news.

She grinned. "We have the satphone's location. Wolfe and Tobin are meeting an assault team in Turkey and—"

"They are on their way? Now?" It was Brian.

Of course it was.

"Yes, now. They will meet up with the assault team in nine or ten hours. I don't know the plan after that, just that they are going to get Bella."

And crush those who took her, her mind supplied.

"Finally!" Rusty shouted.

"Yes, finally. Now, if you don't mind, I have a few things to do, *but* . . . I think we all deserve a break today. It's Saturday, too, so take the rest of the day off. I'll man the phones while I'm finishing up the details Wolfe asked me to see to. When I'm done, you-all can switch off here, two at a time, throughout the day and evening. Sound good?"

"I hardly know what to do with myself," Gwyneth said.

Jubaila grabbed Gwyneth's arm. "I vote for a movie—and popcorn!"

Brian's head snapped up. "Popcorn?"

The bullpen couldn't have emptied faster if someone had yelled "Zombie attack!"

Jaz got busy. She had already tinkered around the edges of the FBI's system and the remote server farm where their files were backed up weekly, exploring the FBI's cybersecurity protocols. They were robust, and it wouldn't be easy for her to accomplish her task, but her brain had already problem-solved until she had ironed out her plan of attack.

Her complete strategy would evolve over two nights. However, she had to get the ball rolling today or risk a week's delay.

It's going to be much easier making the FBI get rid of those files for us than me trying to do it, she told herself as, keystroke by keystroke, she dug her way—carefully—through the remote server farm's firewall.

After twenty minutes of scanning directories, she located the FBI's New York weekly file backup. The backup was on tape—and you can't hack tape. Instead she wormed her way into the server farm's "restore" functions, the software that, in the event of data loss or corruption on the FBI's network, restored the most recent backup of the FBI's files to their network servers.

She opened a text file from her personal library, copied from it, and pasted onto the "restore" functions' handshaking parameters. The "restore" functions would now perform how and when she intended them to.

Very good, my pretties. Very good.

Jaz backed out of the server farm without triggering an alarm. Before she moved to her next and quite-convoluted task, she made herself a cup of tea. She forced herself to drink it slowly while rehearsing what came next—because it was not enough for Jaz to successfully complete her tasks. She had to do so without triggering any alarms or leaving a trail.

I'll start with a low-level employee with basic network access. Let's call him Ralph. Then I'll worm my way into Ralph's personal life. I do hope Ralph is married or has a love interest. If he doesn't, Ralph becomes Reject Ralph, and I'll have to replace him with Ralph 2.0, someone who fits my needs.

Setting aside her empty cup, Jaz opened a command prompt, dumped preformatted text into it, and tweaked it for her present scenario. A few minutes later, she stared at the list of users on the New York FBI's network—but she made no attempt to breach the network's firewall.

She toggled to a new screen outside the FBI's network and ran a search on her initial mark, looking for the man's personal email account, while she hummed the melody to Hammerstein's "Getting to Know You."

"There you are, Ralphie, and thanks for playing today."

"Getting to know all about you" is easy enough, right, Ralphie? I'll just hack your home email account.

Once inside his personal email account, she dug through Ralph's inbox and found an email he'd sent from his FBI email account to his personal account.

Good. Now I have Ralph's FBI email address. Next, I'll find and hack his sweetie's email account. Then I'll send an email from her account to Ralph's FBI email account.

"Let's see," Jaz whispered to herself. "What should Ralphie's sweetie ask him? 'Can we go see this movie?' Yes. That will work."

Jaz prepared the email Ralph's girlfriend would send to him at work. The text 'Can we go see this movie?' was a link to which Jaz attached her Very Special Worm Number 1.

Because on any given workday, when Ralph saw an email from his girlfriend's account in his FBI email inbox, he would open it, yes? Perfectly safe. He trusts her, so he would even click on the attachment to see which movie she wanted to see. The attachment—my attachment—*is also quite convincing. He'd never believe the email wasn't from his girlfriend.*

Jaz snickered. "But, since this is Saturday and Ralph *isn't* at work today, I'll have to open the email and click the link for him."

True, she could have just as well sent the email from some random account, clicked the link herself, then deleted the email—but if, by some fluke, the FBI suspected a network intrusion and began an investigation, she preferred they find ready suspects at hand rather than have them looking farther afield.

On one screen, she sent the email from the girlfriend to Ralph at work. On the other screen, she hacked into the FBI's Outlook email system and into Ralph's FBI email account. When the girlfriend's email arrived. Jaz opened it, clicked the link, and waited.

Once my Very Special Worm Number 1 does its work, Ralph will have temporary administrator access to the FBI's entire Outlook email system.

"Yup. Here we go." She was in.

Jaz scanned the staff directory within the FBI's Outlook program and identified appropriate HR and IT department personnel. She created an email distribution group for the IT department staff and saved it. She then hacked the email account of a mid-level HR employee and sent a group email purportedly from the HR department to all IT staff members.

The email announced upcoming mandatory training and contained an attachment with the training schedule.

"Totally legit, boys and girls," Jaz whispered, "and even though it's Saturday, some bottom-of-the-pecking-order help desk guys are always on duty. Whichever one of them opens the schedule first—with my Very Special Worm Number 2 attached—will grant me *their* network administrator privileges, letting me view the entire network tree, even the classified partitions. I don't need read-write access, just need to see the file structure and all file names."

Jaz unwrapped a stick of Black Jack, folded it in quarters, and put it in her mouth. She chewed and watched carefully for a quarter of an hour. Finally, someone clicked on the "training schedule" and activated her worm.

"Bingo. Yes, I'm that good." She opened the network directory in her new administrator role and found everything she needed—including the directory containing the Ukrainian mob's encrypted files.

To minimize the chances of her scheme being found out too soon, Jaz recalled the first email from HR, and all the unopened emails disappeared. Then she fired off a second email from HR only to the recipient who had opened the first email. "We apologize for our mistake in sending you notice for the upcoming training," Jaz read aloud as she typed. "IT is not the intended target audience for this training. Please disregard the previous notice. Thank you."

Just needs to hold water for two more days.

She returned to her target directory and the folder storing the Ukrainians' files. She could even view the files themselves. But the only action she took was to grab a screen shot of the folder and its files. She pasted the image into a new document and saved it to her laptop.

She would never attempt something so ignorant as altering or deleting the files. No, any such attempt would have set off mega alarms. Might even have triggered a "restore" from the tape backup.

Jaz laughed aloud at her own joke. "Now who would want the FBI to do that?"

Using the screen grab as her guide, Jaz replicated the folder in an admin directory and populated the folder with the same number of files as her screen grab. It was a time-consuming activity, because she had to ensure that every file was named correctly and was exactly the same size as its twin. The contents of each new file were total nonsense—but all of the files were as highly encrypted as the mob's financial records.

Now I need to view the FBI's security alarm system. I'll only tweak it a little. Just a teensy weensy bit.

With her modification to the security alarm system done, she completed her last task, adding one further step to IT's normal backup cron job. Then she erased all trace of her presence in the FBI's system.

Rusty and Vincent strolled into the gym. "Hey, Jaz. It's been three hours. Do you want us to spell you on the phones?"

"Yup. I'm pretty much done here. Glad you guys are taking over—I mean, the phone lines have been *on fire*, and I'm just worn out answering the hundreds of calls flooding in."

Rusty and Vincent laughed. Rusty added, "Don't worry. I'll keep the fire extinguisher by my desk."

"Good move," Jaz answered. While they got settled, she reviewed her work, inaudibly murmuring each step in sequence.

"The weekly backup will run tonight, midnight, writing the FBI's files to tape. Immediately after, the additional step in the cron job will overwrite *to the same tape* the fake Ukrainian directory and files I planted in the FBI's network—after which that directory will disappear. Erased.

"Tomorrow night, midnight, an unscheduled system restore will commence. While the sad little, bottom-of-the-pecking-order IT guys on night duty try to figure out why a restore is running and if they should abort it, it will be too late. The only directory overwritten will be the one holding the Ukrainians' financial records. When they view the directory, however, nothing will have changed. Even the timestamps in the directory won't reflect the restore point—score another round for Vyper.

"Their IT gurus will scratch their heads and cross their fingers, hoping and praying they haven't fallen victim to a world-class hacker like me. If they should sense anything amiss and decide to restore from the *previous* tape backup? Sadly, they will discover that the entire tape has already been erased and reformatted. Twice."

She chuckled softly. "Bottom line? The Ukrainian mob's original encrypted files will be gone. Blotto. The cherry on top is that the FBI has never been able to decrypt the mob's files. Hard to make the case that they've lost the files' contents when they can't testify to what they had in the first place. If they ever do decrypt the files? They'll find reams of complete junk."

Jaz sat back and treated herself to another stick of gum.

Behold the power of the Venom Queen.

Chapter 37

LP

WHEN WOLFE AND TOBIN landed at Incirlik Air Base in Turkey, they were thrown seven hours ahead of their own time zone. They had snatched a few hours of sleep on the plane, but when they descended from the jet, what should have been an hour before midnight was a bright winter morning on a little chunk of America dropped into a foreign nation.

The leader of Wolfe's assault team met them on the tarmac.

"Good morning, sir."

"Good morning, Mr. Fenelli. Marshal Quincy Tobin? This is Tony Fenelli, Wolf Pack Team Lead, designation Wolf Pack 1."

Fenelli and Tobin shook hands. Then, with nothing more than a "this way, sir," Fenelli led them to an idling vehicle and drove them farther down the tarmac to a C-130 Hercules already warming up. His five-member team was waiting for them.

After Fenelli introduced them around, he said, "Our assault gear and cargo are loaded, and our helo is pre-positioned on the LZ outside Grozny as directed by our Russian counterparts. Additionally, sir and Marshal Tobin, we have gear for you to change into on the plane. We are good for go on your say-so."

"And AGFA's hideout?"

"Reconnaissance of the coordinates you provided show that the separatists have occupied a defunct mine. Old blueprints of the mine, obtained by the Russians, indicate only one way in or out of the mine. However, because we believe AGFA has occupied the mine for three or more years, we cannot guarantee that they haven't found or made another point of egress. Certainly they have done extensive tunneling to accommodate the size of their militia.

"When we land in Grozny, we will meet and spend the afternoon reviewing plans and tactics with our counterparts, then spend the night on their base. The operation will commence zero four hundred tomorrow."

"Thank you. If we're ready, let's go. Time's wasting," Wolfe said.

"Uh . . . sir?"

"You have something more to say, Mr. Fenelli?"

"Yes, sir, two things. First, because you're the boss and can stipulate that you and Marshal Tobin accompany us to the drop, you will be geared up and armed. However, as Wolf Pack's team leader, I won't endanger the lives of my men by ordering them to babysit two untrained participants. I will insist, sir, that you and the marshal observe from where I tell you and obey every command without discussion or hesitation."

"Understood. Second?"

Fenelli chuckled uneasily. "Just wondering how in the world we wrangled up a joint op with the Russians on their own turf. Not exactly SOP—or even precedented."

"Let's just say that someone with enough pull owes one of my people a big favor, and I'm calling that favor in."

"Roger that, sir."

Fenelli shouted to his team. "Wheels up! Let's go, let's go!"

THAT EVENING, ASMEEN and Mariam dropped two slices of bread to them—the bread taken from their own dinner plates. Ksenia devoured her slice. When Laynie saw her looking at the other piece, she gave it to her.

Laynie was grateful for the jugs of water Asmeen had lowered to them, but she soberly considered that she and Ksenia would soon suffer from lack of nourishment.

"Dear one, listen to me. We must tell Asmeen and Mariam not to give us their food," Laynie whispered. "They receive barely enough for themselves as it is."

Ksenia didn't answer, and Laynie knew the girl was facing the ugly truth of their situation—that starving was a horrible, lingering way to die.

It would be better not to drag out the suffering.

A while later, Asmeen called to them. She carefully lowered a water jug tied to her veil, which was tied to Mariam's ratty veil.

"They say we are to empty this water into one of our jugs. They will share their water with us."

Ksenia reached up high to untie the jug. She couldn't quite reach it, but Laynie could. She stretched and stared all the way up the cistern wall to where Asmeen's silhouette hung over the edge. Laynie was about to untie the jug when, from out of nowhere, an old memory surfaced.

Ahead of them loomed the wall.

Fifteen feet high.

"*How do we get you two up and over?*" *Black asked.*

"*Stand back while I make a stirrup.*"

"*You don't need to lift me; I'm pretty sure I can sprint toward it, jump, and catch the edge.*"

"*It's not for you. I'm going to throw Red.*"

Laynie's problem-solving ability, the part of her that operated on its own and presented fully formed solutions to her conscious mind, slipped into overdrive. Frowning at her churning thoughts, she handed the jug to Ksenia.

A moment later, the answer arrived—an idea, a series of steps so daring that Laynie trembled.

She let go of the tail end of the lowered niqab. *But Lord? I would be putting their lives at risk.*

A whisper in her spirit floated back. *This is according to my word. For you died, and your life is now hidden with Christ in God. Asmeen and Mariam, too, have chosen me. Trust me with them—for their lives are mine.*

Laynie exhaled. "As you say, Lord."

Ksenia had emptied the jug into one of theirs and handed it back to Laynie. Before Laynie retied it to the niqab, she took Ksenia's hand.

"Ksenia, I believe the Lord has shown me a way out of this cistern and out of this place. I need you to tell Asmeen and Mariam to come together to talk to us when they return from the soldiers late tonight. They should wait until the other girls are sound asleep. If we are asleep, too, they are to awaken us. Please—tell them it is very important."

Ksenia relayed Laynie's message. Asmeen thought on it for a moment, then promised to come.

After Asmeen had pulled the jug up and disappeared from view, Laynie said to Ksenia, "Remember when I told you that I had special training to work as a spy?"

"Yes, *Mader*. Fighting and . . . and other things. I have seen you fight. You fight better than some men."

Laynie laughed a little. "Thank you. I had training for other things, too, like how to escape from difficult places such as this. Now I am going to train you."

"Oh?"

For the next hour, Laynie worked with Ksenia, explaining, then slowly showing. The work was scary and demanding for the girl who'd had little opportunity to develop athleticism. She cajoled and ordered Ksenia to do things the girl had never dreamed of. At the same time, Laynie had to grind her teeth and push herself beyond the agony of her bruised ribs and infected arm.

Lord, even though this idea is from you, and I do believe it is, it will be difficult.

Laynie closed her mind against the tentative ache of a fever making itself known in her bones.

That infection in my arm? Please, Lord, hold it back. Don't allow me to sicken before I get my little chicks away from this evil place. I will need all my strength for what is ahead.

KSENIA FELL ASLEEP that night huddled against Laynie's side. Laynie was glad Ksenia could sleep. The girl was exhausted from the grueling exercise Laynie had put her through—on an empty stomach.

Laynie was just as exhausted, but she couldn't trust herself to sleep. What if Asmeen and Mariam called down to them and couldn't rouse her?

Laynie shivered, but not from the cold of the cistern. Her arm had swollen and was weeping. It was wrapped, and she had dampened it with what vinegar water they could spare.

She must have dozed off anyway, because the distant sounds of the girls as they were released into the cell startled her. They took their normal time relieving themselves before settling into sleep.

She prayed. "Please, Lord Jesus. Please help Asmeen and Mariam stay awake—and, oh God, strengthen them. They will need to be braver than they have ever been if they undertake the dangerous thing I will ask of them."

Perhaps a half hour later, several pebbles bounced off the floor of the cistern. Laynie looked up. She saw only the outline of Asmeen and Mariam's heads.

"Ksenia, wake up. I need you now."

Ksenia jolted awake. "I-I'm ready."

Laynie hugged her. "Good. Now, you must tell Asmeen and Mariam exactly what I say."

Laynie's instructions were short and straightforward. Four steps. That was all. Convincing Asmeen and Mariam took longer.

In the end, they agreed.

ASMEEN AND MARIAM RETURNED to their mattresses and the cold remains of their earlier campfire. Mariam glanced at the mattress that, until two evenings ago, had been Laynie's, then at Asmeen. Asmeen nodded.

Mariam crawled across the mattress and found the rock Lay-nee had told her about. She reached behind it and felt along its base. Yes, there was a hollow where a bit of the rock had chipped off. Her fingers found the key Lay-nee said would be there.

She and Asmeen tiptoed to the gate. They stared into each other's faces in the faint light.

"Oh Jesus, please hide us," Asmeen whispered.

"Amen," Mariam echoed. She reached through the bars and slipped the key into the lock. Turned it. The gate made a soft, metallic cry as it swung open.

The girls froze, their eyes searching the darkness of the cell where the others slept. When no one sat up or cried out, they slipped through, closed the gate without locking it, and scurried down the tunnel. At the junction where it joined the next tunnel, they were usually led to the right. Lay-nee, through Ksenia, had told them to turn left and watch for other cells on their left.

And she had warned them. "*At each cell, tap the key gently on the bars. Some cells may be empty. Others may be occupied by someone else. Do not show yourselves or speak a word until you are certain it is the right cell.*"

BLACK HADN'T BEEN ABLE to sleep more than an hour at a time. He had no idea when Sayed would choose to deal with him, but the next time his cell gate opened would be the last opportunity he had to escape this place. The problem though, was that the route was through one or two guards and Sayed himself.

I'll take the chance, whatever the odds. I won't go down without a fight.

So he held himself ready for whenever they came for him.

Late in the night, he heard the thin tap of metal on the barred gate to his cell. He flattened himself against the wall beside the cell gate. Raised the jar that held his water, ready to bring it down on the first guard through the gate.

The tapping came once more. He frowned. Remained quiet.

Then, the breathlessness of padded feet. Moving away. He leaped to the bars and spotted the swishing hem of an abaya disappear from view.

"Hey! Hey!" he hissed.

The padding halted. Crept back toward him. He heard whispers but saw no movement.

He called under his breath, "Magda?"

Two forms appeared in front of his cell. One of them slipped a key into the gate's lock.

The other, a young girl, said three words to him. She spoke in parroted, highly accented English. "*Come*. Black. Magda."

"Magda?"

The girl nodded vigorously.

He eased out of the cell, and she motioned to him. "*Come*. Black. Magda."

They led him down the tunnel toward the main junction near the cavern. More than halfway there, they turned into the side tunnel to the *kafir* women's cell.

The grate across the tunnel was unlocked. The girls put their fingers to their lips before stepping inside. When Black didn't immediately follow, one of them returned to his side and took his hand. Tugged on it.

"*Come*. Black. Magda."

LAYNIE PEERED UP TO the edge of the cistern for the hundredth time. *Time*. Time was ticking away, and the edge of the cistern was out of her grasp.

O Lord, I plead with you to cover my little chicks, to hide them, lead them to Black, and bring them back here safely.

Ksenia shivered inside Laynie's arms.

"It will be all right, my little daughter. I trust Jesus."

Do you hear me, Lord? I trust you! I believe you—and like that man in the gospels, I'm asking you to help my unbelief.

Pebbles dropped onto the floor. A large silhouette hung over the edge.

"Magda?"

"Oh, dear God! Thank you!" Laynie breathed. "Yes. We're down here."

Laynie could barely hear his answer. "How do I get you out?"

"I'm going to toss her up to you."

Silence for ten tortured beats of her heart.

"What's her weight?"

"Think of Red."

"Got it. Wait one."

Laynie envisioned Black evaluating the situation, instructing the girls to sit or lie on his legs as a counterweight, then hanging as much of his body over the edge as was feasible.

She turned to Ksenia. "This time, I'm going to toss you higher than before, as high as I can. When I do, I need you to keep your arms pointed straight up. Fly as high as you can and reach for Black. He will catch hold of you and pull you out."

"Wh-what if he doesn't? What if he misses my hands?"

"Then I will catch you the way I have before. You will not panic. You will fold up as I taught you, and I will catch you. I will not let you fall."

During the past day, Laynie had asked Ksenia to remove her cumbersome abaya and her sandals. She had put her own back against the wall and taught Ksenia to stand within her intertwined fingers, to crouch with her arms held straight over her head, and to spring up only when Laynie tossed her like an arrow, up, up, up toward the edge.

But their practice during the day had been more technique than execution. Laynie had tossed Ksenia only a few feet—and caught her every time she came back down. This time, Laynie would be throwing her as high as she could, using all of her strength.

The reality was that Laynie's strength was sorely diminished by her swollen, inflamed arm, and every throw and every catch had tugged and torn at her raw, burned skin.

If Black missed his hold on Ksenia and she came back down? Yes, Laynie would catch her—even if it was the last thing she could manage.

Black's voice floated down to them.

"All right. We're ready."

"One sec." She said to Ksenia, "Give me your sandals."

Ksenia took them off. Handed them to Laynie.

Laynie whispered up the cistern. "Catch!" One at a time, she tossed Ksenia's sandals up to Black's waiting hands. It took several tries to loft them to within range of his grasp, but they got it done.

Could she really do the same with Ksenia? On the first try?

Then Laynie took Ksenia's trembling hands in hers. "Lord Jesus, we are calling on you. Please help us do this right."

"Ready," she told Black.

She grabbed Ksenia's shoulders and, because they could not see each other in the dark cistern, placed her forehead against the girl's forehead and spoke earnestly to her.

"You must do your very best, my daughter. You must fly as high as you possibly can. I will only be able to do this one time."

"Because of your arm?"

"Yes. So, I am counting on you to put your trust in the Lord and in what I've taught you. Trust God. No fear."

"Y-yes, *Mader*. Trust God. No fear."

They both looked up. Black was on his stomach, hanging far past his armpits, his arms extended.

Laynie stripped off her abaya and asked Ksenia to do the same. Laynie pressed the small of her back against the cistern wall. Folded into a squat until her weight was centered over her legs and she was in a near sitting position with the wall providing balance and stability.

She motioned to Ksenia. The girl stood in Laynie's twined hands and flexed her knees. Laynie began to gently bounce, warming and readying the muscles of her legs.

"Here we go. One. Two. *Three!*"

Laynie's legs thrust her body upward while her hands and arms did the same, using all her reserves to launch Ksenia into the air.

The girl flew up, up, up toward Black's outstretched hands. There was a pause, a moment of silence . . . before Ksenia's little shriek told Laynie that she hadn't flown high enough, that Black had missed catching hold of her.

"I will catch you, Ksenia! I will!"

Oh, Lord Jesus! Please help me!

All Laynie could see were flickers of shadows as Ksenia's body hurtled toward her—but she had prepared herself to catch the girl, no matter the cost to her own body. Laynie collapsed and crashed onto the cistern's stones, taking the brunt of Ksenia's fall.

Ksenia climbed off of Laynie.

"*Mader!* Are you all right?"

Laynie bit back a groan and answered, "I think so." But when she sat up, she realized the skin on her infected forearm arm had split open. Fluids now dripped from the veil she'd wrapped around her arm.

"Magda! Mags!"

"We're all right," Laynie called softly.

"Listen, we're not done. We're . . . we're going to lower the girls' veils to you. Tie yours and Ksenia's veils to them. We'll bring them up, make a rope, and haul her up that way."

"The veils won't hold, Black. The fabric is old. Rotten."

"Send us what you've got. We'll tear them into wide strips and braid them into rope and reinforce the worst places. We'll make it work! Besides, Ksenia doesn't weigh much. Like you said, 'Think of Red.' She weighs, what? A buck ten, right?"

Asmeen and Mariam's veils, tied together, came down. Laynie, gritting her teeth against the pain of using her injured arm, tied Ksenia's two veils to the end and added her own veil, the one she'd wound around her waist before defying Bula's men.

Laynie staggered to the cistern wall and leaned against it. "Take them up," she whispered.

Ksenia was quiet while they waited for Black and the girls to braid a rope.

Too quiet, Laynie finally realized.

"Ksenia?"

A sniffle. "I am sorry, *Mader.*"

"It isn't your fault, Ksenia. Don't worry. We'll get you out yet. Trust God. No fear. Remember?"

Ksenia didn't answer.

Laynie caught herself dozing off. She slid down the wall and gave in to her fatigue.

Must rest while I can . . . make sure Ksenia gets out.

It may have been only minutes or it could have been an hour before Black's hushed voice floated down to them.

"Heads up."

A braided fabric rope snaked down the cistern. Laynie caught it, felt the toe loop in its end. It hung near her chest.

"Ksenia? Give me your hand."

She felt Ksenia's fingers and led them to the loop.

"This loop is for you to put your foot in. I will squat against the wall again. I need you to stand on my thighs, put your foot in the loop, then latch onto the rope, up high. Can you do that?"

"I will not disappoint you again, *Mader.*"

Laynie grasped Ksenia and hugged her close. "You have not disappointed me, sweet girl. This is a problem to solve, like many of life's problems. The Lord will help us figure this out."

She backed into the wall. Squatted. "Come, now. Climb onto my thighs."

Ksenia scrambled up and perched herself, wobbling a little, on Laynie's thighs. Laynie handed her the rope.

"Put your foot into the loop. It will be uncomfortable but only briefly. You'll be up and out in a few seconds."

Ksenia whispered, "I am ready, *Mader*." Her voice shook.

"Hang on with both hands under your chin. Hug the rope tight to your body. *Do not let go*."

Laynie called up the shaft, "Pull!"

Black, Asmeen, and Mariam pulled. Ksenia rose several feet. Laynie heard creaking as the braided rope stretched—followed by the unmistakable sound of fabric tearing.

Laynie was weak, close to despair. *Lord Jesus, please help, I don't know if I can catch her again!*

But the *snap* of the rope letting go did not reach her ears—and Ksenia did not fall. She disappeared over the cistern's edge.

Laynie sagged against the wall in relief.

Thank you! Oh, thank you, God!

Black's silhouette reappeared over the edge of the cistern. "Next?"

"Send down the rope. I'll send up Ksenia's abaya."

The rope of scarves came down. She tied Ksenia's abaya and her own to it. They hauled them up.

A moment later, Black whispered, "Your turn."

"Take the girls out of here, Black. Get them to safety."

"What? No! We need to get you out next."

"You can't. The rope barely held for Ksenia. It will tear under my weight. The best you can do is to let Wolfe know where I am."

"Uh-uh. No way. You're coming with us—in fact, I can't get past Sayed and his guards without you."

He must have conferred with the girls. When he finally spoke again, he said, "We've tied knots in the rope where it is weakest. The knots made the rope shorter, but we will be able to pull you up now."

Laynie thought for a long moment and considered the note of false hope she detected in his voice. Black had to know how rotted the veils were. This was his last-ditch effort.

If the rope gives way while they are hauling me up, I'll fall again—and that'll be it.

"Please don't waste any more time, Black. *Take the girls and go!*"

Instead, the end of the rope of veils floated before her eyes. Not enough length for her to get a foot into the loop.

Black's voice came down. "Ksenia says, 'Trust God. No fear.'"

Laynie muttered under her breath, "Typical teen . . . throw my advice back in my face."

Laynie felt her hot, swollen arm. The swelling was making its way into her armpit. Only one option remained open to her. She put her good wrist through the loop, then wound the rope twice around her palm so her wrist would not have to bear all the stress.

"Pull away."

Laynie's felt her arm go taut when the rope took her weight. Her shoulder complained—and then it screamed.

As Black and the girls grasped for additional purchase, the rope went a little slack. When they hauled on it, she felt the bone in her shoulder slip out of joint. The pain was excruciating.

Laynie shut her mouth and her mind to the agony.

She was unconscious when they hauled her over the edge.

CHAPTER 38

LP

LAYNIE AWOKE WITH FOUR anxious faces hovering over her. She tried to move. "Where are we?"

"Hold on, Magda." Black slowly moved her right arm. "How's that feel?"

"Sore. Not too bad. Oh. Yeah."

"Yeah, we dislocated your shoulder pulling you out. You were out cold, so we carried you halfway down the tunnel, away from the other girls so we wouldn't awaken them. While you were unconscious, I—*we*—popped your shoulder back into place."

He still looked concerned. "Your other arm, though, is in bad shape."

"I know. It's infected, but I need to power through and take care of it later."

"Well, the only way out of here is the escape ladder inside Sayed's quarters."

"A ladder? How far is the climb?"

"Pretty far."

"I see."

"We'll worry about that when we're there. Our next step is to get past the main junction and into Sayed's salon. If we can surprise or ambush Sayed's guards and take their guns without raising an alarm, we should be able to subdue Sayed himself.

"And actually, I think Ksenia has come up with a workable idea. She's going to lure the guard away from Sayed's door . . . right to me."

AN HOUR BEFORE DAWN, two American Sikorsky MH-60 Black Hawk helicopters lifted off from an isolated airfield outside of Grozny. They followed four Russian Armed Forces helos, variants of the Russian military's Mil Mi-8 combat helos.

Two of the Russian helos were serving primarily as troop transport for the thirty-six crack ground troops riding in their bellies. The remaining two helos were gunships bristling with fearsome armament—each carried KV-4 12.7mm nose-mounted machine guns, two door gunners hanging from either side, and a full complement of S-5 rockets—tank killers.

The combined force was in the air, headed due south from Grozny, into the dense Chechen mountains not far from the Chechen province's border into Dagestan.

The Americans were prepped for a hard-fought rescue. The Russians were primed for an extermination—after their rescue assist to the Americans. The Russian troops intended to lop off the head of the particularly vile separatist group known as All Glorious for Allah.

Tobin and Wolfe, strapped into the second Black Hawk, wore the same basic combat gear as Fenelli's assault team: fatigues, tactical boots, body armor, and helmets. Tobin carried a modified first-aid kit in a light pack. He and Wolfe wore sidearms and carried extra mags. That was the extent of their similarity to the American assault group.

Fenelli, good as his word, had told them hours ago, "Our Black Hawk will drop us on the ground outside the entrance to the tunnels. Your helo and its door gunner will fly overwatch—with you in it. As you have no need for rifles, you will not carry them. You may listen to my radio communications and monitor the assault along with the pilots.

"When we have penetrated the cave system and subdued AGFA forces, I'll radio your helo permission to land and send an escort to bring you inside. If the rescue is successful, your people will ride with you and our medic back to Grozny. Any questions?"

"No, sir," Tobin had answered.

Wolfe shook his head.

Now, as they approached the battle, Tobin prayed. *Lord God. You have moved mountains to get us this close to bringing Laynie home—and I am grateful. I pray for every soldier entering into this battle. O God, be merciful to them . . . and to Laynie, I ask in Jesus' name.*

KSENIA, ALONE, WALKED quietly into the junction. She peered into the cavern and down the main tunnel. Seeing no one, she signaled behind her.

Black ran forward and disappeared into the cavern. When he rejoined Laynie and the girls in the side tunnel, he was armed with the coal shovel from the cavern's furnace.

Ksenia advanced again, just as quietly. She walked into the junction and turned left into the passage leading to Sayed's quarters. When the guard standing post at the entrance to Sayed's salon noticed her, she whirled around and quick-walked back to the junction, then toward the cell's tunnel.

"There is but one," she whispered to Black as she walked by. When the guard entered the junction looking for her, he saw her partway down the tunnel—just past the side tunnel to the *kafir* women's cell.

"Hey!" he called softly. "What are you doing out here?"

She beckoned to him. As he drew closer, she pointed farther down the tunnel and walked that way.

The guard never saw Black emerge from the side tunnel behind him with the shovel in his hands. They dragged his unconscious body into the side tunnel and bound and gagged him with his belt and socks.

Black handed Laynie the man's sidearm. She could fire it one-handed. He took the rifle. The five of them retraced the guard's route and stepped into Sayed's salon without being seen.

"Behind that tapestry," Black pointed. "I will take care of Sayed."

Laynie led the three girls to the tapestry and drew it back. The alcove within was utterly dark.

"Hold hands." They joined hands, forming a single line.

When the tapestry dropped behind them, they could see nothing. Laynie felt her way toward the farthest wall, pulling the line along with her. There. She ran her hand along the wall, looking for the opening Cossack had told her she would find.

She gathered them close. "Ksenia, you will go first."

"Asmeen must go first, *Mader*."

"Why?"

"Because I am to make sure you can climb. I will push you, if you need it."

Ksenia continued, "Asmeen, Black says slide on your back for three feet. The passage will open over your head. Stand and find the ladder. Climb. Do not stop. We will be right behind you."

Laynie had Ksenia add, "It is a long climb. Rest a minute if you need to, but don't give up."

Asmeen and Mariam started up the ladder, following Ksenia's instructions.

"Now, you, Mader."

Laynie found Ksenia's cheek in the dark and kissed her. "My good girl. I'm very proud of you." Ksenia reached her arms around Laynie and hugged her—until Laynie hissed and pulled back.

"I am sorry. I forgot your arm."

"We have many years of hugs ahead of us, little daughter."

"You will . . . you will not leave me behind when you go to your home?"

"No. Asmeen and Mariam have families they can return to. But you? Even should we be separated temporarily, I would come back and claim you as my own."

"All right, ladies," Black whispered behind them. "Time for that later."

"Did you find your phone?"

"Yes. In the same drawer where Sayed's servant keeps the satphone."

"And Sayed?"

"I found him asleep in his bed. I woke him, let him see me, then knocked him out and left him trussed up like a Christmas turkey. But on the off chance someone raises the alarm? I'll remain here and hold them off until you reach the top and are safely out."

He felt for her hand, placed something in it. "Take the phone. I've already activated the beacon. As soon as you hit unobstructed air, the orbiting satellites will pick up the beacon's signal."

Laynie tucked the phone into the pocket of her abaya. "Thank you, Black. I . . . I won't forget what you've done for me . . . for *us* in this place."

"I won't forget, either, Magda, but you don't owe me anything. No, it was me. I owed you, and I . . . I couldn't believe it when I first realized you were here. I still find it hard to fathom why, of all people, it was *you* . . . except that we had unfinished business, you and I. So I'm glad . . . I'm *thankful* that we were here, together. That we are both able to put that chapter of our lives to rest. At long last."

He nudged her. "Now go, Mags. Leave this cursed place and go back to that lucky man you told me about. Don't worry about the climb. Ksenia will push you from behind if you tire or your arm gives out."

Laynie smiled in the dark alcove. "She told me."

"Then go—"

The sound was unmistakable. The rumble of an explosion followed by heavy weapons fire, far down the tunnels, in the direction of the mining cars at the entrance. An assault.

"Get going, Magda. Don't slow down and don't stop."

Laynie lay on her back and tried to propel herself backward into the first part of the tunnel, but her swollen left arm was nearly useless.

"*Mader*, stiffen your legs. I will push you."

Ksenia pushed Laynie until she could sit up, reach the first rung, pull herself to standing, and begin the arduous climb. Each step was more than difficult—it was tedious and agonizing. She had to hook her swollen elbow around a rung while she reached for the next one to pull herself up. This she did, time after time, making slow but steady progress. When her limbs began to shake from the stress, Laynie leaned back and rested against the opposite wall.

She knew Asmeen and Mariam were far ahead of them. Would reach the exit long before she did—until, above her, Mariam called softly down the shaft.

"What did she say, Ksenia?"

"She says Asmeen has reached the end of the tunnel and there is only rock above her, not a way out!"

Laynie's fatigue and pain were so great, that at the realization they might have placed their hope in an unfinished escape route, she momentarily blanked out.

"*Mader? Mader!*"

"I-I'm all right. Tell . . . tell Asmeen to run her fingers all around the tunnel walls. Tell Mariam, too."

Laynie and Ksenia waited, silent and somber, in the utterly dark shaft.

Mariam called again. Laynie could hear the relief in her voice.

Ksenia relayed to Laynie, "Mariam says there is another tunnel in the wall behind them. It does not go up but seems to lead away from the ladder, sloping a little downward. They must leave the ladder and crawl down this new tunnel."

Laynie roused herself. *Not up? Then it has to be heading toward a valley. it has to be heading toward a valley.*

Mariam spoke again.

"Asmeen took off her abaya so she could crawl. She is pushing it ahead of her."

"Yes, a good idea," Laynie replied—but she shuddered as a wave of claustrophobia washed over her.

O God! We are wholly surrounded by rock, yet still in your hands. Please lead us out of this darkness!

Laynie shook with fever, but she forced her body to repeat her slow and painful upward course.

Hook elbow around rung. Ignore pain. Reach up. Step up. Pull up.

Hook elbow around rung. Ignore pain. Reach up. Step up. Pull up.

Hook elbow around rung. Ignore pain. Reach up. Step up. Pull up.

When instead of the next rung, she banged her hand against unyielding rock, Laynie stepped down a rung and reached her hand to the wall behind her.

Empty space. The edges of another shaft. Nearly horizontal, but sloping downward.

"Take off my abaya," she murmured to herself. She rolled it up and pushed it into the tunnel ahead of her. Belly-crawled inside. Inched forward.

Move. Keep. Move. Keep. Move. Keep. Move.

Laynie must have stopped, because she felt Ksenia's fingers wrap around her ankle.

"Jesus, help *Mader*, please."

Move. Keep. Move. Keep. Move. Keep. Move.

And then Mariam's voice flowed over Laynie. "Lay-nee! Lay-nee!"

"*Mader!* Asmeen has opened the door at the end of the tunnel!"

A cool breeze touched her and light stung Laynie's eyes.

Yes. Move. Keep. Move. Keep. Move. Keep. Move.

THE BLACK HAWK SLOWLY circled the valley just south of the mine entrance. After the initial assault, Tobin and Wolfe could see nothing of the battle raging below them—within the mountain. They could only imagine it.

An hour passed. The dissident defenders were well-armed, but they had no ammunition resupply available to them. As the Russians and Americans pushed farther and farther into the cave system, slowly taking ground, the dissidents would eventually run out of ammunition and space to retreat. If it weren't for the hostages inside, the Russians would have simply set charges and brought the mountain down on top of the enemy. End of story.

"Sir!" The copilot sought Wolfe's attention, tapped his headphones. "Sir!"

Wolfe's head came up. "What is it?"

"Message from your home office was transferred to us, sir—status *urgent*. According to the call, NOAA picked up a personal locator beacon signal from this location fifteen minutes ago."

"From *this* location? Here?"

"Yes, sir." The copilot rattled off the beacon's number.

Wolfe recognized it instantly. He turned to Tobin and mouthed, "*Cossack*."

Tobin signaled that he understood.

Wolfe said, "That beacon has to be transmitting in open air in order for NOAA's polar orbiting satellites to pick it up." He asked the pilot, "Can we go lower and circle the area, scan for people on the ground?"

"Makes us more vulnerable to ground fire, sir."

"Wouldn't we have already taken fire if there were hostiles on the ground? I have a man down there *right now*, calling for immediate extract."

The pilot shrugged. "Yes, sir. Descending now—gunner at the ready. Vasquez? Keep your eyes peeled."

Wolfe and Tobin grabbed binoculars, and both of them strapped themselves into door gunner "monkey" harnesses that hooked to points on the cabin floor. The door gunner was already standing in the open starboard door. Tobin sat in the doorway beside him, legs hanging in the open air, scanning the ground below them. Wolfe stood behind him.

Tobin tapped Wolfe's foot and pointed. "Two o'clock. That's a directional antenna."

"For AGFA's satphone?"

Tobin nodded. He trained his binoculars around the antenna, looking for a hatch or for Wolfe's operative. But the protruding shoulder of the mountain, while an ideal location for the antenna, would require the use of climbing gear for a man to descend into the valley.

The valley. Tobin walked his glasses down the mountain toward the valley, then shifted them and walked them back up—

"Director!" Tobin pointed straight down. "Six o'clock!"

The pilot banked right. Beneath them, four Muslim women huddled in the snow on the slope, an open hatch nearby. One of them turned her face up to the helicopter.

Tobin adjusted his binoculars. The woman's face came into focus—and his heart thundered in his chest. "Oh, thank you, God! Wolfe, look—it's Bella!"

"Bring her around," Wolfe ordered.

As they circled again, a man climbed from the hatch. He pulled a rifle out of the tunnel after him.

The gunner exclaimed as he brought his gun to bear, "Sir, that's an enemy combatant!"

"No! Hold your fire!" Wolfe shouted. "Hold your fire. That's my man."

In a calmer voice, he said, "Now, if you please, take us down. Close as you can. Those are our people."

THE CHOPPER FLARED AND inched toward the ground. Tobin unclipped and dragged off his harness. He was out the door, running, before the wheels touched down. He clambered up the rugged slope, scrambling over rocks and through patches of snow and ice.

Wolfe's agent, Cossack, slung his rifle and watched impassively as Tobin worked his way toward them.

Out of breath, Tobin finally reached Laynie. "Bella? Bella?"

She smiled a little but didn't move. She was sitting in the snow while the others stood. A woman—a girl, actually—put a protective hand on Laynie's shoulder and spoke in rapid-fire Russian.

Cossack translated quietly, "She says, er, *Bella* is sick and needs a medic ASAP. Her left arm is severely infected."

Tobin frowned. "You're Cossack, yes?"

"I think that code name is blown, but yeah. And you are?"

"Quincy Tobin. US Deputy Marshal and utterly out of my jurisdiction."

Cossack looked him up and down. Slowly nodded. "You're Tobin. Okay. Got it."

The faintest frown of confusion flickered across Tobin's face and was gone. "Wolfe's in that helo. I'm going to get Bella aboard."

"*Director* Wolfe? He's here?"

"Yup. Your beacon was picked up and relayed to us not five minutes ago. Come on—let's move it."

Cossack addressed the girls. They gathered around Laynie and began to help her up.

Tobin gently muscled them aside. "Please. Let me. Let me. I got her."

As he lifted Laynie, her head lolled back, and the veil she had half-removed slid off her head into the snow.

Tobin choked. "Marta! Oh dear God! Sweetheart, what did they do to you? Oh, Jesus!"

Laynie's eyes fastened on him. "Quincy! How did you . . ."

Tobin blew out a breath. Again. "Tell you later, m'kay, buttercup? You-you just rest now."

The girl who seemed particularly protective of Laynie picked up her veil and motioned to Tobin.

"Magda is running a fever. She's afraid Magda's head will get cold." Cossack murmured.

"Roger." Tobin knelt in the snow while the girl wound the fabric around Laynie's head with quick efficiency. When she finished, he started down the slope, bearing precious cargo, taking his time.

A line of black-garbed goslings trailed behind him. Cossack brought up the rear.

Wolfe was waiting for them outside the rotor wash.

"Bella's sick," Tobin said. "We need to evac her to Grozny, like *now*."

"Get her aboard, Marshal."

WOLFE EXTENDED A HAND to Cossack. "I'm glad to see you in one piece."

"Not as glad as I am to see you. Frankly, sir? I need a vacation."

Wolfe chuckled. "I think you just might have some leave stored up. I'll ship you straight back to the States, but," he gestured to the three girls, "what about these, er, young ladies?"

"They had better come with us. Magda—or Marta or Bella, or whatever else she goes by these days—has developed some attachments."

"Right. We'll sort it out in Grozny."

It took Cossack several minutes to convince the confused and terrified girls to join Laynie on the chopper. When Cossack climbed in, they finally consented to board, too. The cabin was crowded, and they found Laynie lying across a row of four jump seats, half-asleep, her head cradled on Tobin's lap. Cossack, Wolfe, and the remaining two girls took the row of seats opposite Tobin and Laynie. Ksenia took the seat at Laynie's feet and studied Tobin's possession of Laynie with uncertain eyes.

Tobin, for his part, seemed to sense and understand her trepidation.

He put his hand to his chest. "Tobin."

Ksenia looked away.

"His name is Tobin," Cossack said to her. "I think he is Magda's special friend . . . come all the way from America to find her. Why don't you tell him your name?"

She chanced a nervous look at Tobin. "Ksenia."

"Her name is Ksenia, Marshal."

Tobin nodded at Cossack. "Thank you."

He held out his hand, palm up, toward the girl. She flicked a glance at Cossack, who gestured his approval.

She put her small hand into Tobin's. He gently brought his other hand down and just as gently pressed hers. "Ksenia," he said. Then he grinned.

That earned Tobin a shy smile from the girl . . . and a notch in Cossack's estimation.

I hope you'll find a lifetime of happiness with this man, Magda.

They were rising into the air moments later.

Wolfe got on the radio to Fenelli. "We have our people, Tony. The Russians can blow the place to kingdom come if they've a mind to."

"No . . . no . . ." Laynie moaned. "*Kafir* women. Save them."

Cossack explained. "She's talking about the captive girls Sayed used . . . to service his militia. They are down the first tunnel to the left past the main cavern."

"Charming fellow, Sayed."

"You have no idea."

Wolfe spoke into the radio again. "Look, change of plans, Tony. Tell the Russians there are more hostages, female, first tunnel to the left past the main cavern. Oh. You have them? Good."

Cossack tugged Wolfe's sleeve and pointed down. The Black Hawk had crossed the valley and was nearing the entrance to the mine. Russian soldiers were herding the surviving dissidents into the open, sorting the wounded from the unwounded.

"Director? I'd like to get out here. Help identify Sayed and Dr. Gupta."

"So that lying traitor made it here after all. Yes, you do that—*do not* let her escape."

Cossack's expression went flat. "You have my word."

Wolfe asked the pilot to put down near the entrance. As the Black Hawk approached, Fenelli and his men emerged from the mine. Fenelli jogged to them. Cossack and Wolfe got out to meet him.

"Outstanding job, Tony," Wolfe said. "Give your men my best and send your after action report soonest." He motioned to Cossack. "This is my inside man. He can identify Sayed. Then make sure he gets back to Turkey with you. I'll arrange a flight for him back to the States. Thanks.

"Oh. By the way, my other operative is quite ill, and I'm calling for my plane to meet us in Grozny, so this is goodbye for now. Again, outstanding work. Thank you."

WHEN WOLFE RETURNED TO the copter, he tapped the copilot's shoulder and said, "Radio my pilot in Turkey, please. Tell him I need him in Grozny the soonest he can manage—and tell him to bring an Air Force flight nurse cleared to fly with us to Ramstein. Then radio ahead to Grozny. We'll need medical attention for a severe infection when we arrive."

As they approached Grozny, flight control ordered the Black Hawk's pilot to put down on the landing zone outside the base's triage unit. A Russian medical team was waiting for them and wheeled Laynie inside. Wolfe, Tobin, and the girls accompanied her.

Wolfe explained to the doctor that he needed Laynie stabilized for the flight to Ramstein Air Base in Germany. The doctor, a seasoned combat surgeon, took one look at Laynie's arm and started shouting orders.

Wolfe translated for Tobin. "Cellulitis—a bacterial infection of the soft tissues—in addition to severe dehydration. He's quite concerned and is calling for immediate fluids and an IV antibiotic. Once my plane gets here, we can load her aboard and keep going. Get her to an Army specialist."

"Good. She's burning up." Tobin frowned. "So, you speak Russian, Director? Didn't know that."

Wolfe gave him an enigmatic smile. "I wasn't always the Director, Marshal, and in a role like mine, one must have ample field experience."

"Uh, right."

Wolfe noticed a man standing a few yards away. Waiting.

"I think I'm needed over there. Excuse me."

He knew the man by his photographs. Tall, still lean, in his mid-fifties, no longer as youthful as his smile in those photographs often made him appear.

Wolfe offered his hand. Addressed him in perfect Russian. "Jack Wolfe. I want to thank you for your assistance."

"Is that her, behind the curtains? The woman I knew as Linnéa Olander?"

"It is."

"I am glad you rescued her. Might I . . . see her?"

Wolfe pursed his lips. "She's not looking or feeling her best just now."

"She is seriously injured, then? In danger?"

"Seriously, yes, from a bad infection. Your people, however, are addressing it—for which you have my deep appreciation."

"*Da*. You are welcome." He glanced away before changing the subject. "I have received an initial report from the assault commander. With your information and help, we have rid ourselves of a particularly troublesome radical militia."

"That's what we in America call a 'win-win'—a win for you, a win for us."

"Yes, but you will please tell her, whatever you call her now, that the favor she said I owed her is now paid."

"I'll tell her—however, she did save your life, did she not? Such a cruel, agonizing death swallowing hydrofluoric acid would have been, being slowly eaten from the inside out, your bones melting away. For rendering you such a grave service—against orders, I might add—I assume your people won't be looking for her in future? After all, she is no threat to you any longer. And, as you say, with our information, your people rid Russia of a particularly troublesome militia. A 'win-win.'"

The man studied Wolfe. "She disobeyed orders to save me?"

"Yes."

"I am surprised. Yes, surprised. There are many things, looking back, that I regret."

He sighed. "Then perhaps you are right and I owe her more. If . . . if I have your word that she will never again meddle in our affairs, I believe I can persuade the appropriate authorities to leave her be. Let her live out her life in peace."

Wolfe again held out his hand. "My word, then, Vassili Aleksandrovich."

The Russian took Wolfe's extended hand. "Safe travels, Dzhon Ivanovitch."

Wolfe walked away. He hadn't permitted his surprise to show.

Interesting. Haven't been called by that name in a couple of decades. And I did think all those who knew me by it were dead.

Yes. Interesting.

SIX HOURS AFTER SETTING down in Grozny, Tobin helped Laynie from the wheelchair at Wolfe's jet. Still running a fever but somewhat improved, she insisted on getting onto the plane under her own power.

"Up the steps, Marta, okay?" He went ahead of her, tugging gently at her hand.

She nodded and started up the steps, praying the fog would clear. So much of what had transpired in the past twelve hours—or was it eighteen?—was a blur. Surreal. She'd be fine one moment, then her mind would twitch and she'd be back in Sayed's escape tunnel, a fresh jolt of adrenaline telling her she needed to move faster . . . Then she'd see Tobin and remember.

Tobin. He had his sweet hazel eyes on her.

Because I stopped halfway up the steps.

She shut her eyes, squeezed away the mist, and got herself going again.

Tobin saw her into a seat on the starboard side of the narrow aisle. Wolfe joined them. An Air Force nurse waited behind him, her kit under her arm.

"We'll be wheels up in ten," Wolfe said.

"How long before we get home?" Laynie asked. Her voice seemed distant.

"Turns out, we're not going stateside right away," Wolfe answered softly.

"We're flying you directly to Ramstein Air Base first. The base is five miles from Landstuhl Regional Medical Center, run by the Army. They'll check you out. Deal with any injuries or underlying health problems."

The nurse who'd been hovering nearby spoke up. "Ms. Garineau? I'd like to check your IV line. Get a fresh bag of fluids and antibiotics flowing. Take your temp."

Laynie wanted another stranger touching her like she wanted leprosy. She moved her feverish gaze from Wolfe to Tobin. Tobin was trying so hard to keep the worry out of his voice. Out of his eyes.

"You need this, Marta. Okay?"

Oh, yeah. Guess he saw the mess my arm is in. Like Daniel in the lions' den, you saw me through the pit, Lord. You'll see me through this.

She looked from the nurse then back to Wolfe. "Ksenia? Asmeen and Mariam?"

"The girls with you?" Wolfe asked

"Yes, but they . . . they're only children. Need our help. Asmeen and Mariam . . . to their families . . . Azerbaijan. And I-I . . . keeping Ksenia."

Wolfe drew himself up. "Sorry, what? Are you talking about that little spitfire who hovered over you like a mama hawk during the flight? Keeping *her?*"

Pride rose up in Laynie. "Yes. *Mine.*"

Wolfe moved his head up and down. Slowly. "All right. Didn't see that coming, but I'll get her on the plane with us. Ramstein has a history of receiving refugees. Don't fret. I'll get it sorted." He left immediately to make the arrangements.

"Thanks," but the word came out after he'd gone.

Laynie leaned toward the window and turned inward. She didn't notice when Tobin gave up his seat to the Air Force nurse. Didn't see when the nurse drew up her sleeve to view Laynie's wound and hissed through her teeth. Didn't react when the nurse started fresh IV antibiotics.

Laynie's head slowly drooped and rested on the window. Minutes later, Wolfe showed Ksenia to the seat beside Tobin facing Laynie, but Laynie had drifted off to a state of peaceful rest.

CHAPTER 39

LAYNIE WAS ADMITTED TO the Army's hospital in Landstuhl, Germany, where the medical staff worked to find the right course of antibiotics to wipe out her multiple infections. The cellulitis in her burned arm was most concerning, but other bacteria had found their way into some of the several wounds on her head. The worst was the cut she sustained when she was thrown into the cistern and that now bore five sutures.

She slept much of the time—a healing sleep, the doctors assured Tobin—but she was not a sight for the faint of heart. Her face was purpled and swollen, her body thin to the point of emaciation, her scalp a harsh landscape of stitches, scabs, bruises, and dabs of antiseptic ointments.

Ksenia refused to leave her side and would shout, "*Nyet! Nyet!*" if anyone attempted to move her.

A nurse took Tobin aside. "What the story with the little Muslim girl?"

Tobin put his hands on his hips. "Don't have a complete answer for you. I know her name is Ksenia and that Bella befriended her. I don't think, though, that she's Muslim. She . . ." Tobin had a hard time getting the words out. "She was kidnapped by a radical Islamic group and . . . used."

The woman had been an Army nurse for a long time, and she'd seen her share of horror. "That girl needs an exam. And a shower. No telling what she's gone through or what the damage."

"Well, I doubt you'll pry her out of this room without a war."

"Maybe she doesn't need to leave the room."

She returned later and introduced Tobin to a female physician and a female Army translator.

"We're going to admit her overnight and give her the other bed in this room, but not before we've established a rapport with her. Sergeant Fattah will attempt to identify her native tongue and explain why we'd like her to take a shower, then convince her to let Major Toomey do an exam."

The translator walked up to a wary Ksenia and spoke. She tried three languages before she hit on Kurmanji and Ksenia answered back. When Ksenia gave her permission, the sergeant pulled up a chair and spoke with her further, asking a few questions, pointing to Laynie, and nodding multiple times when Ksenia opened up and spoke for several minutes, gesturing at Laynie more than once.

In the end, Ksenia consented to a shower, and Tobin left the room to give her privacy. When he returned over an hour later, the curtain was pulled around the second bed in the room, and Sergeant Fattah was standing nearby in case translation was required.

The young woman grinned. "You should have heard her in the shower. She loved it. Know those little soap and shampoo samples the hospital provides? She used every bit of them. And she sang! I didn't realize she spoke Russian until she started singing 'Amazing Grace' in Russian with the water going full blast. We couldn't get her out until she'd exhausted the hot water." She smiled again. "Guess she'd never taken a shower before."

Sergeant Fattah shrugged. "But that was before they ordered her into a bed and I had to tell her to stay put."

The nurse pulled the curtain back, and Tobin spied Ksenia, worried and confused, wearing a drab hospital gown and confined to bed, her whole being dejected with a capital D. The doctor motioned to Tobin to join her outside the room.

"Hold on a sec. Is it all right if she wears this? Picked it up at the base commissary. They let the base spouses sell homemade goods there on commission."

"Sure. That's fine."

"Thanks." Tobin looked at the translator. "Would you mind helping me with this?"

He walked up to the bed and placed the garment on Ksenia's legs. "Ksenia, I thought you would like something pretty to wear."

The sergeant picked up the gown sewn from pink flannel dotted with white rose buds. She showed Ksenia the ruffles on the hem and cuffs while she translated for Tobin. She ran her fingers over the fabric. Ksenia did the same and said something to the sergeant.

"She says it's very soft. She's never worn anything so soft or colorful."

"Okay, squirt?" Tobin asked with a hopeful uptick.

Ksenia looked from the translator to Tobin, then replied—exactly as he'd said it—"Okay?"

Tobin chuckled as he nodded. Then he joined the doctor and nurse in the hallway.

The doctor sighed. "I'll be brief. This poor child. I won't bother testing her until there are fewer things to test for. I'll prescribe meds for every sexually transmitted disease out there and for worms, lice, and other parasites. I'll give orders for her to be scrubbed daily with medicated soap and shampoo and all her linens and clothes managed carefully. We'll reevaluate in a week."

"What about Bella?"

"I'll contact her doctor and recommend the same."

That night, after Ksenia was sleeping soundly, Tobin pulled a chair close to Laynie. He needed to be near her in private, even if she was sleeping. He wanted the privacy to watch her without anyone watching him. To pray over her. To tell her how he felt and what he wanted.

Tobin had spoken to her doctor and obtained his permission before he bought the sweet-smelling lotion. He poured some into his hands, rubbed them together until the lotion was warm, and oh-so-gently applied the lotion to her hands. She sighed in her sleep as he did the same for her feet—although he was taken aback when he encountered a recently healed injury on her ankle. After washing his hands, he warmed more lotion and dabbed it on her scalp, tenderly massaging it over the numerous scabs—courtesy of Gupta's madness.

If Laynie had wakened, she would have heard him whispering, "Now, Father, you know this ol' country boy loved this girl's hair. It was her crown of glory. And you know that if I think on it too much, I'll start hating that old hag, Gupta, for what she did to Marta. Bella. Er, *Laynie*."

He sighed. "Sorry, Lord. I shouldn't have called Gupta a hag, even if she was one. Well, I forgive her, Lord. I do. I forgive her and ask you to be merciful to her, because I figure she's standing before you right now with a heap of sins to account for. Besides, my Marta's hair ain't *her*. I love the woman she is, Lord, hair or no, and that's the gospel truth."

THE FOLLOWING MORNING, the hospital commander, on hearing that a non-military flight had landed for emergency medical care, decided he should pay the patient a visit. A cheerful and efficient military bureaucrat, he walked in unannounced while Tobin and Ksenia, in her pink flannel nightie, were sitting with Laynie.

Tobin stood to greet the man. Ksenia, leery of everyone in general—even Tobin—but all the more of anyone new, hid herself behind Tobin's bulk.

The administrator offered his hand to Tobin. "Colonel Cooper Swift, Commander of Landstuhl Regional Medical Center."

"Quincy Tobin, US Marshals Service."

Swift's glance passed from Tobin to Laynie's bed then returned to Tobin. Jinked back to Laynie in a startled double take.

He lowered his voice and whispered to Tobin. "Good God—was this poor woman pulled from a gulag or a POW camp?"

Laynie may or may not have been sleeping, and she may or may not have heard the visitor's hushed question, but Tobin didn't much care either way. The stillness that came over him was so profoundly dangerous that Ksenia—who was fine-tuned to danger—felt it and her eyes widened.

She also didn't understand what the visitor said, but she saw how Tobin reacted to it—which, if it concerned Laynie, was good enough for her. She moved to his side and peered up at his face, took in the steely contempt fixed on the stranger, and assumed the same fiercely protective expression.

Tobin took hold of Colonel Swift's arm. "I'll just see you out, Colonel." He steered and half-pushed the man to the door and out of the room.

"*Ow!*"

"That couldn't possibly have hurt."

"Not you. *Her*. She kicked me!"

"Did she now? Wonder why." Tobin gave the girl a quick, approving squeeze.

Swift looked from Tobin to Ksenia and back. "Uh, I suppose we may have gotten off on the wrong foot."

"I suppose."

"My apologies. Terribly unkind and unprofessional of me. Is there anything I can do for you? Get you?"

"Thank you, *no*."

Ksenia had already picked up on "yes" and "no." She parroted Tobin perfectly. "*No*."

Tobin gave the girl an approving nod. They were in complete agreement.

Swift tried once more. "I, um, I could arrange for a visit from the chaplain?"

Tobin exhaled. Got himself under his usual control. "That would be appreciated."

THE CHAPLAIN APPEARED within the hour, and caught Laynie during one of her awake spells. The gentle old man read a Psalm over her, prayed for the three of them, told a few jokes that Laynie translated to Ksenia, and generously loved on all three of them.

He even knew a bit of Russian and drew Ksenia into a sweet and simple conversation where he assured her that God loved her, that she was safe, and that she could come to him any time if she needed anything—thoroughly earning Tobin and Laynie's respect and gratitude.

"Anything," the chaplain reiterated.

"Anything?" Laynie asked.

"Within my power? Absolutely."

Laynie, Tobin, and the chaplain then spoke a while longer, although Laynie's part of the conversation was mainly nods and short, murmured phrases due to her fatigue.

"Well, it's going to be tricky," the chaplain declared at the end of their visit, "but I'll do my best."

WHEN LAYNIE WASN'T sleeping, Ksenia and Tobin urged her to eat. The infection, however, seemed to have stolen her appetite. That is, until Tobin brought two milkshakes up from the cafeteria. He gave one to Ksenia and coaxed Laynie to take a sip on the other. She held the soft sweetness in her mouth a moment, swallowed, and her taste buds sprang to life.

She sucked the shake down in record time, giving herself "brain freeze" twice. Afterward, she begged for a hamburger.

"Now, that's the Bella I know," Tobin laughed.

Ksenia on the other hand, had never had a milkshake. Or ice cream for that matter. When she was discharged and each day thereafter, Tobin took her over to the base commissary and bought her a different flavored shake. He might have bought her *two* in a day, but he'd never tell Laynie. And although Ksenia loved to try new flavors, she learned how to say "black cherry," declaring it was her favorite.

SURPRISINGLY, WOLFE REMAINED with them in Germany during the six nights Laynie was hospitalized. He commandeered an office on the base and busied himself with numerous phone calls and reports.

His first call when they arrived at the base was to Broadsword. Richard gathered Bo, Harris, and the members of the task force in the conference room where, on speakerphone, Wolfe spoke at length on Laynie's rescue, the condition they had found her in, how long she would require treatment, and their tentative return date to the States.

Interspersed between his normal duties back in DC, several of his other calls were to the US State Department where he used his considerable influence to clear the way for Ksenia to enter the US with Laynie, and to arrange with the Russian commandant in Groszy for the "*kafir* women," including Asmeen and Mariam, to be returned to their homes and families. Other calls and emails were with Fenelli and Cossack as he followed up on the fate of the surviving AGFA soldiers.

Certain details proved surprising, but all things considered, quite satisfactory.

WHEN LAYNIE WOKE ON her fourth day in the hospital, she found Ksenia dressed in jeans, a sweater, and sneakers. Ksenia had seen a different world on the base, a world where girls her age wore pretty things and their faces and hair were seen by all.

On her daily visit to the commissary with Tobin, he had taken her to the teen clothing section and motioned that she should select a few items. Tobin had, without comment, bought whatever she brought to him.

Laynie drew the girl close to her. She touched Ksenia's long, curling brown hair. She ran her fingers along the curve of her cheek, studied her serious eyes, the same shining color as her hair.

"You are so beautiful, little daughter," Laynie murmured.

Ksenia leaned into Laynie's embrace and wept. When Laynie sought Tobin's reaction, he'd turned his back to stare out the window. But Laynie thought she'd heard a suspicious little catch in his throat and saw him swipe at his eyes.

A few minutes later, he dragged a chair to Laynie's bedside. Pulled a pocket New Testament from his coat.

"Now that you're on the mend, thought I could read aloud, and you could translate for Miss K here. She's a-catchin' onto English fast as a brush fire, but maybe we could start with you translating."

Laynie peered into Tobin's heart. "Start?"

"Sure. We should begin as we mean to go on—shouldn't we?"

Then it was Laynie who was sobbing.

TWO DAYS LATER, after a last but important visit from the chaplain, Laynie's doctors released her from the hospital. Laynie's arm was in a sling and would be for a while, but when she, Tobin, Ksenia, and Wolfe boarded Wolfe's jet for America, she walked across the tarmac and up the stairs on her own.

Wolfe sat far forward in the plane when he made the call he'd been putting off. The rear of the plane, with Laynie, Tobin, and Ksenia laughing over Uno or Old Maid, was too rowdy for this conversation.

He'd waited on this particular call, not out of an overabundance of caution, but to provide a timeline he was confident in.

KARI THORESEN PICKED UP the phone. "Hello?"

"Ms. Thoresen? Jack Wolfe calling."

Kari's heart nearly stopped. She grabbed the edge of the kitchen counter to steady herself. To surrender her will to God. Again.

Father? I need not fear. You are my ever-present help in time of trouble.

She caught Søren's eye. "Yes, Director. This is Kari Thoresen."

Søren reached his arm around Kari, undergirding her, adding his strength to hers.

"Ms. Thoresen, I made Laynie a promise before she left on her last assignment. I promised her Christmas with you—with her family—at your home in New Orleans."

Kari's mind snagged on the phrase "her *last* assignment" in Wolfe's preamble and jumped from one numbing assumption to another, colliding with the worst conclusion imaginable.

"Ms. Thoresen, I'm calling to ask you to please pack up your family—"

Lord, please help me to trust you in this moment.

"and return to New Orleans."

Kari sobbed against Søren's chest.

Please, God, not again! Not another funeral!

"Ms. Thoresen, I'm keeping my promise to Laynie. In three days, I'm bringing her to you."

THE TWO CARS WOUND slowly up the road to Broadsword. Tom Parker drove Wolfe and Seraphim in the lead vehicle while Harris drove Laynie, Ksenia, and Tobin in the second. The men at the checkpoint called ahead to let the task force know.

Harris pulled alongside the gym, and Tobin got out. He opened the front passenger door and helped Ksenia out. She glommed onto his side like she was a magnet and he was her steel. He swallowed her little hand in his bear paw. She smiled up at him, trying to hide her nervousness.

"It's okay, squirt."

He continued to hold the rear door while Laynie slid slowly across the seat.

A thousand things bumped and jostled around in her thoughts, so she sat there, at the door, delaying getting out. She was nervous, too, so she patted the scarf twined around her head. She wasn't used to it, but some sort of covering was necessary. She felt the absence of her hair in every frosty winter breeze but also in every curious glance or outright stare.

I see their pity. They think I have cancer. I don't, of course. I just don't have any hair. Gupta cut it off.

Laynie exhaled. *I forgive her, Lord. Again. I'll forgive her as many times as I need to until it "takes."*

Besides, my hair will grow back.

I think.

In a month, it should almost be respectable.

But it will never be long again.

Sure it will.

Not like it was.

Give it time.

Time.

She didn't know whether it was the cold or the fact that she'd be facing her team in a matter of moments, but an icy shiver rippled down her spine.

My team. They will have so many questions.

My team—are they? Are they still my team? Told them I'd be back in five days, but I've been away . . .

She kept telling herself it had been less than eight weeks since she departed Broadsword.

Her heart knew it had been a lifetime.

A life. A death. A resurrection.

I don't have to imagine how Lazarus felt, walking out of that tomb.

And I am coming back with Ksenia. My new life will be—it must be—different going forward. Should probably stick to intelligence gathering. No more field work.

Because I have a daughter to care for now.

Things to "figure out" with Quincy.

SHE BLINKED AND WAS standing in the gym doorway, not certain how she'd gotten there. Her task force stood in the bullpen. Staring. Waiting. She wouldn't look at their faces—that would be a mistake. If she did that, if she watched their reactions, she would be undone before they began.

Can't have that.

A wide-eyed Ksenia peeked out from behind Tobin's protective bulk. And he had his hand under Laynie's elbow. Nudging her forward.

Because I keep stopping. Blanking out. Might be a while before I stop doing that.

Laynie gently removed Tobin's hand and, keeping her eyes at chest height, walked toward her team.

"Hey, everyone. Sorry I'm late . . . getting back."

The intake of individual breaths wasn't simultaneous, so Laynie heard their shock like an undulation, one slow gasp following another, ending in a single, whispered curse word with an exclamation point.

That last was Brian—and not Jaz for a change.

Jaz reached her first, and the familiar scent of anise twitched Laynie's nose. Jaz said nothing, just stretched her arms around Laynie, careful of her arm, and hugged her. Held her. Laid her head on Laynie's shoulder. The others came then. Many arms encircling her. A great wall of love molding them together.

Jaz whispered in Laynie's ear. "We thought you were dead, Bella. When we knew you weren't, I prayed. First time, really. I prayed he would bring you home."

Laynie nodded slowly. "Guess he heard you, huh?"

"Yes," Jaz sobbed. "He did."

"Guess you and I will need to talk about what that means, hmm? You know, if God is real and all."

Jaz wiped her eyes, smearing liner and mascara. "Yah, I figured."

Tobin caught Laynie's wink and brought Ksenia toward the knotted lovefest. Laynie pulled Ksenia to her and turned her around so that she was nestled under Laynie's chin.

"Everybody? I'd like you to meet someone. This is Ksenia."

The team studied the girl and, one by one, greeted her. Overcome, she dropped her eyes.

Laynie whispered in Ksenia's ear, and she smiled. Then Laynie said, "I don't know how else to say this, so I'll just ask it straight out. How would all of you like to be honorary aunts and uncles?"

Gwyneth gave a little squeal. "I knew it! I knew it! You're going to adopt her, yes?"

"Yes, and we want you-all to be part of her life, too."

"Does that mean you're staying, Bella?" Vincent asked.

"Whew. I'm glad you asked," Rusty exclaimed. "I was getting myself all psyched up for the 'it's been great and all, but it's time for me to move on' speech."

"Of course I'm staying. Quincy, too—but as of today? I'm swearing off field ops."

"I vote for that!" Jubaila called from behind Soraya's shoulder. "I can't take any more nail-biters."

"Yeah, me either," Soraya said.

"No more nail-biters," Laynie promised. "So, what do you think, Uncle Brian?"

He grinned. "I can roll with that!"

"You, Aunt Jaz?"

Jaz had stepped back. "Dunno about the honorary stuff. I don't do Aunt Jaz."

Ksenia, her eyes wide, walked away from Laynie, straight up to Jaz and pointed at her purpled-tipped hair. "*Mader*, look! Black cherry!" She touched the purple strands and giggled.

Jaz stared into Ksenia's soft brown eyes, shuffled her feet, looked again. "Well, I guess maybe Aunt Jaz could work . . ."

Laynie hugged Jaz. "Thank you. I'm so . . . so very grateful for you, for this team, for so many things."

Worship bubbled up in her chest. "Oh, Jesus! Oh, my Jesus, you've been so faithful to me. Thank you for bringing me—bringing *us*—home."

"Yah," Jaz added, "I . . . agree. Um, so be it."

WOLFE AND SERAPHIM stood aside until the emotion of Laynie's homecoming subsided, until Bo and Harris took Ksenia to meet Broadsword's horses, and the team realized Wolfe and Seraphim were waiting on them.

While Vincent posted two conspicuous signs on the boards, the team took their usual seats and settled. Wolfe had told Tobin and Laynie that he had business to wrap up and news to report to the team, but they hadn't heard it yet.

"Okay, people," Wolfe began. "Before I release all of you for a much-deserved three-week vacation, I want you to know how all your hard work and dedication shook out.

"And," he pointed to the signs Vincent had posted that read CLASSIFIED BRIEFING, "although I shouldn't have to remind you, I always will. This is a classified briefing. Nothing of what you are about to hear or any subsequent discussion is to leave this room. Understood?"

"Yes, sir." It was a unified response.

"Very good. The first point I'll make is that we in the intelligence world rarely get to wrap things up with a nice little bow on top. This is one of those quite rare moments. AGFA's third and most devastating attack on the US never materialized because the US Coast Guard took possession of the carfentanil shipment the moment it entered US waters."

He looked around the room. "*You* people averted that disaster. You figured it out and you suggested I meet directly with the Ukrainian mob to resolve the crisis. Because of *you*, the poison has been safely disposed of."

He cleared his throat. "You will receive bonus pay and there will be commendations—all classified, of course, but bestowed and received nevertheless—along with additional funding for this task force. And from myself and from those far above my pay grade? A hearty *well done*."

A roar of delight erupted through the room. It went on until Wolfe raised his hand.

"As for AGFA's US-based jihadis, I have it on good authority that they are off the board."

Svitlanya Davydenko's email had been short and concise.

Director Wolfe,

We have satisfied our part of the bargain. Below you will find the location of a refrigerated semitrailer. Your people may pick up and catalog the bodies, each one tagged with the name he or she used while operating in the US.

Cordially,

SD

Wolfe continued. "Next, AGFA's primary stronghold in Chechnya. Our assault team assisted Russian troops in storming their cave system and removing every individual from it before the Russian demo team blew it up. Among those rescued were eleven Kurdish and two Azerbaijani young women. The US State Department, in conjunction with the Russian government, has repatriated them back to their families."

Wolfe looked up from his notes. "I have here, handwritten notes from the families of two of those girls, Asmeen and Mariam, to Bella. They and their families are grateful to you, Bella, for rescuing their daughters, for the friendship and love you showed them, and for the *hope* you instilled in them while you were incarcerated with them in a most hopeless situation."

Laynie couldn't speak, and she couldn't hold back joyous tears.

"Wait. Hold up, Director." Brian, of course. "I'm confused."

"Not the first time," Rusty quipped. "Not the last either."

"Really, Rust Bucket? Sheesh. Give it a rest already. Sorry, Director. We can't take him anywhere."

"Get on with it, Brian," Jaz nudged him.

"Yeah. Okay. Director, you said *our* assault team operated on Russian soil? How in the world did the Russians agree to that?"

Seraphim stepped forward. Choosing her words carefully, she said, "It seems that an influential Russian politician was instrumental in authorizing a joint operation against AGFA's stronghold."

Rusty frowned in concentration, then guffawed. "Wait a sec. That Russian politician wasn't in the US recently, was he? Saved from a horrible assassination attempt?"

Amid laughter, even from Seraphim and Wolfe, Seraphim recovered her composure and replied, "I can neither confirm nor deny your assertions, Rusty, nor would I ever suggest that a member of our task force played a role in averting said *alleged* assassination attempt."

She was smiling. Wolfe smiled with her. The team high-fived.

"Good one, Seraphim!" Rusty grinned.

"Yeah, but what about AGFA's head guy, Sayed? What happened to him?" Brian. Again.

Wolfe consulted his notes. "Our team's after action report states, and I quote, 'Mohammed Eldar Sayed, leader of the most volatile arm of AGFA, perished in the battle to take his mountain stronghold.'"

"And the traitor, Rosenberg?"

"This will take a few moments to unpack. Unknown to us or any of her coworkers, Dr. Bhagya Gupta, a longtime employee of our organization, converted to Islam in 1979. She returned to visit family in India several times in the succeeding years, twice for six-month sabbaticals. During those sabbaticals, also unknown to us, she crossed from India into Pakistan and then into Afghanistan.

"We can only presume that she was radicalized and recruited during these visits and became a sleeper agent in our organization. She later studied to switch her medical specialty from gynecology to psychology.

"When she became a counselor to our organization's people, including active and returning operatives, she often passed on to her handlers operational details obtained during their sessions. Somehow Gupta even obtained the network logins of several high-level clients, giving her access to classified operational plans and details. It's no wonder we had difficulty identifying the mole in my management staff.

"At some point, she grew enamored with Sayed's vision for a new Islamic caliphate and became his eyes and ears within our organization. When we uncovered her treason, she fled the US to Sayed, escaping our surveillance. She, too, perished in the battle to take AGFA's mountain stronghold."

He looked up, smiled, and said, "That is all. Your extended leave begins today. Please report back to Griffin Industries in Germantown on Monday, February 11. You are dismissed."

He turned to Seraphim, and she nodded. Neither of them would ever reveal what the remainder of Fenelli's action report had said. How Cossack had gathered the remaining young *kafir* women from the survivors, and suggested to the girls that they choose a fitting punishment for Mohammed Eldar Sayed and Halima bint Abra.

It had taken the girls only a few minutes to tell Cossack what they had decided. They accompanied Cossack and Fenelli back into the caves, leading the two Russian soldiers who held Sayed and Gupta in their custody. They marched to what had been the *kafir* women's cell. Then to the cistern.

The girls had insisted that the Russian soldiers lower Sayed and a screaming, cursing Gupta into the cistern rather than throw them in. The grate across the kafir women's cell would be locked—just in case Sayed or Gupta somehow managed to climb out of the cistern—but the girls wanted Sayed and Gupta alive after the demolition team brought down the cavern and the tunnels leading to the surface.

At the girls' insistence, the demolition team—experts in their field—promised not to blow the tunnels beyond the cavern. Sayed and Gupta would have ample "together" time to think on their crimes before dehydration ended them.

Wolfe and Seraphim had decided to keep that portion of the after action report to themselves.

JAZ SAT DOWN AT HER desk and started to repair her smudged makeup. Wolfe sidled up to her and perched on the corner of her desk. She looked up from a mirror, guileless and unflappable, but he could tell that she knew *exactly* why he was there.

"Director Wolfe, sir. So many great outcomes. And I'm really glad you, Tobin, and Bella made it home safely."

"Me, too, Miss Jessup. Me, too."

A half-empty pack of Black Jack gum and several empty wrappers lay near her keyboard. He picked up the pack of gum and sniffed it.

"Licorice, yes?"

"Close enough. Anise or aniseed. It's an acquired taste. Care to try it?"

He put the gum down and smiled amiably. "Care to guess who I spoke to a couple days ago while we were in Germany and Bella was in the hospital getting treated?"

"No, sir. Should I know?"

"I think you could probably come close. Try this—the Assistant Director in Charge of the FBI's New York field office. He'd already left three voice mails, but as I was rather preoccupied with getting Bella out of AGFA's stronghold and then to a hospital, I didn't return his call right away. However, it's not generally a good omen when the Assistant Director in Charge of an FBI field office rings you up—repeatedly."

She didn't so much as blink or flick a brow. "Huh. I suppose it had to have been important?"

"It was. Seems their IT department suffered some form of cyberattack a week or so back. Their cybersecurity specialists have been in a furor ever since, trying to figure out why someone would start a full backup of their files. Remotely."

Jaz frowned. "Right. Why would someone do that?"

"They didn't know either, but since it was the same IT department where the encrypted Ukrainian financial records are stored—in a secure directory of their own—they were concerned it was an attempt to delete them. *Very* concerned."

"Whoa. Did someone actually manage to purge the mob's files?"

"No, they're still there."

"Whew. Glad to hear it. I assume the FBI's security is pretty tight."

Wolfe picked up one of the gum wrappers, unfolded it, refolded it.

Oh, we can do this little dance all day, Miss Jessup. Frankly, I'm rather enjoying it. Learning a few things, too.

"The ADIC *did* say one of their best IT guys noticed something . . . a touch off concerning the mob's files."

"What's that?"

"Well, seems that they had recorded the exact size of the directory and all its files—right down to the smallest increment. You know, megabytes, kilobytes, and plain ol' bytes and tiny bits? Not a thing had changed. The directory had all the right files with the right file names, nothing misspelled, the correct date and time stamp on the directory and files, and so on.

"But here's where things got interesting. When they went to look at the backup tape from the week previous—"

"Did the hackers steal files from the backup tape? Wow. I didn't think you could to that!"

"No, that's not what they found."

But great deflection, Miss Jessup. I'm impressed.

"No, instead, they found that the entire backup had been erased. Completely, I'm told. Unrecoverable."

Jaz was frowning. "The hackers purged a backup tape. What does that get them?"

"Not sure, but here's what their best IT guy did notice, the single difference—one file on the FBI's drive belonging to the Ukrainian mob, just *one* mind you, was smaller than it should have been."

"What?"

You're a little too surprised, Miss Jessup. Did you honestly make a mistake? Maybe I should log the date and time. Have it witnessed. And notarized.

"The size was off by a single byte, I'm told."

"A byte? That's not right. Shouldn't have changed at all. Period. Do they need help figuring out what happened?"

"Do you mean did they call me to ask for *your* help?"

Jaz shrugged. "Just a thought. It is my area of expertise."

"Huh."

"Sir?"

He stared at her.

She stared back. All innocence.

"Well, I was just glad to tell the ADIC, with utter confidence, that no one working for me would have ever attempted a breach of their systems."

"No, sir."

"Nor would anyone working for me have ever reached out to the new head of the Ukrainian mob or cut a deal with them in order to, say, save one of our own."

"Sir, I can promise you that no one working on this task force reached out to the Ukrainians."

I remember quite clearly, Director, that Svitlanya Davydenko contacted me, *not the other way around. Sure, Tobin made me promise to keep my hands off until his god "acted." Well, I did that.*

Wait. Did I just admit . . .

Wolfe was impressed with how Jaz handled herself.

Yes, you are good at this, Vyper. A little parsing of the words, and you're telling me your version of the truth. I'm rather pleasantly surprised.

"We need to talk about your future with us, Miss Jessup. We could, with proper field training, expand the scope of your duties."

"Sir?"

"You lie with the best of us professional liars. We should make better use of you."

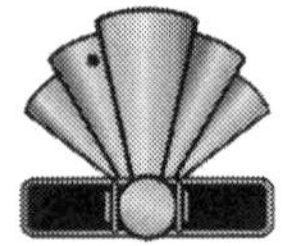

POSTSCRIPT

THEY WERE A DAY EARLY, and Laynie hoped it wouldn't be a problem, but she just couldn't wait another day. Another minute. She, Tobin, and Ksenia waited on the front porch for someone to answer the doorbell.

Laynie was suitably impressed with the house—and they'd only seen the exterior.

This isn't a house. It's a few bricks shy of a mansion.

"This here might not be a mansion, but it's within shoutin' distance," Tobin muttered, like he'd been in her head.

Laynie grinned. She didn't mind him "in her head." They had spent hours, while she was in the hospital, on the flight from Germany to the US, and while they were at Broadsword, just talking. Laynie had shared what Jesus had done inside Sayed's stronghold. Tobin mostly listened, but he did tell her about Jaz's prayer.

He grinned back and placed a tender hand on her lower back. Just a touch that said, "I'ma with ya, Marta-Bella-Laynie-Elaine. Got yer back. Always will."

Ksenia looked up at Tobin. For her, the transition from an orphaned slave locked in a cell inside Sayed's stronghold to the hope of a loving family in America was—and probably would be for a while to come—overwhelming.

Tobin chucked her chin gently—very, very gently. "You okay, squirt?"

Ksenia knew "okay" and Tobin's pet name for her. From the moment Laynie had introduced them, it had been "squirt."

"Okay," she answered and smiled tentatively.

Lord, you will help us, Laynie prayed. *Ruth will help us, too. This is her gifting, by your grace helping hurting women. She will be your hand, guiding us through troubled waters as Ksenia's heart and body heal.*

The door opened with an excited jerk. Shannon stood there, her eyes flitting from Laynie to Ksenia to Tobin, back to Ksenia, so excited she was practically vibrating.

"You weren't supposed to be here today!"

"Hi Shannon," Laynie said. "I know we're early. May we come in anyway?"

"Oh. Oh, sure." She stepped back, still staring at Ksenia.

Under Shannon's scrutiny, Ksenia cast her eyes down, onto her feet.

It will take a while for that behavior to change, Laynie thought, *but with love, it* will *change.*

Laynie reached out and hugged Shannon as tight as she could. "I'm so glad to see you again, sweetheart."

Shannon gulped. "Me too, Aunt Laynie. I never wanted to come back here for Christmas if you weren't ever going to be here with us."

"Here I am. God has been good to me."

She let Shannon go and said, "I believe you've met Marshal Tobin?"

"Oh, yeah. Hi."

"Hey, Shannon."

"And, Shannon, this is Ksenia. I brought her home with me from Russia."

Laynie spoke to Ksenia, introducing Shannon. Ksenia raised her face and nodded at Shannon.

"Hi, Ksenia. I'm twelve. How old are you?"

Laynie interpreted. A pained expression came over Ksenia's face as she answered.

"We're not certain yet, Shannon, but we'll get it figured out. Let's call it either fourteen or fifteen for now, okay?"

"I . . . okay. What language are you talking to her?"

"Russian."

Shannon went goggle-eyed. "You speak *Russian?* Like *real* Russian?"

Ksenia didn't know what was going on, but she giggled at Shannon's pop-eyed astonishment.

"I speak Russian, Swedish, Spanish, a little German, and horrible French. You do not want to hear my French. Where is everyone?"

"Oh! In the kitchen. I'll get them!" She ran off, hollering as she went, "Mom! Dad! Aunt Laynie's here!"

Within moments, Laynie's entire family was gathered around her, hugging, crying, rejoicing. Laynie kept Ksenia tucked safely under her still-healing arm with Tobin on Ksenia's other side, his arm around Ksenia, too—a little Ksenia sandwich with Laynie and Tobin as the bread.

Then Laynie began introductions. "Mama, Dad? This is Ksenia." She repeated the intros in Russian. Ksenia, prompted, said carefully, "Hello. Nice to meet you."

From her wheelchair, Polly reached for Ksenia and patted her hand. "You are a beautiful young lady, Ksenia."

Laynie translated. Then she took a deep breath and smiled.

"Everyone? We have happy news. While we were in Germany, Quincy and I decided to adopt Ksenia. Together. It was a bit tricky at the outset, but the base chaplain helped us. We've already started the paperwork to make her ours."

Her parents and Kari stuttered, but Shannon embraced the idea instantly.

"You and Quincy are adopting Ksenia? Like Mama and Dad adopted me and Robbie?"

"Yup. Just like that."

"Cool! Well then, does that mean you and Quincy are getting married?"

Laynie laughed at Tobin's chagrin. "Oh, goodness! I'm sorry. I guess I blew it. Skipped ahead. Cart before horse? That was the tricky part of our paperwork, wrangling a special license, changing my last name to Tobin."

She smiled bigger. "Because, you see, we already got married."

The End

About the Author

Vikki Kestell's passion for people and their stories is evident in her readers' affection for her characters and unusual plotlines. Two often-repeated sentiments are, "I feel like I know these people," and, "I'm right there, in the book, experiencing what the characters experience."

Vikki holds a PhD in organizational learning and instructional technologies. She left a career of twenty-plus years in government, academia, and corporate life to pursue writing full time. "Writing is the best job ever," she admits, "and the most demanding."

Vikki and her husband, Conrad Smith, make their home in Albuquerque, New Mexico.

To keep abreast of new book releases, sign up for Vikki's newsletter on her website, **http://www.vikkikestell.com**, find her on Facebook at **http://www.facebook.com/TheWritingOfVikkiKestell**, or follow her on BookBub, **https://www.bookbub.com/authors/vikki-kestell**.

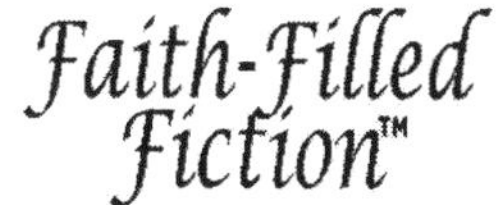

www.faith-filledfiction.com | www.vikkikestell.com

Made in the USA
San Bernardino, CA
06 June 2020

72407040R00206